Mr. Stitch

A Novel

BY

Chris Braak

Mr. Stitch

Threat Quality Press
1299 New Gulph Road
Gulph Mills, PA 19428

The characters and events in this book are fictitious. Any
similarity to real persons, living or dead, is coincidental and
not intended by the author.

ISBN 978-0-9828884-1-4

1

ONE

I cannot but think that the highest act of the created is to become the creator himself. Is not grasping Reason a gift bequeathed to us by solemn Divinity? There are atheists among the scientific minds, this is true. These men consider that all moral law is as nothing before the application of Science. They consider that there should be no field beyond the bounds of man's intellect, and so engage in an even-handed fashion all of those pursuits deemed heretical by the Church.

I believe this to be an erroneous conclusion in the first part, and that in the second part it leads to discoveries that are haphazard and ultimately foolishness. The truth is this: it is not simply the case that there is no scientific heresy, but rather that those elements of study which seem by most to be heretical are the ones demanded most by the Divine.

Science must not be merely faithless, but truly blasphemous, for only in this way can we show that the act of Reason is the truest expression faith.

--from the journal of Harcourt Wolfram, 1785

The undercroft of Vie Abbey is considered by most to be no fit place for any sensible person to spend their time. It is a monstrously large labyrinth of catacombs, built on top of a monstrously large system of caves—tunnels hollowed out by the prehistoric antecedents of the River Stark, which spent the early years of prehistory honeycombing the bedrock that is the foundation of the city of Trowth. Certain maps of the catacombs are available, though unreliable; the assorted Abbots of the Church Royal—many of whom had peculiar and salacious appetite—had historically found good reasons to keep certain quarters of the undercroft secret, and likewise to reveal certain portions in order to discredit their predecessors.

No trustworthy maps of the caves are available, nor is there any information about how many they are, where they lead to, or how deep they go. This made the entire complex a haven for superstitious heretics, who preferred the religiously-charged environment of the undercroft to the more secular mysteries of the Arcadium. Something about practicing heresy right at the heart of the Church Royal was appealing to certain oneiricists and chimeratics.

And the ectoplasmatists. Elijah Beckett, detective-inspector of the Royal Coroners, found that, in his old age, he detested the ectoplasmatists more than any of the other heretical scientists. *At least*, he found himself thinking, as he waded through some kind of ankle-high sludge, deep in the undercroft, *at least necrologists have laboratories where they need to keep things* dry. *What is this, anyway?* It was an idle thought, and one that he quickly crushed. Survival in the Coroners meant developing a resistance to the disgusting, and after many long years, Beckett found that the most formidable resistance was, "don't think about it."

Beckett shuffled along, carrying a small heat-lamp; it sizzled and sparked and cast flickering shadows with its red light. He didn't like the noise it made, but there was nothing for it—Second Winter had brought its omnipotent chill all the way through the city and into the undercroft; without a heat source, he'd be dead and frozen in a heartbeat. Frost rimed the stone walls, even where the weight of the earth should have kept the temperature constant.

His knocker clattered something unintelligible on a nearby wall, and made him pause. He couldn't understand the code—in fact, he hadn't been able to interpret the telerhythmia of any of the knockers they'd saddled him with since he lost Skinner—but he was made anxious by the fact that James was trying to communicate with him. Was he warning him? Beckett tried to pry meaning out of the rapid double-rap on the sooty stone wall by his side, but it was useless. Something was down here with him, he knew that much, but whether it was ahead or behind, near or far, the knocker couldn't tell him.

Useless, Beckett grumbled. He slipped his revolver back into its holster, and pulled out a flask of veneine-laced brandy. He was finding that he needed more and more veneine to keep the pain at bay but, paradoxically, the hallucinations it caused were coming more easily. He sipped at it, the sharp edge of the veneine satisfying the feeling in the back of his mouth that was both a sense that he was bleeding deep in his throat, and a craving for the drug. He swallowed, and steeled himself against the wave of strangeness that washed over him; the world flickered and distorted, as though he were seeing it briefly through a curved mirror. There was a sense of shallowness then, that the faintly illuminated stones in the undercroft were just painted on top of something deeper, vaster, that the whole world was a tiny, visible island set atop an enormous, incomprehensible abysm...

The feeling passed, and something flickered in the periphery of his right eye. Since the fades had taken his left, he'd found that his good eye had become unusually sensitive to sudden movement.

"Shit," Beckett said, dropping the brandy and clutching at his revolver. *The lamp, don't drop the lamp,* he whirled and drew his weapon. Something had come up behind him, a hunched shape; it carried its own lamp like a glowing red eye, but was black with shadow behind the light—its edges shimmered and shifted, as though they couldn't be bothered to hold to the shape that nature had given them, and Beckett thought suddenly of a face, twisted into a hideous rictus, lolling on a broken neck...

Beckett fired at once, and the sound of the Feathersmith revolver and its echoes stuttered along stone walls like a rolling thunderclap. The first shot missed, drawing sparks and stone chips from a low arch. The shape was moving, ducking down, its red eye glaring. Beckett drew a bead on it as the sound of the gunshot died down, and the thing's voice resolved in the darkness.

"Beckett! Beckett, stop, it's me!"

"Valentine?" Beckett put up his gone. "What the hell are you doing down here?" He could see the young man now, as he stepped into the light from Beckett's own lamp. Valentine Vie-Gorgon was tall, with a lean frame entirely disguised by the huge, heavy winter coat that he wore. Heat washed over them both, as they stood within the range of each other's lamps.

"James didn't tell you I was coming down?"

"He did. I just..." Beckett looked around for his flask of brandy, now probably lost forever in the sludge at his feet. "I must have mis-heard his signal. I thought...I thought he was talking about another—"

"DOWN!" Valentine shouted, suddenly shoving Beckett out of the way. He had a silver-plated revolver in his hands and was firing into the dark, the explosions from the revolver deafening them both, the muzzle-flash blinding.

Beckett held up his hands to shield his eyes as he crashed into the stone wall; it would hurt later, he knew, but for now the veneine helped him feel nothing. Lit up by the brief flashes from Valentine's gun, he saw a man duck away down a side passage.

"Stop," Beckett said. "Stop!" He grabbed Valentine's arm. "Enough, he's gone down the side." The knocker's code was rattling furiously against the walls, but it was all gibberish to Beckett's ears. "Come on!"

Beckett ran, but was outpaced by his partner, whose longer legs and limitless enthusiasm propelled him in a reckless sprint down the tunnel and around the corner, only to suddenly duck and spin away from the aperture as gunshots rebounded off the walls. Valentine dove to the side and pressed his back against the wall just as Beckett, crouched low with the gun held at his hip, fired into the darkness, even before the figure resolved itself.

Not the figure, he saw, but figures. There were two men in the dark, Beckett saw in the split second before he shot, one that tried to take off farther down the tunnel, and a second that was running towards him. Without thinking, Beckett fired on the nearer shape, only to feel a sinking feeling in the pit of his stomach as his bullets splashed harmlessly through it. *Wrong one*, he realized too late, even as Valentine reappeared, gun blazing, taking potshots at the retreating shape.

Beckett lashed out with his lantern just as his target came in range; red light spilled over the form, revealing it to be made of thick, silvery-gray smoke. The sparking emitters from the lamp touched it, and it became immediately a gout of fire, hot and orange in the dark, before vanishing utterly. The dark tunnels of the undercroft were obscured by red and purple afterimages; Beckett couldn't see Valentine tearing off through the sludge after the ectoplasmatist, though he had no doubt that it's what the young coroner was up to. Instead, he stood with his arm in front of his eyes, waiting for his vision to clear.

Another gunshot, painfully loud after the brief moment of quiet. Beckett looked up, squinting in the dark for the red glimmer of Valentine's lamp.

"Got this one," the young coroner said, as he returned from around another corner.

"This one?" Beckett asked him.

"Yeah; didn't James say? He heard a second one, that's why he sent me down."

"A second..." Beckett blinked again, then looked down at the sludge at his feet. He lowered the lantern slightly, casting its lurid light across the floor of the tunnel...

...which was covered in thick, silvery-gray smoke in the shape of hands and eyes and faces, that churned and roiled and reached out for him, hands gripping at his wrists, trying to hold lantern and gun at bay, faces crawling thickly up his body, struggling to get into his mouth, clutching at his throat, trying to crush the life out of him...*so much, how can there be this much?* Beckett thought, as panic struggled inside him. There was a river of that weird emanation, *we've been wading through it!* Ectoplasmaticists made the stuff from their own substance, how could there be this much of it inside a person?

Valentine cried out, firing his gun in the dark, stumbling, dropping his lamp...

Oh. Beckett thought, as he saw the sparking red emitters drop to the ground. *No.*

The undercroft became an inferno as the ectoplasm that had filled it ignited in a flash of light and heat. Fire washed over the two coroners, stinging at their eyes, singeing hair and clothes, sucking the air from their lungs.

The fire was gone in a less than a second. Beckett took a deep breath, and looked up at Valentine, who was gingerly touching his face and attempting to ascertain whether he'd just burnt off his eyebrows.

"All right?"

"I think so," Valentine said. "I think it was too fast to cause —"

A ragged shape leapt on him, emerging from the weird cascade of shadows that the heat lamps had made. Valentine grunted and staggered, the black form clinging to him.

"Damn it," Beckett muttered. "Valentine, stand still!"

Valentine continued to stagger, but managed to take a few drunken steps towards the old coroner, who drew his arm back and struck the ectoplasmatist across the side of the head. The man went limp and slithered to the floor.

"Oh, ugh, have I got any on me?" Valentine asked, checking his coat.

Beckett squatted down next to the unconscious ectoplasmatist. "This one was real." The man was lying face down on the filthy, damp floor of the tunnel, which was now mercifully clear. Beckett rolled the man onto his back and would have gasped, had not thirty years of horrible sights thoroughly inured him to the deformations of human misery. The man was gaunt and starved, with sunken eyes and hollow cheeks, skin as thin as paper and so pale it was nearly transparent. It had a peculiar, waxy quality to it, as though he was really just a skull onto which an oily picture of a face had been hastily painted.

Ectoplasmatists drew on their own substance to create the sticky white gunk called ectoplasm, but Beckett had never seen anything like this—never a heretic able to create a full body, never one that could fill the floor of the tunnel with the stuff. No wonder the man looked starved; he must have torn out and rarefied all his own flesh to create so much.

The man opened his eyes, suddenly, and they rolled in their sockets as though there wasn't enough muscle left to hold them in place. "The asphyx," he whispered, "will sustain..." his eyes widened in horror then, and his mouth opened and stretched. He began to make a gagging sound, then all at once vomited a thick fountain of white hands and arms and staring eyes, that boiled from his mouth and grappled with the coroners. The man on the ground went rigid and arched his back, as though the ectoplasm had a life of its own, as

6

though it were wrenching itself free of his body, a spirit made manifest and disdainful of the rotting meat that housed it.

Sticky thick gluey ectoplasm surrounded them, but before it could find purchase, Beckett drew his gun and shot the ectoplasmatist in the head. The ectoplasm continued to slither around his body, trying to crush his lungs, struggling to get control of his arms; fear slivered past Becektt's veneine haze, as he saw Valentine almost suffocating beneath the cloud of vomited-up emanations. Beckett managed to shoot again, and again, shattering the dead man's skull, but the weird fluid remained, heavy and congealing on his arms, keeping the red-hot lantern emitters at a distance, closing around his face, struggling to get past his scarf and into his nose and mouth.

Then, at once, the plasm evaporated, leaving behind no trace except for a persistent greasy feeling that Beckett knew would persist for several days. The old coroner permitted himself a small sigh of relief.

"Gah," Valentine said, as he sagged back against the wall. "That...does it usually do that?"

Beckett looked down at the dead ectoplasmatist. The man's head was fully destroyed, but little blood or brain matter had splashed from it. There seemed to be little of anything left in the man's body. "I've never seen it last so long after the man died," Beckett told his companion. "Usually...usually it just disappears."

"So...what's different?"

The coroner began rifling through the man's pockets. He found himself weirdly squeamish about coming into contact with the withered body, but ignored the feeling; the veneine had been shaking loose all sorts of new sensations, lately. There was something dry and ragged in the ectoplasmatist's inside coat pocket; Beckett got a hold of it and drew out a weathered, folded-up quarto.

"What's that?" Valentine asked him. He leaned in close to look at it. "Huhm. 'On the Life Suspire.' That...what is that?"

"The 'life suspire' is what ectoplasmatists call their goop." Beckett settled down against the far wall of the tunnel. It was cold, and so he held his lantern close, bathing in the dry heat. "They think that, beneath the Word that made the world, there's a...I guess a whisper. A secret meaning that only some people can understand. They think it lives inside them, and they can draw it out and use it."

Valentine looked around the tunnel. There was no sign of silvery ectoplasm, but that strange feeling of greasiness remained. "That's heresy. I mean, real heresy."

"It's all real heresy," Beckett told him, but he understood what the young man meant. Ectoplasmatists were unique among heretical scientists in that they fully embraced the idea that what they were doing *was* heresy. Necrologists, geometers, even the oneiricists usually acted like the Church Royal had banned their sciences in some fit of drunken power. There was nothing in the heirologue or the grammars that prohibited necrology, really; it was just the Church trying to keep control of people.

But the ectoplasmatists — they really thought they were tapped into a secret, true religion that the Abbots were trying to hide. That was why ectoplasmatists loved the undercroft so much. They found some perverse satisfaction in practicing their obscenities right beneath the seat of religion in Trowth.

James was clattering with his telerhythmia on the walls, still garbled nonsense. "It's all right," Beckett said loudly, knowing that the knocker's clairaudience would spirit the words out of the croft to where the man was waiting. "They're dead. Send down the kirliotypists *first*, this time. Are you listening?" The rattling stopped. "Send them down first. I want pictures of every inch of this place before anyone touches anything. Then send the trolljrmen down. Have them take the bodies to Ghad's hospital and put them on ice. I don't want Ennering-Crabtree cutting into them unless I'm there. Understand?" In his bid to end what amounted to three decades of frustration in the Royal Coroners, Beckett had begun ferociously demanding information and documentation. He'd ordered maps commissioned, demanded that local gendarmeries report every murder, theft, and rape that happened in their purviews, insisted that every crime be document, kirliotyped, and filed in the office in Raithower House, whether they were heretical science or not. Since the destruction of Hightower Square, the old coroner had found this information flowing freely. It inundated his office, and threatened to drown the young corporal who'd replaced Beckett's secretary.

There was a complex triple-rap against the wall, which Beckett took to mean "Yes."

"You," he said to Valentine. "Come with me."

Outside of the undercroft Vie Abbey brooded, dark and substantial, a compact fortress atop a hill, a contrast to the sprawling tangle of buildings, arches, and towers that comprised the Royal Palace at the other end of the city. Trowth spread out between these two illustrious edifices, along the iron-black ribbon of the River Stark. Dry, icy air whipped about Beckett and Valentine, as they made their way past the ten kirliotypists that Beckett had hired, past the two great trolljrmen—largely protected from the cold by their bulk, but their feathered crests still held in close—past James Ennering, the new knocker, as he sat in the coroner's coach and tried to coordinate everything.

Beckett took Valentine to a nearby djang-house. It was crowded; during Second Winter, the people of Trowth more easily overcame their natural standoffishness, as the desperate need for any sort of heat or warmth drove them to huddle close, to pack into pubs and shops, even to stand a little nearer each other on the street. Second Winter was an enemy that every man shared in common, and led them to great lengths that they should keep it at bay.

Still, the charcoal suits and the grim mandate of the Coroners bought Beckett and Valentine a little space in the dark, hot, suffocating djang-house, and a small table in the corner. Valentine immediately ordered a cup of the stimulating djang; Beckett asked for nothing, and only scratched at a persistent itch by his eye.

"This," Beckett said, as he placed the quarto on the table, "I don't know what this is."

"It's a pamph—"

"I know it's a pamphlet, Valentine. I mean, I don't know where he got it. I've never seen anything like this before. It looks like an instruction manual for ectoplasmatics."

"Well, maybe that's what it is."

"Ectoplasmaticists don't like instruction manuals. They don't like writing things down at all. So, where did this come from?"

Valentine pursed his lips and held the quarter up to the dim lamp at their table. "Well, this is definitely Southend parchment; that's the cheapest one you can get," Valentine Vie-Gorgon's family was the Vie-Gorgons of Comstock Street. They had, in an effort to distinguish themselves from the more famous branch of the family—the Raithower Vie-Gorgons—succeeded in establishing a near-monopoly on the printing industry of Trowth. "I think you can buy a ream of it for a half a crown. The type's Flood New Face, which is the kind they use on those new typing-machines. You could make this in your own basement, if you wanted."

Beckett nodded. He'd suspected as much; even if an ectoplasmatist had managed to conquer his natural reticence over print, there's no way he'd risk taking heresy to a genuine press—but those new machines were cheap, and widely-available. "Read it," he told the younger man. "Tell me what you find."

"Don't you…" Valentine trailed off, a little awkwardly.

The fades that had been ravaging Beckett's body had, recently, passed on to his left eye. The whole orb was invisible, leaving yet another dark, bloody red hole in his face and making him look even grim and skull-like. The eye was completely blind, as the creeping transparency caused whatever it touched to fail. Between his vanished eye, transparent nose, and the hole in his cheek that showed off his white teeth, Beckett looked horrifically grim—a man already dead, still lurching through life by nothing more than the sheer force of his obdurate will.

"My eyes," the old coroner said, "Aren't what they used to be."

Two

After nearly a decade of drawn-out conflict, messy skirmishes, costly, bloody occupations, and disastrous engagements, the Ettercap War finally ended. *The White Star*, which broadsheet traditionally served as the voice of the Emperor and his ministries, announced an unconditional victory for the Trowth Empire. The precise details of the victory were lost in the flowery praise, grandiose claims, and the repeated insistence on the glory of the Empire in which the editors of *The White Star* had never lost faith.

In fact, the details of the victory were never fully-established by any of the many broadsheets, though speculation was rampant. *The Observer* insisted that the cost of phlogiston was substantially lower after the end of the war than it had been before the start — so, once a decade of crippling fuel prices had been eliminated, the Ettercap War could be counted a success. Other papers claimed that the war had been nothing but a failure, a pointless waste of lives and time, to satisfy the lust for conquest of William II Gorgon-Vie (Rex Imperator Trowthi, Word Preserve Him and Keep Him). One insisted that William II Gorgon-Vie was not the emperor at all, but some kind of heretical doppelganger fashioned by the remnants of the Corsay Trading Company.

The Ministry of Information, tightly-controlled by the Raithower Vie-Gorgons, quickly and quietly silenced any of the papers that were too critical — though they were perfectly content to allow the propagation of the most outlandish rumors. The presence and persistence of these entirely unbelievable claims at least served the illusion that all points of view were being expressed in the broadsheets. The Vie-Gorgons preferred a light touch when it came to affairs of state, and the more their involvement could be disguised, the better.

With the end of the war, thousands of soldiers, many of whom had been forced into service against their will, were brought home. Many, if not most, were crippled — often with legs, arms, hands, feet, or eyes missing. Some were crippled psychically, irreparably damaged by the oneiric munitions of the

Ettercap. The remainder, healthy as they may have seemed, all nursed the trauma of the dragging, dirty war in Gorcia. They were taciturn men with wan faces, who wanted no company but their own. They were uncomfortable around bright lights and enclosed spaces. At night, they gathered in each other's homes, and sat in tense, silent circles, and if some sense passed between them, it was invisible to the world outside.

In response to the return of Trowth's young men, women who had been called up to work in their absence were sent home. Some women, pleased to see their husbands, brothers, fathers, and sons returned to them—damaged though they were—were happy to leave their work to the men. Some, accustomed to the agency that employment had provided, resisted. During Second Spring, they demonstrated; they wore sashes and marched in front of government buildings. During Second Winter, when the sub-zero weather made public demonstrations potentially lethal, they published pamphlets, articles, monographs. They held meetings in their homes and discussed what it would take to enable them to return to work. Thirst wetted with a taste of equality, they began to consider even more drastic and improbable ideas: equality. Independence. Suffrage.

William II Gorgon-Vie reacted to the mounting unrest in his capital city in the traditional style of the Gorgon-Vies: bluntly. He declared the formation of a Committee on Moral Responsibility. Their mandate passed directly from the Emperor and into the world: they were to prevent morally salacious ideas from becoming commonplace. Committee members sent agents to all of the publishers at once, to ensure that no more incendiary tracts were printed. They went into every ministry, every government institution, every business that had even the smallest effect on social policy, and delivered the Emperor's message to the women of Trowth: "Thank you for your help during the war. It's over now. Get out."

This was how, after six years of loyal service, Elizabeth Skinner lost her job with the Coroners. She was summarily dismissed, without even her last week's salary. In fact, because the Coroners had continued to employ her for a full month after the formation of the Committee on Moral Responsibility, there had been veiled threats that *she* might owe *the Coroners* money, for illegally collecting pay during that time.

When the political officer—a thin man in a tweed suit, one of the lesser Gorgon-Ennering-Daior cousins—had come to Raithower House to demand compliance, Beckett had only sat, sunk deep into a chair in the sitting room, glowering. Forty years in the Coroners, and he'd become used to being jerked around by politics and bureaucracy. He'd learned that there was no way to fight

12

it, or avoid it, that it wasn't given to him to decide the rules, only to do his job within them as best he could.

It had been Valentine — naturally — that had risen to her defense, and nearly gotten himself arrested for assaulting a Committee member. He had attempted to defend her quite forcefully. For her part, Skinner had quietly collected her things and gone home.

Now, she sat in a small djang house that ought to have been structurally incapable of housing as many people as it clearly did. Their voices blurred together into a constant noise, a pulsing ocean of a conversation. The warmth from their bodies and the heat lamps on the walls made the air stifling. Heat and sweat made her itch under her corset, and under the silver plate across her eyes.

She quietly sipped at her djang, relishing the bitter tang of it on her tongue, and considered what she ought to do with her last six crowns.

"Miss Skinner." Peter Wall had pushed his way through the crowd of customers in the shop. His father owned the djang house — had, in fact, been one of the early advocates for the medicinal, social, and culinary benefits of djang when it had been introduced from Corsay — and Peter had worked there since he was old enough to carry a plate.

"This is yours," Peter said, clattering a plate down in front of her. Skinner heard him set a fork down, carefully placing it by her left hand.

She quickly tried to calculate how much of her dwindling funds this might represent. A penny for a cup of djang she could afford, but she needed to be a little stingy with her food. "I can't — "

"On the house, miss, you know." Peter told her. "Da don't like to see anyone hungry, if he can help it. Gives him a sour belly all day, and then mam's got to feed him bread pudding for dinner…well, it's a right mess, if you take my meaning."

Peter left before Skinner could thank him. She was half-tempted to try and follow him with her clairaudience, to see what his father *really* had to say about it, but, as the smell of food wafted up to her nostrils, found more important things to occupy her mind. Her belly rumbled, and she set to the meal with gusto.

It was not hearty, the way traditional Trowth fare was, but the concoction of sweetly-pickled apples and pears, minced nuts and dates, and liberal application of white pepper was more than enough to quell her appetite. In the short-term, at least. There was still the matter of living on six crowns in a city that was legally forbidden from giving her work.

Most of the women that had been employed during the war had still lived at home; sometimes with fathers or grandfathers, too old or too respectable to be pressed into service, but just as often with mothers and sisters. They could easily, though sometimes uncomfortably, return to those households and wait patiently for a husband or gradually retire into spinsterhood, as they saw fit. Skinner did not consider either future especially appealing, and, moreover, had neither the interest nor the ability to return to her family's home.

The situation left her with a feeling of inevitability, a sense of impending doom that she couldn't shake off. There was no work. There was no way home. No matter how she looked at it, she was stuck with a handful of coins to her name—a need that exceeded her means, and no ready solution.

Skinner finished off her food and sipped at the djang, taking the opportunity to soak up as much warmth as she could before she had to go back into the cold. She stayed at the djang house until about mid-day. The city, still freezing, was at its warmest then. It would turn into an icy nightmare when the sun went down, and since she'd have to walk...well, people still died from Second Winter in Trowth, and not just the indigent and destitute. Skinner decided to walk home shortly before tea.

Bundled in a thick coat, with heavy mittens and a fur hood, Skinner took the short, ice-slick path back to her boarding-house. It was in Chapel Height, a modest, clean little neighborhood near New Bank, and a fully-entrenched Crabtree-Daior outpost in the Architecture War. Skinner had always supposed that this meant low buildings with flowery downspouts and baroque styling, but had never seen it herself. She preferred the Crabtree-Daior style because of its sturdy walls and moderately-wide hallways, which were much easier to navigate sightlessly.

Skinner lived on the first floor of the boarding-house, which had been established only a few years earlier precisely to give young ladies a place to live—peacefully, and without the threat of scandalous assignations with rambunctious young men—while they worked the jobs of the absent soldiers. It was managed by Mrs. Crewell, a gentle woman who took great care of her charges—perhaps as a way of spiting fate for her name, or perhaps because she simply enjoyed the irony of it. Mrs. Crewell was a particular sort of stout, gruff, middle-aged woman so numerous in the city that they might as well have been their own species and had, by fair means and foul, acquired a significant number of grandchildren. She made particular use of their youthful energy and agility in maintaining the boarding-house.

"Miss Skinner," Mrs. Crewell called, when the ex-coroner arrived. Skinner could hear the woman bustling about in the living room, waging her lifelong crusade against grime. "Miss Skinner, if I could have a word."

Rent, Skinner thought immediately. *She wants this month's rent. How far am I behind? Only three days...she can hold out until the end of the week, at least, certainly —*

"I...there was a visitor, today," the woman said. "From the Committee. They're...well, they're to encourage women to be going back to their families, and all that. So..." Skinner could hear the soft brush as Mrs. Crewell wrung her hands. "So, I've to close the house down. By the end of the month, they say. Now, don't you worry about the money; I've plenty by me, and Word knows there's little more you can do. But you'll need to find a place for yourself, and soon as can be."

"I..." Skinner's stomach flipflopped, and her hand went involuntarily to her mouth. *At least she doesn't want the rent for this month.* She choked off a bitter, perverse laugh at that. "Yes. I understand. Thank you, Mrs. Crewell, you've been very kind."

"Course, course," Mrs. Crewell said, softly. "Oh! Someone's left a letter for you. Fancy paper, looks like. Have you got a gentlemen, Miss Skinner?"

"No," Skinner said, firmly. It was probably a bill from the Committee, asking for her salary back.

"Shall I read it for you?"

"No. Not...I'd just like to sit down for a minute, Mrs. Crewell."

"Oh dearie, of course," the housekeeper replied. "You go on up to your room, I'll send Roger in to you in a few minutes." Roger was one of Mrs. Crewell's innumerable grandchildren. He was only ten, and just learning how to read, so Mrs. Crewell employed him as Skinner's reader. The arrangement actually worked out fairly well; while ten-year-olds are not notable for their ability to keep secrets, Roger was just young and incurious enough that he hardly understood a word of the messages that he relayed to the knocker.

Not that it matters, Skinner thought. She was unlikely to receive any missives from the Coroners any time soon. "Yes, all right," she told the housekeeper, and, shucking her coat and gloves, made her way to her room.

She sat in her small chair, and held her cane between her hands, wondering what she should do. She had little in the way of personal items or clothes, so packing them up should be no great trial. Except that she had nowhere to take them, nothing to do with them. If she went down to Red Lanes, maybe, or into Riverside. The indige had different ideas about their women, one that the Empire tended to tolerate. Maybe they'd let her rent a room there? Six crowns would buy her a little more than a month, if she set something aside for food. That would take her to the end of Second Winter, at least. She'd never afford movers, though, or a coach, so she could bring only what she could carry. A few dresses, and she'd have to be diligent about laundering them herself. The

15

guitar was light, but would not hold up well in the freezing cold air, even in the short time it took to get across the city. She'd have to wrap it up in her smallclothes. And then what? Once she got there, once she was living in Riverside, then what?

Don't think about that. You can't do anything about that. Solve the problems that are in front of you first. Skinner noted, with a wry grin, that her inner voice had begun to sound an awful lot like Elijah Beckett.

"Mum?" Roger rapped on her door. "Mum, I've got your letter, mum."

"Come in, Roger," Skinner told him, and suddenly realized that her room was freezing. She'd left the heat on low when she went out. "Go ahead and put on a light, and turn the heat up a little, would you darling?" She heard the faint screech of the lamp-switch, and felt the warmth from the heater. "Good lad."

"Gram says I'm to read this. All right?"

"Yes, please."

"Uhm." The sound of paper rustling, as the boy opened it. "Oh! There's a fancy crest on it, looks like. I don't know what it's supposed to be…"

"It's all right, Roger, just read the letter."

"Uhm. To. Miss Elizabeth Skinner. It has come to my at…attent…"

"Attention."

"Attention. That you and I share si-mi-lar in-terest. Interests. I wooled—"

"Would."

"Would. Be pleased if you joined me at the Royal the-a-ter. Oh! At the theater. I shall send a coach for you. At seven. Yours…" The boy stopped, and Skinner heard his breath catch. "Oh. Emilia Vie-Gorgon." Even a ten year old knew the Vie-Gorgon name. The Vie-Gorgons were one of the most famous of the Esteemed Families of Trowth; their legendary feud with the Gorgon-Vies was one of the defining elements not just of politics, but of the Architecture War, of culture and entertainment, of virtually every aspect of the Empire. The Vie-Gorgon family was second from the Imperial Throne, and Emilia Vie-Gorgon's brother was next in line to be Emperor. An invitation from her—an invitation to someone like Skinner—was like…well, it wasn't like anything. Nothing like this had ever happened before. The Families didn't associate with the commoners unless they had to, and even then it was only appropriate for the least relevant members—fourth or fifth sons, like Valentine, or else secondary or tertiary cousins. Emilia Vie-Gorgon…if Trowth had a princess, Emilia Vie-Gorgon would be it.

"It don't say," said Roger, "if you want to accept or not. Shouldn't it say that?"

Emilia Vie-Gorgon probably didn't consider that someone might want to turn her down. "I wouldn't worry about it, Roger. Tell me, do you know what's on the playbill at the Royal tonight?"

THREE

Beckett sat at his desk and stared. It was piled high with papers — with the reports that he'd been demanding. Arrest reports, biographies, kirliotypes. Pictures of crime scenes, spattered with blood, pulsing with strange auras. Stacks of clippings from the broadsheets, relating tales that ranged from the mundane ("Abundance of Rats in Red Lane Gutters") to the unpleasant ("Third Severed Hand Found in Mudside") to the purely outlandish ("Gendarmes Replaced With Ectoplasmic Dopplegangers: Who Can We Trust?"). There were reports of looted crypts, hospitals that had been robbed, men that had been found bleeding dreams into the streets, or wandering about with scaly arms grafted to their bodies. There were lists of men in custody, trolljrmen who'd unwisely practiced their chimerstry away from the secrecy of their hospitals, of indige geometers who'd been brought in for engaging in heretically hyper-spatial mathematics, human men rounded up from the duetti clubs where they'd been purposefully over-dosing on veneine…

Beckett scratched at the itch by his eye, and leaned back in his chair. His forearm throbbed a little from where he'd injected himself, but mostly the veneine left him feeling detached, floating. His left eye, despite its blindness, detected no small number of thin, writhing black shapes that wriggled across the walls of his office, but Beckett did not find himself concerned. Nor did he find himself concerned by the damp stains on his walls, or the shallow puddle of water by his feet. The warmth and peace of the veneine high would last only a little longer, and the old coroner was determined to enjoy it wall it lasted.

Soon enough, the cold and anxiety began to creep back in. Distant aches in his knees and back began to sharpen, the numbness in his face and fingers demanded more of his attention. The water dried up, though the wriggling black eels remained, making it difficult to concentrate on his papers. The Committee on Moral Responsibility had forced him to fire Karine, his indige secretary. The new man they'd found — a timid, shell-shocked young man who'd worked primarily with the quartermasters during the war—was purely incapable of distinguishing useful information from dross, so Beckett found himself obliged to wade through the mess himself.

The papers seemed unlikely to yield up their secrets any time soon. In the last few months, the sheer amount of information to come across Beckett's desk had increased exponentially. Heretical science was spreading through the city like a disease, cropping up left and right, everywhere from dingy public houses in the Arcadium to the fancy homes of New Bank. There was no clear point of origin, no source, no connection between any of the heretics. It was all just a tangled, unnavigable mess of half-formed leads, each one turning a half a dozen corners before it dead-ended in a corpse somewhere.

This had been the story of Beckett's life for years. Find evidence of a heresy, find the heretic, kill them. As often as not, their own foolishness did the job for him. But it never stopped. No matter how many lunatic scientists Beckett ended, there was always one more. And now, now every time he put a stop to an ectoplasmatist or a necrologist somewhere, a half a dozen more seemed to spring up in the wake. Forty years of work in the coroners, and every day the problem just got worse, and worse, and worse.

A hysterical frustration rattled around in Beckett's mind, as he rubbed his hands over his face. The veneine, he was sure, was shaking him loose. It was harder and harder for him to maintain that cold detachment, that sense of duty that let him just tackle one job at a time, and not think about the rest, not think about the implications, not think about the never-ending chain of more death and more misery that waited for him every day, and would wait every day until he finally gave up. He slapped at a report at random and picked it up.

Brass bones? Everything was making less sense to him, lately, and Beckett started to worry that it was the disease, eating away at his mind. Would this have made sense a year ago? Someone had found a chunk of brass in the shape of a shoulder-blade in a pile of offal in Red Lanes. The gendarmes, pleased to finally have a lap into which they could dump all of their weird crap, had gleefully passed it on to Beckett. *Who...why would you even do that?* He looked back at some of the other reports, accompanied by kirliotypes of men who'd starved themselves to death by vomiting ectoplasm, or whose hearts had given out trying to support extra limbs. Dead-ends, all of them. *Well,* he thought. *I'd better check.*

The officer from the Committee on Moral Responsibility was, as usual, taking tea in the sitting room. One of the privileges of being cousins to the Emperor—even eighth-cousins like the Gorgon-Ennering-Crabtrees—was the possibility of getting a job in which your primary responsibility was taking tea in places. He wore a dark blue suit, with bulls embroidered in a delicate green around his sleeves. *Edmund? Edelred? Ed-something,* Beckett thought. *Whatever.*

"Going out, Mr. Beckett?"

Beckett turned his gruesome, death's head stare on the man, but said nothing.

"Ah. Hm. *Inspector* Beckett."

The coroner said nothing still, and began the laborious process of shrugging into his winter coat. It was heavy, and his sore joints had begun to impede his mobility. *Should have shot up before I left,* he thought to himself. *Too late, now.* He had no desire to let Ed-whatever Gorgon-Ennering-Crabtree see him use the needles.

"Where are you going, Inspector?" The political officer asked again. He had a little notebook with him, presumably to help him keep track of Beckett's moral failings. When the coroner failed to respond yet again, the officer raised his voice. "Mr...Inspector Beckett, I'd appreciate it if you'd keep me apprised of your activities." Beckett wrapped his red scarf around his face; it hid his mangled-looking nose, at least, even if it left his empty eye socket staring at hapless passers-by. "Mr. Beckett. Excuse me. Excuse me!"

As he turned to leave, Beckett found the hallway obstructed by the huge, misshapen form of Mr. Stitch. The reanimate, built over a century ago from spare, dead parts, watched impassively from the brass lenses in its eye sockets. It still wore its huge, heavy coat, but had removed the three-cornered hat that it usually wore.

"Beckett." Stitch said, with its terrible, sepulchral voice. It took a deep breath from the billows that had replaced his lungs. "Where?" Stitch had been about its enigmatic business. Beckett thought it had been consulting with the Emperor's doctors.

"A lead," he said. "One of the Red Lanes cases." He grimaced as he heard the political officer scratching something in his notebook.

"Valentine?"

"He's...working on something else for me." More scratching from Gorgon-Ennering-Vie and his notebook. Beckett gritted his teeth, resentful of having to have to explain himself, resentful of the political officer and his incessant inquiries, resentful of the whole situation.

"Take. Gorud." Stitch rasped, then shambled off towards its office, the metal braces on its legs clanking. Mr. Stitch had a difference engine for a brain — an engine of miraculous complexity. It was capable of perfect memory, of limitless calculations, of astonishing insight. Mr. Stitch was almost never wrong, and its advice invariably turned out to be not just useful, but the best possible advice that anyone under a particular set of circumstances could give. Beckett hated it.

He hated this particular advice as well. Gorud was a therian, a kind of ape-man native to Corsay. Small numbers had been brought to Trowth; because of their linguistic dexterity, they were used often as translators or interpreters. Since the end of the war, the numbers of therians in the city had increased. They were generally a pleasant, good-natured people, though unused to the frigid temperatures of the imperial capital. Gorud wore a bulky coat that fitted him poorly, despite the fact that it had a hole cut out for his tail.

If Beckett didn't like Gorud, it was certainly nothing personal, as the therian was as good-natured an example of a member of his species had could be desired. It was not even a particular specism on Beckett's part, though he did tend to lean towards the human-centric. In fact, Beckett just didn't like it when things changed. He spent all his time trying to get on top of things, trying to manhandle the elements of life and work in to place, to make everything *just so* — and then, invariably, he was saddled with something new. Just when he'd gotten everything figured out, gotten everything *sorted*, the therians came along, or the sharpsies went mad, or something equally frustrating and inconvenient happened.

"You," Beckett told the therian, who sat on his heels on the couch. "Come with me."

Gorud, sensitive to Beckett's disdain, said nothing, and padded after the old coroner on four legs. They found the Coroners' regular coachman, Harry, in the guardhouse outside, and set off for Red Lanes.

Beckett and the therian rode in relative silence, as the coach creaked and clattered along. Outside, Harry had been outfitted with his best winter gear, and a variety of small heating elements — small bands he could wrap around his hands, an emitter that sat next to him. It was a waste of energy that would have been unthinkable a year ago, but since the end of the war, fuel was cheap and plentiful.

Inside, Beckett watched the therian. Gorud had a strangely long, leathery face, that seemed largely impassive, except for a pair of quick, roving eyes. He sat on his heels, his arms wrapped around his knees, as usual. "Do you know Red Lanes?" Beckett asked him.

Gorud twitched and puffed out his cheeks. "Live there," he said. "With some cousins." Gorud had a warm tenor of a voice which always surprised Beckett with its clarity and timbre.

"Know any of the gendarmes?"

The therian looked up at him with an unreadable expression, and shifted in his seat. "One," he said, finally. "Nasty thing, with a mark on his face, like this." He drew a number five in the air with one long, agile finger. Therians were predisposed to illiteracy, Beckett knew, but at least they could recognize symbols. "He kept trying to move us from the eyrie, but we didn't like it."

"And?"

The therian yawned, abruptly, displaying a huge mouth and four canine teeth each as long as Beckett's thumb. "Haven't seen him in a while," Gorud said, and made a popping sound with his lips.

"Hnf." Beckett replied, and silence predominated for a while. As they clattered down the hill, Gorud abruptly perked up. "What?" Beckett asked him. "What—" A faint rumbling reached his ears growing in intensity, the sound of a massive wave rolling towards them. "What is that? Do you hear...?"

The rumbling turned into a ringing sound in his ears, and suddenly black water crashed through the windows of the coach, washing over him, tearing him from his seat and out, out into the dark riptide of salty ocean that choked him, strangled him, struggled down this throat and threw him hard against smooth rocks. Beckett's head banged against metal; he felt a rib give way.

The water retreated then, leaving Beckett on a smooth brass beach that sloped steeply downward, and he fell, sliding along its length, still coughing up seawater; he saw the moon beneath him, green and leprous, luminous with its own baleful light, black cities crawling across its surface, as hands reached out from the hot, red-gold brass and clutched at him, hands that were made of tangles of fat, black, boneless leeches, that sought out bare skin with their tiny, puckered mouths. The hands gripped him, and something like a mouth appeared, a nest of teeth with no lips or throat, just independently shuddering dentition that stretched and jittered and longed to puncture...

And then it was gone. All gone, the vision disappearing with the same sudden completeness as ectoplasm gone up in flame. The hands on his arms were Harry's hands—ordinary, rough coachman's hands. The face made of curved teeth was only Harry's face, his ordinary, ugly old face.

The ringing began to fade from Beckett's ears. "—eckett!" Harry was shouting. "Mr. Beckett! Are you all right?" Gorud had retreated to a corner of the coach, watching, his eyes wide.

Two dark green shoots sprung from Harry's nostrils, tendrils with sharp thorns, springing from the soft places of his body, curling back to scratch at his own eyes.

"What..." Beckett asked, his voice hardly above a whisper. "Garrett? Garrett, your dead," the old man declared, as the twin green vines blossomed into blood-red flowers.

"It's me, sir," Sergeant Garret said, more thorny vines pouring from his mouth, "it's me, it's Harry, sir. Can you hear me? Are you all right? Do you know me sir?"

No, Beckett told himself. *It's Harry, it's just Harry. Garret died.* They were still inside the coach. Beckett was wedged against the seat; his ribs were still sore. "What happened? What was that?"

"There's something up ahead of us, some kind of explosion," Harry told him, the vines gone, his face his own again. "Shook the whole place up. I came to see if you was all right, and then..."

"You fell," Gorud picked up. "When the shock came. Your eye did this," he rolled his eyes up in his head, so that only the whites were visible. "And then you coughed and choked, and then Mr. Harry came in to help."

Beckett coughed wetly, wiped his mouth, and pulled himself upright. "Explosion?"

"Something up ahead, sir."

Beckett scrambled from the coach, a sinking feeling in his stomach. He barely noticed the bitter cold outside, as it struck out at his already-senseless extremities. His good eye raced over the narrow, high-peaked and gabled Ennering-Crabtree buildings; houses, offices and shops that had been converted from old abattoirs. People were timidly peeking out from their doors and windows, a few braver souls actually taking to the streets, consternation on their tongues.

At the end of Augre Street was the smoking husk of a building, a great slaughterhouse that had been repurposed, as the city expanded, into some other professional edifice. Its pointed roofs, now crooked and tumbled, would have looked out of place even if they'd remained intact. Smoke poured from its windows, and a hysterical gibbering rose from the inside.

Beckett limped down the hill, Harry and Gorud at his heels. He drew his revolver, swiveling his head from side-to-side, struggling to reconstruct what had happened. A man in a blue coat stumbled from the building; he was covered in soot, and his eyes were wild and white-rimmed.

"...the overwhelming way of winter's seven towers," the man was screaming. A dark, thick fluid dribbled from his mouth and nose. "I saw the red gold walls and the ivory-towered teeth." He charged at Beckett, grabbed his wrists, tried to bear him to the ground. "There are men in the dark," he said, weeping that same black fluid from his eyes. "There are stone sounds.."

"Get off!" Beckett shouted, twisted his body, trying to let the man's momentum throw him away. Harry managed to get hold of him and pull him off the coroner, but the strange man continued to lash and struggle and wail, blubbering nonsense as the foul ooze began to poor from his eyes and mouth and nose.

Beckett struck the man across the face with the butt of his revolver, and the stranger went limp. It seemed merciful; the twisted rictus on the man's face relaxed away.

"Tommy," said a soft voice nearby. Beckett turned to see a young man, very pale, staring at the smoking building with a strange absorption. His left sleeve was empty, and pinned up to the shoulder.

"Tommy?" Beckett asked him. "Is that his name? What happened here?"

"It's Tommy, innit?" The young pale man said. "They dropped them bombs on us."

Beckett clutched at his revolver, ready to knock this man senseless as well. "Tommy *who*?"

"Vinegar Tom," the man said, still not looking at the coroner. "The Ettercap."

The Ettercap. The Ettercap used oneiric munitions—bombs that had a psychic component as well as an explosive. The damage caused by concussion and shrapnel was trivial compared to the disorder, chaos, and damage that could be caused by turning the survivors of an attack into raving madmen. The air around the bombed-out former slaughterhouse was growing thick and syrupy. Weird colors and puissance began to flicker in the smoky windows. Beckett could smell saltwater. *Dream poison*, he thought. More mad gibbering rattled around inside the building.

"Look," he said to the young man. "Hey, boy, listen." He seized the man's arm and forcibly turned him. "Look at me. I need you to go and get the local gendarmes, all right? Go to the gendarmerie, bring me back some men…"

"The gendarmerie?" The young man said, his eyes dreamy, unfocused. "That *is* the gendarmerie."

FOUR

Skinner heard the explosion fifteen seconds before it happened. The sound began as a peculiar ringing over her guitar strings, an echo overlaid across the tune she'd been playing. Her hands paused at once, and the ringing remained, a high-pitched whine, followed by a strange, reverse echo — a rumbling that grew exponentially louder as it led up to the event itself, and then stopped.

Light from the munition reverberated off of the obscured architecture of the city and filtered past her silver eye-plate to tease her peculiar senses. It was pale white, with a faint rainbow hue at its edges; all of this was clearly visible in her mind's eye, though no product of her own imagination. She could tell its distance, its location — just inside Red Lanes, she knew — and she recognized it as an oneiric weapon immediately. The dream-precipitates used in such charges were largely inconsiderate of local laws regarding space and time, and their effects could be felt by sensitives in a way out of joint with ordinary reckoning.

When Skinner had joined the Coroners, her first assignment had been outside the city — to a town near the seaside called Seagirt. It had been a small place, a population less than a thousand. A man, a former scientist at the Royal Academy of Science and a near-cousin of the Rowan-Czarneckis, had retired to Seagirt after certain improprieties in his research had come to light. His connections and the Estimation of the Crown had kept him from further investigation, and probably execution, but, perhaps not surprisingly, the threat of the Coroners had not been enough to keep him from more experiments. It hardly ever was.

The man had attempted to build an oneiric reactor, a machine that could seize on the repressed psychosexual energy of sidereal consciousness and turn it directly into power. He had failed to take any reasonable precautions, and in a real way, this had not been his fault: because oneiristry was a Forbidden Science, there was little information as to exactly what reasonable precautions would be. The results of Eiger Feathersmith's experiments on oneiristry, a hundred years prior, had been suppressed by the Church Royal, so this Rowan-Czarnecki scientist could not have known what would happen when his reactor went critical.

In instances of catastrophic oneiric events, the Coroners' mission is simple. Locate damaged minds, and kill them. A man exposed to an excess of oneiric radiation would suffer dream poisoning; he would no longer be lucid, his mind would be unrecoverable, and his condition could become contagious. By the time the coroners had reached Seagirt, the entire population was infected — a whole city of raving madmen, the conscious-subconscious membrane dissolved by corrosive dream radiation — they tore at their flesh, struck out at each other, murdered, raped, burned, engaged in every foul and heinous desire that they had secretly feared to indulge.

Isolated as it was, the extermination of the infected at Seagirt had been a simple, if arduous process. An oneiric event in the middle of the densely-packed city — even a small event like the one she'd just heard — could be infinitely more dangerous.

She was on her feet at once, and had pulled on her heavy coat and gloves before she recalled that she had no professional interest in the matter. She was an ordinary citizen, now — in fact, according to the Empire, somewhat less than an ordinary citizen. She was now prohibited from involvement both by her dismissal from the Coroners, and the purported delicacy of her natural condition.

Screw it, she thought, defiantly. "Roger!"

"Yes, mum?" The boy responded from nearby. He must have been in the kitchen.

"Roger, come with me, I need you to help me hail a coach."

"Yes, mum. Only, ladies aren't s'posed to be alone."

"That's why I've got you."

They called a coach, and then Skinner found herself having a startlingly similar conversation with the coachman:

"Can't let you ride with just the boy — "

"The boy's not coming."

"Well, I can't let you ride alone, neither."

"I won't be alone, *you'll be driving me*."

"Well…"

"Do you know what the word 'emergency' means?"

Skinner finally promised to pay him double his usual fare if he could get her to Red Lanes at once, and the coach began clattering and creaking through the streets, while the driver shouted out people to clear the way, furiously threatening them with all manner of bodily and psychological harm in order to secure his passage. The heater inside the coach was on the fritz, and an icy breeze squirming into the cab and playing across Skinner's face.

She ignored it, and projected her hearing to its greatest distance. It was not extensive — certainly, she couldn't project across the city. But it did give her some early warning about what was happening before they arrived. Red Lanes had become noisy; men were shouting, screaming at each other, running back and forth with heavy boot-steps and rustling coats. Below it all was an eerie ululation, a strange gabbling that seemed almost a kind of harmony — the symptom of shatterbrain.

Skinner cast her ears around until she found a familiar voice, gruff but calm, shouting orders insistently but not hysterically. *Beckett*. He was trying to establish some kind of perimeter, to keep something contained — the mad voices at the epicenter of the event. Each one had become its own weapon, a ticking bomb ready to escape into the city and bring devastation in its wake. She rapped on the ground at his feet in a clean, precise way that the old coroner recognized at once.

"Skinner?" He said. "Where are you?"

Hundred yards. Approaching.

"Word and fuck. Good. Can you hear them, in there? It's the gendarmerie headquarters in Red Lanes."

Yes.

"I'm going to have to go in — "

No.

"I have to, Skinner. They're poisoned. If I don't take them down now, they could get out, and start infecting others."

Wait.

"No time. How far — wait, is that you? There's a cab coming down Augre Street." There was a sudden knocking on the door at her side; it startled Skinner's senses back to her. "Skinner?" Beckett said, opening the door.

"Beckett, you can't go in there by yourself," she said, climbing out of the cab and accepting the hand that she knew he'd offered. "You don't know — "

"I'm not going by myself. I've got men."

Skinner paused.

"Who?"

"Men. Never mind, come up to the line, I need you to keep track — "

"*Who?*"

"Gorud. He's a therian. Attached to the coroners. Skinner, we haven't got time for this. Whatever happens to me in there, it's going to be worse if we let the men in there get out. Now. Start listening."

She pursed her lips, irritation giving way to the particular satisfaction to be had by returning to old routines. Skinner pressed her hearing outwards, tracking down the street and into the hollowed-out gendarmerie, setting her shoulders and steeling herself against the eerie wail of gibbering shatterbrained men, using her preternaturally refined senses to extract voices from each other, following echoes down ruined halls, up and down stairways, sorting out the shape of the building, prying the collage of noise apart until it became a map in her mind.

She heard Beckett's footsteps, as familiar to her ears as her own — though slower today than she was used to — make their way towards the building, followed by the peculiar four-footed lope of the therian.

Five, she rattled to Beckett. There were bodies...she shook her head. There was organic matter in the hallways, absorbing the echoes. A substantial amount. The men...the targets had been fighting each other. Five would be easy to handle. This was good news; she could feel sorry for the dead men and their families when she and Beckett were done.

Five

There was comfort in the knowledge that Skinner was back with him. Beckett picked his way around the debris in the doorway of the blasted-out gendarmerie headquarters, and drew his revolver. The revolver was also comforting; a good, solid weight in his hand. He'd been carrying the weapon for so long it was practically an antique. He flexed his free hand, wincing as his knuckles popped, and stepped inside.

The lights had been the first things to break when the bomb had gone off. There was a little daylight that had found its way in from cracked walls and deep crevices, light already weakened from the struggle to break Trowth's omnipresent cover of fog and pollution. The gloom inside was thick and almost palpable, barely disrupted by the narrow shafts of pale sun.

"Can you see anything?" Beckett whispered to Gorud.

The therian snorted. "No. Am not a cat," he muttered. There was a faint rustling, and the hall was suddenly awash in blue light, as the simian creature produced a small phlogiston lantern. Gorud narrowed the beam, slightly, shining it on the black stone and charred wood that littered the floor, letting it play about the walls.

They were in a relatively large receiving room; its function in a slaughterhouse was obscure to Beckett, but as offices for the gendarmerie, its purpose was relatively clear. There was an upturned desk, splintered and broken in half, where the citizenry might have come if they had a complaint, or to make a report. There were overturned benches where people could wait, torn scraps of paper fluttering in a faint breeze, the remnants of broadsheets that had served as entertainment in idle minutes.

There were bodies scattered across the floor. Half a dozen at least, and most twisted and sprawled away from the center of the room. Beckett surmised that they had died in the initial blast, dying mercifully as a result of physical trauma, instead of the unbearably painful psychic damage of the munition. The throbbing pulse of freed-up psychic energy beat around them; surfaces, even under the dim glow of Gorud's lamp, took on peculiar textures and characteristics, impressing colors into Beckett's mind. Stone suggested it might be sticky to the touch, wood seemed like paper, about to be snatched away by an unseen hand. The floor...the floor was wet, damp, brackish water over dark brass...

Skinner rapped on the floor at his feet. *Five*. Beckett sighed with relief as he realized that the coding of her telerhythmia was perfectly clear to him — as easy to understand as any conversation. He had not been losing his mind; the new knocker really just was unintelligible. She relayed the positions of the men still in the building. Two on his level, three more on the floor above. This was a small blessing; at least the three men on the second floor would be unlikely to escape.

"What is it?" Gorud asked him, his voice pitched low.

"She's telling me where the targets are. Two down here. You have a weapon?"

Gorud made a sound like a cough. "No. We are not permitted."

Stupid. Why would you let someone join the Coroners, and not give them a gun? "If things get tight, stay back, keep the light on them." Becektt considered just how helpful the creature would be in a fight. Moving on all fours, he was about as high as Beckett's waist. It was hard to be sure beneath the heavy coat and thick fur, but the coroner suspected that Gorud's frame was replete with strong, rangy muscle. Still...unarmed, against a strong man? "Run if I tell you to. Understand?"

The therian made that same coughing sound. "Yes."

Beckett nodded towards a yawning black doorway at the far end of the room. Gorud moved towards it, one hand holding the lantern aloft, the other on the ground, helping him move. Beckett followed close behind, gun ready. Skinner rapped softly at his side, letting him know how close they were. Three raps, spaced evenly, represented his distance. The faster they came, the closer the target was. It was an unnerving process; the rapid taps could make anyone tense.

Three taps, very close together, and Beckett knew they were practically on top of the man. He could just faintly here the madman's muttered glossolalia.

"There," Gorud whispered, and shone a light down a narrow hallway. It fell on a shadow in the shape of a man, white eyes glittering in the dark. The man looked up at Beckett and screeched, pronouncing syllables in a language the old coroner had never heard, if it was a language at all and not just the meaningless gibbering that all lunatics held in common.

Beckett's weapon kicked, hard, as he put a bullet between the madman's eyes. The man fell back as though his feet had been kicked from under him, and hit the ground as still as stone. *Easy. This is easy. This will be easy.* "One more on this floor," Beckett told the therian. "Then we need to find the stairs."

They found the second man in an adjoining room. He was huddled in the corner, the body of another man sprawled out in front of him. There was something black and sticky about his mouth; it was impossible to tell the color in the blue lamp-light, but Beckett had a fairly good idea of what it was.

The man just looked at them as they entered, and whispered to himself. "…she didn't *know* she was me, if she'd *known* she'd have been, she'd have been, she knew, she'd have been somewhere. Somewhere else if she was. Somewhere—"

Beckett shot him in the face; he twitched, and lay still. While he waited for the spots that the muzzle-flash had left to clear from his good eye, the coroner took the opportunity to open his revolver and dump out the two spent shells. He reloaded and snapped the weapon closed. "Come on," he told the therian. "Upstairs."

There was a sudden rap at his side, an irritated quadruple-rhythm on the wall—the telerhythmic equivalent of a curse. "Skinner. What is it?"

She tried to tap something back to him, but there was now a second phantom rhythm on the wall, a garbled mess of long and short sounds, that made communication impossible. *Shit,* he thought to himself. "Whoever else is listening, be quiet. I can't understand what you're saying." There was a pause, and he heard Skinner's rapping again. He had time to make out a word, "Trouble," and then the second knocking returned, louder this time, loud enough that Beckett was worried it would be overheard.

"Be *quiet*," he insisted. "You are drawing attention. I need you quiet," he spat through gritted teeth. After a moment, Skinner's telerhythmia vanished, and Beckett was left with the new knocker, who softened his voice, but could make himself no better understood. "James, I know that's you. I need you to get me Skinner. I can't read you. Do you understand me? I can't tell what you're saying. Let Skinner talk to me."

Silence, for a moment, and then James' garbled knocking stubbornly returned. Beckett turned to the therian. "Can you understand this?" Gorud silently shook his head. "Crap." The old coroner adjusted his coat. "Crap. Crap. Crap." The veneine high was beginning to fade; the warm blanket that protected Beckett from the pain in his joints and the aches in his muscles was beginning to unravel. A sharp spike drilled into his knee. "Upstairs," he whispered.

The path upstairs was by a narrow stairway at the far end of the hall. The steps were wooden—old and nearly rotten, and the creaked and crackled as Beckett climbed them. The therian followed, his long arms and prehensile feet giving him confidence in the face of the structure's potentially catastrophic failure.

The muttering of damaged minds was just audible when they reached the second floor, spilling down the cramped, claustrophobic hallway, from any one of a number of rooms with crooked, broken doors. James' knocking along the walls was no help; he used some means, unfamiliar to Beckett, to describe distance and direction. It didn't sound like speed or volume, and the coroner found himself disinclined to take the time to puzzle it out.

"James," he spat through clenched teeth. "I can't understand you. Just shut up." The knocking continued for a moment, then stopped. Beckett sighed, then winced as a myriad of tiny sharp pains in his neck and shoulders saw their way clear through the drugs. He held his hand out to Gorud, indicating that the therian should hold back, then eased forward towards the first door. There were scattered, huddled shapes. None of them moved. The mad chattering was weirdly delocalized up here; no matter where he seemed to move, its volume and distance seemed to persist—as though those gabbling voices were not real sounds at all, but some alien part of his subconscious that had suddenly been given voice.

Beckett shook off the feeling, and carefully moved to the next room. This one, too, was empty. The third room...nothing moved in the third room. There were no huddled shapes, only one man on the far wall, who hung limply from where he'd pinned his left arm into the mortar with a short sword. Blood colored the length of the limb and most of his torso, and continued to expand in a smooth-edged circle away from his feet. A weird, puissant rainbow of half-formed, effervesced dreams flickered in a halo around the body.

There was no sure way to tell how long ago the man had died. Was he one of the three that Skinner had spotted upstairs, one that had finally succumbed to the self-destructive ravings that the oneiric weapon could draw out? Better to assume that there were still three left to go. He shook his head and moved on.

As the veneine faded, so did Beckett's protection against the existential misery that lurked in his soul. Another dark hallway, another dangerously-disturbed man. Another threat, another monster. Navigating black, dangerous corridors, all while his body rotted out from beneath him, this had been his life for as long as he could remember anymore. And it would be his life until the fades finally claimed something irreplaceable—once they reached his heart, or lungs, or liver—he would die on his feet, pointlessly hunting some foul heresy. And when he was gone, men would continue; continue to threaten the safety of the Empire, continue to make monsters of themselves. The gloom shivered in his mind, strengthened by the reverberations of the oneiric weapon.

The fourth room was empty, too, just piles of broken furniture. Gorud shone his lantern across it, while Beckett gave it a cursory glance. The muscles in his gun hand throbbed fiercely now, and quivered in a way that presaged a cramp. *Empty*, he thought. *No, wait.* Beckett gestured to the therian, and pointed towards a far corner, towards an overturned table.

There was something…something moving there. He could see it, or he thought he could see it, through his blind eye. A flickering silhouette, a shape..a man drew himself up from his crouch behind the mislaid furniture. Blood caked his mouth and his hands twitched and writhed abominably, as though his fingers were struggling to violently detach themselves from their parent limbs. He chewed at his arms and shoulders, compulsively, like a dog trying to get at flees.

His mouth was a strange flower, an even circle of luminescent white teeth, long and curved like fishing hooks, like the petals of a lotus, they whirled and pulsed as he worked at his arms, cleaving meat and flesh away, freeing the strangeness within to the charged air that would give it shape and substance, congeal it from the imaginary to wickedly real…

No. No, Beckett thought. *That's wrong.* His mouth was an ordinary mouth. A human mouth, with human teeth and bloody lips. He stared up with glittering white eyes and shuffled past a body on the floor Beckett saw now was still twitching. *Was he one of the live ones? Is this two, or just one? Three?*

"Mr. Beckett?" Gorud whispered. "Mr. Beckett!"

The man leapt forward, and Beckett screamed as a hideous, shrieking, twisting pain coiled through his arm. The agony brought him to his knees and caused the muscles in his fingers to clench—the gun went off, but the bullet went wild, tearing a chunk of stone and plaster from a far wall. His hand knotted into a fist, Beckett found he couldn't release the trigger to fire again, couldn't even let go of the gun…

Teeth gnashing the madman fell on him, frenetic fingers clutching, as he tried to secure a grip, tried to bite a chunk out of Beckett's face. The coroner tucked his chin down, tried to keep his head low, as he struggled to tear the gun free from his frozen hand.

Gorud sprang forward then, leaving the lantern on the ground as he snatched at one of the madman's arms. Using momentum to make up for his lack of mass, the therian managed to spin the human around and off of Beckett, then, still holding tight, dropped low and curled up, sending the dream-poisoned gendarme rolling over his back and into the darkness. The man crashed painfully to the ground, but was on his feet again in a second. Gorud howled, great teeth bare, prepared to bite.

Beckett held his clenched hand up and fanned the hammer of his Feathersmith with his good left hand. The gunshots were miniature explosions, again and again as the massive revolver punched holes in the stranger's body, sending him staggering into the far wall. He opened his mouth and stretched it wide; for a moment, Beckett thought he saw that strange, toothy flower of a mouth again, before it was obscured by the colored spots left behind by the Feathersmith's muzzle flash.

There was silence, then, broken by James' sudden, furious spectral knocking. "All right?" Gorud asked him, over the noisy rattling.

"I can't...can't let go of the gun," Beckett grunted, the pain in his arm brought tears to his eyes. "I can't..." With one last heroic effort, he managed to lever the revolver from his right hand. The freed fingers immediately closed up, thought the pain remained. Panic surfaced too, as the sense that the muscles in his hand had been twisted around each other violated his body's sense of integrity. "Damn it, James!" Beckett shouted. "I can't understand you!"

The rapping continued, seeming to take on a panicked, hysterical edge to it. An alarm? A warning?

Gorud heard it, too. "Someone's coming."

"No," Beckett said, a sudden realization dawning. "Someone's getting out." He groaned and lurched to his feet. "Shit. Come on."

Gorud quickly grabbed the lantern, its light swinging nauseatingly across the walls, the hallway seeming to roll back and forth like the deck of a ship. The ground pitched wildly, and Beckett gripped his oar tightly, falling to his knees on the deck of the longboat. Up ahead, far, too far ahead, Fletcher's cigar pulsed dim and red in the dark. He turned to look at Beckett, thorny green vines crawling from the black holes where his eyes were, and then his whole shape dissolved into a pale nimbus of light, revealing another man. A stranger, stumbling down the stairs at the end of the hall, trailing a thick smear of black blood and an aura of half-formed dream images—smiling faces, women with sultry eyes, spiders with long, snaking tales and hands with fingertips made of ice.

Beckett fired, left-handed, missed. He fired again, and the hammer clicked on an empty chamber. "Damn it!" He ran after the man, outpacing Gorud, whose lantern cast the coroner's shadow ahead of them. *It doesn't matter, I know where he's going*, Beckett thought has he plunged into the dark, opening his revolver and stuffing it into the crook of his right arm while he fumbled with the bullets in his pocket, trying to reload. The old coroner crashed down the stairs, nearly falling, tumbling into the open receiving area, in time to see the poisoned man flee into the fading afternoon light that had crept in through the building's devastated entryway.

"No, no," Beckett muttered, "Come on." He tried to press a last bullet into its chamber, but dislodged the revolver. It fell to the ground with a clank, and scattered its ammunition across the floor, bullets vanishing into the scattering of shadows. "No!" He dropped to his knees, gasping as he felt the joint in his right leg explode, trying to ignoring the screaming pain as he searched for a bullet, just one bullet to load into the weapon. Something, anything. Gorud appeared beside him, nimble fingers playing across the debris-littered floor.

Driven by the violent, churning engine of fever-dreams that had grown in his heart, exploding outwards as radiation from the oneiric explosion had corroded the delicate partitions of his mind, the raving gendarme ran. The light burned at his eyes, but he pushed himself towards it as new, strange senses that itched about his skin told him of other minds and other pairs of eyes, and the new, blooming, degenerate and venomous lust drew him on, demanded that he vomit his stomach of poison and bile into their minds, to free them from the husks of rotting flesh into which they had suffered the misfortune of being born. He fled into the afternoon light, and looked out upon the looking eyes that saw him.

The thunder of gunfire stopped him short, and he didn't bother to look down as he felt his dreams bleed free of his wounds. He felt his body dissolve into meat and filth, and the new strange minds inside his mind wondered if the world would still be there when he left it.

SIX

Chretien [Crabtree-Daior] has come to me with a new project. He is of a mind with me regarding the nature of true Blasphemy, and is enthusiastic in his work, but misguided in his direction. Certainly, the ichor is a fascinating substance, but simply reinvigorating dead tissue is an insufficient means to create life as life was created. It is not the composition of a thing that makes it live, but the way the thing behaves: autonomously, with sensibility and awareness. That is the new life — not the demands of flesh perfected, but mind unencumbered by the demands of flesh at all.

I will enter into this project with him, but I must think more on the core truth of it.

--from the journal of Harcourt Wolfram, 1785

"All right," Beckett called, from the dark, bombed-out shell of the slaughterhouse. "It's me. It's Beckett. Don't shoot, all right?" He heard a sound like affirmation, and then limped into the last dregs afternoon sun. The air was bitterly cold now, the icy night threatening to fall on the city like an avalanche.

The last of his veneine high washed away, leaving a thousand little agonies in his limbs. His right leg felt like someone had smashed the knee with a hammer. His right hand felt like it had been tied up in torn, tangled knots. Beckett focused on the bitter thirst for veneine in the back of his throat. *Another shot,* he thought. *Just get to the coach, and take a shot.* He lurched past the dead gendarme, brushed past Valentine, who stood just beyond the exit, silver-plated revolvers smoking, an unreadable expression on his face.

Beckett slumped in the coach and if the men outside were talking he couldn't hear it. The sounds of the world were drowned out by the pounding in his ears, blood throbbing in his head like his veins would burst. He fumbled beneath the seat for his kit, and struggled to use the syringe with just one hand.

He had to hold the needle in his teeth while he pulled his sleeve up, exposing inflamed red veins and a constellation of tiny pink wounds; the shirtsleeve fell back into place the second he let go in order to grab the vial of veneine, and Beckett almost screamed with frustration.

"Here." It was Gorud. The therian had followed him in to the coach, and Beckett hadn't even noticed. The simian creature took the vial and syringe in his strong, dexterous fingers. Beckett pulled his right sleeve up, and Gorud shook his head. "No. Other arm."

The coroner nodded, and scraped his left sleeve up with his crippled hand. The skin was less damaged here; only a few pink pinpricks showed livid on his pale skin, and then blood vessels seemed less damaged. Deftly, the therian gripped Beckett's wrist, found a vein, and made the injection. He used the syringe precisely; no blood washed back through the needle.

It took a moment for the warmth of the veneine to spread about his body, and the relief was an incalculable joy to him. The pounding in his head receded, the aches faded. His hand began to relax and he flexed his fingers, mercifully, narcotically unconcerned by the cracks and pops he heard. He smelled saltwater then, and imagined rivulets of brackish fluid dribbling down the walls inside the coach, leaking in from the doors, pooling at his feet.

"This is dreamsnake venom," Gorud said. "This is too much."

"I—" Beckett began, then broke off. The absence left by the veneine-banished ringing in his ears was filled with a familiar voice.

"—not going in," Valentine was saying. "If he wanted to talk to you, he'd be talking to you. He doesn't. Now. Move back, before I move you."

The veneine was warm and rich and sweet, filling his mind with honey, dragging his eyelids down, soothing his battered body. Beckett wanted to lie down in the back seat and sleep. Instead, he raised his voice.

"It's all right, Valentine." The old coroner levered himself to his feet again, while the therian watched, silent. "It's all right. I'm coming out." He sighed and shivered in the cold despite the drug. He found Valentine standing, arms crossed, outside the coach. The Moral Responsibility officer was standing cross from him, huffing importantly. "You. Edly. Edder."

"Edelred."

"Good. Where's Skinner?"

"*Miss* Skinner went home, where she belongs. You are fully-equipped with knocker support," he gestured towards James, who stood off to the side, eyes covered in a band of silver, mouth twisted in a sour grimace. "There is absolutely no need to contribute to the constant erosion of our moral bedrock that employing a woman—"

"Can I ask you something?" Beckett asked, his voice suddenly good-natured. He knew he should be angry, should glower and glare and growl, and all that, but just couldn't find it in himself to do that right now. He was suffused with a sense of well-being, and had no desire to disturb that. "Do you believe all that, that you're saying? I mean," he leaned in close to the Gorgon-Ennering-Crabtree, "when they found you. To put you on the Committee, did they just ask around for men who were uncomfortable thinking about women? Or did they look around for sycophant cousins, who'd parrot any line of bullshit they were given if they thought it meant getting some crumbs from the Emperor's table?"

"I—"

"Never mind!" Beckett grinned, such an unexpected and appalling gesture that even Valentine took a step back. "I don't really care! Valentine, come with me."

"Mr. Beckett," Edelred Gorgon-Ennering-Crabtree spluttered. "I mean. Inspector Beckett. May I remind you that I am a member of an Esteemed Family?"

Beckett turned back to him, no longer grinning. His missing eye, the bleeding black rents on his face where his flesh had faded from sight, the glittering white teeth added up to a particularly gruesome expression nonetheless. "You may."

"Well," said Edelred. "I've got a job to do, too, Mr. Beckett, and that means sending your woman home. Mr. Ennering is your assigned knocker. You will use him for any future engagements. Do I make myself clear?"

"No," Beckett said, his voice dangerously quiet. "No, you don't. Because it sounds like you're giving me orders. That doesn't make a lot of sense to me."

"I have the authority," whispered Edelred. "To have you removed from your position. Is *that* clear enough for you?"

His temper had nearly made its way back through the drug, and Beckett found himself on the verge of saying precisely what Edelred could do with his authority, and considering also adding a few comments about what Edelred must have had removed in the first place to take a position with Moral Responsibility. He held his tongue when he saw Mr. Stitch.

The huge reanimate was shambling down Augre Street, and if it was bothered by the cold, or the situation, or anything else, there'd be no way to tell. Its grotesque, patchwork face was just as impassive as ever, the brass-ringed lenses of its eyes giving away nothing more than their constant sense of intense interest. Its limbs moved deliberately and awkwardly, careful with its mismatched joints, but covered ground quickly because of its long legs.

"Beckett." It said at last, in its tortured whisper of a voice. "Report."

"There was a high-intensity oneiric event. I established a perimeter and then went in to eliminate the survivors."

"The woman," interrupted Edelred, "that was *released* from the coroners was—"

Stitch wasn't listening. "And?"

"I succeeded," Beckett told him. "Valentine took out the last one. There's no one left alive inside, so the oneiric damage should be minimized."

Mr. Stitch nodded and looked away, those cold, inhuman eyes delivering data directly to the miraculously complex difference engine it had for a brain. It raked its gaze over every inch of the street and the bombed-out gendarmerie headquarters. Beckett knew that the reanimate would soon go inside and study every piece of wood, every stone, every broken pile of furniture, every corpse. In time, it would wrestle the truth from uncooperative evidence.

"Thoughts?" Stitch asked.

Beckett shrugged. "Oneiric munition, I think. Could be the ettercap, treaty or no. They've attacked in the city before. But there was a lot brought back by our own soldiers, a lot misplaced. Anyone could have gotten a hold of something like that."

"So. Why?"

"It could be the gangs," Valentine put in. "Anonymous John works in Red Lanes a lot. They've been getting bolder, lately."

The old coroner allowed that this could certainly be possible. "It could be…" Beckett muttered. "It could be sharpsies. I know most of them ran, but…you could hide an army in the Arcadium. It'd just take one with a grudge." He rubbed his face, over his blind eye, ignored the eerie sensation caused by the numbness. "Hell, it could be anyone. Just carrying a weapon like that around could drive you insane. He might have dropped it on the gendarmes because they'd chased him off from some doorstep, or because he was hallucinating and thought that it was the imperial palace. He might have thought it was his mother's house."

Stitch nodded. "I. Will. Investigate."

"Hm," Beckett replied. "Fine. Fine."

The giant reanimate shambled off, its subtle aura of menace seemed to drag James away, causing the knocker to follow after it like a small moon pulled into orbit. Beckett watched them for a few moments, then turned to Valentine. "All right. Did you read that pamphlet?"

"Oh! Yes. Here, hang on, I made notes…"

"Not now," Beckett said. "Not here. Come with me. Have you met Gorud?"

Seven

While she rode back to her boarding house, Skinner chewed and spat and flexed her fingers, itching for the chance to snare Gorgon-Ennering-Crabtree's neck and just crush it. The thought was deeply satisfying, though she knew the act would be far more trouble than it was worth. Still, it didn't hurt to think about it, and so she allowed herself several minutes of purely murderous daydreaming. The fantasy passed, and left her with a slick sickness of shame at her joy. Skinner set it aside.

At the house, she left the coachman behind, who muttered about the fare and seemed nearly courageous enough to demand it from her, involvement with the Coroners be damned, and likewise damned the dishonor implicit in demanding money from a blind girl. If he might have complained, he was stilled by the presence of Mrs. Crewell. Skinner could hear her at the door, great lungs full and ready to lay into the man, whether his request was reasonable or not.

If anything came of it, Skinner never found out. She retreated to her room and sat by her window, pressing her hearing out where she knew it was quiet. Mrs. Crewell's boarding house had its back to the Daior Chapel necropolis. Skinner listened to the dead, and let them soothe her.

Silence, to a knocker, is a strange phenomenon, and especially strange in a city like Trowth. The city's sighted inhabitants often ignore it, preoccupied with the desolate loneliness of gray stone and worn, green bronze. Their eyes distract them from the merciless quiet of the city, whose cavernous stone underbelly, thick fogs, and bitter cold seem to muffle the casual sounds of daily living. During Second Winter, there are not even beggars in the street, or ragmen or bone-pickers harvesting their merchandise. There are no rats, or crows, or seagulls to hunt the empty city streets for scraps — all life that has no home to go to retreats deep into the Arcadium, ceding ground to the inevitable icy onslaught.

Despite the ringing, resonant quiet of the city, the eerie underpinning of stillness that quietly draws the life from the most animated conversations, there are very few places that were truly silent to Skinner's preternatural hearing. Always, above that black gap of quiet was a haze of tiny noises — of hurried breaths and distant echoes, ruffling wool and rattling footsteps. The myriad sounds of humanity drew her clairaudience to them, exerting a nearly-imperceptible pull on her senses.

It was often thought that knockers were capable of communicating with the dead, and this was because of how they often chose to live near graveyards. The misconception stemmed from the average citizen's inability to understand what it meant for the knockers, that their hearing should be so painfully acute. Knockers listened to the dead not because corpses were noted conversationalists, or because they had eldritch secrets to impart; they listened because the dead were so benignly *quiet*.

The Vie-Gorgon coach came for Skinner sharp at seven, rolling to a stop just as Chapel bells finished tolling the hour. The echo faded, and dissolved into the sounds of Mrs. Crewell, busying herself about the house with a housekeeper's native self-importance. She would not suffer a spot of dust on the day that the Raithower Vie-Gorgon coach came to her hotel, even if it carried a man of such small importance as the Raithower Vie-Gorgon coachman. Coachmen talk, Mrs. Crewell well knew, and she'd not have any gossip about the state of her house.

The coach was warm, and of a style that Skinner was unfamiliar with — she shared a large compartment with the driver himself, separated from him by a mesh partition, rather than having him sit outside, warmed only by portable heating mechanisms. Skinner could hear him breathing and shuffling about behind the screen, whickering softly to his horses as the need arose. He did not speak to her, though, and Skinner felt strange raising her voice to him. Was it appropriate to speak to a coachman if he was sitting inside with you? It would be rude to say *nothing*, wouldn't it? But he was also a *Vie-Gorgon* coachman, and the Vie-Gorgons took propriety very seriously. Surely he'd be offended if she said something. Or not? Perhaps he hated the stifling conformity demanded by polite society, and was really itching for an ordinary conversation with an ordinary person, and was just waiting for her to say something?

Am I nervous? Skinner thought to herself. *Is this why I'm losing my mind?* "Do you," she said, then cleared her throat. "I mean, have you been to the Royal, before?"

There was a moment of considered silence, and Skinner worried again that she'd made the wrong decision. When he spoke, the coachman had a grizzled old working-man's voice that seemed out of place. "Once. Miss V gave me and the missus floor tickets."

"What did you see?"

"Oh. Hm. Conscious...*Conscientious Assignations*, I think it were called. Big fuss about it in the papers, you know? That Eveham fellow was all over it, and he's a laugh for a read, but I can't say I've ever much cared for anything he's got behind. Couldn't find nothing particularly interesting about this one. Closed quick too, didn't it?"

"Closed quick" might have been an understatement, Skinner thought. *The Conscious Assignation* had played at the Royal for a week, billowed by favorable reviews from Andre Eveham, the drama critic at the *White Star*. If he was actually a poor arbiter of theatrical quality—and, as some suspected, really just a mouthpiece for the Empire's preferences for the theater—he made up for it with a brutally clever wit. Eveham's reviews were the most widely read in the city, but seemed to have little bearing on the success of their subjects.

"You didn't like it?" She asked.

"Well, it didn't make sense, did it? Fella's keeping that woman safe, right, because her uncle's after her? And so he's got her in that little house, right...did you see it?" He coughed. "Er. Uhm, sorry miss. I mean...did you...had you...uh..."

"I was there opening night, sir," she told him, a small smile on her face. "I like opening nights."

"Yeah, well, all right," the coachman went on. "So he's got her in that house, right? But there's never no, you know. Touchin', or nothing like that. And they're goin' to be married at the end of the play, we think they're in love and all that, right? But he's been to that little room every night, and not once have they put hands on each other."

"Well. I think that'd be more than a trifle scandalous, wouldn't you? Hardly a *conscientious* assignation, then."

"Yur, well, I know. Can't do none of that stuff on the stage, can you? Some committee or other would be on you in a minute. Still, how'm I supposed to believe that two young people like that are all hot and bothered for each other, but don't never do *nothing* about it? They don't even say something like, 'Oh, I want to put it to you somethin' fierce, but we can't...' now, nevermind how I says it, I'm not a writer or such, but you know what I mean?"

"You didn't believe it."

"That's it. That's right, right there. Didn't believe it. Didn't believe a word of it. Like the fella—who wrote it, what's-his-name?"

"Bertram Sitwell."

"Sitwell, right, he's just writin' about how he *thinks* people should be. But they ain't that way, if you know what I mean, and maybe if he weren't a writer, and maybe got himself around a little bit, got down to the Riverside once or twice," he coughed again. "Er. Excuse me, miss. I do go on sometimes. Not a fit subject of conversation for a lady."

I've personally killed six men, and participated in the execution of over a hundred. There's not a lot you can talk about that's going to upset me. "Of course," she said, but she did not pursue the topic, and the driver had little else to say.

A long silence that sounded to Skinner like a constellation of tiny sounds, and then they had arrived at the Royal. The driver politely lead her inside, past a noisy, chattering crowd, and upstairs to the Family boxes.

Emilia Vie-Gorgon was waiting for her, along with another young lady. Neither said anything until the coachman had left—his departure a bold violation of the ordinance that all women were to be accompanied by chaperones while in public. Skinner gingerly found a seat for herself to occupy, while the other two women sat in silence.

"Miss Skinner," said Emilia Vie-Gorgon, abruptly. The youth of her voice was surprising, though perhaps it shouldn't have been; famous as she was, Skinner realized, upon a certain amount of reflection, that Emilia couldn't have been more than twenty. "I would like you to meet Nora Feathersmith. Nora, Elizabeth Skinner, formerly of the royal coroners."

This was an event nearly as intriguing as the invitation itself. Nora Feathersmith was the youngest daughter of Ephraim Feathersmith, patriarch of one of the most peculiar families in Trowth. Like all major families in the Empire, the Feathersmiths had their own special area of business—Ephraim continued a long tradition of excellence and control over engineering and manufactury. Feathersmith factories built everything in Trowth that had more than two moving parts—from revolvers to typewriters to train engines. And yet, unlike the Crabtrees or the Daiors or the Ennerings, the Feathersmiths had never received, nor, to anyone's knowledge, even *sought* Estimation by the crown.

That is, the Feathersmiths were a family, but not a Family. They were highly-esteemed by both the public and their colleagues in industry, but never Esteemed. In many ways, this served as quite an extraordinary advantage against many of their competitors: by never finding favor with an emperor placed on the throne by one Family, they never found themselves in *dis*favor when a new Family secured control of it. This permitted the Feathermiths to remain at the top of their industry since its earliest incarnation as weaponeers during the reign of Agon Diethes, to weather crises of interregnum, revolution, and the exposure of certain of its members as heretics. Peculiarly, by shunning the power that Estimation brought with it, Ephraim Feathersmith's antecedents had found themselves a broader freedom.

"Miss Feathersmith."

"Nora, please," the young lady responded, lazily. She took a long drag on a cigarette or cigar that smelled of tobacco and dreamsnake venom.

"And you must call me Emilia," said Emilia Vie-Gorgon. "We are, I think, going to be great friends. You know my cousin, don't you?"

"Valentine." Skinner replied.

"Oh, he's a charmer," Nora put in. "And such lovely hair…"

"Generally," Skinner replied, a little stiffly, "I find him to be rather irritating. Is he..is that…why…how you know me, I mean?"

Nora chuckled faintly, and Emilia was silent. That silence was profound in a way that Skinner had never heard from another person before. Ordinarily, she could make out the character of a silence — a thoughtful hesitation, an embarrassed lack of a response. From Emilia, she gleaned nothing: it was as though the young woman had vanished off of the face of the earth, hid herself deep in the aethyr while she contemplated a correct response.

"No," when her voice came, after that strange, total silence, it was softly shocking. "We have another friend in common, actually, one who thinks very highly of your abilities."

"Hm. Perhaps you should have him talk to the Emperor."

"Yes. Perhaps." Emilia replied. Was that the hint of a smile behind her voice? A barb? There was no getting past the wall of smooth confidence that sheltered her private feelings. Emilia Vie-Gorgon was the kind of woman that could lie to her mother with the calm, casual certainty that ordinary people used to remark on the color of the sky. "Ah, the show begins!"

If it was a tradition to be silent during a play, it was apparently a privilege of box seats to offer commentary. Emilia and Nora snickered furiously from the opening — a simpering detonation of music from Corimander's last symphony — through each and every scene.

"Oh, this is lovely. Can she walk? Maybe they should get someone to carry her onstage."

"That's it, love. Say the words *louder*. That'll improve them."

"Oh, he can't help it, Emmy — he's sad. Sad people say things LOUDLY."

"Yes, and so do ANGRY PEOPLE. And so do HAPPY PEOPLE."

The commentary greatly improved on the play — *Alas, My Love* — which was, in Skinner's estimation, utter tripe. A new play by the now thoroughly-defamed Bertram Sitwell, *Alas, My Love* was modeled after the old pastoral-royal comedies of the 17th century, where every shepherd turned out to be a king in disguise. They were all an oblique reference to the ascendance of Owen I Gorgon as the first Emperor of Trowth after the interregnum, and meant to legitimize the Gorgon-Vies' claim to the imperial line. The Gorgon-Vies spent a great deal of time attempting to legitimize their claims to the imperial line, and usually in as thoroughly a ham-handed fashion.

"Oh, he's gone up on his lines."

"Well, can you blame him? I've only had to hear it once, and I'm already trying to forget it."

"There's the cue card boy. Oh, look, he's lovely! They should just have him play the role."

"Certainly, he couldn't be worse, unless he turns out to be a deaf-mute."

"Not at all; I should think not having to hear the script would be a categorical improvement. Miss Skinner?"

Skinner had been sitting, quietly amused, though not comfortable enough to participate. She perked up when Emilia addressed her. "Elizabeth, please. And, yes, I imagine there are innumerable ailments that might be alleviated with a precipitously silenced performance."

Nora Feathersmith giggled enthusiastically, and Emilia certainly sounded like she could be smiling.

"We shannot be," the lead actor proclaimed during the pause, "together this day. Fate shall keep us all away, as does the winter stray the mourning dove, we are alone, alas, my love."

And then, mercifully, it was intermission. The intermission revealed another privilege of the box seats, which was complimentary, catered dinner. Quiet, discreet gentlemen—Skinner pegged them as typical theater ushers, conscripted perhaps, or else rewarded, with the task—brought in trays of warm food: spiced meats, soft bread, deliciously sweet fruits. Someone left a decanter of wine on a small tray at Skinner's side, and she carefully located a glass.

The wine was superb, rich in flavor, but smooth as water. It was like drinking spring sunshine on her face. She sipped at it carefully, though. Intoxication was more than a little dangerous to a knocker, who required great focus to keep their senses under control.

"I take it, Elizabeth, that you aren't enjoying the play," Emilia said, after they'd had a few moments to set to their meal.

Skinner swallowed a bit of lusciously soft bread. "I am quite enjoying the *experience*, certainly. I will admit that I've heard better work from Mr. Sitwell."

There was another one of those vacant, absolute silences from Emilia. "Yes," she said, after a moment. "He has rather gone downhill, hasn't he. What was his first one...?"

"*The Bone-Collector's Daughter*," Nora put in. Skinner could hear her lick crumbs from her lips. "That was an interesting one. He'd probably have been hanged if he'd put it up in Canth, of course. And it surely never would have played here."

"No," agreed Emilia, "but then, someone who desires to keep you quiet is the surest sign that you've something important to say, isn't it? Wouldn't you agree, Elizabeth?"

There was something strange about all this, and Skinner suddenly felt like an animal wandering about in a forest full of traps. Pits and snares all around her, disguised beneath the impeccable camouflage of polite conversation. "I...suppose."

"Of course it is," said Emilia, quietly. "If you want to say only what everyone would *like* you to say, then it hardly needs to be said at all. Maybe that's why we're drawn to it. The forbidden ideas, I mean."

Forbidden. Skinner felt a knot in her stomach. *Is she talking about the Sciences? Surely...surely not. They don't expect me to participate in heresy...*

"Oh, but Miss Elizabeth knows all about things forbidden," Emilia said lightly. "Yes?"

"I think that, perhaps, I ought to leave," Skinner said, as she stood. "I doubt very much you'll find me amenable to...what I suspect you have in mind."

"Oh, dear, do sit down. I assure you that you will be amenable to the idea. I know, because I am certain you've *already* been a part of it."

"I...what?"

"Please. Sit."

Skinner did, and wracked her brain. What could Emilia mean? Had someone been implicating her in heresy?

"You know, Mr. Sitwell hasn't been very popular since his first play. His later works seem to lack a certain...*something*."

Oh. Skinner realized at once. *That.* "Yes. Gratitude, perhaps?"

"Gratitude, that's lovely. Did you know, Nora," Emilia said to her friend, "that a selection of the *Bone-Collector's Daughter* was published in *The Observer* fully a month before the play opened?"

"Why," said Nora Feathersmith, with obviously feigned surprise, "I had no idea!"

"It's true! And in it, he credited a collaborator, who must remain nameless...oh, why was that? I can't remember the exact words..."

"For propriety's sake," Skinner responded. "Which was a load of horse… well, nonsense. Sitwell had been looking to dump his…collaborator… ever since they'd started working together. Probably because he felt she threatened him and his over-blown ego."

"She?" Nora Feathersmith asked. "That seems a little peculiar. Woman aren't permitted to write for the stage. Even during the war, they never let us do *that*."

"Did I say 'she'?" Skinner replied. "Must have been a slip of the tongue."

"Oh, come now," Emilia put in. "This is a private booth. I assure you, there is no one to overhear us. Nora, did you know, I found out who Mr. Sitwell's nameless collaborator was?"

"Really!" There was that feigned surprise again, and Skinner realized she was well and truly snared. "Who was it?"

"Why, a woman working for the Royal Coroners by the name of Elizabeth Skinner."

"My goodness!" Nora said. "Is it true, Elizabeth? Did you help him write *The Bone-Collector's Daughter*?"

For most of her life, Skinner had felt herself a woman with a calm disposition, not given to flights of aggravation, or suffering from an excess of pride or choler. If she had seethed inwardly when the Committee on Moral Responsibility had taken her job, she had displayed outwards nothing but good grace. If she was furious at Edelred Gorgon-Ennering-Crabtree for forcing her to abandon Beckett in that slaughterhouse, she had presented a face as cold as a marble statue.

And yet. Perhaps she'd never discussed something so close to her heart. Perhaps her tongue was loosened by the wine. Whatever the case, she found herself unable to restrain the bitterness in her voice. "Help? Help *him* write it? You seem to have Mr. Sitwell confused with someone with talent. *I* wrote that play, and Bertram struggled to drag down every word. If I hadn't needed him to see it produced, I'd have kicked him to the curb after he crossed out a single line. The man can't string ten words together to order *breakfast*, and can't so much as touch a sentence without turning it to gibberish. Word and fuck, half of *this* play," she gestured towards the stage, where the inanely innocuous *Alas, My Love* had recommenced, "is plagiarized from Henri Montcour's 1787 version. All he's done is translate it badly from the Sarein and then cram it with his own personal brand of prattling nursery rhymes."

There was silence for a moment, and the lead actor's voice reached them in the box. "The king dost keep a revel here tonight, we shallst run first, or else take flight!"

Emilia Vie-Gorgon and Nora Feathersmith at once broke into helpless laughter. Skinner compressed her lips to a thin line, and then felt herself compelled to join them. It took several minutes and an entire carafe of wine before they were able to regain control of themselves. Their hysterics were of such a fortitude that the poor actors, still valiantly trying to maintain the seriousness of the scene, were obliged to stop and start from the top no fewer than three times.

"Ah," Emilia sighed, "Nora, I do believe we've found the person that we're looking for. What do you think, Elizabeth?"

"I'm sure I have no idea what you mean."

"Goodness, you're right," Emilia said, as she filled Skinner's wineglass. "I've gotten ahead of myself. We'd like you to write a play."

"Yes?" Skinner said, gulping down some more wine. "Any play, or a particular one?"

Nora laughed again. "We've one in mind, actually."

"Do you know," Emilia asked, "*Theocles*?"

"Oh my," Skinner whispered. "You are a pair of wicked young ladies." *Theocles* was a 15th century poem about the second Emperor of the continent — Theocles the Tall, who had assassinated Agon Diethes and usurped the throne. He'd presided over a particularly oppressive regime, and had begun a foolish, ill-advised war with Thranc. His martial failures had led to the Second Reconciliation of the Powers, which had broken the Empire into its component parts and seen Theocles deposed and executed.

The parallels were close enough to the reign of the current emperor that Skinner could have found herself arrested for writing it even if she *weren't* a woman. The poem itself was on the Empire's black-list. And these two young ladies, daughters of two of the most rich and respected families in the Empire, wanted...what did they want? To see it onstage? To get themselves arrested?

"No one will do it. There's not a producer in Trowth that would touch a play like that with a ten foot pole."

"Oh," said Emilia, with that enigmatic sound of a smile. "We'll find someone."

"They should do it here," put in Nora, and her grin sounded fearsome. "Right at the Royal."

"Never," Skinner replied. "They never will."

"It's a wonderful idea, Nora," Emilia said. "We shall arrange to have it performed right here at the Royal Theater."

"How do you plan to do that, exactly?" Skinner was still grinning around her wine, not entirely convinced the two girls were serious.

"Didn't you know, darling?" Emilia Vie-Gorgon asked her. "I own the Royal."

Eight

It was a common misconception among many of the Trowthi people that the strangling bureaucracy of the Emperor and his assorted Ministries was something that had been inflicted on them. No sooner, for instance, had the Committee for Public Safety been dissolved than the Committee on Moral Responsibility had replaced it. The pressgangs had been dismissed, and almost immediately the gendarmeries monopolized law enforcement. In fact, much to the bitter resentment of the opinion-makers, editors, and columnists of the broadsheets, many of the men in the new committees were the very same ones who had been unemployed when the old committees were extinguished.

This misapprehension on the part of the people was based on an error of assessment: because these committees had *names*, it was quite natural to think that they were entities independent of the public itself. A thing with a name is a thing distinct, a unique creature with its own boundaries and habits, its own patterns of behavior, it's own birth and life and death. When it grows troublesome, it can be killed and, to the mind of the average citizen, that should improve the world by decreasing the amount of bureaucracy that he must suffer, however incrementally.

The noisy mouthpieces of the public complain imagine that they are making a certain progress, or else feel that progress is frustrated: either they have succeeded in murdering a troublesome beast that sees the public as its prey, or else they are rightly frustrated by *yet another* meddlesome creature that's been foisted upon them.

For any man who took a longer view, their frustrations were obviously misplaced. Bureaucracy was not a thing *imposed* on the population. It was something that grew up *from* the population. The bureaus, the committees, the ministries, the innumerable degrees of rank and office, the impossible tangle of hierarchies and authority were not some alien feature thrust upon the Empire, but a direct product of the psychology of the very men involved. It was the need

51

to dominate that demanded the creation of hierarchy; the need to rank oneself according to one's peers—to prove himself better, or to plan out whom one must overcome next—that created the ranks. The need to gain more and more from his fellows is what drove a man to make the ranks complex, to carve out his own little bailiwick in a world filled with men struggling to do just the same. Trowth could not rid itself of its addiction to bureaucracy any more than it could rid itself of its addiction to water or fresh air (though black-smoke-belching factories did struggle mightily to break that last habit).

Valentine didn't know any of this at a conscious level, but he had spent his life deep in the cut-throat politics of the Esteemed Families, and had made the following similar observation: there were two kinds of men in politics. The first kind took everything personally, viciously avenging themselves of insult and offense, cold-bloodedly conniving or scheming, or just outright murdering their way to the top of their fields. The second kind took nothing personally, and found themselves a niche, out of harm's way, disengaged and uninvolved where they might have a few moments of peace without checking every glass of wine for poison. The first kind of man was often successful and rich, but was never permitted to stop fighting to maintain that success. The second kind of man rarely accomplished anything of note, but was rarely perturbed by this condition.

In his youth, Valentine Vie-Gorgon had graciously bowed out of the fight for dominance among the Comstock Vie-Gorgons, and with the Vie-Gorgons in general, and with every other beady-eyed, raisin-hearted and mercenary-minded member of the Estimation. He found a niche for himself, and decided that he would occupy it come hell or high water, and if his father was disappointed that he'd never be fit to run the family businesses, at least there was never any worry that some lesser cousin might see him as an obstacle to be removed.

All of this was to the point that, when Valentine realized he was being followed by a pair of agents from the Committee on Moral Responsibility, he didn't take it personally. This, after all, was just how the world worked; he could no more blame the men for following after him than he could blame the sky for raining on him.

It was early morning, and the strained watery light that flickered off the mountain of stormy architecture of Trowth did little to alleviate the cold, though it was actually one of the warmest periods of the day. The early morning--when warm air swept briefly in from the sea—and the late afternoon were the only times during Second Winter that pedestrians were common; a small, muted collection of passers-by and vendors had tentatively come out into the cold streets above St. Dunsany's. The air was just barely tolerable, and tasted faintly of salt and fish. Even the normally antisocial and solitary citizens of the city would take the time to wander about for a few hours, gamely trying to catch a fleeting glimpse of the sun.

Valentine discovered the two men completely by chance. They were ordinary-enough looking gentlemen; clean-shaven, reasonably well-dressed, though not so ostentatiously as to attract notice. One of them seemed excessively pale, which could mean he was a Family member, or it could mean that he'd spent a long convalescence after the war. Valentine spotted them the first time when he realized he'd forgotten his bill-fold at Raithower House and had turned around to go back inside. He spotted them a second time while, on his way back out to Vie Abbey, he had a sudden whim for a cup of djang. He called to the coachman to stop at the next stall and, when he got out, noticed the very same two men, chatting amiably and seemingly entirely unaware of his presence, passing by in a hansom cab, their faces lit by the red glow of a pair of over-hanging heat emitters.

Valentine nearly dropped his cup when he saw them, then did his best to appear like a man unruffled by surprise. *Maybe they haven't realized that I've made them.* He failed at this endeavor, his own natural enthusiasm and nervous energy immediately overwhelming all attempts to appear calm and collected, but it was to Valentine's particular fortune that the men in question were unfamiliar enough with his ordinary behaviors to note it.

"Here, now," Valentine whispered to the driver, a young man whose name Valentine had somewhere misplaced. "Go on ahead without me. I'll meet you up at the abbey."

Just because the men had no personal malice against him was no reason to make their job easy, reasoned Valentine. He had been making certain plans for losing tails when they arose—undaunted by the fact that he had to his knowledge never before been tailed in his life—and was eager to try them out. He stood still as his coach rolled away, and sipped at his hot djang, ostensibly pretending to look in the window of a merchant shop—one that sold ladies' undergarments, a fact which would have made the whole deception quite obvious if either of the two shadows had noticed it—while he surreptitiously watched the men out of the corner of his eye.

Sure enough, they stopped their cab, and made a great show of animated bargaining over the price of a meat pie at a nearby stall. Valentine smiled, and decided to put his plan into action.

It was an act of supreme will that permitted him to walk sedately—rather than sprint—towards Haypenny Street. He took the narrow, crooked lane into the dark of the Arcadium beneath him, ducking beneath a low stone arch.

This stretch of Trowth's undercity was lit by the eerie, cool blue glow of the phlogiston lamps, and occasional drums where oil fires flickered. It created a strangely shifting, purple-hued light, but actually made the whole place quite warm. It was no wonder that the claustrophobic covered streets were littered with human detritus: homeless men and women and children, indigent bodies that huddled against the stone, wrapped in ratty blankets, too cold or sick or tired to even beg, clustered around those warm oil drums.

Valentine slipped along Haypenny Street, quickly making his way a little deeper into the labyrinthine depths. His scheme, which was uncharacteristically well-thought out, had been to memorize a dozen entrances and exits into the vast network of narrow alleys and roads, a handful of passages between them, and a few landmarks so that he could find his way back to a familiar route. He now knew that, wherever he was in the city, he was no more than a half a mile from one of his points of entry — provided he wasn't all the way out in Mudside or Bluewater, or something. He could chose from a variety of exits at random, and the rapid succession of sharp turns, switchbacks, and stairways that extended both back to the city above, and below to even further-buried streets, meant that unless his followers were literally right on his heels, they had no chance of keeping up.

Even the echoes contrived to his advantage, something that had not even occurred to Valentine when he'd made the plan: should he ever be tailed by a knocker, the plentitude of stone walls and arches, bronze sculptures, and bridges overhead would exponentially multiply the echoes of his footsteps, and make tracking him nearly impossible.

So it was with a sense of elation that Valentine, after a brief jaunt through the dark tunnels in Trowth's underbelly, emerged near the Royal Mile. That sense persisted as he hailed a cab, and took it to the outskirts of the city, back to Vie Abbey, which had been his goal from the outset.

The elation only faded when he arrived, and saw another small hansom, parked at a short distance from the entrance to the Abbey, where a third gentleman, this one wearing long moustaches, looked very much like a tourist haggling with his driver over the cost of his fare. *Of course they had someone just follow the coach, too. Idiot*, Valentine thought to himself. *Oh, well.* He approached the mustachioed man. "Hallo, chum," said Valentine in his brightest, cheeriest voice. "Shouldn't be too long there. An hour or two, maybe, if you want to hop off and get a tipple before we resume." He handed him the now-empty djang cup. "Oh, and would you mind dropping this for me with Christo, over at Haypenny, if you get around there any time soon? Thanks much."

He left the astonished man, holding the used cup, and headed up towards the abbey gates, nodding and smiling at the uniformed guards who stood, miserable and frigid in the icy air, eternally at attention.

"I can't let you look at any of those things, of course."

"What do you mean, you can't?" Valentine asked the bishop's secretary's adjunct. "You have to. Look at the little badge, for fuck's sake." He waved the copper coroner's shield in front of the man's face.

"It's illegal, for one," said the man, middle-aged, with graying hair and a sturdy familiarity with his job that he was plainly loathe to forgo. He wore red and purple robes with an ornate white and gold shawl; finery deeply at odds with the man's stubbornly ordinary features. He looked as though the real secretary's adjunct had stepped out for tea, and just thrown a cassock over a local shoemaker and had him fill in. "And it's a heresy for another. Do you want me to get in trouble?"

"You *can't* get in trouble," *you fucking idiot,* Valentine said. "I am the Coroners. If someone were going to come here and arrest you and execute you, it would be me, and I'm already not going to do that." *YOU FUCKING IDIOT.*

The man had wet lips that he kept licking nervously. He pouted suddenly. "How do I know this isn't some kind of a trick?"

Valentine suppressed the urge to pound his head on the desk. It was a lovely wooden desk, in the adjunct's small, tastefully-appointed office. There were books on the shelves, weathered and worn as though they'd actually been read, and a podium with a great, leather-bound copy of the Grammars on it. "Well, that's a good point. But, how do you know what my plan is? Maybe I'm here to arrest you for impeding an official investigation, and I'm just trying to trick you into not letting me see the books."

The adjunct paused, and actually seemed to consider the idea, which nearly had Valentine chewing the carpets in frustration. "All right," the man said, after a moment. "But you've got to make sure that you sign in."

He led the coroner through the corridors of Vie Abbey. The Abbey had been built long before the Architecture Wars, and so well before the Vie-Gorgon's had settled on their long, thin, narrow style of design. The Abbey had an old-world feel to it — broad hallways, fat columns on geometric plinths, galleries and balconies everywhere. What wasn't dull gray granite was covered in rich, vibrant tapestries, depicting the history of the Goetic Church and the Church Royal all the way back to the Immolation. They followed the halls down past the library, to a dank, wooden room filled with rough tables and dirt.

"You have to wait here while I get the ledger," the man said, and left.

Valentine sat down on one of the benches and tapped his feet. He'd begun to read the quarto that Beckett had found, as per instructions, but was having a certain amount of trouble. It wasn't that the text was unclear: it was, in fact, almost frighteningly clear. And specific. And simple. It was the kind of text that could have instructed a ten-year-old in heretic science and produced quality results. The problem was simply that Valentine had nothing to compare it to—whether this quarto was more or less simple than traditional ectoplasmatic texts, whether it conformed to establish beliefs on heresy or church doctrine, the coroner had no idea.

One of the troubles, he mused, while he waited for the adjunct to return, *with secret information is that those of us who are charged with finding it won't recognize it when we see it.* The Coroners were given scant little information about the nature of the crimes they were to investigate—only the effects. Beckett had gleaned more than a little just from his history, but Valentine was stumbling about in the dark. And, lucky stumbler that he was, the young man had stumbled onto an idea: the Church Royal, he knew, made a habit of collecting heretical texts. They were rare, of course, and access was restricted. But if he could just get in and have a look at one or two, it might give him…well, he didn't know *what* it might give him. He only knew that he didn't know anything now, and could only think of one way of knowing more: the library.

"Here it is," the church official said as he returned, carrying a huge, dusty book whose pages looked brittle enough that they might crumble to dust from being looked at too closely. "You've got to sign in, and I've got to make you sign an oath." He opened the book and set it in front of Valentine.

The coroner put the date, and then wrote his name in—the second name on this page. The previous entry was someone with a last name that looked like "Feathersmith," and was dated more than a hundred years ago. Valentine would have to turn the page to see any of the earlier entries, but he was genuinely worried about the integrity of the book.

"All right, the oath, hang on." The man took a small piece of paper from the pocket of his robes. "Dost thou swearen, upon…er…sorry, it's in Middle-Trowthi, I don't think anyone's updated it in about five hundred years. Just say yes when I'm done. Ah. Swearen that thee lawfulle secretes herein enclosed, by sondry means and many, shalle by Holie Saviour and Pyre and Worde, remaine fit and kept by hearte to ende?" He paused and, after a moment, nodded at Valentine.

"Uh. Yes."

"Okay, come on." The adjunct took Valentine through another old wooden door, and down a set of stone steps into a long, dark, room. The light that spilled down from the stairs only served to illuminate a small semicircle around the two of them. The coroner could see three shoulder-high sets of bookshelves, extending off into the dark. They were packed with books, withered, decaying pamphlets, rolled-up scrolls, and little tin plates with glyphs etched on them.

The adjunct muttered something, and then threw a great knife-switch by the door. Immediately, dozens of blue phlogiston lamps pulsed to life, buzzing faintly, bathing the room with their light.

It was *enormous.*

This sub-library must have stretched for a hundred yards off at least, and was nearly fifty yards wide. And throughout the entire space those long, low bookshelves stretched, each one packed full of books and papers and words.

"Welcome to the Black Library," the man said. "Ectoplasmatics are numbered 300 through 800, right hand corner over there."

"Wait...wait. What is this?"

The adjunct looked at him skeptically. "This is the Black Library. It's where we put all the heretical documents so no one can read them. We've been filling it up for...oh, about nine hundred years now, I think."

"All of this?"

"Oh, sure. I imagine a lot of it's pretty repetitive, though. I remember, the church found a great cache of books about chimerastry a few years back, and most of them were just attempts to recreate Shandor's sixteenth."

"His sixteenth what?"

"Pamphlet. He wrote twenty-two, I think, about all sorts of things. Five of them are heretical — fifteen through twenty. The last two were about waterwheels."

"What did the heretical ones say?"

The adjunct harrumphed importantly and fiddled with his belt. "Well, I don't know, do I? They're heresy. I never read them."

"Then how did you know the ones that you found were heresy?"

He rolled his eyes. "Well, they said what they were doing right in the title. Besides that, the church has people look through them. Never more than a page at a time. Then, they give a summary to the Bishop, and the Bishop reads all the summaries and decides whether or not there's heresy. That way, no one actually reads the whole thing. Look are you going to look through this stuff or not? I can get in a lot of trouble for bringing you down here."

Valentine dismissed his concerns with a wave of his hand, as he threaded through the shelves towards the ectoplasmatics section. "Aren't you worried? About me reading this stuff?"

The adjunct shrugged. "I don't suppose. I mean, if we can't trust the Coroners to know what heresy is, who can we trust?"

This was a valid point, and one that Valentine could not dispute. In fact, it led him to some serious questions as to why, as a coroner, he hadn't been required to read all of this material in the first place. It was surely no wonder that thousands of heretics were constantly operating directly under the noses of Beckett and his fellow inspectors when they had only the barest idea of what to look for. *Something*, Valentine thought, *to bring up with Stitch. Maybe he could read them all, and at least print up a bunch of notes for us to look at?* Valentine could not recall having read more than the most skeletal descriptions of the thirteen heretical sciences, and what kinds of things precisely counted.

It was all in one pamphlet, with a number of columns. "Healing the sick," for example, was in the "acceptable" column. "Raising the dead" was in the "heretical" column.

The ectoplasmatics section of the Library was arranged ostensibly alphabetically, but more than three quarters of the books, papers, quartos, folios, and scrolls were anonymously attributed, and so the bulk of the material was arranged by date of confiscation. This was more than a little confusing, because a late date of confiscation didn't necessarily indicate a late date of creation. There were a number of dirty, weathered rolls of vellum that had to date back to Agon Diethes' time, but which hadn't been discovered until 1808 — and so they were shelved more recently than a pamphlet that had been seized in 1788 and couldn't have been more than a year old when it was picked up.

Valentine looked at the daunting array of material and sighed. Hundreds of confiscated books, along with probably ten times that many executions, and the stupid bastards *kept writing them.* How many centuries of history does it take for men to finally give up on something?

"Well," he said aloud, as he ran his finger lightly along the volumes. "Of course they're crazy. That's why they're heretics." He found a fat black volume, brought to the Black Library during the 17th century, and drew it out. It was in an old-fashioned Sarpejk dialect that Valentine found he could read tolerably well, and he sat down to muddle through it.

It was only an hour or two before he gave up, and turned back to the shelves, looking for something else. He found a pamphlet from only half a century ago and breezed through it, looking for key words or phrases, jotting down notes when he was of a mind. He continued this process — picking a book at random and skimming it, trying to just get some idea of what ectoplasmatic texts were *supposed* to look like, for the better part of the day.

Valentine had been chewing one particularly tough text in Old Middle Thranc—lost in a tangle of increasingly-obscure descriptors that he couldn't determine were bad metaphor, a secret code, anagogic theology, or just a peculiarity of 15th century Thranc grammar—when the adjunct rushed back into the room, face ruddy and panicked.

"Mr. Vie-Gorgon. Inspector. Sir," he said, gasping for breath. "They sent...your driver sent...sent me." He gasped again. "They need you. In Red Lanes. There's been...an incident."

Nine

"So, I've been reading this stuff," Valentine was saying, but Beckett wasn't really listening. "Some of it, you know, not too much, because then, well, it's just complicated isn't it?"

They were in the dining room of the Hotel Jaise, which offered a bill of fare that would have been fantastically intimidating to anyone except for Valentine, who immediately began to proceed through all five courses of dinner. Beckett picked at some kind of complicated fish plate—some intricate arrangement of smoked fishes and pickled fruits, slathered with a tangy, reddish-brown sauce whose origins the old coroner couldn't place. Rich, the way they made all the sauces in Sar-Sarpek these days, but spicier. Probably another Corsay transplant.

Beckett forced his attention back to Valentine, whose explanation was only interrupted for the length of time it took him to shovel some delicious new morsel into his mouth, at a speed that must have made actually tasting the food impossible, and was no doubt a great insult to the chef. "...mmmfgh. Anyway, look, the old books, the ones in the Abbey library? They're a mess. Every last one of them. I mean, I didn't read every one of them. But all the ones I looked at, and I think it's a safe bet that no one really knows what they're talking about. They can't..." he swallowed a spoonful of fruit concoction. "...mggh. Can't make up their mind, I mean, whether they're trying to talk in a secret code and just *allude* to what they mean, or if they're giving instructions, or what. I mean, we know that ectoplasmatics is a science, right, but none of the ectoplasmatists seem to know it. Like the science is just an accidental..." he had some more fruit. "This is really good, by the way. Tart, a little sweet, but smooth. Sorry. Right, the science is just an accident of the religious stuff. They're doing science, but they *think* they're praying, you know what I mean?"

Gorud was watching Valentine intently, but Beckett had no idea whether or not the therian understood him. How smart were they? The coroner knew that he tended to think of them like children. Or else, to think of them as they appeared: unusually intelligent monkeys. But being smarter than a monkey wasn't the same thing as being as smart as a person. Therians could speak all different languages, Beckett recalled, but they couldn't read. Is it possible to be intelligent but illiterate?

The therian was looking at him, suddenly, while Valentine droned on. Gorud had bright orange eyes, a fiery gold color in the lamplight, with a black sclera. He blinked rarely, just stared at him with those close-set eyes and heavy brows, from atop his elongated muzzle. He sometimes puffed out his cheeks. The ruff of fur around his face quivered as though stirred by a gentle breeze and, unaccountably uncomfortable, Beckett turned away from him.

Someone had let birds into the dining room — a pair of small white snowbirds that flittered around the ceiling beams, chasing each other around. They were fighting, or mating, Beckett wasn't sure how to tell. The birds were very white.

"Beckett?"

Valentine was speaking to him. "What?" Beckett muttered. "What is it?"

"I was asking if...are you all right?"

"Of course I'm all right." He looked down at his fish. "I'm just not especially hungry. Had a big lunch."

"Yes. Okay, right. Well, have you seen something like this before? The pamphlets are typewritten, right, so they must be new. The pamphlets must be new, I mean, but maybe there were earlier forms...?"

"Well," Beckett snapped at him. "Did you *see* any in the library?"

"Ah. No."

Beckett shrugged, and picked at his fish again. It kept shifting away from the fork in tiny increments, as though it were ever-so-slightly trying to avoid it. He couldn't blame it. If he were chopped up on a plate, he probably wouldn't want to be eaten either.

"...and there's a city made out of brass, on the other side of a stormy ocean, and there are things that live in that city — "

"What?" Beckett's attention snapped back to Valentine. "There's what?"

"Uhm." Valentine looked over to Gorud, who did not respond. "I said there were diagrams. In the pamphlet." He was gesturing to a stack of rumpled papers — notes that Beckett had not seen him pull out. "I made a sketch, see? It's something to do with the lungs and the four humors, but, you know, like I said, I didn't want to read it too closely..."

Beckett nodded again, and was then possessed of a sudden urge to look beneath the table. He gently drew the table cloth up, to look down at his feet, and saw that he was standing in water. He looked up and around, and saw that the entire width of the floor was covered in six inches of black, swirling brine. The other diners swirled their feet in it. The waiters splashed through it as they brought people their meals.

"I..." Beckett began, but hesitated. Isn't there *supposed* to be water on the floor? That's where they get the fish from. He could, indeed, see small, slim-bodied animals wriggling through the water, yellow lights glittering off of their backs. *Not fish.* Were they eels? The animals began wriggling towards his ankles now, and one turned upwards, opening a tiny mouth that was just a round aperture filled with tiny little barbs, whirling in a little circle.

He stood up with such speed that he unconsciously caused his chair to be knocked to the floor, splashing black water over the other diners, who seemed little perturbed by it. "I don't..."

"Beckett?" Valentine was saying, from a very long way off, down a tunnel or a well, his voice an echo reaching out over an incomprehensible stony distance. "Beckett? Are you all right?"

The old coroner shook his head to clear it. "Yes. I'm fine. It's...hot in here. I need some air."

"I'll go with you —" Valentine said at once, but Beckett interrupted him.

"No. No, I need...I need you to do something else for me."

"All right."

"Go back to Raithower House get Karine..."

"Karine doesn't work there anymore."

"The secretary. Whoever's handling the reports now. Get him to look for break-ins in..." munitions depots. Where were the munitions depots? "Arkady Green." They'd moved the vaults there while Old Bank was being rebuilt. "Reports from the gendarmes."

"You think the weapon was stolen...?"

"It," Beckett fumbled with his coat, carefully trying not to attract the attention of the leeches, which would dart toward him if he moved too suddenly. "It could be. Or someone could have made it. So we check. If no one stole it, then we'll know."

"I will, but it can wait until morning, Beckett, at least let me get you a cab..."

"No." Beckett snapped, putting his coat on, numb fingers struggling only slightly with the buttons. "Now. The longer we wait, the harder it gets." He splashed out of the dining room and into the cold, cold night air.

The stagnant water in the Hotel gave way to a small stream that ran along the gutters of Red Lanes — once gutters that held blood and offal from the district's butcher shops and slaughterhouses, emptied of their carnal waste as the city grew and the abattoirs were pushed farther and farther away. They held briny water now, fluid and untouched by the cold, when any but the most sidereal waters would have frozen solid.

The Second Winter of the year before, the city waterworks had had to run their heat emitters in shifts. Phlogiston was rationed, and without the flow of that miracle fuel, everyone was required to cut back. Second Winter had dropped on the city like a landslide, then, and during one of the off-shifts, certain pipes in New Bank had burst. Water had poured out of them and down the streets and sprayed across walls and gargoyles and downspouts and statues, and frozen almost at once. A few hours after the incident, a whole quarter of the city was covered in glittering white ice, like a fairy kingdom in a wonder-story. Enterprising children had made use of old shutters as sleds, and spent an afternoon sliding down the steep hill of Demogorgon Street, skidding to a halt, all apple-cheeked cheer and breathless laughter, just where New Bank gave way to Chapel Height.

Wet water didn't last long in the city in Second Winter, but there was Beckett, following the tiny river down dark streets, frigid air clutching at his lungs as he drew deep breaths, jogging slightly, then running, then...

Then he was at the waterfront, at Bridge Street, where a delicate Crabtree-Daior bulwark served as a railing for young lovers to lean against, should they ever be out strolling and of a mind to observe the flow of the River Stark. The briny stream rushed through the gaps in the stone barrier, and splashed soundlessly into the body of the river. On the far bank, the city loomed; jumbled stone architecture giving way to a red desert hill, where far atop a the block, walled city of Kaarcag stood, a monument to heresy, casting its black shadow through time and space.

The Stark was deep and swift, and it never froze, not even in the depths of winter. Tiny little islands of white ice bobbed in its currents, drawn from eddied pools upriver, carried without circumstance to the sea. The Stark was cold, always cold, even at the height of Summer. A man could still die from hypothermia in the Summer; he'd die in minutes if he leapt into the water now, if he looked out at its hypnotic whorls and by some trick of the senses, became convinced that its horrific cold was a kind of warmth...a soothing stillness of the will...

"Inspector Beckett."

The coroner turned away from his contemplation of the Stark, noting with some surprise how close he was standing to the railing—his hips were practically pressed against it, he could feel the cold stone pulling the warmth from his body, right through his heavy coat. Loping down the street in his peculiarly-canine, four-legged gait was Gorud, wrapped in heavy wool, eyes fixed and unblinking.

"Inspector Beckett," the therian said again, as he approached. "Mr. Valentine had some worries of you, and sent that I should inquire."

"I'm fine, Gorud. I just needed some air."

The therian sat on his heels, beneath a blue-glowing streetlamp, eyes shining eerily in the dark, and did not say anything.

"I'm fine," Beckett repeated, slipping his hand into his pocket and feeling for the grip of his revolver.

Gorud yawned, then, displaying those huge canine teeth. He got to his feet and crept closer. His gloves and shoes were a soft whisper against the cobblestone. "You see the Water, sometimes?"

"What?"

The therian made an incomprehensible gesture with its long hand. "When you use the venom, you see the Water? Like the ocean. It smells like salt."

Cross the Water. The first stage of veneine overdose. "Yes. Sometimes. Do you...how do you know about that?"

Gorud bobbed his head and puffed out his cheeks again. "The venom comes from Corsay. My people drink it, sometimes, for..." he gestured with his hands, groping for the word.

"A ceremony?"

"Like a ceremony, but not like that. We drink it. If a *thukeri* drinks too much, he sees the Water."

The old coroner relaxed the grip on his weapon. He shuddered with sudden relief whose source he could not quite ascertain. "Yes. The water. Sometimes...sometimes I've been past the water. The City of Brass. Do...your people...know that?"

Gorud said nothing at first, just scratched at the end of his nose. "*Humankeri*, you. Where do you think the world is from?"

If he was startled by the sudden change of topic, Beckett did not show it. "The Church Royal says that the world is a Word, the voice of the Speaker. He Spoke, and here we are."

The therian shuffled forward, its gruff voice low and conspiratorial. "And. Was there another Word? A different Word than this one, you know?"

Beckett shrugged. "Some people thought so. Harcourt Wolfram did. He was a scientist. He thought there was a whole stack of Words, right on top of each other, and he thought he could find a way to move between them." He saw a face, frozen in a terrifying rictus, head lolling about on a neck like it was broken, a shimmering panoply of real and unreal limbs. "He might have been right. But if there are other Words…we don't do well there."

Gorud nodded. "We think something like this. But not a Word. There is a Dreamer, yes, and this is his dream. One day he will wake, and all of this will vanish." He made a popping sound with his lips. "Poof. But this is not the first dream. The Dreamer once woke before, and all that dream went away. But it didn't *go*, it just isn't. Somewhere, He still dreams it. He dreams of a Brass City and an Ocean. That is the place the dreamsnakes come from. That is where their venom takes you."

"Takes me? It's not a real place. It's a hallucination."

The therian spread his hands. "I do not know, 'hallucination.' It is not a real place the way this is a real place. But it is a real place. Some things still live there."

They were quiet for a while then, as icy wind whipped around them. The water that Beckett saw had trickled to a stop, and the veneine warmth began to boil off his body and into the empty night air. The beginnings of a headache lurked around, just outside his field of perception. His knees and elbows throbbed, his right hand was sore. "Hmf." Beckett said, eventually. "It doesn't matter."

"You use too much," Gorud said. "The Water is dangerous. The City is worse."

Beckett didn't tell the creature about what was beyond the Brass City, about the black basalt towers on the moon. About the things that he thought might live there. "It doesn't matter. I need it."

Gorud nodded. "It…tastes bad. To be without it. Hurts."

"It hurts all the time," Beckett spat, as his headache began to ring in his ears again. "It feels like there's broken glass in my joints, like someone's been driving nails into my head. I can't even *get up* without the stuff. I can barely move." He pulled down his scarf and showed the therian his ruined, half-transparent face. "Do you know what this is? It's called the fades. You get it from working in factories that use flux. Usually children get it. It kills them before they turn fifteen. Sometimes, it doesn't show up until you're an adult. But it kills you just the same. Two years, ten years, no one gets away from it. And it just rots your body away."

"You worked in a factory?"

"For two years, after my father died. A long time ago. Before they knew what caused it, made them start ventilating the factories better." Beckett snorted. "The first factory regulations were put in place the year after I quit to join the marines."

Gorud said nothing for a moment, then, "Still, it's too much."

"No. I need it. I can't work without it."

"You think the world will fall apart if you stop working? Will He wake up?"

The old coroner rubbed at the number corner of his mouth. "Huh. No. Probably not."

"So. Why?"

Beckett shrugged. "What else can I do? It's this, or lie in bed until I die." He sniffed and looked around. "It's cold. We should go. You drink djang?"

"Haha," Gorud said. It was not a laugh, exactly, but a sound meant to indicate that he was laughing. "Where do you think you got djang from? *Thukeri* have invented djang."

"Well, come on then," the coroner said gruffly. "I'm thirsty."

Ten

Emilia Vie-Gorgon was nothing if not generous, and with the nearly bottomless wealth of the Raithower Vie-Gorgons at her disposal, she could afford to be. When Skinner had returned to her boarding-house, late that night, she found that most of her belongings had already been packed up and burly-sounding men with heavy, competent footsteps were in the process of moving them out. Mrs. Crewell, astonishment plain in her voice, had been waiting for her with a handful of letters, details of the arrangement between the former coroner and the Vie-Gorgon heiress.

"It says there's a house in Lanternbridge," Mrs. Crewell was saying, as men tromped past with trunks of clothes, "leased under William Vie-Gorgon's name that's mean to be for you and your assistant. There's a cook there, and a maid that should come in once a day, and you're to be given an allowance of…my goodness." She quoted a figure substantially higher than Skinner had ever made with the Coroners, but must have still been paltry compared to the funds that the Raithower Vie-Gorgons regularly had access to. "If you don't mind my asking, Miss Skinner, what…what is this all about?"

Skinner permitted herself a truly enigmatic smile, one that she ordinarily reserved for the most outrageous of circumstances. These were certainly circumstances that might qualify, even if the wine and good company hadn't managed to coax her humor to the surface. "I have found an opportunity, Mrs. Crewell. I imagine that you'll hear about it, soon enough. Let me thank you for your good nature and excellent hospitality. I surely cannot imagine a better host than you have been. Do not!" She suddenly raised her voice to speak to the movers. "Do not even *think* about moving that instrument without wrapping it in cloth, first. Have you any idea what the cold weather will do to the strings?"

She traveled by coach from Chapel Height, skirting the lower edge of New Bank, and into Lanternbridge. The neighborhood was near one of the sinuous curves of the Stark, built near one of the first bridges across its length. Centuries earlier, when Trowth the city had really been a half a dozen loosely-connected little villages, an enterprising family member—probably an Ennering, but historical documents differ—had put three long lines of bright yellow lanterns along the bridge, and ensured that they burned at every hour of the night. Travelers, merchants, tinkers, and anyone else that might bring a coin or two of commerce to one of the competing districts were, once the sun went down, quite naturally drawn to the brightly-lit bridge, and the neighborhood found its inns and taverns always full come evening.

The good trade made Lanternbridge one of the wealthiest districts in the area, a characteristic which persisted for many years, until the sprawling mass of Trowth finally, by virtue of dozens more bridges across the river, spread out to the far side of the Stark, and pushed its travelers' lodgings with it. Lanternbridge fell into disrepair for nearly a century then, gradually sliding down the inevitable decline into slumhood, until the Great Forfeiture. Once the wealthy families abandoned Old Bank for Lanternbridge's neighbor, New Bank, the place underwent a kind of cultural renaissance. All of the decently-paid servants, craftsmen, cobblers, haberdashers, tailors, and restauranteurs relocated to be nearer to the wealth, and Lanternbridge was where they found themselves.

By Skinner's time, it was known as a clean, quiet, safe neighborhood, with an exciting mixture of solidly middle-class, cheap journeyman shops and startlingly luxurious fashion houses and dining rooms. It was a common place of residence for moderately wealthy, not-quite-Esteemed merchant families, for up-and-coming and ambitious young people, and for certain relatively famous and popular actors and theater managers.

The house in Lanternbridge was a cozy three-storey building, not a mansion by any means, but by far more comfortable than any house Skinner had ever hoped to own. She took a few minutes to insist that the movers tour her around the space—getting a feel for distance and location, locating the stove without actually having to risk burning her hands—then hastily ushered them all out. It was far too late at night to begin work, to begin even pondering the work, and so instead she took advantage of the huge, soft, warm bed that had been provided her.

When morning came around, and anemic sunlight sifted through the gritty black clouds that made up the roof of Trowth, Skinner decided that she would likewise took advantage of a late morning, stirring only faintly as the maid brought her breakfast—covered over, with a tiny heat emitter at the base of the tray, it would stay hot for hours she knew—then pushing her face deep into downy pillows and sweet, satisfied dreams. The weak sunlight crept across the floor of her room, warming and brightening it. Gas lamps along the walls burst to life, bringing with them more light and heat, but Skinner would not be moved.

It was nearly noon when she finally roused herself, sampling the bacon, eggs, and toast that had been left for her breakfast and was, indeed, still hot. Years of early mornings, to get a start on the day's inevitably macabre labors caused her a twinge of guilt when she realized the time, but she resolved that she would not regret starting to work as late as she liked. *Late mornings,* Skinner thought to herself, *Are the privilege of the artist.*

Skinner chose a light dressing-gown for herself, rather than struggling to strap herself into the substantial undergarments required by her coroner's suits. Not having to get fully-dressed in the morning was another luxury she had rarely enjoyed. Waking up in a house, being beholden to no one — it was almost impossible to imagine that, the very day before, she'd planned on renting a rat-trap flat in Bluewater to stay off the streets.

Downstairs, company was awaiting her, and Skinner recalled that the letter mentioned she would have an assistant who would share the house with her. She'd assumed an arrangement would have to be made, as the knocker required someone who could take dictation for her, but had quite forgotten that the assistant would be living with her.

"Miss Skinner?"

Karine. She recognized the voice at once, and of course it was Karine. The young indige women had lost her job at the same time Skinner had, and there couldn't be anyone more qualified to assist her. "My dear," Skinner said, "It's so good to hear your voice."

"They didn't tell me who I would work for," her voice smiled, "I am glad it's you, miss."

Skinner experienced a fleeting moment of worry, at the astonishing extent of Emilia Vie-Gorgon's information. How on earth did she know about Karine? The Vie-Gorgon heiress must have men everywhere. Skinner shook off the thought.

"Well, have you eaten, Karine? I'd like to get started, but we're not in any hurry, just yet."

"Oh, yes, miss. I am ready whenever you are."

"Good. How well do you take dictation?"

There was a peculiar sound then, a mechanical tapping sound, and then the turn of a dial. Skinner had never heard anything quite like it before. "Yes," Karine said. "I have been working for my cousin, who is a broker for airshipping. I have learned to use this...the Feathersmith machine." She did something with her hands, and a machine clacked and rattled alarmingly. "It is like a tiny printing-press."

"Well, then I suppose we had better get started," Skinner said, gamely, as she sat down and prepared to work. It did not take her more than a few minutes of silence to realize that she had absolutely no idea how to begin. The silence hung awkwardly between them.

The work on *The Bone-Collector's Daughter* had been different—the product of an inspiration that had seized her while she had been wholly occupied with something entirely unrelated. When it had blossomed in her mind, she found that the play had practically written itself; Skinner was herself taking dictation, listening to the play speak in her head and then just repeating it to Sitwell in one of their aggravatingly-long sessions. And, for as successfully as she'd been with *The Bone-Collector's Daughter*, she'd really never written anything else before, and was altogether unsure as to how to go about it.

"Miss?"

"All right," Skinner said. "Let's just...start. With...something." *It's better, it must be better, to just right it down, whether it's good or not. If it's bad, we can always change it later.* "With Theocles. We'll start with the poem. Do you know it?"

"No."

Merciful relief, as Skinner found she could spend a good hour reciting the epic story to Karine—working easily from memory, not striving to build something new. She told her assistant the whole story, but had her just write down the main thrust of each of the sixteen books. When they'd finished, Skinner was strongly of a mind to break for the day, enjoy a well-cooked meal, drink some of the liquors that the movers had helpfully pointed out to her the night before. She resisted the impulse, out of an old habit that she'd learned from Beckett: whatever you didn't solve today was what would bite you in the ass tomorrow. Of course, writing a play hardly had the same urgency or stakes about it that tracking down renegade necrologists did, but the principle could correctly be said to be the same.

"So," said Skinner, as Karine's clattering typing ground to a halt. "So, what is this about?"

"It's about Theocles."

"Yes," Skinner agreed. "Wait. No. No, Theocles is *who* it's about. *What* is it about, though?"

"He...takes over the empire."

"That's what happens. What is it *about*?" Skinner asked again, and Karine said nothing. "All right, I know what this is about. It's about a man who is thirsty for power. He wants more power, he thinks he *deserves* more power…no. No, he thinks he can do a better job. He thinks he can do a better job, and so he starts doing bad things in order to get the power."

"That's not in the poem. The poem just says he's jealous of Agon Diethes."

"Well, we're changing it. We're allowed to, there's no rule. It's more interesting if Theocles thinks he can do a better job. Or maybe both. Maybe he secretly thinks he can do a better job, but then something happens…that makes him sure of it." *What…how could you make that happen? It needs something weird. Something creepy.*

"He fights that troll in the second book. In Daeagea, before my people made a kingdom for themselves, there were all just tribal hetmen. And if a man went out and killed one of the kriegbats or lannershrikes, it was seen as a sign of his destiny."

"Yes. The troll." *No, wait. The Loogaroo.* "Wait, all right, I've got it. First scene. First scene is Theocles and his friend in the forest. After…after a battle. It's a stormy night. Are you writing this down?"

What followed was a rough cut of a scene in which two tired, bloody, dirty old soldiers encountered a compelling oddity in the woods. Theocles, still at this point content to be a humble servant of the Emperor, did not fight a troll, but instead came upon two bogeys, behaving in the strange and off-putting way that bogeys do.

"Steeplechase," Skinner said, with a sudden burst of inspiration. "And Mumbletypeg are their names."

They spoke mostly gibberish; Skinner borrowed liberally from the weird monologues that she'd heard dream-poisoned men spout off, or the terrifically peculiar rants of a man deeply lost on veneine. But in the middle of those weird speeches, they spoke directly to Theocles. They hailed Theocles as a general, and a king, and told him of an impossible future.

No grown adult in Trowth would admit to believing in bogeys—not anymore, anyway. And few of them would confess, except in their darkest and most private moments, to believing in the Loogaroo. Only on quiet, lonely nights, on desolate windswept roads, when that solitude transmuted into an unbearable feeling of *presence*, when men and women picked up their paces and hurried back to well-lit parlors and warm fires, would a person acknowledge that there were times when they still feared a fairy-tale like the Loogaroo.

The Loogaroo was the king of the bogeymen, the Nightmare Prince. It was a dark shadow of a thing, a wicked dissonance in the nature of the Word. The Goetic Church still insisted that the Loogaroo existed, and was present as the black cruelty in the heart of every man — an actual, living entity that, in some small way, possessed a portion of each and every human being's soul. It was an evil, but a necessary evil, meant to give dimension to the Word. Good, the Goetic Church said, is meaningless without a corresponding wickedness. The Church's position is why a play suggesting that a doctor of theology might secretly be a servant of the Loogaroo — a play like *The Bone-Collector's Daughter* — would have been condemned as heresy in Canth.

The Church Royal, on the other hand, maintained the official policy that the Loogaroo was simply a metaphor for mankind's native tendency towards wickedness. The various bogeymen named as its subjects — often given allegorical names like "Lust," or "Greed," — were simply poetic personifications of natural phenomena. It was *real*, but not really what it seemed to be.

Skinner liked the bogeys in the first scene; there was still enough of a sense of mystery, a willingness to indulge in fantasy, among the Trowthi people that their monstrous prophecies *could* be true, but a history of painting the creatures as conniving, scheming demons meant that Steeplechase and Mumbletypeg could just as easily be liars.

As though rediscovering the Loogaroo had burst some levy in her imagination, scenes and incidents and speeches began to pour out of her. Theocles making a pact with the Loogaroo. The bogeymen summoning the Loogaroo. The Loogaroo haunting the coronation ceremony, finding a place for itself at the celebratory banquet. *Just write it all,* Skinner thought to herself, as they worked through dinner and late into the night. *Just keep writing it, we can always cut it out later.* By nightfall, they had produced no fewer than seven full scenes, and a dozen more speeches and snippets of dialogue that Skinner liked, but wasn't sure what to do with.

When they had finished, Skinner slumped in her chair and absently scratched at the edge of the silver plate across her fate. She had been snacking on a small piece of roast that the maid had brought, but now found herself ravenously hungry.

"Why do you think," Karine asked, her chair creaking as she leaned away from the Feathersmith machine, "that Miss Vie-Gorgon wanted *this* play?"

"Oh, who can say with the Families? They're always up to something obscure and confrontational. The Wyndham-Crabtrees and the Crabtree-Daiors own the Public Theater, don't they? Maybe just a way to draw the audiences off from there."

"It sounds... *Theocles* sounds like, a little bit like what the Emperor is like. Now, I mean." She coughed lightly, then added, "Word preserve him."

"Yes, it does sound like that."

"Do you suppose he'll be mad about it?"

Skinner was quiet for a long moment, apprehension and pride warring over her face, vying for the chance to change it to a frown or smile. "If I were quite honest with you," she said, smiling as her apprehension about what she was risking by writing a play like this lost out to the pride she took in her ability to do it, "I would say that that is precisely the point."

ELEVEN

I believe I have met with some success. I have devised a calculating engine, vastly different in design from our ordinary engines. This new engine relies on a kind of imprecision, an accommodation of likelihoods rather than precise calculation. It therefore does not require that all elements of a question or problem be input directly into its mechanism, but can act and calculate beyond its own parameters.

I have done this through the use of [lacuna; three pages of the journal are excised by the author. In their place is the following note: *"As I suggested, certain events have come to light which make me loath to share my methods. I am not altogether confident that this experiment will result in a positive outcome. Until I am sure of it, I mean to keep my procedures from the world at large, for fear of unexpected consequences."*]

--from the journal of Harcourt Wolfram, 1785

Stuck. A month in, and Skinner was stuck. Dead in the water, floundering, as unable to think of a decent simile as...as someone who was stuck. Emilia would be by today for more pages for the actors to chew on, and Skinner had absolutely nothing to give her.

The first few scenes had gone easily enough. Once she'd worked out the bits with the Loogaroo, a panoply of material had presented itself, ripe for the plucking. And then, when she'd run out there, she just started adapting scenes directly from the poem, changing bits here and there to mesh with her idea for the piece. And now she'd reached a point where everything that might reasonably be stolen from the poem was stolen, and everything inspired by her flirtation with the symbolic dark heart of humanity had done it's inspiring, and Skinner had no idea what to do next. The play wasn't hanging together, didn't feel real enough, didn't feel like it mattered.

She would not tolerate being the author of an inoffensive drama. The sort of play that might be enjoyed by a few wealthy families, and then filed away in one of the Groheim collections where it would sit among equally unspectacular dramas, minding its own business on someone's bookshelf while audiences spent their nights out lusting for meatier fare. Her play would fascinate and hurt, would land like a punch to the gut. It would make people sit up and realize…

Realize what? Skinner didn't know. She could hear Karine, waiting bored and patient by her machine, ready to resume the work. Skinner sat with her chin in her hand, tapping her cane against her shoe, waiting for an idea.

No one, she thought to herself, *is going to realize* anything *if I never finish the damn thing.* She likewise was starting to grow concerned again about where she would live, and what she would eat. Emilia Vie-Gorgon was certainly generous, but it was doubtful that she was generous enough to provide so much without the expectation that Skinner would produce something.

"Miss?"

Skinner sighed. "Karine, let's…take a break for now. I don't have anything to write today."

"Miss Vie-Gorgon is going to be here this afternoon. She'll want to see pages."

"Yes, I know. I'll talk to her."

There was a pregnant silence then, a kind of silence that Skinner recognized: the sound of a person who was hesitating to say something.

"Yes?"

"…I don't…Miss, I don't want to worry you, at all, but…"

"It's all right, Karine, just say it."

"Well. I like working for you, miss. I'd like to keep working for you. So. So, I suppose…"

"I suppose I'll have to think of something soon, right?"

There was another pause.

"Yes, miss," Karine said, slightly more enthusiastically. "I'm sure you will."

"Hmph." Skinner returned her chin to her hand, and slumped in her chair as Karine bundled up her things and left. She would be out window-shopping for hours. Karine was a very frugal young woman, and did not make extravagant purchases even now that she was, comparatively, quite flush — but she took a great pleasure in *looking* at fancy and expensive things, in imagining her life with them, in imagining what it would be like to be able to purchase a new silk dress for every day of the week entirely unmindful of the cost. This imaginative pleasure ensured that her trips around town were both long and unremarkable.

Emilia Gorgon-Vie arrived sharp at two, while Skinner had spent the intervening time somewhat guiltily enjoying the pleasures of her house. She was sitting in the bedroom, experimenting with a new musical scale that she'd heard at a djang house, recently, when Emilia's man came knocking.

Skinner did her best to explain the situation as plainly as she could: that writing a play was not like building a chair, or tallying a ledger. The work was not there, waiting to be done, but it could only be done when the author was of the correct mind to do it. And this was a fickle, slippery condition, not subject to deadlines or motivation, but only through inspiration. Art cannot simply be commanded, or produced to order, it comes only in its own time.

She managed to deliver the entire explanation with a single, convoluted sentence, avoiding giving Emilia the opportunity to interject a question or a comment. But she was destined to have to stop talking eventually, and when she did, she'd have to suffer the Vie-Gorgon heiress's response.

That response, as Skinner had expected, was silence. Emilia Vie-Gorgon's peculiar absolute, untouchable silence that, if it persisted for too long, was liable to make a blind person believe that the young heiress had actually left the room. They'd nearly passed this threshold, Skinner holding her breath ever so slightly, Emilia dead silent, when the woman finally spoke.

"Very well, Miss Skinner. If you'd care to come with me?"

"Ah. Yes? Where?"

"To my coach, Miss Skinner." Her voice was icily controlled, perfectly modulated, utterly inexpressive. It was an emotional feat that Skinner felt was quite unprecedented. "I've something I think you might be interested in."

As ominous as this sounded—and Skinner could not deny that the whole thing sounded very ominous—she could think of no practical reason to refuse. It was not as though she was doing anything else, at the moment. She put on her coat, and joined Miss Vie-Gorgon in the young woman's coach, where they sat in quiet for several moments.

"Do you know," said Emilia at once, giving Skinner a mild start, "Much about my family, and the Emperor's?"

The Vie-Gorgons and the Gorgon-Vies—of course Skinner knew *of* them, and knew as much about them as was published in the broadsheets, or taught in history class. "They…you have been feuding for six centuries. About the legitimacy of Owen Gorgon." Owen Gorgon was a hero in Trowth. He appeared at the end of the Interregnum, and claimed to be the last descendent of Gorgon himself. He'd married Elthea Vie—whose family could reliably trace their ancestry back to the first cousin of Agon Diethes — to cement himself in the Empire, and had crowned himself ruler.

The Gorgon-Vies asserted that Owen Gorgon was in a line of legitimate offspring from Gorgon, and so the Gorgon name ought to come first. The Vie-Gorgons insisted that, since there was an interruption in the line of legitimate Gorgon heirs, Owen must be an illegitimate child, and therefore the Vie name should come first. The family had split, with cousins all taking one side or another, and thus was born the defining relationship of the Empire.

"The feud began," Emilia said, "over the legitimacy of Owen Gorgon and his name. But while we fought, we were obliged to take positions against each other on principle. If the Gorgon-Vies advocated for a stronger monarchy, the Vie-Gorgons lent their support to a stronger parliament. If the Vie-Gorgons favored an isolationist policy regarding our neighbors, the Gorgon-Vies immediately proposed an aggressive one. If we favored slim towers with narrow windows, they started building square buildings with wide ones."

"That all seems," Skinner said, after a moment, "fairly stupid."

Deathly silence. Skinner discovered it was becoming a little easier not to find her heart in her throat when that happened, now that she was more used to it. "Yes," said Emilia. "It is, generally. Except that the Gorgon-Vies, and this *particular* Gorgon-Vie, are wrong. I don't mean that they're wrong to fight with us, or to disagree with us. And I am not asserting the principle of my family, which is that *whatever* the Gorgon-Vies do, it *must* be wrong — though you would be forgiven for thinking that. What I mean is, they are *actually* wrong. The Emperor has made nothing but poor choices since his coronation.

"Do you know why he waged the war against the ettercap? Not because they were a threat to us, but because the Gorgon-Vies desired absolute control over the importation of phlogiston, rather than the shared control that had been forced on us. This is implicit in everything the Gorgon-Vies do: they believe in autocracy. That who holds the single most powerful element is the person who controls the most power. The Empire runs on phlogiston; who controls the phlogiston, controls the empire."

"That seems a reasonable assumption," Skinner said, recalling how close the city had come to turning into a mass grave the previous Second Winter.

"Yes? While the Gorcia pipelines were shut down, how did we get the little phlogiston we had?"

"Trains, I suppose," Skinner said. "Indige airships."

"Both of which the Vie-Gorgons own a controlling stake in. Shutting down the pipelines tripled our family fortune. We gave most of that money away. To charities, sometimes, or to funding certain public works projects. Do you know why?"

"I hadn't known there'd be a test, Emilia. If I had, I suppose I would have studied harder."

"Because goodwill is cheaper than armed guards. The Gorgon-Vies spend money to protect themselves against angry peasants; the Vie-Gorgons spend it to ensure that it's the Gorgon-Vies with whom the common people are angry."

"Is that what this play is about? Is that why you're having me write it? To keep attention on the Gorgon-Vies."

"Yes," Emilia said. "after a fashion. An Emperor should be accountable to his subjects, shouldn't he?"

Skinner pondered the implications of this question, and of the fact that it was Emilia Vie-Gorgon asking it. The Vie-Gorgons controlled the Ministry of Information—shutting down broadsheets, arresting and discrediting critics of the Emperor, tightly controlling what was known about him—what could any of that have to do with forcing him to be accountable?

"Certainly..." she began, "there are times when I wish that the Emperor...realized the consequences of his edicts more thoroughly." Worrying about how to feed herself with six crowns, about where she would live when her boarding-house was closed. "Though I suppose that he is, in his mind, acting in the interests of the Empire."

"You are quite right—*in his mind*. By his judgment, he is doing what is best for Trowth. But what assurance do we have that his judgment is correct? It was not judgment that sat him on the throne—certainly not *his* judgment, anyway. Why should we ascribe the characteristic of judgment to a man simply because he has *become* Emperor?"

"The Word? Divine provenance?"

"Miss Skinner, I am surprised. Tell me, in all your years as a coroner, have you ever seen the Word *actually* affect the world? Anything to suggest that humanity is anything except entirely on its own?"

"No, I suppose I haven't."

"The Word does not choose our kings. We do. And their judgment is not any better than ours—so, it seems only right that we should attempt to improve on it. Now. We seem to have arrived."

"Arrived where?"

Emilia moved about in her seat. Skinner could hear the rustling of her skirts. "This is a hospital. One of the casualty homes."

The casualty homes. There were a hundred of them, all over the city. A few were built from old trolljr hospices — sturdy, roomy, airy. They were great complexes where the sick were meant to be healed. Not all of them were as clean and neat as Dhagu's hospices, though — the number of injured and wounded men brought back from Gorcia well exceeded the city's existing capacity. Dirty heated tents, sweaty and diseased, festering with necrosis and illness, they grew like a poisoned fungus in the worst corners of the city — by the Break, and the Little Break, on the burnt remains of Mudside.

"What...what are we doing here?"

"We're going inside, Miss Skinner." The door to the carriage opened, bringing in a gust of chilly air. "You said you needed inspiration."

"I can hear from the coach. The clairaudience..."

"You *can*." Emilia stepped out into the air. "But I suspect it's more inspiring if you don't."

"Wait..."

"No."

The hospice was a makeshift building near the old Break. Skinner could hear wood creaking and the peculiar whine of stretched canvas — a low, almost inaudible hum. The inside was hot, oppressively hot and damp. Heat emitters buzzed at regular intervals around the space. Skinner was hesitant to use her telerhythmia here to establish the boundaries of the room, but based on the quality and number of voices she was hearing, it was somewhere fairly large. There was no effective way to regulate heat in a room this size; the hospice workers had no choice but to dump energy into it, or see the men freeze.

The room stank. It smelled like blood and rotten garbage. It smelled like stale sweat and vomit. It smelled like ichor and iodine. The odors whirled together in a potent cocktail of disgust that coated the inside of the throat at once, and nearly made her sick to her stomach.

Men are dying in here, she thought to herself. *The least I can do is keep my breakfast down.*

It was the sound of the place that was the worst. Above the unnerving structural rattle of its jury-rigged edifice was an orchestra of misery. The place was full to bursting; there were hundreds of men inside. Skinner couldn't see them, didn't know how they were arranged, and it felt to her like they must have all been crowded around her at once, whispering in her ears. They moaned, and they whimpered. Some men prayed to the Word — praying for an end to the pain, however it might come. Some men choked and puked and coughed. One man, his voice strangely modulated as though he were moving about the room like a ghost, sometimes far, sometimes painfully near, only sobbed his dry sobs.

Skinner could hear nurses and trolljrmen moving about the bodies — the former resolutely quiet, the latter with heavy footsteps and taciturn by nature. She could hear whispered entreaties by some of the nurses, and thrumming, bone-rattling responses from the trolljrmen.

Emilia led her deeper into that sour, foul place, while the voices of suffering men weighed on her shoulders like a mountain, bearing her down, building up a terrible density above her, so that it seemed that every step forward was really a step down, down into a horrific cellar well below the surface of the earth. The anguish of the men was a tunnel around her, a wall at her side, a cave that she had no choice but to descend into.

"Here," Emilia said softly. "Joshua. Tell her what you told me."

"You've been here before?" Skinner whispered, but Emilia hushed her.

" I never thought…" a boy spoke, with a voice like an open wound. This must be Joshua. "…we all knew it was bad. But I didn't…I signed up, though. Towards the end, when they started to give bonuses if you signed up. Since my da were dead, I thought…I thought if I signed up, I could give my ma the bonus to help her. You know?

"They put me on an ironside ship, and sent us around. Gorcia is this red place. All rocks and mountains and plants with black leaves. They gave me a gun, a long-pin rifle, and a handful of skin-colored bullets that looked like a man's severed thumb. They sent me down into a cave, then, with a thousand other men. That's where the ettercap all live, underground in these long tunnels. We walked shoulder to shoulder, packed tight in, men at the edges carried lanterns.

"We could smell…it smelled like vinegar. Someone said later that the ettercap make it. With their bodies, somehow, they spray it…but you could smell it. It was strong, and it got stronger the deeper we went. The caves got smaller, so only four men could walk side by side. The lanterns didn't send light far enough ahead. Just a little bit of light at your feet. You could see the man next to you.

"When they came…there was this…sound. This chewing sound. It…we thought it was at the end of the tunnel, but it wasn't, it was all around us. They came at us. There were openings in the top of the tunnel. We hadn't seen them, in the dark. It was a trap. They came at us with this great…they were like claws or teeth or I don't know…you could see their mouths. They had mouths like human beings. Lips. Little white teeth. Pretty mouths, like a girl's. And when they come you go a little crazy, and you think, 'I could kiss a mouth like that.' They come at you and it's…you can't see anything…there's just men shouting and you shoot your gun off and try and hit whatever you can and…

"You can't back up, because there's men packed in behind you. You can't go forward, because there's men ahead of you. You just shoot and shoot, and the men around you get snatched up or bit in half or something long and black stabs them in the heart, and if you're lucky they'll go away before too long. Then you start to pull back out of the tunnel and regroup. Then they send you in again. And again."

The man was silent for a moment, then he whispered softly. "It's dark in here. I don't like it. Do you have any light?"

There was a faint scratch of the key in a phlogiston lantern, and Emilia said, "Here. More light." She laid her fingers faintly on Skinner's arm. "Joshua lost both of his hands after his second battle. His arms had to be amputated at the elbow, because of an infection that accompanies ettercap injuries. There are mechanologists working on replacement parts for him, but there are many injuries, and not much money to build brass hands for them."

In the coach, Skinner snapped at her patron. "That was horrific. Why did you do that to me? To him?"

"Because it was horrific," Emilia replied, smoothly. "I am given to understand that writers are rarely inspired by the purely quotidian."

"I worked for the Coroners for years, *Miss* Vie-Gorgon. I don't need an object example from you about how disgusting humanity can be. I don't…how dare…how *dare* you. Do you honestly think I'm struggling with this because I don't understand the horrors that men have had to face? Do you know how many partners I went through before I was paired up with Beckett? Three. The first was taken apart by a Reanimate in the cellar of a mansion in Swindon. Not just killed, not at first—just torn limb from limb, the way a child plucks the wings off a fly. And I had no choice but to sit and listen to it, to keep track of the Reanimate's position so that we could send *someone else* in after it. You don't need to…" Skinner took a deep breath, tried to tamp her anger down. "What exactly did you think I was going to do? That I'd take the misery of these men and find a place for it in the play?"

Silence as only Emilia Vie-Gorgon could be silent. Was she evaluating what she was about to say? Trying to evaluate Skinner's state of mind, and how she'd respond? Reconsidering the whole project? Was she amused, angry, offended, or just tired?

"Well," said Emilia, eventually. "Will you?"

"There was no way out, trapped in that box canyon. We could neither advance nor retreat, nor move save to swing our swords to save our lives. We were surrounded and outnumbered, and we would have died there to the last of us, had not Theocles, bedecked in gore like his own armor…this is good." The actor scratched his nose and looked at his pages again. "I like this. So, I'm going to be, what, like bloody and bandaged up here?"

"Yes," the director responded. "We're going to have you start off the whole thing, just come in all gruesome like that. It should give a nice ambience to the rest of the piece."

"Isn't it weird that I'm *praising* Theocles, though? Like making him out to be a hero?"

"Yes, that's the *dichotomy*, Charles. We want to set Theocles up as a war-hero in the beginning, so that his descent into cruelty is heightened."

Skinner sat in the back of the theater, listening. She was in the dark, and none of the actors would have recognized her as the writer, anyway. They'd been receiving the pages of the script anonymously. While she still felt a twinge of guilt, using the story she'd heard like this, she had to admit it had helped. The visit to the hospice had given her a broad brush with which to paint the horrors of war across the script, lending both a dark, gritty reality to the story, and helping to generate a depth of sympathy for Theocles' character.

Is it all right if I'm doing it for the right reasons? She wondered. *If it leads to a more conscientious rule, to less of a willingness to wage war…does that make it worth it?*

Twelve

True Spring came, with the comfortable regularity of all of Trowth's seasons, and if there was one time during that city's long war against its elements that could even remotely be described as comfortable, it was True Spring. Second Winter thawed, snow melted, and the streets ran thick with cold, clear water. Crisp, salty breezes snuck past Trowth's ancient sea-wall, and came close to dispelling its omnipresent umbra of cloud and pollution. The sun warmed the city's old stones.

The end of the season would turn raw and rainy, of course, as heavy, damp air poured in from the sea, but, every year, for two weeks at the beginning of the season, Trowth enjoyed as close to perfect weather as the benighted metropolis was capable of. The Armistice, as these two weeks were commonly called in deference to the unacknowledged campaign that the weather waged against the town, extended to every aspect of Trowthi life. Old enmities were forgotten, debts were — if not forgiven — at least suspended, no harsh words were offered. Two weeks of clear, warm weather after the annual nightmare of Second Winter was enough to cool even the hottest-tempered ruffians; well-to-do citizens and irascible low-lifes alike poured into the street, and no man or woman even considered marring these days with violence or misdemeanor.

Shutters were thrown back, doors and windows left open, and warm feelings and good cheer filled the vast honeycomb of houses, pouring out into the streets, where men and women promenaded late in the lengthening days. All of the human and indige need for human contact, pent up and repressed for the rest of the icy year, found expression during Armistice, and seemed determined to make up for lost time.

It was no surprise that the Armistice was also a time for theater premiers; both the Royal and the Public saved all of their most promising work for the warm True Spring grace period, during which time audiences were traditionally larger and more well-disposed to spread positive word of good performances. Very occasionally, the theaters used this temporary period of universal largess to support plays that, otherwise, might have raised violent objections. *Theocles*—published, for propriety's sake, under the innocuous nom-de-plume "E. E. Beckett"—would have earned approbation simply for its first ten minutes, so clever and vicious was Elizabeth Skinner's excoriation of the Emperor and his war. It was hardly a surprise that Emilia Vie-Gorgon had arranged for the premiere of *Theocles* to fall on the second day of Armistice which arrived, as all seasons in Trowth arrive, precisely and dramatically.

Valentine Vie-Gorgon was entirely unaware of his cousin's machinations, or indeed, her or of Skinner's involvement with the play at all. What he did know is that his long-exasperated but always-affectionate father had given him a ticket for the reviewer's box, and there was little the young coroner enjoyed more than the social and artistic entertainment provided by a night at the theater. Valentine shared the box with Roger Gorgon-Crabtree, a noted reviewer for the *White Star*. Roger was a very fat and conspicuously charming man, whose affable, almost vapid demeanor belied a razor wit and an almost encyclopedic knowledge of his subject. He was, in short, absolutely the ideal companion for the premiere of *Theocles*.

Roger met Valentine at the theater's entrance, where they were permitted to go directly to their seats—tickets having already been collected. A substantial crowd milled pleasantly outside, eager for admittance and simultaneously pleased at not having to have to hurry to avoid the cold, or the rain, or mind-bending psychestorms, or the sharp-edged calcite hail that would come in late Summer. If anything, the low-rated families and well-off merchants and shopkeepers that represented the majority of the crowd seemed disinclined to waste the beauty of the Armistice by going inside at all, and if they could have waited in line until the sun was long set, and the late-night chill found its way back into Trowth, they probably would have.

"Have you heard much about this one, my boy?" Roger was asking him, as the two men settled into the plush chairs in the critics' box.

"No, it's new, isn't it?" The theater was full of warm chatter, almost necessitating that Valentine shout to his companion. "Based on the poem?"

"That's right," Roger was saying, sipping at the complimentary punch provided in hot steaming bowls for the box seats. "Though I've heard — and mind you, you're not to repeat this — that the writer, a Mr. Beckett, was also the unnamed collaborator on the *Bone-Collector's Daughter*."

"I don't think I know that one."

"Oh? Played at the Public about two years ago. Caused quite a stir, if I recall correctly, religiously outrageous and all that. At least, as outrageous as Canthi pantomime can be, if you take my meaning."

Valentine did not, as he had paid very little attention to his literature classes in school but, not wanting to seem like the sort of man who had wasted a very expensive education, allowed that he did indeed take Roger's meaning, and it was more than a little extraordinary that the play ran as long as it had.

"Quite right," Roger replied. "Quite right, my boy. But you know, the crown is always hesitant to shut the theater down. I don't know, I suppose you don't remember it, but there was a play, ten or fifteen years ago. A silly thing, but it made a few jokes at the expense of our beloved Emperor — Word protect him and keep him! He had his men close it down after a week, declared it an affront to the crown, put it on the Black List. And wouldn't you know, a month later and someone's *published* it. Just printed up pamphlets of this script and sold them for pennies on streetcorners. He probably made a fortune."

"People bought it?"

"Well, no one would *admit* to it, obviously. Sh, sh, it's starting." Roger had an unpleasant habit of talking during the performance, making snide and sometimes astute observations, or asking innocuous questions, and then shushing Valentine before he had a chance to respond. He also carried with him, to support his bulk, a heavy wooden walking stick, that he was perpetually tapping on the box's railing as a way of showing his good favor. Still, there was something interesting about Roger's perspective — his sense of history and structure served to inform what turned out to be an astonishingly deep text.

"See that? That's a reference to the sharpsie riots. Oh, very clever." Tap, tap, went the cane.

"Wh—"

"Shh, shh."

Later:

"Ah! Did you catch that? The Minister of Defense is going to choke on his breakfast tomorrow!" Tap, tap, tap.

"You mean—"

"Shh, shh."

All in all, the experience was both frustrating and strangely entertaining. Valentine found himself, at first, spending as much time craning his neck towards the other box seats in order to gauge the responses of the Families and Ministry members—the ones that Roger named as the butt of certain obscure jokes—as he spent watching the play itself. And despite all that, there was something about the piece, something he couldn't quite put his finger on, that struck him as being familiar. It wasn't the story itself, which was clearly a dangerously accurate allegory for current imperial politics—he knew that one off the top of his head. It was something else, something to do with the structure of the language, some quality of sound or syntax that he had trouble shaking off.

And yet as the play progressed, Valentine became aware of a compelling spirit, as though beneath the social referents some deeper truth had been brought to light, and all the complexity, the humanity, the reality of the characters, seemed to shrink away in the shadow of that truth. That something was being *revealed* was an undeniable sensation, and it drew Valentines eye back to the stage, time and again, to watch the haggard face of the actor playing Theocles, whose voice changed from the throaty rasp of the soldier to the dread thunder of the wicked king, to the quiet horror of the man whose circumstances had outpaced him. Here was a man cast adrift from his own humanity; Theocles, in service to his nation, had lost touch with certain elements of his soul, and found what replaced them was bloody-mindedness and growing paranoia. All in all, Valentine found Theocles to be a far more compelling character than the actual, present emperor upon whom he was based.

When intermission came, he seized on the opportunity to stretch his legs, and it was while he walked in the lushly-appointed halls behind the Royal's balconies that he ran into Skinner.

This was not literally true; for though Valentine had been carelessly eyeing the elaborate woodwork along the doorframes while he walked, and certainly *would* have crashed headfirst into anyone that had the misfortune of walking in the opposite direction, Skinner herself had a long and practiced sensitivity to the location of bodies in space. She heard Valentine's carpet-muffled footsteps, and carefully stepped to the side as he approached.

"Valentine."

The young man nearly stumbled. "Skinner! What are you doing here?"

Skinner permitted herself a small smile. "I heard there was a play tonight."

"Oh, right. Well, right. Hey, did you notice the author? E. E. Beckett? You don't think...that's not El — I mean, that's not *our* Beckett, right?"

"I don't think so," she replied, challenged now to keep a broad, self-satisfied grin off of her face. "Surely we'd have heard?"

"I wonder if it's a relative."

"Does he have relatives?"

"Younger brother, I think, in Khent-On-Stark. A bootmaker. Hm. I guess I should ask him? Maybe I shouldn't. I won't." He seized her shoulders, all grins and good cheer. "But what are you doing *here*, I mean? I thought you'd left the city! And you don't have a box up here, do you?"

"No, a friend is letting me use hers. Someone I think you know, actually. Isn't Emilia Vie-Gorgon your cousin?"

"Third cousin. I — hm."

Skinner could hear the frown in his voice. "What is it?"

"Nothing. Nothing, I just. She's...how do you know Emilia?"

"She found out that I was in some distress after losing my job, and was good enough to offer some assistance. Why?" Her voice took on an edge as she spoke.

Valentine drew his friend to the side of the corridor and spoke in a low voice. He didn't suspect Emilia was at this performance, but there was no telling what sorts of stray words might find their way back to her. "Nothing. It's just. Emilia...I've known Emilia for a long time, Skinner, and she doesn't *have* friends. She just *wants* things, and so she *gets* things. I mean, I love my cousin — "

"Enough, Valentine. I'm a grown-up. I can take care of myself. And I don't recall very many people offering to help. If I have a friendship with Emilia..."

"I just think you should be careful, is all."

"I'll take it under advisement," Skinner replied, coolly. "Now, I think you might want to find your seat. The show's about to resume."

"Yes. Right. Sorry." He coughed and cleared his throat. "Look, I am sorry. I don't mean to...to be a busybody, or anything. I just. Was concerned."

"It's all well to be concerned now," Skinner snapped. There was something, something ludicrously vulnerable about Valentine's voice that roused her temper. "It's all very well to be concerned that someone has decided to help me. Where was your concern when I was down to my last six pennies? Where was your concern when I was being thrown out of my *house*?"

"I didn't know, look, I'm sorry, I didn't know about your house..."

"...where was your concern when the Moral Ministry took my job?"

"I'm sorry, I just, wait..."

"Nevermind. Forget about it, Valentine." She took a deep breath. "I'm sorry I shouted at you, all right? Just go sit down, don't worry about it."

"I'm sorry," Valentine muttered again. "Sorry." He cleared his throat again. "That's...uh. That's a nice dress, by the way. The blue suits you."

"I wouldn't know. Emilia gave it to me."

And with that last icy comment, she was gone. Valentine stood, blushing and sheepish, cursing himself, wishing he could go back in time and punch himself in the teeth before he had the chance to open his idiot mouth. Instead, he settled for returning to the critics' box, where Roger was engaged in an animated discussion with another critic.

"I just think," the man—a raw-boned fellow that Valentine thought wrote for the *Observer*—was saying, "that real tragic art should be transcendent of political circumstances. You can't make a good play that's too topical—"

"Shh, shh," Roger interrupted. "It's starting up again." He tapped his cane imperiously on the balcony, the red-gold house lights dimmed, and the play resumed.

The second act of *Theocles* was a marvel; a piece of such blistering intensity that even Roger's lively tongue was stilled. Valentine sat on the very edge of his seat and leaned as far on the railing as he possibly could. A lightheaded euphoria filled him as the raw passions of the actors seemed to dredge his soul up and tear it free from its moorings.

Partly, this was a purely mechanical effect. The new director of the Royal had perfected a way to use an array of lenses and phlogiston and incandescent lamps to produce a bright, narrow spotlight that could range in color from bright white to a pale, ghostly blue. Theocles stood in a circle of strange, denatured light, and his cheap theatrical armor was transmuted into something real, ragged and bloody. Pools of blue light illumined the bogeymen that the wicked king, in his desperation and his arrogance, returned to — their leather masks were made into vivid and leering faces that Valentine found uncomfortably familiar.

Theocles, pursued to the last battlements of his fortress, haunted by vengeful ghosts, was finally cut down by Arden Wyndham, who had lost his family to Theocles' bloody ambition. When Wyndham returned the stage, now illumined by a wash of lurid color, bearing the head of his enemy on the tip of his sword, the audience roared — not approval, not anger, not exactly. It was a kind of pure, undifferentiated feeling, something more primal than fear or sadness or rage, something that had been building during the enforced stillness of the preceding scenes, something worked to a fever pitch and then finally freed itself.

Valentine was on his feet at once without even realizing it, applauding fiercely. Even Roger was lumbering to his feet, ruddy-faced and grinning like a madman, pounding his cane on the balcony floor. The fat old critic tried to shout something to his companion, but Valentine couldn't hear him over the sound of the ovation.

"What?"

"….trouble…come…morrow…" Roger repeated, then turned back to the stage where the actors were taking a fifth curtain call. Valentine clapped harder, and for the first time in many years of attending the theater, did not wonder how long it was going to be until the actors stopped bowing.

THIRTEEN

The applause did eventually die down, though its echoes still thundered in Valentine's ears. He was just about to take his leave of Roger Gorgon-Crabtree — the critic was unlikely to even notice, as he was embroiled in an uproarious, though good-natured, argument with another man — when a commotion amongst the floor seats caught his eye.

The coroner leaned over the edge of the balcony and peered out into the theater. The house lights had been lit again, but the cavernous space was still very dim. Among the audience members, pressing against each other as they began their disordered exit, there was a kind of ripple of anxiety. Valentine couldn't precisely say what it was, but there was definitely a sense…a tension of palpable and growing intensity.

"What…"

"What?" Roger asked. "What is it?"

"Something…" Valentine replied, unhelpfully.

Voices were raised, tinged with the timbre of hysteria. Men and women began pushing at each other, struggling to get away from something, turning violent in a clear violation of the long tradition of goodwill that was supposed to pervade Armistice. They began moving faster, panicking…

"Something's wrong. Shit, something's wrong," Valentine muttered. He missed his guns. Who carries guns during Armistice? The idea of carrying so much as a pocket-knife was anathema. "Your cane," he said to Roger. "Give it to me, I…"

A woman screamed, and they both heard the sharp retort of a revolver, followed by a strange crackling echo, as if a hundred phantom revolvers had been discharged in response. There were more raised voices now, and the audience on the floor began to fight each other, crowding into the aisles, climbing over the seats. A green light glimmered near the stage.

"Now!" Valentine snapped, and snatched the cane from Roger's slack hand. "Shit." *How do I get down?* The stairs were too far…but the red curtains that hung down between the boxes. *Oh, all right. All right. I always wanted to try this.* He stuck the cane into his belt, reached out, and grabbed hold of the plush red fabric, and swung out over the seats…

…and hung there. He had, perhaps, expected that he would slide slowly down the length of curtain, or that it would give way at a reasonably slow rate, gently lowering him to the ground. But the curtain remained stubbornly affixed, and Valentine suddenly found himself wondering if he'd take his skin off trying to slide down it.

"Shit," he muttered. "Okay. Just…okay." He kicked out his foot, tried to hook it back over the railing, pull himself back to the balcony, when suddenly the curtain *did* give way, with a catastrophic ripping sound, and Valentine found himself dropping like a stone with two yards of heavy red fabric coming down on top of him. He landed with a teeth-jarring crash, and immediately began the laborious process of trying to free himself from lengths of cloth.

Finally free and on his feet, Valentine tried to make his way towards the stage, past a streaming, frightened crowd; theatergoers in their clean suits, women with their elaborate hats, terror printed on their faces. There was another gunshot, another peculiar web of echoes. More screams. Valentine stood on the arms of a seat, balanced precariously above the bobbing heads, trying to get his bearings. Two people had been shot—one gentleman in a fine suit, who had been hit in the chest. Red blood stained what had been a snow-white shirt front. He twitched feebly; Valentine could see that he would be dead soon.

A woman lay sprawled across some nearby seats, weeping. Blood stained her dress where she had taken a bullet in the arm. She kept trying to crawl away from the gunman, who now seemed to have completely lost interest in her.

The gunman…two men…three men at least were at the edge of the stage, dressed in identical, ragged blue trousers and shirts. They were waving revolvers around, and green light glimmered from their eyes. They shouted, furiously working to be heard over the noise of the crowd, gesticulating wildly, desperate to make themselves *understood*. One man was on the theater stage, shouting up into the flyspace, as though he were addressing an adversary hiding in the withdrawn curtains. A second man was kicking at the chairs in the near rows, turning his head this way and that, on a wild hunt for some unknowable prey. A third man clattered around the orchestra pit, knocking down instruments and music stands, his intentions indecipherable.

On each man's face, glowing from somewhere in the depths of their skulls, was a sharp point of light—bright white at the center, fading to a surreal green at the edges. It made skin and muscle transparent, obscured eyes and features, so that each man appeared to have no face; only a leering skull surrounded by a halo of viridian light. *Daemonomaniacs*, Valentine thought. He tore the cane free from his belt and held it like a sword. "Out of the way!" He shouted. "Coroners!" All to little effect; the crowd ignored, though it was mercifully thinning.

One of the men fired his revolver off into the air; the other two responded. Yet a fourth sounded right nearby, nearly startling Valentine from his perch. The one who'd fired looked just the same as the others—the same ragged blue shirt, the same green glimmer across his face.

"Here!" The stranger shouted, "It's going to start here. I'm going to stop it! Don't you understand? I have to stop...to stop it!" His empty sockets turned towards Valentine, and the coroner could just make out the opaque, jade green sclera of his eyes. He leveled his revolver, and Valentine snapped the cane at his head, aiming right for that weird light on his face...

He felt the walking stick connect, and felt his arm draw back simultaneously, felt himself hesitate a second too long and take a bullet in his chest, felt himself crack the man's skull before the gun could go off, felt a dozen possible past and future moments fracture in a spiderweb of disrupted causality...

And then the man was gone, and in his place was nothing but the absolute certainty that there had never been anyone there in the first place.

"Aw, nuts."

The crowd was gone now, pressed to the far exits and finally squeezed outside. Valentine saw five men now with their guns, and two people—a man and a woman—lying across the chairs, bleeding from wounds in their chests. The green-glimmer men were casting about wildly, shouting incoherently about stopping...something.

Of course they were mad. Or, really, *he* was mad, Valentine realized, as some of the identical-looking men were really causal doppelgangers—a peculiar effect caused by the daemonomania. Four men were weird hallucinations, and their bullets were harmless. One man was real, and definitely deadly. *Which one?* The young coroner knew he didn't have the means to tell them apart: though he couldn't recall precisely, he had a vague and uncomfortable feeling that none of the doppelgangers really *were* doppelgangers until he actually tried to test one. It had something to do with actualizing lines of causality, and Valentine had actually dozed through much of that lecture when he was being trained.

"This moment is the end," the men shouted—that, or some variation on it, each glimmering figures words colored by slight causal variations. "This is the last time. This is the edge of now. All past and future moments are echoes of this one!"

Nothing for it, Valentine told himself, grimly. *I'll just have to take them all.* He clutched the cane like a sabre and tensed, choosing as his first target the man kicking his way through the orchestra pit. He kept checking under things, as though he were looking for something. *Now, or never.*

"Valentine!"

The coroner looked around; he'd know Skinner's voice anywhere. After a second, he saw her in Emilia's box seat. She stood with her head cocked to the side. Pointing.

Pointing at the doppelganger on the stage, the one that was stamping his feet and frothing. *Oh,* Valentine Vie-Gorgon thought. *Please be right, Skinner.*

Like all young men of his economic class, Valentine Vie-Gorgon had an extensive and expensive education. It covered many topics, including the arts, science, literature, politics, and military strategy. It also included training in a number of "gentlemen sports"—a euphemism for the violent soldiering techniques that, as a member of Trowth's elite high society, Valentine would never be called on to use. They included boxing, wrestling, and, of course, fencing.

93

It was generally considered true among both habitual fencers and habitual brawlers that there was not any particular difference between hitting a man with a sabre and hitting a man with a long stick—the wound it delivered was different, but, mechanically, the process was essentially the same. All of this is to say that, when Valentine leapt at the daemonomaniac man—dropping low to avoid being shot, kicking his leg out behind him and off at angle in a technically perfect low-long-pass (called a *vaeda socz* by Sarpeki fencing masters), and thrusting firmly with Roger Gorgon-Crabtree's cane right below the daemonomaniac's sternum—he was not altogether mad in thinking that this would be an effective course of action.

Nor was he altogether wrong; the blow was strong and well-placed, and good enough that the daemonomaniac lost his breath and staggered, firing wildly above Valentine's head. However, in common with many men who have trained as fencers, but have had little opportunity to actually fight with a sword or stick, he was wrong in thinking that this strike alone would be enough to end the fight. It was Valentine's peculiar luck—the same one thought to accompany drunks and idiots—that the daemonomaniac dropped his gun before leaping on Valentine, as the young man paused after his perfectly-executed lunge.

"Ow, get off!" Valentine said, while the daemonomaniac grunted unintelligibly, and did his level best to get his fingers around the coroner's throat. "Shit, get…" he lost his balance, and the two crashed heavily to the floor. Valentine tried to get a hold of him, to pin him, to do something, but the man fought with the strength and reckless abandon of a madman, and the light that glared from his face pulsed and grew brighter, seemingly in concert with the daemonomaniac's desperation.

A gravelly voice shouted, "Hold him! Hold him still!" It was barely audible over the pounding blood and adrenaline in Valentine's ears. Another figure loomed into his vision and gripped the daemonomaniac by the neck. At once, the struggling man began to relax, his breath returning as his anger left, his voice resolving into strange, muttered inconsistencies. Valentine shoved him away.

"Beckett?" He said, when he caught his breath. "What are you doing here?"

The old man looked at him with one good eye, and one dark red pit where a second should be. He had a brass-furnished syringe in his hand. There was a tiny amount of milky-white veneine still remaining. "He'll be out for a little while," Beckett said of the daemonomaniac. "We need to get him somewhere copper-lined and secure, before the doppelgangers manifest again."

Valentine nodded. "He was saying something...something about 'it starting here,' like that..."

"They always say that," Beckett spat, disgustedly. "Daemonomaniacs think that they can get in touch with some kind of oracle mind so they can predict the future—it always makes them think that something terribly important is about to happen *right now*, and the only way they can stop it is by shooting people."

"It's a hallucination?"

"Probably. Who knows?" Beckett shrugged. "If you think about it, what's ever happened that *couldn't* have been prevented by shooting someone at the right time? How would you know anyway?" He gestured at the comatose man. "They always lose their minds before their predictions come true, anyway. Check his pockets."

Valentine began at once. "What am I looking for?"

"Another of those pamphlets. That's why I don't want this one executed, yet. I want to know where he got it."

"Are you sure he's got...oh wait. Here." The coroner held up a weathered quarto with "The Causal Mind" printed neatly on the first page. "To attune oneself to the daemon that knows the precise location of all the universe's atomies, and so to know their paths, and so to know the paths of all objects —"

"Enough. We'll take it to the Church. Or Stitch. Get a report on it. Last thing I need is for you to come under suspicion, too."

"I'm a coroner, Beckett."

Beckett snorted. "I don't know if you've noticed, but the new ministry is keeping a closer eye on us than anyone else. I can't protect you if they want to take you in."

"I have —"

"Your name won't protect you either. Help me get this son of a bitch out of here."

Grunting, Valentine slung the man over his shoulders and, somewhat wobbly, managed to get to his feet. "So, what *are* you doing here?"

The old coroner shrugged. "I go to the theater sometimes. Not every day a play comes out with my name on it."

Fourteen

Quickly, with a practiced efficiency, Beckett and Valentine bound the madman, commandeered a Family coach, and brought the daemonomaniac to the coroners' new holdings cells on the edge of Old Bank. The bars and walls were sheathed in greening copper, which metal's alchemical properties served to gradually divest the man of the shimmering green light that poured from deep within his skull. Beckett decided to let the daemonomaniac sleep off his veneine dose in the interests of questioning him once the madness had fully abated. Moreover, the old coroner knew from experience that a dose that high would leave the subject with a terrible headache and painfully dry mouth afterwards — two features that might aid in his interrogation.

Afterwards, the two coroners stood on Terrace Street which, ever since the *Excelsior's* unfortunate reactivation had swallowed a substantial chunk of Old Bank, had a view of the whole of Trowth, all the way down to the bay. The city, with its vast intricacies of architecture, green bronze and copper statuary, crooked roads and canted buildings, was all tangled shadows in the last dregs of red spring light. Trowth seemed then to be a great stone wave, frozen in the act of rearing up, ready to crash with apocalyptic thunder onto the iron stillness of the Agon Bay. There was a mass to the city, a feeling of unstoppable inertia, as though some terrible machinery had been set in motion and, by virtue of its weight and power, would not stop until it had finally destroyed itself.

"Well," said Beckett, his ravaged face as impassive, as always.

"Well. Daemonomaniacs. I didn't think anyone still did that."

"There's always a few," Beckett replied. "The Brothers of the Mad Wind—you know, the ones that go out in the psychestorms, hoping for enlightenment?"

"They're daemonomaniacs?"

"Technically. Any time someone uses flux to distort their own consciousness. The Brothers are mostly harmless, though. Real daemonomaniacs use etherized-flux..." the old coroner trailed off, staring at the city. The night air had cooled and sharpened; blue phlogiston streetlamps flickered on, waging a losing battle against Trowth's deep shadows.

After a moment, it became clear that Beckett had no intention of continuing. "Why don't we...er..." he prodded, "Prosecute them, then? The Brothers?"

Beckett shrugged. "No point. They're all over. The second you go after one, the rest just disappear into their little bolt-holes. Usually into the Arcadium. I have someone keep an eye on them, instead. Sometimes, they lead us to real heretics." He paused for a moment. "Not usually."

"No?"

"There's..." He shook his head. "The....there hasn't been a serious daemonomaniac in Trowth in. Ten years. Thought they'd really. Died out." He let out a low, ragged, sepulchral chuckle. "Of course they didn't. It never goes away, does it? Once it's out there once...as long as *someone* knows, it will never go away. Ideas are a poison worse than any plague." His shoulders seemed to sag, then, as though the effort of holding himself upright had suddenly grown beyond his last reserves of strength.

Valentine watched him for what felt like a long time, possessed of an inexplicable urge to reach out to the old man, put a hand on his shoulder. He contented himself with, "Are you all right?"

"Have Karine check for...flux. Shipments that have gone missing, warehouses."

"Beckett."

"Warehouses that have been broken into."

"Beckett, Karine doesn't—"

"Someone knows. Fuck, they're supposed to *report* it..." The old man had a hand to his head, as though he were overcome by a sudden wave of dizziness.

"Beckett!" Valentine snapped. "Karine's gone, remember?"

"What?" Beckett grunted. "I know she's gone. Just have...whoever. Whatever-his-name-is check into it."

"Are you all right?"

"I'm fine. Just." Beckett shook his head again. "Fine." He turned, abruptly, and strode off into the night.

For a moment, Valentine watched him go, wondering if he should follow. If the old man was losing his grip...Valentine shook his head. He couldn't believe that; if there was anyone in the world that could keep it together, it was Elijah Beckett. And, even if something *was* wrong, how to talk about it without rousing the man's pride and ire?

Valentine Vie-Gorgon decided that he would look into the flux issue himself.

FIFTEEN

Beckett waited until the following afternoon to interrogate the daemonomaniac. He took Gorud down into the basements of Raithower House, far away from the weak but welcome sunlight of Armistice, where it was deep and dark enough to feel like the middle of the night.

Though they were not used often, there were two old vaults beneath Raithower house that served as temporary holding cells. They could be accessed by a dark, narrow stair, and they were cramped and humid. In the winter they were deathly cold, in the summer they were broiling hot in the summer, and during Armistice they were possessed of a suffocating humidity. They were unpleasant places to be quartered. It was unusual for the Coroners, whose mandate was so extreme, to actually make arrests; the dangers of certain sciences being themselves often so tremendous that permitting a heretic to live long enough to transport him to a safe location represented an unacceptable level of risk to civic safety. However, the vaults were equipped with rough cots and heavy locks, and in the few instances when Beckett felt the need to interrogate a prisoner at his leisure, he was able to do so.

The daemonomaniac was crouched in the corner of the vault, glaring with eerie green eyes that were not quite luminescent. His third, atemporal eye, had vanished. In his withdrawal, the man quivered and shook, and chewed on his twitching, spidery fingers.

Beckett approached the bars of the cell, Gorud at his heels. The therian carried a small phlogiston lantern equipped with a red filter to keep its light dim. Daemonomaniacs often suffered unpredictable reactions — including painful and even deadly sublimations — under bright phlogiston light.

The old man had left his hat and scarf and coat in his office. He stood, impassive and immobile, glaring at the madman, trying to intimidate him with his hideously ravaged face. The empty eye and skeletal shadows cast in the red glare of Gorud's lamp were certainly horrific enough, but the daemonomaniac's

100

mind was damaged beyond caring. He did not even appear to notice the two coroners, but instead gnawed enthusiastically on his abraded, skittering fingers.

"Name." Beckett said.

The man stared off into the distance, not looking at Beckett at all, instead keeping his eyes focused on some invisible item that was of incomprehensible fascination to him. He said nothing.

"What's your name?"

Nothing but the wet sound of the daemonomaniac chewing. His fingers were red and raw beneath his teeth.

"He doesn't know," Gorud said. "He has forgotten his name?"

Beckett nodded. "The 'daemon,' the intelligence that they think they're in touch with, is supposed to expand their minds. It's a delusion, of course, but their minds don't know that. They fill up with nonsense, crowd the rest out. If we're lucky, there's still something we can use." He reached out and slammed his hand against the bars. "Hey. What's your name?"

The man looked up at them with a sudden start, and his eyes, briefly, snapped into focus. He opened his mouth to speak, but instead stretched his jaw wide, so wide that Beckett could hear the joint pop, and his eyes glazed over again. At once, he began to speak in a hoarse, raspy voice. "Huhk. Gurat. Torroketetetet—"

"Glossolalia," Beckett muttered. "Nonsense."

"—kaitor get...get...get out. Get out. It's ours. It's ours! OURS!" The daemonomaniac began to scream, the words dissolving into guttural croaking shouts as he leapt up from his corner and threw himself crashing against the bars. Gorud hopped back as the hinges and locks creaked, but Beckett remained still. The locks held. The man hammered impotently against the bars of his cell, shrieking and spitting like a mad animal.

"They're starting from here," the daemonomaniac's voice dropped to a frantic whisper. "Here. No! Don't tell them that."

"Where did you get the flux?" Beckett demanded.

"They can't know yet. They don't know yet. Theyuk, arctorus keret gai phorthent."

Beckett asked again. "The flux. Who gave it to you?"

"Gorret kora, kirakari ta net!"

"Listen," the coroner said. "You're talking nonsense. You think you're speaking Trowthi, but you're not. The part of your brain that understands speech—"

"Harep," Gorud spoke up from the dark. "Kara dettu priata?"

Very slowly, Beckett turned to face the therian, who was huddled behind his lamp, his eyes wide, his canine face impassive. The coroner said nothing, and for a long moment, neither did the daemonomaniac.

"Exhu," the daemonomaniac said, his voice soft, almost cogent now. "Garrakt for dett. They know."

"Shingoru dettu parak. Exhu diri otomen." Gorud shook his head. "Exhu borak."

The man tried to speak again, but no words emerged. He worked his jaw, his eyes bulged, veins throbbed against his head. He threw himself against the iron bars, again and again, entirely silent except for the labored breathing through his flaring nostrils. Finally, he staggered back against the far wall, his body still wracked with pain, and shrieked. The foreign words exploded in a torrent from his throat.

"Agatta! Exhu agatta! Exhu agatta!" He broke off into a piteous wail and wept and screamed as he arched his back. The atemporal eye began to glow behind his skull, illuminating its morbid contours, humming faintly in sympathy with the metal bars.

"Damn it," Beckett said. "He's seizing." He began fumbling with the keys at his belt, his numb fingers clumsy, his haste paradoxically slowing him down.

The man's screams grew louder. "Exhu agatta! Exhu agatta!" The light from his skull was enough to see by, and his back had contorted so sharply that it looked as though it meant to crack.

Beckett finally fit key into lock, as the daemonomaniac's scream built to a fever pitch, was cut off by a strangled choke, and abruptly sound and light and all were gone. The daemonomaniac was still as a bronze statue, frozen at that twisted painful angle, his outline just visible in the dim red light from Gorud's lamp. Beckett sighed, and let the door of the vault swing slowly open.

"Dead." He cautiously approached the man to examine him. Seizures of this nature were not uncommon with flux overdoses and, while gruesome, were somewhat less frightening to see than a full sublimation. Whatever daemonic sympathies the man had created in the recesses of his mind had overburdened his system, filling it with the psychoactive radiation of the flux. The mild synaesthesias that the mineral sometimes caused were nothing compared to this: the nerves that should control the heart were diverted to the tongue, eyes to the lungs, muscles in the arms and legs scrambled with internal organs, speech centers, memories. It was as if a giant hand had reached into the daemonomaniac's nervous system and twisted everything into a deadly tangle of misguided signals.

"Dead," the coroner said again, as though the idea had become stuck in his mind, and he couldn't move on from it. "Dead, dead, dead." With a splintery creak of ruined joints, he bent down to look at the daemonomaniac's hands. They had been chewed unnaturally thoroughly. The skin wasn't just red, but broken in many places, bleeding, scraped all the way down to the bone. No mentally-undamaged person was capable of doing such injury to their own body.

"Is this typical," Gorud asked, as he brought the light around, and removed the red filter. The room was suddenly an order of magnitude brighter. "The chewing?"

"No," Beckett said. "I've never seen it before. But. Daemonomania is idiosyncratic. Not everyone responds the same way." With a grunt of pain, he stood up. "What was that you did? You were talking to him." The coroner turned to face the therian, who had now retreated a few steps. It was hard to tell, because the creature's face did not reflect its emotions the way a human face did, but Gorud seemed pensive.

"It is. Karak. Theri, you call it," he said. "My language."

"How did he know theri?"

Gorud shrugged. "I do not know. Perhaps he knew some of my people? There are not many of us here in the city. Perhaps he came from Korasai?"

Beckett looked back down at the man. "Skin's pretty pale. No tan lines, no sun damage. He's been in Trowth for a while, anyway. Maybe Corsay when he was younger. What did he say?"

Gorud was quiet for a moment, then shook his head. "Nothing. Nonsense." Beckett stared, waited to see if the therian's reserve might be overcome by the pregnant silence. "He said...he said he must kill her. He said that someone was coming."

"Who?"

"I don't know how to say it." Gorud puffed his lips out thoughtfully. "What is the word, for a person that is not from here? That is not like us?"

"Foreign. Strange."

The therian ducked his had enthusiastically. "Yes. Strange. Exhu, 'strangers.' The strangers are coming." He shuffled uncomfortably under his coat, and fiddled with the controls of his lamp. The sounds were very loud in the now-quiet vault, crisply echoing from the stone walls. It gave Beckett the feeling that he and Gorud had bored deep into the center of the cold earth and were now pounding madly and pointlessly against the walls of a rocky prison, far from anyone that could hear them, far from anyone that could help. After a moment, the ape-man shrugged again. "It is meaningless, as you said. Nonsense. Are we not all strangers in this city?"

For a few seconds, that ominous, dreadful sense of isolation persisted. Then Beckett snorted. "Yeah. I guess we are." He turned back to the claustrophobic stair that would lead to his office, and supposed he'd have to just cool his heels until something useful came along.

Sixteen

The next day, the broadsheets were full of righteous indignation and hysterical ranting. In fifty, no, a hundred years, no soul had ever thought to violate the good will of Armistice! The shooting at the Royal was a travesty, a tragedy, unheard of, deplorable, disgusting! The writers and critics of each and every paper found new depths of vituperative rhetoric to express an outrage that bordered on the cosmic. While they could not agree of what this unprecedented act of violence was a sign—some thought it was representative of a coarsening of the Trowth culture, others a lack of respect for tradition, still others saw it as the first step towards revolution against a decaying monarchy—no journalist could disagree that it was anything but paramount in importance.

With the exception, of course, of Roger Gorgon-Crabtree. Peculiarly, in his review of *Theocles*, there was absolutely no mention of the daemonomaniac and his gun—though, given that between the flowery praise and ebullient enthusiasm there was hardly room for one additional word, this was perhaps not so peculiar. Roger—whom many readers had long suspected was actually morally incapable of liking *anything* unabashedly—had finally thrown his considerable weight fully behind a new play.

The combination of this uniquely positive notice and Trowth's prurient interest in the grim and grisly violation of one of its unspoken taboos served to make the second performance of *Theocles* one of the most popular in the history of the Royal. Patrons were turned away in droves—some even refused, and crowded into the lobby during the performance; maybe they hoped to steal a seat when some ticket-holder was overcome by the drama, maybe they thought they could appreciate the play just by virtue of what could be overheard through the

CHRIS BRAAK

auditorium doors, maybe they just wanted to be seen at the most popular event of any season. Whatever the case, there seemed to be no fear at all of a repeat of the preceding night's incident, so thoroughly was the idea of Armistice imprinted on the minds of the people of Trowth.

Following the performance, Emilia Vie-Gorgon and her brother, Emilio, hosted a small, informal party at the palatial townhome of the Raithower Vie-Gorgons. The actors, of course, were not invited—though they were generously compensated with several bottles of wine and sweet Corsay rum, and it was generally presumed that, wherever actors got off to when they'd finished a performance, they were likely to be enjoying themselves. Skinner *was* invited, though not as the author of *Theocles*—an honor she must necessarily avoid—but as a close friend of Emilia's.

The party, despite being nominally informal, was actually an opportunity for the young gentlemen and ladies of Trowth's upper-classes to demonstrate their opulent wealth and often-questionable fashion sense, indulging in the bright colors, ruffled fabrics, ribbons, jewels, and other ornamentation that were usually considered gauche by public fashion standards. They mingled and danced and drank, gossiped about this or that arcane social event, objects so far outside of Skinner's purview that they may as well have been discussing alchemy. It was hot and noisy, and the only music consisted of a relentlessly cheerful harpsichord and a poor man exhausting himself on a Sarein fiddle.

Skinner wore a high-necked dress in emerald green that, she was assured, suited her admirably, and a diamond broach that Nora Feathersmith had lent her. Skinner found herself disinclined to be social on this particular night—though she had never been a social butterfly by any stretch of the imagination. The young men at the party had lost interest in her when she had refused their invitations to dance; the young ladies had lost interest when she had refused to use her clairaudience to overhear what others were saying about them. Instead, she stood off from the crowd of strangers with their jostling elbows and artificial laughter, lost in thoughtful rumination.

Until: "Ms. Skinner," asked an infuriatingly familiar voice. "Would you care to dance?"

"I am afraid I am not much of a dancer, Valentine."

106

Skinner found her left hand in his right, and his left lightly on the small of her back. "It's all right," he said, "These new waltzes are mostly just to give us an opportunity to see each other's clothes. It's hardly any more work than walking in a slow circle."

"And are your clothes worth showing off?"

"It's a handsome suit," Valentine admitted with mock reluctance. "And I cut a dashing figure in it. But I really felt like you were the one that people should see."

"It's not my dress," Skinner said. "I haven't got anything that isn't coroner-charcoal."

"I wasn't talking about the dress."

Skinner bit back a retort, and smiled in spite of herself. Valentine's lines might be a little sappy, but she was flattered at least that he was trying.

"Can I admit something?" He asked, after a moment of thoughtful silence.

"If you're sure your comfortable with such importune honesty."

"Hm. I spent five minutes watching you, trying to plan out how this conversation should go. The bit about the dress was all I came up with."

"Well, it was very nice. Thank you."

Another shy, thoughtful pause. "I also wanted," he continued, in a low voice, "to…to say I'm sorry. About yesterday, and everything…"

"Valentine…"

"No, just listen, okay? I'm sorry about the other day, and I'm sorry about…you having to leave the coroners. I tried…well, never mind that. I didn't know about your house, anyway. But I just wanted to say…" He took a deep breath. "I know that Emilia is helping you, now, and that's good. But if…if anything changes, you know? Or if something happens…"

"Valentine."

"If something happens, if you need anything, you just…I'll help. I will."

Skinner sighed. "Valentine, you know I could never ask — "

"I know, you don't have to ask. Just say it sometime. Like, if you're walking down the street, and you need lunch, just say, 'Oh, I could use some lunch.' And I'll find out, and get you lunch, okay?" He paused. "No, wait, that sounds weird. I shouldn't have said that. I regret saying that. Just pretend…what…why are you laughing?"

Skinner found herself giggling helplessly. Valentine was just so relentlessly *earnest*, it was impossible to stay angry with him for any length of time. "All right! All right," she said at last. "The next time I need lunch, you will be the first person I call. Fair enough?"

"Yes, and —"

"And you're forgiven for everything you've ever done. You didn't know I was in dire straits; how could you? I never told you. That was positively my fault. All right."

"All right. You're good at this, by the way. Dancing."

"Thank you."

"You know everyone is looking at us?"

"Well, you do cut a dashing figure. Or so I'm told."

In fact, a substantial portion of the party was looking at the pair, usually with hastily averted sidelong glances. This was because new additions to the social circle—namely Skinner, who with her silver eyeplate was a particularly unusual addition—were always watched closely for any sign that might resemble weakness. It was also because Valentine was himself notoriously eccentric, and was often watched closely in the hopes that he might do something strange enough to be worth gossiping about. Aside from dancing with the new woman, this particular party seemed likely to prove a disappointment.

When the dance had proved suitably tiring, Skinner begged the chance to rest.

"Of course," Valentine said, slightly out of breath. "Sure. I…hm. Is that Nora Feathersmith talking to my cousin?"

"Where?" Skinner asked.

"By the door. That's strange. I thought they hated each other."

"Really? No, not at all. They're quite good friends, actually. I sat with them in Emilia's box at the theater a few weeks ago."

"You did? But…but this is all very strange. A year ago they had a very public falling out. Well. I suppose I just ought to pay more attention. Do you want something to drink? Wine? They've made a hot, spiced punch that's very good..."

"I'll have some of that, yes, thanks," Skinner said, as curiosity slowly compelled her clairaudience towards Emilia and Nora. Snatches of conversation sounded in her ears as she projected past the partygoers, but she ignored them until she found the precise timbre of the voices that she wanted.

"...tomorrow, you think?" Nora was saying.

"Yes, I should hope so. If we haven't caught their attention by now, I don't know that we ever shall," replied Emilia, her voice characteristically devoid of any hint of hidden meaning.

"I suppose our principal will be pleased."

"I doubt our principal is capable of pleasure."

There was a pause. Nora hummed softly to the music, while Emilia seemed to vanish from the face of the earth. "Do you really think it will work?" Nora asked, eventually.

"I don't see why not. Remember Adronus, dear heart," Emilia replied. "Wars are won with narrative."

"Here you are!" Valentine's voice brought Skinner immediately back to herself. He gently placed a cup of steaming punch in her hand. It was warm — almost too warm to hold, and certainly too warm for the stuffy salon. "It's good, I think they use that djang fruit in it. That's funny, isn't it? Five years ago no one had even *heard* of djang, now I'm not sure there's food or drink in Trowth that doesn't use it..."

"Who's Adronus?" Skinner asked him, as she let her punch cool.

"Adronus? I'm sure I don't know. Is he here at the party?"

"No, he's...nevermind." She sipped at the punch. It was still too hot. "Someone that you might have read, maybe?"

"Uhm. Constantine Adronus, do you mean?"

"I don't know," Skinner snapped, exasperated. "If I knew who I meant, I wouldn't be asking about him, would I?"

"Well, all right, I don't know. Constantine Adronus was a general, uhm. 15th century I think. Or 1500 something, I get those mixed up. Anyway, he's out of favor, now, since what's his name, the Sarpeki general from the siege of Canth published his book...that whole thing about legs and arms."

"Valentine. Focus."

"Right, sorry. Adronus' big thing was, 'A war is over when the opponent thinks he's lost. A battle is just a pointed argument.' He used to say that wars were really just stories..."

"War is narrative," Skinner suggested.

"Yeah, like that. Have you been...why do you know about Adronus?"

"I was...it's just something I heard, once. I thought you might know."

"Well, that's suspicious. Why would you think that I knew anything?" His voice held a bold grin.

Skinner snorted. "With all those years at fancy schools, I was sure you were bound to recollect something, particularly if it was useless. At the knocker school they only taught us *skills*."

"Well, la-di-da. For your information, gentlemen aren't supposed to need skills. That's what we have butlers for. And tailors."

"That's just like the Families, isn't it? Sustaining their lifestyles on the backs of their servants."

Valentine laughed out loud. "Careful. That kind of talk is generally frowned on in places like this." The music picked up, as the fiddler found his second wind and joined the indefatigable harpsichordist. Skinner and Valentine danced again, and twice more before the night was over.

The idle rich spent late nights, as morning held no particular urgency for them. It was close to dawn when the last, most devoted partygoers finally dispersed, all wavering drunken smiles and over-friendly hands. These were the gentlemen who, now that their late-night's entertainment had waned, would probably find some other dissolute venue in which to practice their only particular ability: hedonism.

Skinner had waited until the end, hoping for a brief word with Emilia, but, after her enigmatic conversation with Nora Feathersmith, the Vie-Gorgon heiress was nowhere to be found. Her major-domo helped the guests gather shawls and coats, and politely but firmly showed them the door. Valentine found her a coach, and repeated his embarrassingly sincere offer to buy her lunch.

The sun had nearly risen by the time Skinner returned to the house in Lanternbridge. Skinner could not see the sky turning red and angry with the day, the clouds unusually thick for Armistice, the black towers of soot pouring from smokestacks as the factories started up. She could not see the sprawling mass of the royal palace, highlighted against the sun, nor the vast expanse of her city stretched out beneath the meager light. She could not see the empty windows, the darkened doorways that looked like so many unfriendly eyes and mouths, yawning open to disgorge their bleary-eyed occupants.

But she could feel something—a hot breath of air, stirring from the south and whipping through the streets, tinged with the bloody taste of burning phlogiston, the acrid smell of smoke and industry. A humming energy, beneath the city's ancient streets, a powerful sense of immanence that surged through the drowsy morning like so much summer lightning.

The truth was that knockers often had such feelings—experiences of unnamable dread or imminent danger, that many times had no reliable connection to the world. And Trowth was a city that lent itself well to such strange sensations, even among its less-sensitive inhabitants. Under the best of circumstances, gargantuan, weather-beaten Trowth was a city that felt haunted by the heat and cold, by damp chills and strange agues. So it was reasonable, and perhaps forgivable, that Skinner thought nothing of the feeling, and collapsed into her bed having given it hardly a second thought.

SEVENTEEN

Beckett sat in his office, brooding. He had for the first time that year opened the heavy, green copper-plated shutters on his windows, an indulgence he permitted himself only during the two weeks of Armistice. These were, in fact, the only two weeks when the weather did not bother him in some way; warm enough not to cause his bones to ache, cool enough that he could still wear his suit and scarf without sweating. It would be an exaggeration to say that Armistice is the only time of the year that Beckett actually enjoyed, as "enjoyment" is perhaps too strong a word to describe what Beckett felt about anything, but certainly one could say that Armistice was the two weeks of the year that Beckett found to be the least intolerable.

Ordinarily. Now, the lightening sky and cheery, amiable atmosphere of the city rang hollow in his ears, a false front of friendship piled up, after so many years of tradition, on top of Trowth's ever-rotten core. There was not, Beckett had been forced to conclude, anything sacred. This was not a revelation that struck him like a thunderbolt, but rather a slow, seeping realization. After many years of work in the Coroners, he had learned that most people did not hold most things sacred, and that those things that above all demanded respect for their sacredness were the ones most likely to be ignored. But he had hoped, or else imagined, or at the very least considered that there were in his world one or two things that everyone chose to respect.

"Should have known better," he muttered to himself. He looked at his desk, cluttered with paperwork for cases that he would never, could never solve. He felt the ugly weight of the gun in his hand. His mind drifted back to his last conversation with Mr. Stitch.

"You perceive. A. Connection?" The hulking reanimate, still as a corpse behind its desk, had wheezed at him.

"There's no question," Beckett had replied. "The pamphlets that are being circulated, they're all made at the same press. We don't know where it is, but we're going to find it. I want to move on these men, now."

"Impossible." Stitch replied. "We. Cannot. Find them."

"You didn't find anything?" Beckett asked. "Anything at all at the gendarmerie bombing site?"

"Nothing." Stitch's voice betrayed no emotion except the constant pain of having to be used at all. "The site. Was entirely. Devoid."

"We can't..." Beckett had begun. He felt his voice grow hoarse, and worried that it would crack. He wondered how he could be so desperate about something, after so much time spent in the regular, dispassionate slog of his work. "We can't let this go. We have to *do* something."

"So. Find. Something."

That was it, and it was depressing. If Stitch and its miraculous engine of a mind couldn't find anything to connect the bombing and the daemonomaniac and the mysterious pamphleteer, then there was little hope that Beckett would be able to. No leads, no anything, like so many of his cases these days. The number of crimes that could be connected to one of the heretical sciences seemed to grow exponentially, but the tools he needed to prosecute his investigations remained stubbornly old-fashioned. Ask people if they'd seen anything. Question notorious career criminals — this was a tradition, and a fairly useless one; since heretics were executed on the spot, there were generally very few people who could rightly have been said to have made a career of them. One advocate in the Royal Academy of Sciences insisted that it was possible to determine a heretic by precisely measuring the shape of his head, but he wanted funding for his experiments *before* he could produce any worthwhile results, so that was fairly a bust.

Nothing. Beckett looked down at his gun again, felt the black iron call to a black spot in his heart, numb and raw and cold. He stared at the barrel, watched it grow, stretching out to encompass him, its dark, empty core drawing him down, down into it with an inexorable gravity. The principle seemed remarkably easy. The barest twitch of his finger would be enough, the gun would do all the work. Wasn't it quite extraordinary that so much pain, so much weariness, could abolished with such a small, simple step?

"Mr. Beckett?" The boy's voice was soft; he had crept into Beckett's office without the old coroner hearing.

"Alan?" Beckett shook his head and looked up. Of course it wasn't Alan, Alan had disappeared, escaped to Corsay probably. It was James, the new knocker. His face was pale and pinched, his jaw always clenched as though he were perpetually fighting back nausea. Ruddy light from the windows reflected off of his silver eyeplate. The plate had been set improperly, and now a string of syrupy black ichor dribbled down his cheek. "James. What?"

"I..."

"What is it, boy? Speak up," Beckett snapped at him, as he set his revolver back on his desk.

James sighed, but said nothing for a long moment. Then, "I was in Gorcia, did you know that, Mr. Beckett?"

Beckett allowed, privately, that he had indeed known that, though he hadn't given it much thought. To the knocker he simply said, "Yes. So?"

"I was at the Proc Offensive. Got...a lot of men had trouble, after that. Going into the caves, I mean. Do you know about it?"

"No," Beckett said, simply.

"It was bad. They moved me off of that, afterward. To Quartermasters." The knocker was silent again.

Beckett grunted. "Get to the point, boy. What is it?"

"I want...I need to be sure. Have you been in the army, Mr. Beckett?"

The old coroner rolled his eye but was, in spite of himself, intrigued. "Third dragoons. One battle, in the Dragon Isles."

"Where?"

"Kaarcag."

The knocker perceptibly shivered when he heard that. "You were at...? Kaarcag was a massacre."

Beckett closed his eye and experienced a momentary flash of thorny green vines pouring from Fletcher's mouth. "We knew it going in, that it was an ambush. You couldn't help but see."

"But you went in."

"We went in. Took ninety percent casualties. The rest of us were discharged."

"Why did you do it? Why didn't you stop?"

"You don't get to stop. The army falls apart if you stop following your orders. Even when you know they're bad...you still have to do it. Suck it up, hope for the best."

James nodded. "I can't...I can't tell you how I know about this. But. The Empire...has been producing oneiric munitions."

The statement should have landed in Beckett's mind like a cannonball, and yet he found himself unsurprised. There was very little he was willing to put past the Empire, these days.

"They were for use in Gorcia," James went on. "When the war ended, most of them were destroyed. Some were brought back to the country. There's a depot in the city. In Small Ash Abbey. The man that runs it is...not altogether trustworthy. I have reason to believe he may be selling his stock..."

"When?"

James was quiet; he cocked his head to the side, twisting himself as though trying to avoid Beckett's gaze, though he had no direct experience of it.

"Tonight."

"Why didn't you tell me? Why didn't you tell Stitch?"

James grimaced, painfully. His face twitched, he seemed almost about to cry. "Orders, Mr. Beckett. You know how...how it is. Sometimes the men...the men you work with. They aren't always...but you can't just..." His voice dropped to a barely-audible whisper. "...you can't turn on them. I told you because I thought you'd understand. I don't know what Stitch understands."

CHRIS BRAAK

EIGHTEEN

We have met with some setbacks. For all I believe that the mind is the key engine, Chretien's work on the body is still incomplete. There seems to be no effective way to prevent the eyes from decomposing. This has led me to certain other concerns. Perhaps a creature could be built with no eyes at all? But how should such a thing think? How could it learn to live in a world of conscious beings? I know that there are blind men who live fully in the world, and are not harmed by this difference. But a blind man has a wholly human mind otherwise, lacking only the single default. What should a mind be if it lacks all the elements of the human mind, as well as its senses? How should this mind apprehend the world?

--from the journal of Harcourt Wolfram, 1785

Beckett tore out of his office, barely taking time to shrug into his heavy coat. "You," he said to Valentine, who was reclining lazily on one of the couches, "With me. Where's Harry?"

Valentine snapped to his feet. "By the coach. The coaches. I think. I assume, I mean. What are we doing?"

"Intercepting. Get your coat on."

Popular opinion had it that the name "Small Ash Abbey" came from the building's miraculous survival of the Great Fire of 1719; the truth was substantially less remarkable: it was the smaller of two abbeys built by the Sar-Sarpek émigré Tyador Azsch in the 16th century. Small Ash Abbey had been retrofitted, sometime in the last fifty years, in the Daior-Vie style; a style of sleek

116

lines and simple geometries, the Daior-Vies had been convinced that it would be embraced as the modern mold from which all future styles would emerge. As it happened, a certain scandal among the most esteemed Daior-Vies left the whole family in disgrace, and the style became an archipelago of clean-lined strangeness that was gradually invaded, overcome, and replaced by the more aggressive and more reputable contenders in the Architecture War.

The Abbey was tucked away in Whitehaven, a district so far from central Trowth that it might have been a suburb. There were no trains here, the stone roads were broken and choked with rust-colored, inaptly-named cheerweed. So far outside the city was Whitehaven that it actually constituted only the first or second, or possibly third, level of construction. There was no Arcadium beneath it, just a dense undercroft of basements and sub-basements that periodically collapsed, taking the buildings above them with it. The result of this gradual erosion of its foundation was a ramshackle Whitehaven, a run-down Whitehaven, a crooked, stony nest that served as a home to the indigent only.

Beckett stopped the coach several blocks from the Abbey. He and Valentine slipped out and approached along the street, sticking close to the buildings where phlogiston-barrel fires had stained the walls black and sooty. There were no streetlights here, and the moon was low behind the city proper, so there were plenty of shadows through which the coroners could pick. Having eventually secured a location that offered a serviceable view of the Abbey's entrance and was still obscured by dark and architecture, Beckett and Valentine proceeded to wait.

And wait.

And wait.

Waiting patiently is, without question, the most prized and important skill that a detective of any stripe must possess in order to catch criminals in the act. It is a skill at which Beckett was practiced, and which Valentine abhorred. That Valentine managed, in this particular instance, to remain still and silent for the astonishing three or four hours that they waited was lost on Beckett, as he was troubled by something that he did not know how to articulate.

As he watched the door to the Abbey, he felt his shoulders clench up, as a tension coiled through his body. Sounds, the sounds of men shouting, of rifles discharging. An eerie wail had picked up, just at the edge of his hearing, the

117

sound of an engine whirring faster and faster. His neck and shoulders spasmed and he shook the sounds away. They were soft sounds, not real sounds, sounds that he knew lurked in his mind. They'd been shaken loose by something, by the drugs or the events at the gendarmerie in Red Lanes. Or by the munitions that must now be waiting in the Abbey.

Beckett closed his good eye and shook his head again, but the sounds only grew louder, the wail raised its pitch, men began to scream, lungs turned to rotten meat by the chimeric gas the Szarkany Rend had unleashed, choking, now, vomiting their hearts up, bleeding from their eyes and the wail, that wail.. Cook stared at him, fallen to the ground. Beckett tugged at his arm. "On your feet," he shouted, voice muffled by his scarf, "come on, soldier, up!" The green fog crawled from Cook's nostrils, drawing blood out with it, suspending it in tiny drops in the air. More cannons sounded, and more detonations. The fog rose in pillars, and reached out with crooked tendrils for tender lungs.

"Beckett! Beckett!"

"What?" Beckett opened his eyes. The noise was gone. The sun had, slowly, stained the shreds of horizon visible through crooked buildings with a vivid red light. Valentine was clutching at his shoulder. "What?" Beckett snapped, "What is it?"

"Look."

Two men, from two different directions, were approaching the Abbey. They had their collars turned up and their hats pulled down low — a reasonable precaution against prying eyes or the chilly snap of early-morning Armistice. With competent efficiency they approached the Abbey, did not call out to each other, did not say a word; the only sign that they might be there for the same purpose at all — rather than simply two suspiciously-dressed travelers who coincidentally arrived at the same abandoned Abbey at the same unlikely hour of the morning — was the fact that the first man held the heavy wooden door, ever so briefly, for the second.

"Think that's them?" Valentine whispered.

Beckett didn't bother answering, instead checked his revolver and steeled himself, pressing fear and anxiety and excitement to one side, evoking the cold dispassion that he wore more comfortably than his uniform. "Come on." With an audacity that was Beckett's and his alone, the old coroner walked right through the front door of the Abbey, on the heels of his suspects.

The inside of Small Ash Abbey prioritized space, as most of the old-century religious spaces did. Empty air was at a premium in claustrophobic Trowth, and the only places that could afford, or would afford, to leave a square cubic inch free of brick or mortar were those places that had some interest beyond what they could rent it for. Small Ash consisted of a square of four long halls with tall, round-arched windows facing its wide inner courtyard; there, a hastily-erected construction of salt-worn wooden timbers obscured whatever took place. Inside the Abbey, there was no sign of the two men.

Beckett laid a finger across his lips for silence, and gestured for Valentine to search the hall to the right, hopefully working his way into the interior courtyard. The two men drew their guns, held them low and ready as they crept through the dark. Once separated from Valentine, Beckett began to notice the hallucinatory sounds again—the faint whine of some eldritch engine, the distant echoes of choked-off screams, a murmuring...

No. The murmuring was real. Real men were talking to each other, in the structure that occupied most of the Abbey's courtyard. Beckett thumbed back the hammer of his gun and tried to slip discreetly past the rusty-hinged doors.

The inside of the structure was not dissimilar to any kind of warehouse: a claustrophobic mountain of plain wooden boxes, towering on either side of a three or four narrow alleys. The place was lit by a few blue phlogiston lamps, hanging high overhead; they were the military-grade lamps, with thick metal shields around the sides to prevent volatile leaks. There was an empty space in the midst of the boxes, where three mean spoke to each other in hushed voices. Beckett took a deep breath to push his fear away, only to find there was no fear or worry--just a raw, empty space.

"Coroners," Beckett said, as he approached, startling the three men. "No one moves, put your hands on your heads." In his many years as a coroner, Elijah Beckett had said precisely these words in precisely this order a countless number of times. In those same years, only four times had the suspects to which he spoke ever complied with the orders.

These men were no exception; they recovered quickly from their surprise, split up, drew weapons, and fanned out in an attempt to surround him.

"Who are you?" Spat the man in the middle, not one of the two visitors, so probably the quartermaster who was arranging things. He was handsome enough, though Beckett thought he wore his sideburns too long. He had a new, nickel-plated revolver pointed at the coroner.

Where is Valentine? Beckett wondered, but the thought had no real traction. No thoughts had any traction, they just floated away from him, along with a whirling line of voices and footsteps and gunshots. *Should I be afraid? These men mean to kill me.* He thought. *The hell with it, I'm not afraid of anything, anymore.* Without the hesitation that plagues even the most experienced shootists, Beckett raised his gun towards the man directly to his left, and shot him in the face.

The sound of his gun, loud and bright like a thunderbolt in his hand, was lost to the soft sounds of gunfire in his mind, and echoed by a return volley of bullets that went mercifully wide, tearing chunks of wood from the empty boxes. The handsome quartermaster was screaming then, not at Beckett, but at the gunman to his right, Beckett couldn't hear him, or couldn't be bothered to hear him, just turned and fired. He hit the gunman high in the shoulder, sending the man whirling to the ground.

"...hit the munitions, you idiot!" The quartermaster was saying. He dropped his weapon. "Look, okay, look! Unarmed. I surrender, all right? I surrender, just stop fucking *shooting.*" Beckett stepped forward and struck the man across the face, using the full weight of his antique revolver. The man fell, and Beckett kicked him twice in the ribs, hard, before he could stand. "Shit. Shit," he gasped. "I *surrender*, for fuck—" Beckett kicked him in the teeth, and he slumped into unconsciousness.

"What...what...are you..." the gunman moaned. "You're supposed to arrest..."

Beckett whirled on him. "Who are you working for?" The man's face was different, now, there was a deep dent in his skull and his were glazed. *Dummies,* Beckett thought, *how did the dummies get here? How did they find their way from Kaarcag?* It would reach out to him, Beckett knew, try and crush him with its stupidly strong hands.

"You're supposed to..."

Here, Beckett told himself. *You're here, in Trowth. He's a heretic.* The old coroner stepped on the man's wounded shoulder, digging the toe of his shoe into the bullet wound. The gunman screamed. "You were picking something up here. Where were you taking it? Who are you working for?"

"You can't—"

Beckett pressed harder, and the man screamed again. "You don't tell me, boy. You don't tell me anything. I have a question, you answer it. That's how this works. Understand?" Beckett leaned in again, coaxing a ragged gasp from the man's throat. "Do you understand?"

"Yes," the man stammered. "Yes."

"Who do you work for?"

The man shook his head, sweat streamed down his face, which now was wracked with pain. "I can't. He'll kill me."

Without warning, Beckett turned and fired another bullet into the dead man behind him. The action was so sudden, the gunshot so sharp, that the gunman at his feet cried out, involuntarily. Beckett leaned down and glared, one eye hard as a polished stone, one just a bloody black pit into the recesses of his skull. "Idiot. What do you think *I'm* going to do to you?" He kicked the man in his wound again. "Who do you work for?"

The gunman coughed and choked and spat out, "John," from behind his tears. "Anonymous John."

"What are you doing?" Valentine whispered, softly. Beckett hadn't seen him enter, barely registered the sound of his voice.

"Where were you taking the munition?"

"An address…in. Bluewater." He nodded towards his dead companion. "He's got it. Written."

Beckett turned to Valentine. "Get it. I'll be outside." He threw one last, spiteful kick at the man's face, and stomped out into the warming springtime air.

NINETEEN

It was after the third performance of *Theocles*, at yet another high-spirited soiree at the home of the Raithower Vie-Gorgons, that the official news of the play's demise was received. It was some time after midnight—considering that the performance was a several-hour affair in the first place, and was combined with six curtain calls and a substantial amount of paperwork required for the royal censor to fill out, this may in fact be regarded as an unusually quick response. In any case, some time after twelve, a messenger arrived from the royal palace at the Raithower home; he was admitted by the Vie-Gorgon major domo, and brought directly to Emilia Vie-Gorgon, who decided to make the announcement to her guests herself.

"Ladies and gentlemen," she began, her voice full of emotion that Skinner could not help but think was spurious. While she was no expert on the subject of Emilia Vie-Gorgon and her many modes of expression, Skinner was fairly certain that she'd never heard the young woman sound so moved about anything. "I have an...unfortunate. A terribly unfortunate announcement. It seems that His Royal Majesty..." here she pronounced the word "majesty" in such a way as to suggest that it was so thoroughly distasteful that she regretted requiring her tongue to say it at all, "...may the Word bless him," pure sarcasm there, "...has found something objectionable in the content of our play." How she managed to say this while sounding completely innocent of purposefully commissioning the most objectionable play imaginable was a mystery to Skinner. "He has, just today, announced that, in his position as head of the Church Royal, he has added *Theocles* to the Black List. Future performances are prohibited by law. Printing a copy of the play is prohibited by law. Owning a copy is prohibited by law." Her voice took on a sly tone here. "I expect that all of you will want to destroy your copies as *soon as possible*."

There were acid chuckles at this, followed by pronouncements of both consternation and indignation, that Skinner suspected were for show. Here in the safe, warm circle of Emilia Vie-Gorgon's attention, critically lambasting the Emperor was acceptable, even expected. Just calling him a petty name or making lewd comments about his mother was likely to garner appreciative snorts of laughter, regardless of how seriously the joker took it. There were no spies for the emperor among Emilia's circle of friends, that was for sure, unless they were Emilia's own spies, placed to evaluate just how much her friends valued her.

But whatever the case, in the cold light of morning, when the assorted Committees of Loyalty and Compliance and Modest Behavior roamed the streets once more, even the most fervent comedian would quell his tongue, and say "Word bless the Emperor, and keep him," and mumble such other obsequies as might satisfy the harsh and demanding eye of the Empire. The more she came to know them, the more Skinner found the Esteemed Families to be peopled entirely by cowards. Emilia, so far as Skinner knew, was the only one that had ever troubled to dare anything.

And Valentine, Skinner thought, as he came muttering back from the punch bowl with a drink for her. Though the line, in this case, between the young gentleman's daring and his simple lack of good sense was a crooked one. "Stupid," Valentine was grumbling.

"You think the Emperor is stupid?" Skinner asked, sipping at her punch.

"No, my cousin. She knew this would get closed down. She's baiting him. It's like...she's waving a red flag in front of a bull. Provoking."

"I thought the Raithower Vie-Gorgons were largely unassailable, even by the Emperor."

"Huh. Maybe. I wouldn't bet on it, though. We...they, anyway, don't have an army of marines and lobstermen to deploy against the dissidents. Sure, shutting down the trains for a few weeks would be a hassle, but it's not like no one else *could* run them." Valentine sucked his teeth, as he considered. "Maybe the Gorgon-Vies couldn't, though. Maybe that's what she's banking on. The Emperor acting without thinking, responding with force, the way he always does, not realizing the wasp's nest he's about to step into."

"Hm." Skinner said, noncommittally. With Emilia's announcement, she'd begun to grow a little worried. The play was done and done for, now, so what would be the point of continuing to employ the playwright? Emilia, Skinner had no doubt, had known precisely that *Theocles* would be shut down; this must all be part of her plan. Maybe more plays? Maybe the plan was to continue to secretly heckle the Emperor until...until what?

"Oh, there she goes with Nora, again." Valentine said. "I wonder what she's up to?"

"Where?"

"By the stairs. Uh. Three o'clock, about ten yards."

Skinner let her clairaudience drift in the direction Valentine had indicated until it caught up with the two young women. " —it?" Emilia was saying.

"Yes. By *post* if you believe it. He must have sent it last week. How did he know?"

"I've given up trying to guess. He's certainly clever."

"More clever than we are," Nora Feathersmith snorted.

Emilia cleared her throat.

"Fine, more clever than I am, anyway. I assume you'll want to burn it?"

"Not at all," Emilia said. "It's hardly a crime to be *sent* evil letters. I save all my correspondence; if all is uncovered, I shall present it and, in a very convincing manner, explain that I have been the victim of a cruel trick."

"Doesn't that seem a little risky?"

The women had moved into a study, now, and one of them—Emilia, probably—was opening a desk drawer. "I don't think so. The privilege of being unable to be responsible for anything is that we are equally unlikely to be held accountable for anything. We are, after all, only women. Surely we could not have devised such a devious plot on our own?"

"Hah. The next step, then?"

Emilia or Nora activated a baffler, then, and Skinner found her hearing clouded with incomprehensible echoes. Not for the first time in the last few years, she cursed the man that had invented it. "Valentine," she said, letting her perception return to her body, and cutting off the young coroner in the middle of an impassioned speech about why playwrights ought not to be censored by anyone.

" —just that, what? What is it?"

"Emilia and Nora are about to come down those stairs," Skinner told him. "I need you to distract them."

"All right. For how long?"

"As long as possible," she said. "I need you to occupy their full attention. There's...something upstairs I need to check on."

"Ah," Valentine said, excited. "An escapade. An exploit. I shall attract attention at once."

Valentine sauntered through the party, then—though she could not see him to be sure, there was something about the young coroner that suggested that sauntering was his natural mode of transportation—and, as Emilia and her friend descended into the salon, he began talking in a very loud voice about propriety and treason, and his suspicions that there was not one but were in fact *several* spies among the partygoers who were insufficiently loyal to the Emperor and, by extension, the Empire. He then challenged to a duel anyone who would dare threaten the Empire's edicts, lewdly grabbed a hold of Emily Rowan-Czarnecki's new silk bustle, delivered a good-natured headbutt to Corwin Daior-Crabtree when the man tried to grab hold of Valentine's arm, and then kicked over the punch bowl.

Though Valentine had always enjoyed many critics, and after that evening added several more to the list, not a one of them could ever say that when Valentine Vie-Gorgon committed to something, he did not commit to it fully.

His antics left Skinner ample opportunity to slip upstairs. She had, by old habit, been keeping track of how far Emilia and Nora walked. Sixteen steps down the hall, then a right turn. The door was locked, so she knelt down and lightly rested her hand against the keyhole.

At the publicly-funded but very, very private schools where knockers were trained, the teenaged savants were kept under close guard, with strict headmasters and rigid schedules. No one was permitted out of bed or out of their rooms past seven o'clock, and all the doors were locked, with bafflingly complex mechanisms, to ensure the knockers remained there. At the same time, the masters of the schools considered it a useful skill for the effectively blind knockers to be able to navigate their way past the innumerable obstacles that they would undoubtedly face. As such, while punishments for violating curfew were severe, there was still the unspoken expectation that Skinner and her peers would try to escape and roam about the grounds — sometimes getting into trouble, more likely just reveling in the freedom that their abilities had finally bought. Using telerhythmia to pick locks was the first skill that a teenaged knocker ever learned.

Skinner began knocking rapidly against the lock's tumbler, creating a tension on the interior pins. Then, a few telerhythmic bursts inside rattled the pins up and down until they stuck, shears opening, and the lock snapped open. She slipped inside the study quickly, clairaudiently canvassing the hall behind her to ensure that no one was coming.

Fortunately, she wouldn't need to put on a light, possibly alerting household staff to her presence. Unfortunately, as was always the case, the room served as a new adventure in relational geometry. She couldn't knock too loudly on the walls to get a sense of the space — not without risking undue attention. Which meant that she'd have to, very slowly and very lightly, feel her way around the room with her cane.

Years of experience building mental pictures of new rooms had given Skinner a good feel for it. Vie-Gorgon studies like this were usually narrow, with the desk directly opposite the door, near the window. There was probably some guest furniture, a low stool or a chair, perhaps, in between...there. She tapped lightly on a wooden chair leg. Reached out, set her hand on it. It was high-backed and plush. She resisted the urge to move quickly; if she had to make a run for it, she needed to be sure where everything was. A few moments of caution now were worth it.

Farther out, more furniture. Then the desk. It was heavy, wide. The desk chair was on the opposite side, between the desk and the window — she knew there was a window, because she could hear the wind whipping against the glass. Around the side, carefully, and she made sure to fix its corners in her mind. Behind the desk, and she lightly bumped into the chair. It was wheeled, and rolled slightly when she touched it. She felt her back brush against heavy draperies.

Now, to find the letter. Slowly, and as quietly as she could, she began opening the drawers. Each one squeaked and scraped against the desk slightly, but also particularly. No two drawers or doors or spots on the floor ever sound quite the same. There, third one down on the left. There was neither time nor means to sort out which letter, precisely, she was looking for; instead, she grabbed the first four and stuffed them into the pocket of her dress.

"...candles for the study."

Skinner jerked her head up. Someone was coming down the hallway. She suppressed the urge to snap her telerhythmia around the room looking for a hiding place, instead reached out with her hands. *The desk? How high is it off the ground? Would they be able to see me under it?*

"I thought Miss Emilia said she didn't like candles in there."

"Her mother wants candles in all the rooms, don't ask me why." The door handle rattled as someone grabbed it. "Oh, she'll chew you out for this, it's supposed to be locked all the time."

The drapes, move behind the drapes. Skinner stepped as close to the window as she could and pulled the heavy drapery around herself. Her hiding place would either be effective, or laughably absurd — leaving the hem of her dress exposed at the bottom, or lying across her face so that its shape was clearly visible. The door opened, footsteps brushed softly on the thick carpet. *I left the drawer open. Shit.* The servants chattered aimlessly as they worked, presumably putting new candles in candelabras throughout the room. *No way to get to it. How will I know if they're looking towards me?*

Matches were lit, and the smell of sulfur filled the air. *They'll see me for sure, now.*

126

"Such a waste," muttered the first speaker at the front of the desk, not a yard away from Skinner. "Candles...just because she likes to see the windows lit up at night." Closer now, he'd moved around to the back. "Wish I were rich enough to burn candles at all hours." There was nothing between him and Skinner except for that thick drape. She could reach out and touch him if she wanted. The drawer's particular voice resounded as the servant closed it.

The pause that followed brought Skinner's heart into her throat. It could not have lasted longer than a fraction of the breadth of a breath, but Skinner must have spent a day, a month, a year with her chest pounding, biting her lip and gritting her teeth, waiting for the man to snatch the draperies away and demand an accounting of what she was doing in Emilia Vie-Gorgon's study.

Such an apocalypse never occurred, and instead the man, after a moment's hesitation, left the candlelit study and closed the door behind him. Skinner breathed a sigh of relief whose force surprised her, as though she might have inadvertently expelled her soul, then after using her clairaudience to make sure the hall was empty, followed the servant out.

She hadn't taken more than two steps into the hall when yet another voice addressed her, triggering yet another precipitous drop of her stomach.

"Miss?" The sternly polite and politely suspicious voice asked. Emilia's major domo. "The guests aren't supposed to be up here."

"Yes. No," Skinner replied, smiling. "I was a little lost, I was trying to find..."

"I fail to see what you could have been looking for that you thought might necessitate you leaving the first floor," the man said, his voice icy with official indignation.

"Yes, well." Grimacing inwardly at the straightened circumstances that forced her into such a pass, she adopted a hang-dog expression and morosely tapped at the silver plate that sealed off her eyes. "It's easy for me to get turned around, you see."

"Oh," the major domo said, his voice dropping with the certainty that only knowledge of the most exquisite faux pas can bring. "Oh, oh, yes. Of course, I'm sorry. Do you...can I help you back to the party?"

"If you would," Skinner said to him. "That would be lovely."

TWENTY

"We need to discuss your recent actions," the Moral Responsibility officer said. Beckett couldn't remember the man's name and this, somehow, disturbed him more than the hearing about his fitness for duty. "Some of the reports coming in are disturbing. Your superiors are worried."

"Stitch is worried?"

"Mr. Stitch is only your direct superior. The people that I work for are superior to him," the man said with a quiet sneer. He had a sheaf of papers in front of him. Beckett stopped listening. His mind wandered back to the last night's raid. It was vivid in his imagination, Bluewater in all its rotten, sagging, destitute glory.

Bluewater was where the poor indige lived. The wealthy hetmen of the indige clans had mansions and townhouses lining the streets of Indigae, where imported gullah-trees and glowing phlogishrubs were maintained at great effort and expense. Indigae was a safe, clean neighborhood, well-patrolled by gendarmes, well-tended to by the city's many civil services, and far from the poison-smoke-spewing factories at the west end of the river Stark. Indigae was so lovely a neighborhood, in fact, that if it were not for the immense social shame incurred by being seen amongst the indige, even the Esteemed Families would have maintained residences there.

Bluewater was not any of those things. The wide boulevards of Indigae were narrow, crowded streets in Bluewater. The little gardens were patches of dead grass or shimmering blue slime-mould on the cobblestones. There were no gendarmes in Bluewater, and if order was kept by the gangs of thugs and criminals that ruled it, it was only by accident. The neighborhood dissolved from warehouses full of cheap imports, warehouses converted to densely-inhabited, multi-family barracks, and warehouses that were too rickety and unsound even to support squatters, into factories that spewed black smoke, blue smoke, green smoke. Factories that dumped brightly-colored heavy metals into the rivers White and Crook, which had long been covered over by Trowth's incessant development. The two swift and underground tributaries took the bright-colored and psychoactively charged mud into the Stark, where it sank to the bottom and bred strange species of fish and lizard.

Bluewater was a wretched place, a place whose inhabitants had yet to see the runoff of wealth from their more successful cousins in Indigae. The indige there were easy prey for Anonymous John and his men, for Dockside Boys and River Rats, for Starkies and the Old Trows. Bluewater was as thoroughly villainous a neighborhood as Trowth had known, and who could blame the indige for choosing gang life, smuggling, drugs, and robbery over the meager existence that they might be fortunate enough to eke out in this disused corner of the city?

"Your violent behaviors...Mr. Beckett?"

Beckett snapped back to himself, looked around the room, recollected the situation. "What?"

"You've always had a reputation for brutality, of course, but recently...some people are concerned that you've become a danger to the organization."

"Which people?"

After Beckett's hasty report, and eager to distract attention from their heretical experiments, the War Powers Ministry detached a unit of Lobstermen to serve in the coroners' raid in Bluewater. These marines, nearing the ends of their terms of service, and therefore doomed, in a few short years, to a slow and painful death, were deployed at strategic locations throughout the neighborhood. Beckett's plan was to take a handful of his own men and a squad of gendarmes directly to the address, and to leave the Lobstermen to cut off any potential escape routes. His fear was that the men in their blood-slick bone armor would frighten the black market dealers into doing something stupid, which the Lobstermen would then respond to with characteristic deadly force.

Dead black market dealers would likely yield up little information, so the Lobstermen were kept in reserve. He and his men approached an unassuming warehouse—fully as unassuming a warehouse as any of the other warehouses in Bluewater, and provoking a hurried conference as to whether or not they were sure that this was the correct address. Beckett glared sullenly until he'd obtained the attention of the gendarmes, and then ordered them into positions surrounding the site. Telerhythmic tapping—in the form of a very specific, very simple signal—indicated that the Lobstermen were all in position, lurking dangerously in the dark.

"Your confederate, Mr. Vie-Gorgon? Claims that you unnecessarily killed, and excessively beat a suspect in order to obtain information."

Beckett blinked. "Valentine? Valentine said that?" He shook his head, then winced at the pain this provoked. "Why would he say that?"

"Did you beat the man at Small Ash Abbey?"

"He had information. I got the information. I don't see what the problem is."

The man shifted in his seat, and shuffled his papers again. "I also have some notes here about the raid that you conducted last night."

"Go," Beckett whispered. James heard, and he, presumably, was sending out the tap-tap-tap that would transmit the order. Beckett and his men moved towards the front door. "Coroners!" Beckett shouted. "We're coming in!" He did not wait for a reply, but let the two gendarmes with him break the rotten wooden door down.

In the dark, inside, there were ten or fifteen indige, glowing faintly blue. They wore tattered clothes, and were huddled together, speaking quietly to themselves. When Beckett and his men crashed through the door, the indige leapt to their feet and began shouting.

"Where are they?" Beckett demanded. "The men, where are Anonymous John's men?" He was answered with a babble of pidgin Trowth and Indt. One particularly bold indige youth stepped forward and shouted directly in Beckett's face.

"No more! No more here! No more here!" The indige said, his face glowing brighter as his choler increased. "No more, us! Just us!" The indige swarmed around the gendarmes, repeating this mantra.

"What do you mean, no more? They're gone?" Beckett asked, his heart sinking.

"Gone, all gone! Just —"

A sudden commotion broke through the shouts. Two Trowthi men in shirtsleeves and worn trousers, burst from a door in the dark. They were being pursued by more gendarmes, who waved cudgels and fiercely blew their whistles. Beckett shoved the indige aside and raised his revolver. "Stop! You two men, stop where you are!"

"No more, gone!" The indige insisted, grabbing at Beckett's shoulder.

The old coroner shrugged him off. "Stop, I said!" The two men had crossed the interior expanse of the warehouse, and were fumbling in the dark with something. A weapon, a secret door? "Stop!" The indige grabbed at his gun arm. Beckett snatched his hand away and struck the youth across the face.

The indige collapsed, bleeding hot blood from his cheek. The coroner fired two bullets into the air. "FUCKING STOP!"

"You struck a young man who had no relationship to the case, is that correct?" The Moral Officer asked.

Why can't I remember his name? "He...he was interfering. He was trying to help the suspects escape. I had...he was *interfering*."

"You didn't feel that eight gendarmes, and a contingent of Lobstermen, would be sufficient to prevent the suspects' escape?"

"What is this about?" Beckett demanded. "What is this really about? I've never...no ministry has ever done this before. My fitness for work has never been questioned before." *Why the hell can't I remember his name?* "I obtained information, I used it to apprehend two men engaged in the sale of heretical instruments. That is my mandate, that's my duty, and I performed it. What the fuck else do you want from me?"

The men froze. The indige froze to see their fallen comrade. The gendarmes, many of whom had never known a moment of fear in the lives — and if they had, joining the gendarmerie had been a means to permanently escape the need for that fear — fell upon the two fleeing men like rabid dogs, beat them, dragged them away from the wall, roughly shackled them. The indige family, or clan, or however they arranged themselves, had knelt around their fallen member and were all whispering softly to him in Indt.

"You," Beckett snapped at the fallen indige. "You, get up." The youth didn't move. *The boy,* Beckett thought. *He can't be more than fifteen.* Beckett kicked him in the ribs. "Get up!" The indige sat up, leaning against one of his fellows. "You lied to me. You told me they were gone. Why?"

The indige, sulking, seemed disinclined to speak. Beckett very nearly lost his temper and hit him again. One more person that was refusing to help, one more person that didn't want to talk. Didn't the boy see that it was keeping quiet that was causing the problem? That they could fix everything if people would just *cooperate*? "Why?" Beckett rasped again.

"He paid," the indige replied at last, shrugging. "He paid."

"Who did?" Though Beckett suspected he knew the answer. Yet another Trowthi selling out their family and their city for a few crowns. And if someone was selling themselves into treason, only one man was paying.

"Anonymous John."

The Moral Officer was silent for a very long moment. Then he put his papers away and stood up. "We're done here. I will contact you if I need any further information." The man left, closing the door behind him. Beckett stayed in his chair, rubbing his eyes, craving a veneine injection. He wanted to yell, to scream his frustration at the Moral Rectitude Commission, at the stupid indige that didn't know he was trying to help him, but most of all at the dangerous amoral bastard whose involvement in Trowth's heretical and criminal operations Beckett was coming to suspect was nearly universal. The indige's voice echoed in his head.

"Anonymous John."

Twenty-One

"Will continue the operation from here. Take no further action." Karine read aloud. "Events proceed apace."

"That's it?" Skinner asked. They were in a café near the Stark, surrounded by a bustling, working-class clientele. Since the events at Emilia Vie-Gorgon's party, Skinner had become increasingly paranoid about being observed. No one could think it odd that she was out with her assistant, of course, and the noise of the café would effectively obscure their conversation from casual eavesdroppers. There could be knockers listening in, and if there was anyone in the city who could afford to retain the services of a knocker it was Emilia Vie-Gorgon. But there was nothing to be done on that score, so Skinner resolved to not be worried by it.

"That's it," said Karine. "It's not even signed."

"Well, of course it's not signed," Skinner replied irritably. "Who leads a secret cabal and then writes their name all over everything? No one." She sighed. "What about the paper? Handwriting? Anything familiar?"

"It's typed," Karine said, "regular paper, I suppose. I don't really know. Maybe Mr. Valentine? Isn't his family in printing?"

"Let's...let's hold off on that," Skinner said. She'd already involved Valentine more than she was comfortable with. Though, it's not as if the irrepressible idiot wouldn't tear off through the city, turning over paper mills left and right, trying to find the precise source of a note that Skinner had stolen from his cousin. He probably wouldn't even ask why. Idiot. "We'll wait. The less Valentine knows, the less he's likely to give away. All right?"

"Yes, all right. Though I don't see why—"

"Never mind why. I'm just not sure of him, yet."

"Not sure of Mr. Valentine? But miss—"

"Karine. Leave it. We'll talk to him about the letter later. I doubt he'd be able to help, anyway, they probably make paper like this ten thousand sheets at a time." Skinner sipped at the last of her *djang*, made a face as she tasted the bitter dregs. "Anyway. I suppose it's time I started looking for a new job."

The trouble with being history's most successful anonymous playwright was that it didn't lead to a wealth of new opportunities. It was still quite illegal for Skinner to hold down legitimate work in the city, but the theater was hardly a legitimate enterprise. Under ordinary circumstances, she could have undoubtedly shown a piece like *Theocles* to a producer, and been assigned a substantial amount of work-for-hire material. Except, since the success of *Theocles*, no fewer than fifteen people had come forward claiming to be the author (and demanding the requisite royalties), some of them fairly well-established playwrights themselves. How could she, the real author, prove that *Theocles* was hers? Not without Emilia Vie-Gorgon's help, and Skinner was loathe to rely any more on the heiress than was absolutely necessary.

"Come on, Karine, let's walk home. We shouldn't waste such lovely weather by spending the day indoors."

The weather at the tail end of Armistice remained delightful, and would almost to the very second that Armistice ended. The change from pleasant early spring to the raw, damp weather of middle spring was a change that came with such reliability that no professional man had ever been hired to predict it, nor had any almanac bothered to record it. Like Trowth's internecine familial wars and the monolithic ruins that served as the city's bones, the weather of the city was so unfailingly regular that Skinner could have easily asserted how mild the temperature, how gentle the salty bay-breezes, how pleasant the humidity, without having so much as opened a window.

Karine and Skinner talked idly while they walked, and Skinner asked her assistant many questions about the young indige's life, about her people, about her ambitions.

"Well, of course I will probably stay behind during the New Exodus," Karine explained, as though this information ought to be of obvious consequence to Skinner. "Many of my people probably will. I've never seen the Capital Cities, so they're really of little interest to me."

"I don't know what that is, the New Exodus. What is that?"

"Oh, I'm sorry. I thought...I just thought everyone knew. The indige arrangement with the Trowth Empire was for a two-hundred and fifty year residence. The *ramos*—these are...I suppose you'd call them priests, or grammateurs...declared that Trowth would be a safe haven for us for no longer than two and a half centuries. In another decade, the ritual calendar and the royal calendar will come together in the Third Confluence and...well, I suppose it's all rather complicated, isn't it?" Karine's demeanor, mild and simple as ever, seemed perversely at odds with such alien complexity.

Maybe, Skinner admitted a little guiltily, *I only assumed she was simple.* "It is, but it's fascinating. Your rammers, or priests or what have you, they made a prophecy?"

"Yes, after a fashion. The calendrical confluences are always supposed to be marked by great disasters or boons or something, and the ramos are predicting things all the time. It's pretty unusual that we actually see anything interesting happen. The Third Confluence is supposed to be the End of Cities, so the ramos are insisting that we'll engage in a Second Exodus and leave Trowth before then."

"And you don't think you will?"

"I think of lot of my people will stay. The plenary hetmen are all rich from the phlogiston trade, a lot of us grew up here. It's hard to care about some prophecy made more than two centuries before you were born. Especially if there's money — oh."

"What?" Skinner asked. "What is it?"

"There's someone…there are men at the house. They're moving things into the street. They're…hey!" She called out. "Hey, those are my things! Don't touch those!"

Karine raced ahead, but Skinner outpaced her with her clairaudience. She tracked footsteps, the scraping sound of a leather-and-brass trunk on cobblestones. Karine shouting unintelligibly in Indt, while the men attempted to mollify her. Skinner approached slowly, hoping to maintain some dignity at least.

"What's this, then?" She demanded, rattling her telerhythmia all around the square, snapping the two men across their broad chests, keeping track of them as she neared.

"Begging your pardon, miss," said one man with a gravelly voice, who did not sound at all as though he were interested in her pardon. "We've been told by Miss Vie-Gorgon to clear out this house, as it's no longer meant to be occupied."

"There has been some mistake, obviously," Skinner said this confidently, but she knew her own bluster when she heard it. It was what Valentine had warned her about: Emilia Vie-Gorgon had gotten what she wanted, and was now finished with Elizabeth Skinner and assistant. A sour feeling clutched at the knocker's stomach, and she tightened her grip on her cane.

"There's no mistake, miss," said the man. "We'll leave the things here, you can call a coach if you like."

"You are not going to leave my belongings in the street," Skinner said, her voice adamant. "And you are not going to throw me out of this house. If Miss Vie-Gorgon would like me gone, you may tell her that she can come here and see me out herself. In the meantime, my assistant and I will be quite happy to remain in our home."

"Begging your pardon," the man said again, again in a voice that did not at all seem to beg for pardon, "but Miss Vie-Gorgon said you might be insistent. Advised us that we might have to be a little rough." The sound of a revolver, gently drawn from its leather holster, is a unique sound, and one with which Skinner was well acquainted. "Now, we've not really the heart to do something cruel ourselves, but you know how orders is."

"*Shoh ahtt!*" Karine spat. "Miss, he's got a gun."

Skinner took a step closer to the man, still rattling all around her with the telerhythmia. This was a desperate ploy; most people did not realize how effectively a knocker could apprehend her surroundings, and Skinner hoped that her widespread knocking would mislead the man as to how closely he was the subject of her attention. "I doubt he's going to use it, Karine. He knows the trouble he could get into for shooting at anyone, much less at me."

"You ain't a coroner no more, Miss, if you'll pardon my saying so." He grinned around a mouthful of crooked teeth in Skinner's imagination. At least one of the imaginary teeth was gold.

Skinner took a step closer. "But I still have friends in the coroners. What was your name, again?" She hoped this was enough to at least wipe the grin from his face. She knew what was coming next; the only remaining concern was how quickly the second man would get to her.

"We haven't time for this, Miss. I don't want to, but I will hurt you if I have to." The hammer on his revolver clicked—low and near his waist, he hadn't brought it to bear, yet.

"I agree," Skinner said, as she snapped her cane out. It was a dreadful risk, but one that she'd spent many hours practicing in school—the tip of her cane connected with the man's hand, and he yelped, dropped the gun to the ground, and hopped away. *No time to let him catch his senses*, Skinner thought as she flicked the switch in the top of her walking-stick and drew out a slender, razor-sharp sword. She slashed viciously at his face, forcing him back towards the wall of the house.

The second man's footsteps cluttered like thunder towards her, and she quickly pivoted and swung her weapon towards him, eliciting another shout and the sound of a heavy body stumbling hard onto damp cobblestones. Karine was running too, but Skinner couldn't devote the attention to keep track of her, as she switched back to the first man, and struggled to keep him at bay with her sword.

"Now," said the man, "let's not be hasty. I—"

He was interrupted by a gunshot, and the sound of a ricochet off of stone.

"Stop! *Ito hak haht!* Stop, right now!" Karine. She'd grabbed the loose revolver.

Oh, good girl, Skinner smiled to herself.

"You take these things inside. Right now!" Karine said, presumably waving the pistol around to emphasize her point. The men were silent, perhaps sullenly, though it was hard to know without seeing their faces. They began the noisy process of transporting Karine and Skinner's belongings back inside.

"Wait." Skinner said. There was no reason to put anything back in the house. It was Emilia's house after all, she could, and would, eventually have them removed legitimately. They needed a new plan. "Wait. Don't put them back inside. One of you call a coach."

"Miss?" Karine asked.

"We are going to pay our respects to a few friends today, Karine. I suspect we shall have to abandon this house. Lovely as it was, it's now served its purpose."

Skinner had initially intended to bring a coach full of luggage and low-quality ne'er-do-wells directly to Emilia Vie-Gorgon's doorstep; to sort out precisely what Emilia meant by all of this right there in public, and leave a steaming heap of scandal in the Raithower Vie-Gorgon's portico. She, after all, had substantially less to lose than did Emilia by airing this dirty laundry. Her cooler instincts prevailed, however, and she resolved not to confront the young Miss Vie-Gorgon without taking certain precautions.

The long coach ride was silent—the sullenness had soured now to an outright hostility, held in check only by Karine's deathgrip on the pistol. Emlia's hired goons sulked, as the coach rolled down the neatly-cobbled Comstock Street.

Skinner called up to the driver. "I don't know what the number is—"

"It's all right, miss, I know it."

It's just temporary, Skinner insisted to herself. *Just a place to keep our luggage while I sort this all out. I am certainly not relying on him. He is, after all, thoroughly unreliable.*

Henry, long-standing and equally long-suffering butler to the Comstock Vie-Gorgons, was quite prepared to turn Skinner and Karine away at the door, regardless of how wildly Karine waved her newly-acquired revolver about. The two were saved from the local gendarmerie only by the precipitous arrival of Valentine himself, who barreled past his butler and skidded to a halt where Skinner leaned against the cab.

"Well! All right, this is a little peculiar," Valentine announced. "Have you brought all your clothes with you?"

"Ahem. Yes," Skinner admitted. "It seems that I've...had a bit of a falling out with your cousin. Karine and I...Karine mostly...are in need of a place to store our belongings. Only for a few days, until we make some kind of alternative arrangements. This is...a bit of an awkward situation."

"Awkward, of course, yes. Listen, why don't you have your men here bring everything into...Henry!" Valentine shouted over his shoulder. "Henry, have we got, can you make up the guest bedroom? We can put everything in there. We'll make up the guest rooms, you'll stay here, obviously. I say, you two," he called to Emilia's goons, "just start bringing that in, third floor, back of the hall." The men glowered, but did not object. "You and Karine will stay here, of course."

"Just the luggage. We couldn't impose," Skinner insisted.

"Well, you've got to stay *somewhere*, and it isn't as though we haven't got the room." Indeed, the Vie-Gorgon townhouse on Comstock Street was notoriously spacious.

Henry interrupted this exchange. "Sir, I'm afraid we've only the one spare bedroom available, right now--"

"Oh, yes," Valentine said, dismayed. He had quite forgotten the eight cousins visiting from the Low Provinces in the south.

"It's all right, Valentine, we don't need — "

"Of course, well," Valentine snapped his fingers, immediately taken by the ingenuity of his new plan, "we'll just make up my room — "

"Valentine — "

"Your room, sir!" Henry spluttered with outrage. "Can you imagine the scandal? It will be in the broadsheets in a day..."

"Well, obviously I won't be *in* it, Henry, you might as well show me more consideration than that."

"Valentine — " Skinner attempted to interject again, but the young man was on a tear, and would not be deterred.

"I'll stay in the guest room at the coroner's office...I'm hardly at the house anyway. Karine can have the small guest bedroom, Skinner will stay in my room. Now...oh, here," he drew a five-crown note from his wallet and offered it up to Emilia's two thugs as a gratuity. The men stared at it, flabbergasted, before Valentine ushered them back into the cab and sent them off. "Now, as I was saying. I've some few things to take care of this evening, but I'll make sure I drop by to ensure that Henry is taking good care of you both, right? We'll want to talk about my cousin, of course, and don't think I've forgotten about our exploit from the night before. Now. Away!"

And with that, Valentine Vie-Gorgon was gone into the cooling evening. Karine, Skinner, and Henry the butler stood there, at the portico of the house on Comstock Street, and each one found him or herself entirely, unequivocally, and unmistakably at a loss for words. This lasted for several seconds and Valentine, had he stayed behind to time it, would have declared it a new record for puzzled silence precipitated by his eccentricity.

It was Henry who spoke first, conditioned as he was to life with Valentine. "I suppose. I suppose I shall get those rooms ready."

Twenty-Two

Constable Harald Increase Frye was bored and pleased to be so. Armistice would be over in two days, and until then Constable Frye was happy to fill out "Not a Significant Incident" reports and send them along to the Coroners at Raithower House. That afternoon, two young men—former servicemen, probably, as at least one limped on an artificial leg—having been taken by the spirit of the season had stumbled into the offices, drunk as skunks in an abbey, and requested that they could sleep the night in the cells. Constable Harald was pleased to oblige them, and doubly pleased to fill out a "Not a Significant Incident" report on the event. When the unmistakable murmur of a gathering crowd outside the office reached his ears, and Constable Harald went outside to discover an impromptu game of dice had broken out in the cobbled streets, Constable Harald was pleased to place a fiver above the line, pleased to accept his loss with dignity, and pleased again to fill out a "Not a Significant Incident" report.

In all, Constable Harald had probably filled out close to a thousand various reports for the Coroners, a task he considered to be usually tedious and wasteful—especially the "Not a Significant Incident" reports. Why, after all, should he be filling out a report on an incident that was, by definition, *not significant*? What could the Coroners possibly want with such information? Usually, he shirked this responsibility a little, and filled out less than a third of those reports. But after an unpleasantly tumultuous Armistice—with suffragists, if not behaving violently, causing rather more trouble than they ought to be, and the Heretic that attacked the theater—Constable Frye was very, very happy to be able to report that no significant incidents were occurring in his district.

Constable Coates arrived, as the first wave of Trowth's panoply of church bells began thundering the nine o'clock hour. He'd brought a small cask of barley wine with him, and offered to share it with Constable Frye before they changed shifts. Constable Frye was pleased to oblige him though, notably, he did *not* fill out an incident report on the subject. Constables Coates and Frye had a wide-ranging discussion then — fueled by the potency of the barley-wine — that touched on many relevant Subjects of the Day. Among those topics were Women's Suffrage, which was readily agreed on as a dangerous threat to the stability of the nation, and a product of an increasingly liberal education system; the Ettercap War, which Constable Coates believed a trial while it was occurring, but all for the best, in retrospect — Constable Frye, whose brother had lost a hand and part of his left ear during the Gorcia campaign — politely dissented on that score; and finally, the brief but extraordinary success of the play *Theocles*.

Neither of the two men had seen the play in question, but Constable Frye was fully-prepared with an opinion on the subject, nonetheless.

"'S not that I don't think we should be makin' plays about...about anything we like. I think we should be. I think tha's what plays is for, right? Saying thin's aloud as maybe you and I are too polite to. And believe me, i's not like I'm always sure the Emperor — Word bless him and keep him — has always done quite right." Constable Frye gulped down the last of his barley-wine, and was dismayed to discover that the cask that Constable Coates had brought was nearly empty. "'S just...this is a...'s a challengin' time is all, and so the...he needs our support."

"That's it," Constable Coates concurred. "S'a challengin' time. No time f'r dissent."

"Challengin', right," Constable Frye concurred.

"Wit' suffragists. 'N them gangsters everywhere,"

Constable Coates concurred yet again, in an effort to saturate the atmosphere with a sense of mutually-agreed on sensibility. "Still, I heard. I heard them sharpsies is still around, too."

"No," Constable Frye responded, spoiling Coates' ambition for universal consensus. "Can't be. Where?"

"The Arcadum," Coates insisted. "They're. Hidin'. *Regrouping*, I think. Plannin'...you know how they are. Crafty...crafty buggers."

"There's no...here, hold on."

A man, shabbily dressed and with a glazed look in his eye, stumbled through the door of the gendarmerie station.

"Here, sonny," Constable Frye said, "what's wrong? You look like death on a plate."

The man opened his mouth to speak, but produced only a metallic clack-clack-clack sound as his teeth snapped together and open again. He turned his head left and right, up and down at random, as though unable to comprehend his surroundings.

"He's drunk," Constable Coates exclaimed — and he was certainly in a position to know.

Constable Frye immediately got up from his chair and attended the man, having some half-conceived notion of escorting him down to the drunk tank, where the stranger could spend the night with his fellow inebriates. He'd managed to get his shoulder under the man's arm and was guiding him towards the back room, when Constable Coates called out.

"Here. What's wrong with his tongue?"

The man's tongue, indeed, the whole inside of his mouth, was black with slimy ichor, as though he'd been drinking it — impossible, of course, as without special treatment, ichor was a fiendish poison to living tissue. "What...what have you been doing, son?" Constable Frye asked, as disused cognitive machinery sought to fight its way through the barley-wine fog. "What's wrong, then?"

The man opened his mouth again, producing another round of metallic clacking, then the scratchy sound of a bad phonograph. A cultured voice, clearly at odds with the man's ragged appearance, emerged from his mouth, unaffected by the working of his lips.

"Gentlemen," said the voice, "I hope you understand that this is nothing personal. If you survive, please give Inspector Beckett my regards."

The stranger then, awkwardly, as though he barely retained control of his limbs, tore his shirt open. Set into his stomach — edges raggedly stitched into the flesh — was some manner of brass engine, with a large flywheel and a canister of glowing blue phlogiston. Next to it sat a lump of greasy brown material. The wheel began to spin, throwing off tiny blue sparks.

"No, oh," moaned Constable Frye as he turned to his companion. "Down! Get dow —"

Constable Coates experienced a strange elation then, as the walls shimmered red and brown and turned to high, arching brass vaults. There was a pressure on his ears, a feeling that something had scooped him out from the inside, and now that empty cavity was trying to suck him inwards, causing him to implode. At the same time, he felt divorced from his body as it twisted away, crumpling to the floor, he felt lifted up, floating, as voices from his childhood reached out to him, his mother's hands on the side of his face, his father's voice whispering to him, gently telling him he was worthless, useless, stupid, a liar, lovingly telling him he was dying now, and should take a special joy in suffering the eternal discomfiture of the Divine Disharmony, soft claws gripped his soul, and then he was sliding back, back down to his ruined body, away from the whispering voices that warned him he would be back, he could never escape them, never avoid them, they would wait and wait until the sun burned out for him to return to them…

Constable Godwin Coates blinked up at the ceiling which was charred black and dripping grey ash into his eyes. He tried to turn his face away, but could not. He tried to lift his hand and found his left arm unresponsive. His right arm moved, and he flopped it over his chest. He did not feel any pain, felt instead insulated from pain, as though his mind was packed around with wool, a delicate glass bauble suspended in the center of a splintered crate. He tried to swallow and choked on dust and ash instead.

Voices continued to murmur at him, though he was sure these were not real voices, that his hearing had been destroyed by the weapon. He felt sure he could feel, through the cloud of shock, blood trickling from his ears. The voices murmured anyway, and though Constable Godwin Coates was sure that what they were saying was pertinent, desperately important to his situation, he could not apprehend a single word, as though they were speaking just below the threshold of intelligibility. He strained to listen, but the more he concentrated on the voices, the more they seemed to recede, and the more a frenzied panic and an intolerable, fiery pain encroached on the edges of his senses.

He surrendered, and began a series of dry, hacking coughs, spasms in the lungs and throat that grew more desperate and painful as the ash gripped him and no saliva was forthcoming. He wanted to roll over, at least, to turn away from the gray and black-etched ceiling, but he could not. Constable Godwin Coates had no idea how long he stayed there, prone and helpless on the floor, before he saw the man.

A man in a dark charcoal suit with a long, charcoal coat. He had a red scarf wrapped around his face, and his left eye and the flesh around it seemed to be missing, revealing a black pit into the depths of his skull. His short hair was gray and thinning, and he carried a charcoal-covered tricorn hat in his hand. The man knelt down in front of Constable Coates, perhaps was trying to speak to him, though between the man's red scarf and an incessant, sourceless ringing sound, Coates could not have said for sure.

Wits scattered by the explosion, it took Godwin Coates several seconds to recognize the man in the red scarf as Elijah Beckett; when he did, Constable Coates did his best to speak. He was not certain if he succeeded, because he couldn't hear himself, but he knew, somehow, that it was desperately important, that he had a vital message to deliver.

"Beckett," he croaked, or thought he croaked, or hoped he did, at least. "Beckett. It was." He coughed again—he was dead certain of that, because it felt like someone had reached down his throat and torn out a handful of lung. He took one last, deep, gasping breath, and prayed that his voice was clear.

"Anonymous John."

The breath left him, and the dark claimed him, and his fear rose to a roiling pitch as it did so. Constable Godwin Coates knew that the voices were waiting for him in the dark.

Twenty-Three

Have been studying the minds of my fellow men at length. Am largely disappointed. All men seem to want only to indulge in their creature comforts. Long time and effort spent carving predictable circles in which to spend their lives, just automatons made of meat and bone. What is the point of making another entity such as this?

--from the journal of Harcourt Wolfram, 1785

Wolfram Hall was the official headquarters of the Royal Academy of Sciences — a lush, well-appointed townhouse on the Mile, right where the Daior-Crabtrees front met the entrenched defenses of the Gorgon-Vie architecture. The consequence of this was a very square building with very wide rooms and very low ceilings, and also an astonishing number of floral downspouts, as though the Daior-Crabtrees, frustrated by their inability to burn the building down and start over, were determined to occlude it with baroque gutter-work.

This was where newcomers petitioned for membership in the Academy, where patents were filed, where a substantial library of monographs and recent scientific periodicals could be consulted. It was staffed primarily by clerks, students at the university, and third and fourth cousins of the major Esteemed Families who needed jobs that were well-paid but not particularly taxing.

No serious scientist spent any time at Wolfram Hall, of course. The real work done by the Academy was in the Croft. At the leading edge of Old Bank, miraculously spared by the second activation of the *Excelsior*, was a vast complex of underground vaults, beneath what had once been the Abbey of St. Chretien. This Abbey was several decades older than the much more prominent Vie Abbey, and had been the center of religious life in Trowth for centuries before the church in Canth was disavowed and then replaced by the Church Royal. For years after that, the building served as the largest bank in Old Bank, and was indeed the bank from which that district originally took its name. After the

145

Great Forfeiture, when all of the bank vaults were emptied in order to refill the royal treasury, Chretien's Abbey stood disused and neglected.

All until Harcourt Wolfram, in dire need of space to accommodate his titanic intellect and increasingly-ambitious experiments, petitioned the crown for a laboratory. The Croft, which subsequently saw the birth of the first difference engines, the first aetheric translators, as well as Mr. Stitch himself, was commandeered by the Royal Academy of Sciences after Wolfram's death, in a vain hope that the residue of his experiments could lead to even more breakthroughs that the great scientist had not considered.

The vaults in the Croft extended for more than a square mile, deep beneath the city, ancient catacombs whose purpose, undoubtedly clear to the early grammateurs who'd built it, was now thoroughly obscure. They had now become a hotly-contested commodity for the scientific community of Trowth, and were the home of the more audacious, unlikely, and undoubtedly extremely dangerous researches of the Empire.

This was where Beckett found himself on the morning after the death of Constables Coates and Frye: descending a narrow stairway deep into the belly of the Croft, to consult with an expert in necrology that he kept on retainer. Beckett had brought Gorud with him, and the therian took his surroundings in with an unflappable aplomb. Two porters carried a steamer trunk, in which were contained the remains of the black-tongued stranger responsible for the attack.

After what Beckett considered to be an utterly unreasonable number of steps, they came to the small offices of the scientists in the Croft — tiny rooms stocked with notes and notebooks, where men like Ernst Helmetag — professor of Life Sciences and Asphyxiology — could consider the results of their work.

"Ah, yes," Ernst cried out, "Inspector Beckett, come in, come in. You men, put that there, that's fine." Ernst had the broad, ruddy features of the northern Trowthi, and a slight burr in his accent that was unmistakable. He wore a walrus mustache and was entirely bald. Between these features and the leather apron he wore, Ernst more closely resembled a jolly brewer than an expert in the animation of dead tissue. "Yes, now what have we here?" He paused above the trunk, then looked over at Gorud. "Ah. Is it appropriate? For that…I mean, the little fellow is surely out of his element here, perhaps he would care to wait…"

Beckett did not respond to this remark, only patiently waited for Ernst to succumb to the discomfiture that the inspector's stony silence would produce.

"Yes." Ernst said at last. "Well." He opened the trunk and peered at its contents intently. After a moment, he took a pair of heavy leather gloves and a brass loupe from the narrow shelves in his cramped office, and began rummaging through sticky black goop and dismembered body parts..

"We shall take this to my workbench," Ernst announced, as he summoned two more porters. Or, perhaps they were the same porters; the men traditionally wore linen masks over their mouths and noses, to protect themselves from deadly fumes, and were thus unrecognizable.

Helmetag's workbench was actually four workbenches, arranged in parallel, occupying a large chunk of one of the modest-sized vaults in the Croft. Bright yellow lamps burned overhead, and a small phlogiston generator powered a large, portable incandescent light. The benches were filled with bits of metal twisted into occult shapes; jars with pickled hands, eyes, organs, tongues, and pig fetuses; long knives with straight blades, serrated blades, curved blades; and a respectable selection of glassware.

"Now," Ernst said, "Ahm. Please don't let...eh...the little fellow touch anything. I know you are curious!" He spoke very loudly to Gorud, as though the therian could not understand Trowthi, but an additional helping of volume might clarify things for him. "Yes! Curious! But you must not touch! All right! Now," he said to Beckett, as he began to draw chunks of black, ichor-smeared meat from the trunk. "Now, of course, I am engaged in the study of prolonging the vitality of living tissue, yes? I do not...I must make it clear...I do *not* attempt to reanimate the dead tissue. Yes?" He looked around, as though to satisfy himself that any invisible eavesdroppers had clearly heard his disclaimer. "I will offer my advice, based on my experience, but of course that is not an admission of knowledge *a priori*, yes?"

"Yes, yes," Beckett snapped at him. The speech was a standard part of his conversations with any of his consultants, and he was tired of it. "Just tell me what this is."

Ernst tutted reproachfully, sucked his teeth, and began work on the remains. He laid the largest pieces beside each other, and gently flensed the remaining flesh with his long knives, revealing bits of skeleton made from brass. He exposed the flesh to currents from his phlogiston generator, applied certain tinctures that he'd extracted from his menagerie of beakers, and emitted some knowing grunts at the results. After an hour of what looked, to Beckett, like aimless puttering, Ernst explained.

"This is a quite extraordinary thing," he said, wiping off his knives and carefully putting them back into arbitrarily chosen positions. "It is a reanimate, yes, that is clear. The flesh has been reactivated with an infusion of ichor, and provided *motis vivendum* by electricity. But look, do you see these bones? The bones are made of metal, and are hollow, you see? Cables run inside.

Ordinarily, in a reanimate---er, that is, I am given to understand, at any rate—current is carried along the outside of the body to envigorate the muscle tissues. But these are a design to allow the current to run inside."

"Why would someone do that?"

Ernst harrumphed, as though speculation on the motivations of necrologists was a pointless exercise. "Who knows? Well, perhaps. I couldn't say for sure..."

"Guess, then."

Ernst twisted the end of his mustache for a moment. "Let me ask instead. Where did you find this thing? It was not, I suspect, used in a conventional way."

"No," Beckett said, pensively. "No, it wasn't. It was used to deliver a munition. An explosive...ah."

"You see? Perhaps." Ernst shrugged.

"Brackets and cables are notable. An internal electrical system would enable the reanimate to pass for human. At a distance, anyway."

"It's unusual. Erm. So I've *heard*," said Ernst. "Necrologists do not usually try to make humans, but to make things that are more than human. It is a strange thing to make a reanimate that is indistinguishable from a man."

"Yes," Beckett replied. "Yes it is." The phantom itching in his eye was suddenly abominable again, and he began to rub at it. "All right. Reanimates that can pass for human. There must be a way to recognize them."

"Ah, yes," Ernst replied. "Yes, yes. The blood, you see, is replaced by ichor, which is black. So, tissue that is ordinarily red—tongue, lips, and so forth. Also, the eyes. Ichor does not preserve the eyes, and they will quickly dissolve. Yellowing first of the sclera, unusually large pupils, then weeping of the aqueous humour. I cannot imagine that these...things...should be useful for more than a week, unless some new method has been found to preserve the eyes."

"All right, professor," Beckett said, at length. "You've been very helpful."

"Yes, of course," Ernst Helmetag replied. "Yes. Mr. Beckett. This is all not usual, is it? Something is happening now."

Beckett did not know what to say to that, so he said nothing.

Twenty-Four

"Believe me, I understand where you're coming from," Valentine was saying. "Loyalty. Loyalty is a great thing, and I respect that, I really do. But you've got to consider you options here." He was sitting opposite the prisoner, Sergeant Charles Codrington, formerly of the Royal Army Light Supply Division, who pouted in the most distant corner of the dank cell beneath Raithower House, where he was chained up pending his trial. "Which is to say, you haven't *got* any options. We've got witnesses, evidence that you were dealing in oneiric munitions. You understand that this is heresy, right? You're getting a trial only because you were in the army, and we can't execute you on the spot. But the army isn't going to let you off easy, you know that, right?"

The Sergeant was one of the two men apprehended on Beckett's Bluewater raid, and Valentine had been trying to coax information out of him for what seemed like centuries. He refused always, just sat in the back corner of his cell, bloody and bruised from the beating he'd taken at the hands of the gendarmerie. He stared out into the distance, as though Valentine weren't there at all.

"So, whatever John is offering you, it's not really worth anything, because you can't spend it when you're dead. Or even when you're locked in prison for the rest of your life. That's assuming a best-case scenario, mind you. And whatever protection John's offering…you have to know he can't protect you anymore, right? We've *got* you. You're *here*. Anonymous John needed a city-wide riot to get himself out of jail last time, how do you think he's going to get you out? Why do you think he would *bother*?"

The man said nothing and Valentine sighed. He thought that Sergeant Codrington's cellmate, a former grocer's assistant by the name of Hawkes, was a more promising prospect for obtaining information, but the man had mysteriously choked to death on his dinner the night before. The entire

149

endeavour seemed unlikely to yield results. Valentine was about to renew his persuasive efforts when Beckett returned.

"No luck, yet?" Beckett asked him.

"No."

Beckett snorted. "Go home. I want to talk to him. Alone."

"I'm. Not sure that's a good idea, Beckett."

"I didn't ask. Go. Now."

Valentine did as he was ordered, because he could think of no reasonable excuse not to. Once Valentine had left, Beckett, very slowly and methodically, began to unwrap the scarf from around his face, revealing the hideous bloody rents made by his gradually vanishing flesh. First he exposed the bare orbital bone below his eye, then the black gap where his nose should have been, then the hole in his cheek that revealed his teeth. When he had finished, he let the scarf drop to the ground, and began to gently tug off one of his gloves.

"You know about the fades, Sergeant?" Beckett asked. The Sergeant said nothing. "I've had them for more than forty years, which is, as I understand, a record. They usually kill you in ten." Beckett removed a key from his pocket and unlocked the cell door. "No one's sure where they come from. They eat your body away, very slowly. Fingertips..." he showed his bare hand, with the bone-white tips of his distal phalanges visible through transparent flesh. "Your nose, ears. Eyes. When the meat turns clear, it dies, and starts to rot away. There's no way to stop it, or slow it down. Nothing." Beckett took from his other pocket a small knife, and gently drew a line across his palm, so that livid red blood spilled out from it. "Once you've got it, you just start to disappear, until your bones crack and your lungs give out and your heart stops, and there's not a damn thing you can do about it." Beckett knelt down in front of Sergeant Charles Codrington, his palm now bloody. "You're not afraid to die, I can see that. And you're not afraid of a lifetime in prison, if the army goes easy on you. But you're still going to tell me what I want to know, because I know how people catch the fades." He held his bloody hand close to Codrington's face. The Sergeant jerked and tried to pull away, but was held fast by heavy chains. "It's through the blood, Sergeant. And I promise you, you will give me Anonymous John, or you will choke on my poisoned blood. I will give you the fades, and let you loose, so you can spend the next ten years of your life watching your body die. In a decade, when you're trapped in a wheelchair, and you're blind and deaf, and you can feel your heart lurch with every second beat, you're going to wonder what you thought was so great about what Anonymous John had to offer." He seized Sergeant Codrington's jaw, smearing blood on his face, forcing the man to look at that black, empty eye socket. "Or, you're going to tell me what I want to know."

The Sergeant talked then, at length, and in detail. Beckett used the information to plan his next raids. Anonymous John had not, historically, been a figure with whom Beckett had had much contact—the gangster was a murderer, yes, a smuggler, and a thief, but only in mundane, ecclesiastically-approved ways. He had never before stepped into the field of scientific heresy, and so there had never been an onus on Beckett to interfere with him. Now, though, that John was trafficking in oneiric munitions, providing daemonomaniacal regeants, and building reanimates, he had become Beckett's enemy, and Beckett was determined to make him regret it.

He took his first steps towards that end the day after Armistice ended, when the chilly spring rains rolled in from the bay like a curtain of water, condemning Trowth and its citizenry to two or more months of terminal dampness. Hidden by the iron-gray precipitation that suffused the air, Beckett assembled more than a hundred local gendarmes and twenty-five Lobsterman— as well as a support crew consisting of fifteen trolljrmen and their ambulance tarrasques—and surrounded a complex of warehouses on Front Street, right where the city dropped precipitously into the bay.

That Anonymous John had been smuggling materiel into the city by way of warehouses such as this was common knowledge—but Trowth's enormous, sprawling docks, which covered nearly every inch of the available coastline sheltered by its great sea-wall, and even spread almost fully up the length of the Stark, were impossible to police effectively. Moreover, Anonymous John had been using a complex, rotating system of import locations, using one while preparing two more, so that he could rapidly move his entire operation out from beneath the scrutiny of local law enforcement. Only a few men were given the full rotation, and unfortunately for John, Sergeant Codrington had been one of them.

The Lobstermen went in first, bedecked in blood-slick bone armor, faster and stronger than any ordinary man, and armed with long-pin rifles, whose deadly rounds flew faster than the sound they made. After a few sharp cracks and the whines of flying bullets, shabbily-dressed men swarmed out from the warehouses and into the waiting arms of the gendarmerie. They were shackled and escorted to local prison cells with a minimum of unnecessary violence—a miracle by all accounts, as the gendarmes were as a whole infuriated by what amounted to Anonymous John's declaration of open war against them. Only a handful of smugglers had arms or jaws or eye sockets broken, and only one, who rather ill-advisedly tried to escape custody while his captors were otherwise occupied, was brought down by two especially enthusiastic men and did not, sadly, survive the onslaught of their nightsticks.

In all, nearly a hundred smugglers had been captured, and thousands of crowns worth of merchandise. Nothing in the goods reclaimed by Beckett and his men appeared to have heretical uses, however; the smuggled wares appeared to consist primarily of suffragist and explicit literature, an unseemly number of brandy casks from the embargoed nation of Thranc, and close to two tons of Sarpeki wool, undoubtedly smuggled in to avoid excessive tariffs. It would be of shoddy quality, of course, and sold at cut-rates to textile mills up the river, before being sent back down the river to populate Trowth's high-end clothing boutiques.

Out of spite, Beckett did not permit any of the smugglers to be remanded to custodies indoors until every single item was accounted for. They were obliged to stand in the chilly, pouring rain for over six hours, until Beckett was satisfied with the inventory, and handed the whole lot over to representatives to the Bureau of Trade, Excises, and Licensure. Though no heretical materials were confiscated, Beckett's raid was generally considered a great success, and evidence that his and Stitch's advocacy for a more empowered Coroner's Division was working precisely the way it was supposed to.

Twenty-Five

"Well," said Valentine, "I did say — "

"Yes." Skinner said, a little more forcefully than she might have intended. "Yes you did, I should have listened, your cousin is an unconscionable monster, et cetera and so forth, I would like to move on to the next stage of the conversation, now."

"All right, all right." Silver and porcelain scraped delicately against each other, as Valentine added sugar to his tea. It was late to be drinking tea, but neither of them found themselves predisposed to sleep. "Well, obviously, you can stay here for as long as you like — "

"I — "

"I *know*, I know you don't want to stay here for long. I'm just saying that you *can*. I suppose that going back to your family isn't an option?"

Skinner thought back on her parents' tiny house in Lower West Seagirt, her mother surrounded by piles of strangers' laundry that she would clean and mend while her father slept the days away, recuperating from his night-shift at the mill. The house deathly quiet and suffocatingly hot, its ever-changing topography of laundry making it impossible to navigate. The unconquerable gap between mother and daughter whose spheres of experience were utterly alien to each other.

"No," Skinner said, quietly. "Not really."

"So. All right, you just need to get your own place. I could rent it for you, that's fine. I mean, it's ridiculous that a grown woman should have to do that...'sword, I'm starting to sound like a suffragist."

"You could do worse."

"Yes, I suppose I could." Valentine slurped his tea, noisily. "Have you got any money? I've got...well, my father has an estate agent who's been looking at properties down by Arsenal Close, that's not too bad a neigborhood."

153

Skinner shook her head. "The theater has all the royalties from the play. I spent my last wages from the Coroners months ago." She clenched her jaw and slowly cracked the knuckles on her right hand, one at a time. "I didn't realize," Skinner said, furious at herself but still trying to keep her voice level, "that I was living on Emilia's sufferance."

"Ahm," Valentine replied, in a way he probably imagined was consoling. "You wouldn't be the first person to make that mistake. Well, I could give you—" He drowned this sentence in a coughing fit as he saw Sknner's expression. "No, well. Well there's got to be a way...I mean, the playhouses have never been afraid of shirking the law before. You know theater-people, they'll do anything. Surely you could get work...?"

"No," Skinner said. "I can't prove I've written anything. Everything was kept so secret. It's a shame, too; now that *Theocles* is on the Black List, it would probably sell like gangbusters."

"Yes...oh. Oh!"

"What is it?"

"I've just devised a plan. A good plan. Oh, this feels nice. Is it always like this?"

"Is what like what?"

Valentine began chuckling to himself. "I can't tell you! I can't tell you about it yet, it will be a surprise." He was on his feet at once pacing back and forth, rubbing his hands together. "This is excellent, oh my! I've got some leave coming from the Coroners," Valentine said. "A few weeks, anyway, that I can take. Beckett will hardly miss me. You heard about the raid on Front Street? He's got a fire under him now. You know how he gets. He's like a bullet now, he'll be tearing Anonymous John's organization apart for weeks. He probably won't even notice that I'm gone."

"Valentine, what are you going to do? You have to tell me."

"No! It is a plan both *cunning* and *secret*. I will say no more about it!" He stopped pacing. "Now, I shall go check to make sure that Karine is settled in all right."

"Oh."

"What?"

Skinner shrugged. "Nothing. Go on. I've got to try and get some sleep."

"Uhm. Yes. Right, so do I. At the office. Where they have cots."

"Yes."

Valentine cleared his throat. Then cleared his throat a second time. Then said, "Yes. Well. Good night."

"Good night, Valentine."

Valentine Vie-Gorgon hesitated only for a moment before discreetly leaving the young lady to her room, exchanging another polite "good night" with Karine, and then leaving his house and stepping into the pouring rain.

Beckett lay on his back, staring at the disorder of plaster swirls on his ceiling. He could feel the exhaustion, in some distant orbit around his body, separated by vast tracts of empty space and the gentle warmth of the veneine. It never came to claim him, though. He'd been using djang—small, concentrated amounts of the stuff that people drank to wake themselves up in the morning—in order to combat the lassitude that the increasingly large doses of veneine brought on.

The doctors told him that he'd likely eventually hit a balance. The veneine would make him tired, the djang would pick him up; in the right proportion, he'd soon reach a kind of equilibrium that would put him back to normal, only with no pain. If that was true, the miraculous balance he hoped to achieve was a long way off. Right now, the djang stopped him from sleeping, but the veneine muddled his thoughts enough that he couldn't think of anything to do but lie in bed and stare at the ceiling.

Sometimes, little snippets of memories would swim up from the murky depths of his mind, fuzzy kirliotypes of past that he thought he'd forgotten. They were never did more than border on the significant. He remembered the Dragon Isles campaign, but the memories that floated up were images of learning to use the bolt-action on his rifle, or Fletcher sitting in the front of the boat, smoking a cigar. Beckett saw images from his childhood, too—the day his father patched a pair of Beckett's boots. Some Armistice from decades ago, when he walked to school carrying a weathered little primer that had been used by generations of students before him. Listening to a record in his office at Raithower House.

None of these memories meant anything, as far as Beckett could ascertain. They just flickered through his head, as though some trapdoor had been carelessly left open to emit a deluge of trivial incidence. Or as though, now that Beckett was at the end of his life, his granite-hard personality was slowly coming undone. The long years of building filters to sort the meaningful from the irrelevant were unspooling, the filters were breaking down, one day he'd be drowned in a flood of his own pointless experiences.

Not for the first time, Beckett considered an early leave from the mess. The spectre of an old age dominated by senility and physical anguish was not appealing. Nor was the prospect of a retirement spent drugged into oblivion, letting the fades gobble him up inch by unrelenting inch while he let his mind drift among hallucinogenic fantasies of black water and brass cities. Surely there was no shame in punctuating a life such as his — one with accomplishments that any reasonable human being could be proud of, one in which a difference was made, however small — with a clean and honorable exit, to forgo the inevitable humiliation of decrepitude?

A gentle chill crept into his body, and he could not feel himself shiver. His vision began to slowly contract, the plaster details of the ceiling blurred. Beckett blinked something from his eye and turned his head. His red scarf hung over the sill of the window, which was buttoned up tightly against the raw spring air. For a moment, Beckett was seized with a desire to snatch the scarf up and rip it to pieces, or toss it into the fire.

The moment passed. Beckett got up instead, glimpsed briefly at himself in the small mirror above his vanity. Dressed in his shabby smallclothes, body gruesomely marred by the fades, he looked like a man with one foot in the grave. Which Beckett supposed he must be. He dressed in his charcoal-colored suit, wrapped his red scarf around his mouth and nose, and decided it was not too early to go to work, after all.

Because of Trowth's notoriously inclement weather, its rapid fluctuations in temperature, and its perpetually salty air, it was practically impossible for any large machine to function with any kind of reliability. Discrepancies in function were often small, but could be compounded in an engine that was required to run all the time. Nowhere was this more apparent than the clocks of Trowth.

With every passing second, the massive brass machines sitting atop office buildings and churches and bourses grew ever more slightly away from synchrony. A small army of mechanics, employed by the Committee on Chronography, a sub-division of the Ministry of Civic Well-Being, worked tirelessly throughout the week in order to keep them running smoothly, efficiently, and, most importantly, accurately — but their task was ultimately futile. There were simply too many clocks, and the differences in time were often close to imperceptible.

This was all further compounded by the fact that, according to royal decree, the clock at the top of Vie Abbey should be the clock from which all others took their measurements. The clock at Vie Abbey was primarily an astronomical clock, seated beneath a vast astrolabe. It was very well able to mark the changing of the seasons, the orbits of sun and moon, and the passage of the planets — but it was not accurate for ordinary, civil time beyond an hour. There were no minute or second hands on the clock at Vie Abbey. So the army of mechanics who tuned the clocks, and who lost time as they traveled from church to office to market, were forced to make their best guesses as to precisely what time it was.

All of this yielded a strange wave of clock chimes throughout the city. The four-o'clock-hour, which is the hour that found Beckett on his way back to Raithower House, began with the heavy bronze thunder at Vie Abbey. Shortly after it began, the clocks nearby, with their orchestra of bells, took up the tolling, and passed it along to those clocks that were nearest to them, and so forth. The entire process, including the strange pockets of early chiming, the clocks that were hopelessly delayed, and the clocks that seemed to be under the misapprehension that it was actually eight o'clock in the evening, took well over twenty minutes, even for as modest an hour as four o'clock. During Second Winter, when the clock-tuners were much less able to effectively tend to their charges, the noon bells were sometimes known to toll for the entire hour until they began again at one.

Beckett reached Old Bank just as that neighborhood's venerable clocks began to take up the clanging of the hour. He passed without delay through one of the many checkpoints he'd insisted on; local gendarmes, accompanied by a therian sniffer, searched passers-by for explosives on the chance that Anonymous John might take it into his mind that he should attempt some kind of reprisal. The therians, peculiarly, were unusually sensitive to the presence of the oneiric regeants used in heretical munitions. They were employed much the same way dogs were — a fact that Beckett found more than a little disgusting, but he was willing to accept it if it meant putting a stop to the attacks.

Old Bank was replete with such checkpoints, all the way into the tangled Arcadium beneath it, and it was beyond consideration that anyone might attack Raithower House with an oneiric weapon. Beckett remained fairly comfortable, then, as he walked towards the Raithower courtyard. A tall, rangy-man in a long dark coat preceded him to the gates — another early-riser, perhaps. Beckett called out to him, but his voice was drowned out by Old Bank's clocks. The noisiest of these clocks, which had just begun to toll at Beckett's arrival, was called Goursehead Clock; it rang four brass *clangs*, of varying pitch and tone, for every one great iron *bong* that tolled the hour.

The man entered Raithower House. Shortly thereafter, the building exploded.

The sound and force of the blast were muffled by the old stone walls of Raithower House itself, so the wave of pressure and heat presented Beckett with only a moment of pain and confusion. It gave way to the old coroner furiously berating himself as he saw blue-white light boil out of the windows, and turn almost immediately to the red and orange of burning wood.

Fifty men looking for oneiric munitions, Beckett thought, *And not one checking for regular, old-fashioned phlogiston bombs.* The wave of chiming clocks passed by, to the sound of men shouting for help, the crackling roar of the fire, and the jangling clatter of the fire brigades.

Twenty-Six

Word of the fire spread quickly — so quickly that a throng of citizens had arrived to support the fire brigades before the five o'clock bells began to ring. The citizenry, ever since the devastation of Mudside during the Sharpsie Riots, was extremely sensitive to the possibility of widespread fire. Fortunately, the rain made that unlikely, but the explosion had caused Raithower house and the adjoining property to collapse, and spare hands were needed to clear away the rubble. The bulk of Raithower House actually extended well below the street line and into the Arcadium, and probably remained largely intact — it's neighboring edifice was not quite so lucky. That house had the misfortune of being built on top of another, smaller house, which too had collapsed from the shock of the explosion, leaving a gaping pit into the city's underside. Stone and brass slid like an avalanche into the hole, but Trowth had seen enough of misery and destruction these last few years, and if there was anyone trapped in there, the people were determined to effect a rescue.

Beckett attempted to coordinate the efforts as best he could, until the djang began to wear off and the veneine lurched forth to drag him into the dark with its oppressive grip. He sat down on a toppled bronze statue of a man wrestling with some manner of lion and watched as the dull flames were finally extinguished, the rocks were cleared away, and charred bodies were pulled from the wreckage. His eyelids were heavy; the sleepless night was catching up with him.

Mr. Stitch arrived some time after that, and Beckett did not notice the hulking reanimate, as it, too, watched the rescue efforts and took stock. Stitch stood very still, taking in every piece of information available, processing it all with its astonishing mechanical brain, breathing its deep, raspy breaths from its artificial lungs.

"What. Happened?" Stitch asked, finally? Not because it hadn't surmised, obviously, but because Beckett's opinion was one more datum to be collected, processed, and stored.

"Incendiary bomb," Beckett replied. "All our security was meant to find oneiric munitions. Should have realized. Firebomb's just as dangerous, probably easier to get a hold of."

"Hindsight," said Mr. Stitch, as it considered the fallen buildings. The upper storeys of Raithower house had collapsed forward into the courtyard, filling the space with jagged spears of stone and splintered wood. Beside it, a crevasse had opened up, cracking the roof of the labyrinth of understreets and vaults that made up Old Bank. This area of the Arcadium had been small flats in use by largely bachelors and students; with luck, most of them had been empty. An outer wall had fallen away from the underground buildings, leaving a honeycomb of disintegrating rooms visible from the surface. Light from the parts of the building that were still burning spattered the scene with a dusky red glow, while the rain washed dirty rivulets of mud and ash across every conceivable surface. "Inside?"

"Don't know. I'd only just got here when the...when it happened. Don't know who was there. Third watch, I expect. That's...uhm." Beckett put his head in his hands. "Heathcliff. Courton. Shit. The knocker from the low countries. What..." he took a deep breath. "Can't remember his name."

"Happes." Stitch turned away from the rescue operation, and considered Beckett in its dead, passionless manner. A nearby phlogiston streetlight had lost its glass panes in the explosion, and now fountained eldritch blue light into the sky. Muddled with the red light from the fire, the lamp made everything the livid purple color of a new bruise. "Plans?"

"Plans, yeah, plans. I don't..." This was supposed to be it, Beckett knew. The final proof. Anonymous John was everywhere, he could get to anyone, he could do anything. There was nowhere safe. John had struck right to the heart of the Coroners, and Beckett was supposed to acknowledge a superior force and surrender to it. If this had been Anonymous John's intention, Beckett resolved at that moment to demonstrate that it represented a serious miscalculation. "All right. He wants a war, we'll give it to him. I'm going to shut him down."

"How?"

"I need. Everything. The War Ministry still has impressment powers, right? And the new Moral Standards Committee, their files. I want to commandeer everything, every man, every piece of information in the city, shut down every port, search every ship and warehouse." Anonymous John's operations had been notoriously difficult to dismantle because they were robustly decentralized—small cells operating under instructions, and barely aware of each other. And the process had been repeatedly hampered by the fact that law enforcement in the city was itself decentralized, and subject to the whims of its neighborhood commanders, to the needs of conflicting bureaucracies, the flailing inconsistency of public opinion. But John's organization was still, ultimately, parasitic — it required the ordinary functioning of the city to survive, and had been permitted to exist for so long because it was more trouble to destroy it than it was really worth. "I don't even care if we never find him. I'll keep all fucking industry in this town tied up until he starves to death. I will dismantle every tiny piece of his operation if it takes me a hundred years."

"Ambitious." Stitch replied. As usual, no emotions betrayed its opinion on the subject. Whatever Mr. Stitch believed, it was keeping it to itself.

"This isn't just heresy anymore, or civil unrest. He's not just bombing some local gendarmerie. The Coroners is a division of the Imperial Guard. Attacking us is *treason*. He has directly compromised the safety of the Emperor himself, and I want unlimited powers to track him down. Fucking *unlimited*."

Stitch was silent, just stared at him with those unblinking, brass eyes, then turned away. Its dead, ichor-pickled muscles creaked audibly as it did so. It was not officially reported, but still fairly commonly-known, that Mr. Stitch was routinely consulted by the Emperor's personal medical staff on a variety of scientific subjects. Ostensibly, as the head of the Coroner's division, there were specific, proscribed — and often intricate and confusing — channels through which Mr. Stitch had to act in order to so much as change the color of the front door of the office. But the fact was that Mr. Stitch had the ear of the Emperor if he it was required, and what Beckett said was true. The Imperial Guard, for the safety of the Emperor and the Empire, necessarily had to be sacrosanct. There should be no citizen that felt anything but terror at the thought of raising their hand against the Emperor's appointed servants of law and order. John's attacks had set a dangerous precedent.

It is possible that these were the thoughts that Mr. Stitch's incalculably complex difference-engine of a brain was considering in that moment, that and a nest of future possibilities, weighed against past experience, evaluated according to their upcoming likelihoods, a treacherous reef of non-optimal outcomes through which the reanimate needed to sail. Future outcomes were difficult to predict, as even the most fervent daemonomaniacs who pretended to absolute causal knowledge of the universe were forced to admit. And, moreover, Mr. Stitch had to accommodate this new information into whatever vast plans for the city it had itself been making for the last two hundred years. It was a daunting task, but if there was any mind capable of it, it was Stitch's.

While Mr. Stitch computed, Beckett became conscious of another voice shouting his name. A familiar voice. "Skinner?" He asked. He looked up. The young woman was wrapped in a dressing gown and a heavy coat, hair loose and plastered across her face by the rain, silver-eyeplate glinting red and blue, as though she'd proceeded directly from bed to the patchwork light that now illuminated what remained of Raithower House. Karine was behind her, somewhat less appropriately-attired, as the indige had different customs regarding what constituted acceptable sleepwear than her Trowthi brethren. They were both panic-stricken; Karine led Skinner by one hand, Skinner clutched at her cane with the other.

"Beckett! Where is he? Is he all right? I don't hear him…" Skinner was saying.

"Who? Is who all right?" Beckett was on his feet at once; too quickly; his head spun.

"Valentine!"

Beckett shook his head. "Valentine's not here, his shift doesn't start for another hour—"

"He was staying here. Beckett." Her voice dropped to an anguished whisper. "Beckett, he let us stay at his family house and he was sleeping at the office."

Beckett felt a sensation like his stomach had dropped out from inside him, swallowed up by some inexpressibly deep pit at the core of his being. "Shit. Shit! Okay, come with me. Now!" He seized Skinner's arm and dragged her towards the collapsed building. Rubble still obscured most of the site; volunteers were working tirelessly to clear it. They had made a chain into the pit that had opened into the Arcadium to pass broken stone out of it. Pale, ash-smeared faces and haunted looks made them look like so many horrid ghosts, condemned forever to labor on behalf of a city that would never care for them. "Listen. Skinner, you need to listen there, all right? If he's trapped inside, I need you to find him."

"Is he—"

"The people we've pulled out so far are dead. But we haven't found everyone, all right? We haven't gotten to the bottom. So I *need* you to find him."

Skinner nodded. Beckett could see the small muscles along her jaw clench, the telltale signs of concentration, as she swept her clairaudience through the rubble. Fear and concern would have made another knocker hasty, likely to make mistakes, but not Skinner. She was methodical, precise, thorough. If anyone could find him…

"There's nothing…wait. Wait, there's…I can hear someone…"

"Where? Where is he?"

"Sh! Quiet." She opened her mouth, stretched her jaw like she was yawning, trying to listen more closely...then snapped it shut. Her face went blank. She slowly sank to the ground, besmirching her nightdress with the muck and ash that had accumulated on the cobblestones around them.

"Miss Skinner?" Karine whispered as she approached. "What is it?"

Beckett already knew the answer, but he shuddered still when Skinner spoke. "Nothing. It's stopped."

"Are you sure—"

"I heard his heart stop, Karine. There's no one else down there." Skinner put her head in her hands. Beckett leaned heavily against a stone wall that had, by some miracle, avoided collapse. They were silent as Mr. Stitch approached. It said nothing.

At length, Beckett spoke. "Get me an army. Anonymous John wants a war. I need an army."

Stitch considered the rubble-strewn catastrophe that had one been the coroners' office. "You. Will have one."

163

TWENTY-SEVEN

Though Beckett had demanded an army, what he got was little better than a mob. Men volunteered for his operations by the score—some were gendarmes, some were former soldiers, some were simply shopkeepers and tradesmen incensed beyond reason. Neighbors began gleefully reporting on each other, listing the criminal vices of their fellows in the prurient hope that someone they knew might turn out to be Trowth's notorious arch-villain. Houses and businesses, warehouses, docks, and ships were raided, and some were burned. Commerce in the city practically ground to a halt, as Trowth's population laid siege to itself.

It was veneine and djang and iron self-control that enabled Beckett to retain even a shred of command over his army. He no longer had the stomach for more than one meal a day—usually of smoked fish and kale--and slept for no more than three hours a night. He pushed himself beyond the brink of exhaustion, living in an almost trance-like state in which his mind had completely divorced itself from the sensibilities of his body, operating it remotely, fully disregarding its needs, as he rode back and forth across the city, doing his best to supervise the rapidly-deteriorating organization of his raiding parties.

During this time, the middle weeks of True Spring, chilly showers and civil unrest proved a fertile combination for the city's pamphleteers, who sprung up throughout Trowth like so many radical mushrooms, distributing literature like it was their fungal spore. There were some pamphlets in support of the Emperor, of course, mostly paid for by the emperor himself. By far, however, the pamphleteers were closer to fomenting revolution than they had ever been in the city's history—free now, while Beckett had seized control of all law enforcement and occupied it with chasing down Anonymous John, to say what perhaps they had always wished to. The Emperor was a tyrant, an oppressive madman, crushing the life from the city with his mad whims. Elijah Beckett was a warlord, trying to seize control of Trowth from its rightful ruler. Anonymous John was a foreign spy, trying to undermine the Empire, or else he was a criminal hero, a freedom-fighter battling the forces of oppression, or else he was a devil, the right hand of the Loogaroo come to visit upon Trowth some divine vengeance.

Somewhere in the core of this swirl of rumor and innuendo, coloring the interpretations and fueling the rebellious tendencies of the city's most fiery ideologues, was one particular pamphlet. Elijah Beckett never saw it, because he had neither the time nor the interest to concern himself with public opinion. Elizabeth Skinner never knew about it, because the only friends she had left were too preoccupied to draw her attention to it. But it had not escaped the notice of the Emperor, and it was the subject of a public address that would later be known as the End of the Presses.

Word of the impending address had circulated rapidly among the citizens, and a throng of people filled the Royal Square in front of the dense, mismatched architecture of the palace. It loomed above the people, craggy gables and jagged merlons, forests of buttresses and arches, looking like nothing so much as a grim deity, prepared to pass judgment against those foolish enough to worship at its feet. Arrayed along the sides of the Royal Square were the closed carriages of the Esteemed Families: the Vie-Gorgons and the Daior-Crabtrees and the Rowan-Czarneckis, hidden from public view in their shrouded coaches; under mandate to attend, but under no particular obligation to permit the ordinary people to get a good look at them.

Emilia Vie-Gorgon was there, some onlookers claimed. They insisted that they had caught a glimpse of her beautiful, delicate features and her ebon-black skin through the white lace curtains of the Vie-Gorgon coach.

On either side of the square, the twin statues of Gorgon and Demogorgon stood as silent, inscrutable sentries, the last relics of the city of giants upon which Trowth had been built. Here, of all places, the sense of transgression for which Trowth was known, the sense of being a trespasser in a stranger's garden, was the strongest. It was undoubtedly why the Emperor chose to deliver all of his speeches here. Yet, despite the natural fear that percolated among his audience — the paranoia that they were suddenly subject to as they looked over their shoulders, the abrupt uncertainty that gnawed them — despite all that, the one document that the Emperor had come out expressly to forbid circulated rapidly, passed from chilly hand to chilly hand, stuffed under coats and in shirts to protect it from the rain.

Someone, somewhere, had begun printing copies of *Theocles*, and selling them for pennies on street corners.

The reasons for the sale were, of course, obscure, but it was serendipitous that whatever rabble-rouser had decided to resurrect the blacklisted play had chosen to charge for it, rather than simply distributing it. The people of Trowth were mistrustful of anything *given*, far preferring the tacit assurance of value implied when a thing was *sold*. If it were free, it would have been deemed worthless, but even the few pennies that the printer demanded were enough to convince citizens of its secret value.

William II Gorgon-Vie was, after the fashion of the Gorgon-Vies, a stout man, barrel-chested and apportioned with a generous layer of fat. He was stocky enough to seem short at a distance, but was actually unusually tall. Close-up, William II's thick-necked frame and slightly rounded shoulders gave the impression, as did most of his family, that he was in fact some kind of bull that had been trained to walk around on its rear hooves. This illusion was supported by his perpetual habit of clearing his throat and snorting.

The affectation of the Esteemed Families was that, the closer the men were to the throne of the Empire, the more plainly they were attired. The Emperor was customarily the most plainly-clothed, in a suit of all black, tailored both to accommodate and to enhance his generous bulk. He wore dark, smoked glasses — a deviation from his traditional uniform that would have been scandalous, had they not been a recommendation from his cadre of doctors as a means to alleviate his constant migraines.

William II Gorgon-Vie was an excellent speaker, though suffered from his tendency to employ poor speech writers. His rhetoric was convoluted and sometimes contradictory, marred by words slightly misused (a flaw for which he was routinely lampooned in the papers), and some fairly unusual substitutions of meaning. He delivered this tangle of literary confusion with a bold voice and an upright posture, a generous suffusion of emotion, and all the pomp and grandeur that might be expected of an Emperor who weighed in excess of two hundred pounds. He was, despite not being particularly comprehensible, always quite convincing.

The thrust of his speech was, or at least, appeared to be that, in the face of Becektt's ongoing war with criminality, pamphleteering had become a serious threat to the stability of the city. It was impossible, the Emperor asserted, for the Coroners Division to achieve any kind of social harmony while indecent and unscrupulous men consistently attempted to undermine him in the opinion of the public. There was even some suspicion, the Emperor revealed, that the most nefarious and seditious pamphlets — the ones calling the Emperor a tyrant and implying that the Empire might be run more effectively if supreme power was held by a democratically-elected parliament — were being printed and distributed by Anonymous John himself, precisely to engender the sort of civil strife in which he and his criminal compatriots thrived.

Emperor William II Gorgon-Vie did not mention *Theocles*, and if he thought that this would permit its presence to be overlooked he was mistaken; there was nothing in his speech more conspicuous than that absence.

Consequent to all of this, when the Emperor reached the climax of his speech — declaring that all printing presses were now the property of the Crown, that all printing activities were, by Imperial Mandate, suspended, and that all the properties of Comstock Street as well as all properties of the Comstock branch of the Family Vie-Gorgon were seized and held in trust until such time as their guilt or innocence in the matter of seditious documenteering could be established — the general consensus was that his primary purpose was to finally quell the distribution of that particular and notorious play.

The speech was met with a stunned silence, as the Emperor went on to reveal that a contingent of Royal Marines had already moved to take action on the decree, and would soon be arriving to clear the Royal Square. The audience, moreover, would be searched and all broadsheets, newspapers, and pamphlets would be seized and burned. The Emperor generously added that no one would be prosecuted for such possessions, conveniently leaving out that arresting and trying fifteen hundred people would be fiendishly impractical.

All of this was largely irrelevant to Beckett, except insofar as it temporarily deprived him of seventy-five blood-and-bone armored Lobstermen, who were the only men he had access to with any kind of discipline. While the Emperor seized the printing presses and shut down the business of the Comstock Vie-Gorgons, Beckett was taking the rest of his men on a rampage along the river Stark.

Twenty-Eight

While William II Gorgon-Vie ended the print industry in Trowth, Elijah Beckett stood in Starkton eating smoked fish. The fish were wrapped in the last issue that would ever be printed of the *White Star*, and had Beckett realized the rarity and potential value in such a document, it is unlikely he would have behaved any differently. He still would have permitted the pages to absorb the salty brine from the herring and saltire fish, still let it soak through with Trowth's famous brown sauce, which had once been a ubiquitous condiment for smoked fish. Beckett would have still let soggy bits of paper fall to the ground, to be washed away by the driving rain.

Beckett ate his fish without tasting it, even though he'd tromped six blocks to find a fish vendor that still served smoked fish with brown sauce. In the last few years, nearly every fishmonger had begun dishing up their vittels covered in Corsay pepper sauce or with pickled fruits, leaving the venerable tradition of the brown sauce — a fluid concoction whose recipe was known only to a small handful of men who dealt in the dressing — far by the wayside. Beckett had not given more than a few seconds' thought to the subject until this day, when he added it to the long list of things that had changed in his city for the worse. This is not to say that he dwelt on the subject with any gravity, but simply that it occupied some small part of his mind that concerned itself with whether or not the next generation of Trowthi citizens would be able to avail themselves of brown sauce.

The better part of Beckett's mind was occupied with the ships that his men had seized at the docks in Starkton. The neighborhood — near the very southernmost bend of the Stark, where it finally began to empty out into the icy bay — had long been an occupied territory of the Gorgon-Vies in the Architecture War, and so was dominated by their signature squat, ugly buildings. Hardly anyone ever complained, as the district was comprised predominately of warehouses, shipping agencies, customs houses, and a myriad other government, institutional, and purely functionary buildings for which architecture served no purpose but utility, and which were generally expected to be squat, square, and ugly anyway.

At the edge of the river, where the mouldering wooden docks jutted out into the dark water, three steam-powered river barges idled. Their engines had been shut down, leaving a mist of spent phlogiston swirling over the swift current of the Stark and smelling like copper and blood. Their crews had all been taken into custody, arrested and held without charge or warrant, while the holds of the ships were searched. They loomed in the gloomy morning light, while gendarmes with flickering blue lamps scoured the ships' decks and excavated their bowels. Meanwhile, Beckett watched, and ate his fish.

Stevedores were dragged off by the score and taken to cells beneath Old Bank where they shivered in the damp and cold. The captains and owner of the three barges were being held in Beckett's de facto headquarters, a former barracks for the War Ministry's pressgang, disused since the end of the Ettercap War. Beckett would have his own men question the ship's captains, or would question them himself, but later. At the moment, the veneine and djang buzzing through his system made it difficult for him to focus; he found his mind flitting from subject to subject, utterly disinterested in even the most mild exercises in concentration.

One of Beckett's conscripted gendarmes approached him; the man had a large moustache and a crooked nose, and the number four branded onto his face. This man, whose name Beckett could not remember (he'd been referring to the man as "Four"), had become Beckett's unofficial liaison to the gendarmerie, pretending some past acquaintance with the Inspector that Beckett also could not recall.

"Well?" Beckett asked, licking brown sauce from the numb tips of his fingers.

Four shook his head. "A few bits of contraband, but nothing unusual for ships this size. Mostly just hiding wool for the northern principalities from the Imperial excises. Nothing...uh. Nothing like what you're looking for."

Beckett grimaced, and tossed the remains of his breakfast away. His blind eye had begun weeping, recently, shedding tears of vitreous humor tinged bloody and red as the fades began to eat away at his tear ducts. The ruddy tears, shielded from the rain by the prominent overhang of his leather hat, drew a dark channel along his cheek, but he did not notice them. Most of his face was numbed by the disease; the rest was numbed by the drugs in his system. He could still feel a throb in the crook of his left elbow, the site of his last injection.

He'd had to switch arms, since there were too many spots on his right forearm that appeared in danger of sepsis.

"No explosives," Four went on, while a sound like the buzzing of angry hornets kicked up behind him. It was the sound of musketballs whizzing by, but he did not move for cover, nor did he even appear to notice them. "No oneiric munitions, no anything. Not with these."

Beckett heard the shouts of men struck down as they tried to climb the hill below Kaarcag and saw the weaponized, sentient foglets swirling around his feet. These were the first sign that the assault was a trap, that the Dragon Princes were prepared. They would crawl up a soldier's leg and down his throat, trying to drain his blood out through his lungs.

Elijah Beckett shook his head. No assault. This was a raid. And the Dragon Princes were gone, he was looking for Anonymous John. This must be a hallucination. "We'll keep looking," Beckett said. Two gendarmes had come down the hill (*Off of the barge*, Beckett told himself), Gorud trailing behind them. The therian seemed, as usual, unmoved by the concerns of the humans around him, content to follow his orders and perhaps secretly marvel at man's strangeness.

"What should we do with the boats?" Four asked.

"Just," the old coroner began. Men began to file off the barges in twos and fours, brushing past Beckett and the gendarme captain. "Just hold them. For now."

"The goods on them, though—"

"Can fucking wait. I don't want to have to sort through this crap again when it turns up at the wholesalers down river. Hold the boats until we're done."

"Yes, sir," said Four, as he turned to shout the order back to his men.

A gust of wind whipped at Beckett's long coat, and he shoved his hands into his pockets, where he discovered, much to his surprise, a small scrap of paper. Mindful that this was probably a hallucination as well, Beckett did not at first draw it out, but instead listened to the wind, the gendarmes shouting, the distant sound of rifle and cannon that echoed from his past. When the paper refused to relinquish its solidity, he drew it out and read it, but was still unconvinced that it was real.

"Gorud," he called to the therian. The ape-man obediently loped closer. "Gorud. Do you read?"

The therian shrugged beneath his ill-fitting coat. Rain had plastered his fur to the side of his head. "My people are not adept at this. I have some sufficiency at it."

Beckett handed him the paper. "What does this say?"

"Truce," Gorud read. "Two days. Hardwicke's, nine o'clock. John."

The old coroner snapped his head around with alarming ferocity. The note, had the note been in his pocket in the morning? Before the raid? He couldn't remember, but he was sure he would have noticed. Someone must have slipped it into his coat just now, which meant one of the men, the gendarmes. One of them was a spy for Anonymous John.

The men that had brushed passed him on the docks had all separated, gone off towards their homes or back to the barracks, and even so, there was nothing remarkable about any of them. Ordinary looking men, with the ordinary compliment of eyes and noses, scars and moustaches, garbed appropriately. How long had the note even been in his pocket? Had there been someone earlier, a stranger on the street? Someone at the fish vendor's? Had Anonymous John snuck into Beckett's house and left it in his coat the night before?

It didn't matter now; if there had been an opportunity to snag Anonymous John, it was certainly long gone. Beckett turned the paper over in his hand, and smiled grimly. If John wanted a truce, it could only mean one thing: Elijah Beckett was winning.

TWENTY-NINE

I have discarded the mechanism for now, while I examine its course of principle action. For the imprecision engine to function effectively, the mind must be built according both to intention, that shall motivate its continued action, and restriction, that shall determine both which actions are good, and therefore repeatable, and which actions are sinful, and therefore must not be repeated. I must create a system of interactions that is the human experience in microcosm. I admit that the opportunity has made me feel almost giddy. This is my chance to finally exorcise the animal darkness from the mind, to create a thing of perfect, inerrant reason, a life truly dedicated to the preservation of life, to the advancement of knowledge, to all of man's noble aspirations that are dragged back into the muck of his primal urges.

--from the journal of Harcourt Wolfram, 1785

Old Hardwicke's restaurant had been a staple of upper-class cuisine for more than a hundred years when it was destroyed by the launch of *The Excelsior*. The owner, Thom Ennering-Hardwicke—venerable patriarch of a small family that had received Estimation for the preparation of an unusually delicious bowl of smoking bishop for Agon XIII Vie-Gorgon—immediately set about rebuilding his establishment at the edge of Lantern Hill. He quickly and happily discarded years of tradition by refusing to employ old-fashioned Trowthi chefs, and abandoned the customary menu of Trowth's old businesses—no more meat pies, smoked fish, boiled vegetables, boiled fish, smoked fish pies, or heavy, gravy-smothered roasts. Instead, he began hiring expatriate Sar-Sarpek chefs, indulging in their predilection for cream sauces, meat that had been wrapped in other kinds of meat, and things cooked with wine.

As Trowth's distant Corsay colony began to thrive, Thom Ennering-Hardwicke's grandson—the now-aged Bardo Hardwicke, who was no longer

Esteemed due to Thom's unfortunate decision to marry a Sar-Sarpek woman — began adding the new Corsay cuisine to his menu: peppers, fruit, fish eggs and small fried birds all joined the Sar-Sarpek fare.

Despite its changes of face and menu, one thing was always consistent about Hardwicke's: it always thrived. Even during the Ettercap War, when wallets and purses had been strained to their breaking point, the well-to-do scratched together the money for the occasional night at Hardwicke's.

How, precisely, Anonymous John could get a reservation there was not something Beckett considered. The reason for this particular restaurant seemed obvious, though: the building was very old, and predated the enclosure of the Arcadium; the first two storeys both had exits into that unnavigable mess of tunnels and alleys. There was no effective way to discreetly police all possible entrances, as any men stationed in the Arcadium would be spotted fairly easily in those narrow passageways.

And Beckett was certainly not interested in doing anything *except* policing the entrances. He had no intention, at all, of negotiating a truce with Anonymous John; his thoughts were instead occupied with how he could best secure the restaurant with his men, and seize John when the criminal mastermind finally showed himself. Not that he really expected that; there's no way John could have really believed Beckett would do anything but try to trap him.

Still, Beckett would have been embarrassed if, in second-guessing John, he hadn't brought any men, and then the man had showed up. It would have made for frustratingly smug dinner conversation, anyway. The old coroner had established three tables with pairs of gendarmes at them — he had gone to great lengths to ensure that the men were scrubbed clean and well-dressed, but still felt the effect lacked a certain authenticity. There were patrols of gendarmes taking long circuits through the Arcadium, making the alleys look unusually busy, but hopefully nothing more than that. In a fit of inspiration, Beckett, sent four of the therians employed by the Coroners to take up positions on nearby rooftops. Trowth was such a claustrophobic city, and a city with such an abundance of intricate stonework, that climbing about on its roofs and gables could certainly pose no more difficulty for the ape-men than climbing around whatever jungle environment they'd been bred to. This, at least, was Beckett's considered opinion.

Old Bardo Hardwicke had conceded to Beckett's demands, had displaced his usual customers, and turned his beloved restaurant into a trap for a degenerate criminal, all while glaring furiously beneath his heavy white brows. He had the weathered, sour look, the thin, hunched shoulders and the bony, clutching hands of a man more than a hundred years passed his prime who was simply too irritated with the world to permit himself a graceful exit from it. Bardo Hardwicke would never give Trowth the satisfaction that he had left it willingly.

The old man had agreed to Beckett's demands, because the coroner had threatened to simply shut his restaurant down, permanently, as he was able to do under the expanded powers that Stitch had acquired for him. Hardwicke had agreed that one night of bad business was better than unemployment, but he hadn't been happy about it — though, in Beckett's defense, it did not seem that Bardo Hardwicke had ever been especially happy about anything during his long and, presumably, very miserable life.

Beckett arrived early, and chose a table in the middle of the room, with his back to the door, relying on his men to warn him if someone came in. He sat alone at his small table, not far from Bardo himself, who sat against the far wall and glowered at Beckett. Beckett glowered back. For two hours, well-past the agreed upon meeting time, these two men glowered at each other. If furious glares could produce actual friction, the angry sparks generated by such a glowering contest would have easily burnt Hardwicke's to the ground, and probably caused significant damage to all of Lantern Hill. In fact, despite the generally-accepted insubstantiality of ferocious gazes, a few of the gendarmes in the restaurant that night privately harbored suspicions that, had the evening gone on just a little longer, something actually might have caught fire.

In the end, the wave of eleven o'clock bells washed over Hardwicke's, and Beckett accepted as true what he had privately suspected all along: Anonymous John wasn't coming. He'd either spotted the trap and stayed away, or else he'd intended some other plan that Beckett had successfully foiled. In any case, the evening had turned out to be a dud.

Hardwicke escorted Beckett to the door — as pleased as he'd ever been — and Beckett's men escorted him for fifteen blocks back to Queen's Riot Close. Two more gendarmes were stationed by Beckett's door, in case Anonymous John or his men had decided to attack him personally. Elijah Beckett nodded curtly to them, then decided that he had no desire to sleep.

"Going for a walk, boy," he told them. "Stay here, I won't be long."

The driving rain of the last few days had mercifully dwindled to a faint spritzing, leaving Trowth's cobbled streets slick and glimmering beneath its blue streetlights. Beckett walked towards the river, following the robust stream in the gutter that carried scraps of paper and horse and dog excrement along with it. The water ran downhill along Eiger street, where the shops' wooden signs clattered in the chilly wind, and finally across Front Street, where it burbled gently into the Stark. The night was quiet, and Beckett was struck by how empty the teeming city could seem, like an abandoned temple, or a skull hollowed out by time and neglect, black windows like empty eyes, staring lifelessly into empty streets.

Beckett tasted the sharp, metallic twinge that was his craving for veneine, and a dull throbbing in the bridge of his nose that he'd come to associate with a need for more djang. He resolved to ignore both of these, until he had stared sufficiently into the black waters of the Stark. He would not, he decided, use the drugs at any insistence except his own, regardless of what his body clamored for. He leaned on the granite balustrade that protected the edge of Front Street from the river, and put his addiction and decay from his mind.

While he watched, the old coroner became conscious of a man shuffling down the street towards him. Beckett pretended he could not see the stranger, though he doubted the stranger believed him. The man wore a heavy, brown wool coat against the rain, and he had tangled, matted hair beneath a floppy hat. His shoulders were hunched, and he dragged one leg as though it had been injured and never healed properly. He was precisely the sort of malformed beggar that most of Trowth's citizens were accustomed to ignoring—a twisted, bedraggled shape that fit so perfectly into Trowth's crooked corners as to be practically invisible.

The man shuffled to a spot along the railing an arm's reach from Beckett, and he, too, stared out at the water. Close-up, Beckett could see that he was very ugly, with a face that resembled the product of a man attempting to carve a gargoyle from a potato, and then giving up halfway through. For all his lumpen ugliness, though, there were no signs of sores or disease, nothing weeping or bleeding or oozing, as any such signs might attract undue attention.

"It's you, isn't it?" Beckett asked, after a few moments, still not looking.

The man said nothing, at first, then gradually reached up to touch his bulbous nose. He pinched at it, and it came away from his face with a faint sucking sound. The ugly man pulled at his cheekbones then, and they came away as well, followed by two marbles where his eyes and been, and lips that looked like fat leeches. He pulled of his hat and a wig of tangled hair, and stood up straight, discarding his hunched shoulders along with his old coat.

What remained was a man in a dark suit, or something that might, for a distance, be mistaken for a man. He had no face at all, just smooth flesh from scalp to chin: pale, clammy skin like a corpse's, stretched taught over the smooth expanse where eyes, nose, and mouth should have been. How he could see, or hear, or speak was a mystery; what had happened to cause such a particular deformity was likewise unknown. Not so his identity.

"Anonymous John," said Beckett.

"The very same," said John, leaning back on the balustrade. His jaw did not move when he spoke, and his voice had a strange vibrato, as though it were produced by a phonograph. "I am pleased to finally meet you."

"Are you?" Beckett asked. "You might have shown up when you promised, then. Saved me a long evening."

"Yes, that was inconsiderate of me," John agreed. "Or, who knows? Perhaps I was testing you, to see if you'd really arrest me if I showed up. Of course you would have, not considering at all that I might have made extensive plans to be enacted in my absence, simultaneously acquitting me of wrongdoing and ensuring that troubles would still plague the city while I was in prison."

"For a while." Beckett shrugged. "Your men would run out of orders, eventually. With you gone, the organization would fall apart."

"Assuming you could hold me, which you can't." Anonymous John chuckled. "Or, perhaps you could? Life is full of surprises. Hah, that's what I like about you, Detective-Inspector Beckett. You don't care about plans or consequences. I've spent a lot of time watching your coroners, you know. I have compiled profiles on all of your men. You were the only one that ever really concerned me."

"Why is that?" Beckett asked, as he slowly let his right hand drift towards his revolver.

"Because you're a killer. You've decided what's right, and you know exactly what you're willing to do in order to get it. Which is: anything. Anything in the name of what's right. You're probably thinking about killing me, right now. Of course, it'd be rude to shoot a man in the middle of a conversation, but you don't care about that, do you?"

"Tell me it wouldn't be worth it."

"It might be, but it'd be dangerous. After all, what about my men? The sharpshooters I've positioned on the roof, waiting for you to make a sudden movement?"

He could be bluffing, Beckett thought. *He probably is; no way to know that I'd come this way tonight. He must have been following me.*

"Of course, I could be bluffing," John admitted. "But I've obviously come here with a purpose in mind. Hear me out, at least, and if you don't like what I have to say, feel free to test me."

Most people who had met Anonymous John knew what Beckett was now realizing: it is virtually impossible to read the truth from a man who has no face. Ordinarily, Beckett would have just shot him, anyway, but the layers of Anonymous John's planning had made him suspicious. If the man did have a scheme, or was interested in making an offer, it might be useful for Beckett to know about it.

"All right," Elijah Beckett agreed, without relaxing his hand. "Tell me."

"Hah. All right. Do you know the first thing that the founders of Trowth built, after they discovered the ruins of Gorgon and Demogorgon's city?"

"A clock," Beckett said. Everyone knew that.

"A clock, yes. It was a very old, primitive thing, with great stone wheels, powered by the river Stark. It's still in the heart of the Royal Palace, deep beneath the Royal Hill. Do you ever wonder about that? A whole city, a nation, an Empire, with a stone clock as its beating heart. That is the people of Trowth in microcosm: complex, yes, but rigid, predictable, regular. We are a nation in which every man knows his place, and every man is pleased to fulfill it, and for two thousand years, everything in Trowth has happened precisely the way that it's supposed to."

"I don't know," Beckett said, thinking of Ettercap spies, of men transfigured by aetheric energies, of dreams poisoned, dead resurrected, and the laws of nature violated, "that I agree with that."

"You wouldn't, of course," Anonymous John agreed. "You are employed by the crown to ensure that things do happen the way they're supposed to. You and the coroners, alone, are permitted to encounter those things which violate the precision-engineered society of the Empire. When something violates that natural order, when someone reaches up to scrawl his name across the stone-carved laws of Trowth, it is Elijah Beckett's responsibility to slap him back down."

"And that's you? The man scrawling his name or what have you? You're a hero for being a criminal?"

"In my own, small way, yes. I am a cog that does not know its place. But if you knew, Beckett! My principal, he is the one that is genuinely new, the man rejecting the hide-bound traditions of the Empire. I have made a fortune breaking the law, you see, but he is the one that has seen the outcome: Trowth will collapse beneath the weight of its own history if it does not change. And he is the one who will change it."

"And who is your principal?" Beckett had assumed that John was the top dog in this scenario; perhaps the night would turn out not to be a waste, after all.

"A secret," John replied, and if he could have smiled, Beckett suspected he would have, "even from me."

"So, what do you want from me? Want me to switch sides, maybe? Give over to your new man to save the Empire?"

Anonymous John turned to Beckett, fixing that unnerving, faceless gaze on him, then turned back out to the water. "That's my assignment. To gauge your willingness to switch teams. I've been advised that, if you thought the stakes were high enough, there's a small possibility that you'd be interested."

"And what are the stakes?"

"High," John replied. "Very high. The Empire is at risk, yes, but so is our very species. So, perhaps, is all life as we understand it. I can't tell you how, or why; I can only tell you that the risk is…unfathomable."

"And I'm just supposed to take your word for it?" Beckett began to reach for his revolver again. "A criminal? A liar and manipulator? A murderer?" He closed his hand on the grip of the weapon, and felt rage boiling up inside him. *Valentine. You killed Valentine.* "Sorry I'm not convinced. What's plan B?" If there were no men aiming at him, John would be trying to close the distance, so the best choice would be to back away, draw and fire.

"I told him you wouldn't be." If there were sharpshooters, John would want to open the distance, so the best choice would be to move forward, strike at his face, then draw the gun. "Plan B is to kill you, ob —"

Beckett leapt forward, swinging at John's head and pulling the gun from its holster. His clenched fist met the soft, spongy meat of Anonymous John's face. Too late, Beckett realized that John wasn't trying to move away at all, but had accepted the blow and moved forward, pinning Beckett's gun against his body. *No sharpshooters,* Beckett thought, as he felt an icy brand between his ribs, the horrific, alien sensation of a foreign object violating his body. *Wrong guess.*

He tried to scream as John wrenched the knife from his side, but the pain was overwhelming; it paralyzed his lungs, and the only sound Beckett could make was a choked gagging. His hand spasmed and fired off a round, that ricocheted harmlessly from the street.

"It's a dangerous plan," Anonymous John admitted, as Beckett slumped against the railing. "I have no idea what will happen to your army without you in charge. But you can't argue that it isn't worth the risk." John slipped an arm under Beckett's and twisted his body.

Beckett felt his hips bang against the stone balustrade, then the sickening sense of weightlessness as he fell. He crashed into the freezing waters of the river. He struggled for a moment, but his clothes were soaked through and impossibly heavy before he could get his face above the water. The cold raced in through his limbs, killing the little sensation that he had left, as he drifted downward, carried by the current, the light closing off above him.

He attempted another half-hearted kick and then surrendered. His sense of being dwindled to a thin slash in the center of his body, a dimensionless presence surrounded by the empty shell of flesh. The pale speck of light above him, dimly blue, perhaps a street lamp, grew smaller and smaller, until all that was left was a hard blue spot, and then only the afterimage of the spot, a trick of his mind, desperate to believe that there was still some light left.

Well, Beckett thought, as the dark finally overtook him. *At least it doesn't hurt.* He had a brief glimpse of tall brass towers, melted like sticks of wax, and then, nothing.

THIRTY

For the third time in a year, Skinner found herself evicted from her home. This time, there had not even been any movers to threaten, nor any luggage to collect—all of her belongings were still locked up inside the house on Comstock Street. It was simply cordoned off, guarded by a few Lobstermen who politely but firmly insisted that she was not permitted inside. Where the Comstock Vie-Gorgon's were was anyone's guess; popular opinion had it that they'd gotten wind of their upcoming troubles, and made immediate haste for their luxurious country estates. Skinner sat in the rain outside the house, and considered her options. Again. They were sparse. Again. The familiarity of the situation did nothing to alleviate the despair that she felt creeping in around the edges, kept at bay only by a firm optimism that she would think of something.

It was Karine who came to the rescue, this time, and the thought of having to have to be *rescued* once again set Skinner's teeth on edge. Two years ago she'd had steady work apprehending criminal scientists. Six months ago she'd written the most popular play in the history of the Empire. Now, she couldn't even afford the train ticket she'd need to return to the countryside and live with her ailing father. When she thought about it, about William Gorgon-Vie, about *Emperor* William, fat and smug on his throne, making the laws that served no apparent purpose except keeping half of the population out of work and beholden to the other half—pets, essentially, kept around to be looked at and bear children, but nothing more, not even permitted to feed themselves—her stomach turned into a mass of churning bile. She wanted to spit in his eye. She wanted...Skinner wasn't sure what she wanted, wasn't sure of anything except that she was ferociously angry at someone, and felt more than a little guilty for snapping at Karine.

"Fine." Skinner said. "It doesn't matter."

"It's just, I'm sure you'd be welcome. Even if it's just for a few days. We haven't much, of course, but..."

Skinner waved her off, flushed a little with shame, but still too angry to apologize. "Fine."

This was how Elizabeth Skinner found herself in Bluewater, in one of the ramshackle tenements inhabited by Trowth's indige citizens. Bluewater was a site of frequent skirmishes in the Architecture War, but little strategic value, and the whole thing had, in recent years, fallen into the gauche and modern style of the Ennering-Vies. Or so Skinner was told; she had little personal interest in the architecture of the city beyond which families preferred high ceilings, as this affected her telerhythmia. Valentine had once tried to explain the many different styles and aesthetic philosophies that underpinned Trowth's most complex and byzantine feud, but he might as well have been describing castles on the moon for all Skinner cared.

The Ennering-Vies preferred low ceilings, which made Karine's family home cramped and hot, and preferred not to spend very much money on houses in Bluewater, which made them leaky and humid. This discomfort was compounded by the unusual numbers that the Akori presented. This group was how Karine introduced them—though she also took the time to provide a given name for every person present, Skinner had not been able to remember any except for Pogo—and Skinner was not sure if "Akori" was a patronym, or some manner of clan affiliation, or simply a regional appellation. Certainly, the tiny house was filled with far more people than might reasonably be expected in any immediately family. Twenty-two at the least, by Skinner's count, though the noise and the panoply of voices made it difficult to be sure.

Though she was determined to spend the night sulking, one of Karine's relatives—possibly an uncle or an older cousin—was determined to cheer her up. This was Pogo, and his constant overtures of good cheer were the reason that Skinner remembered his name. Karine had introduced the man as the *ramo*, which Skinner recalled was some kind of priest. Hardly a minute passed that he wasn't regaling her with a story about how he had to stab Jorgi once for violating the tabu, or the time he'd found a sixty crown note in the gutter. When he wasn't telling stories, he was pressing cups of hot mulled wine into Skinner's hand, or offering her a bowl of starchy fish soup. His charm was aggressive and very nearly contagious, though Skinner struggled hard against it.

In truth, she was happy to just hear someone speaking Trowthi; the family spoke Indt incomprehensibly rapidly, and the only words of that strange tongue that Skinner knew were certain profanities she had hear Karine utter in times of distress. While they found liberal use in conversation, they did not lend any particular clarity to the topic under discussion. Certain words, like *malaka*, which Skinner knew for a fact to be a malign slander regarding the gender and

181

species of a person's sexual partners, were used with verve and laughter, belying the word's clear intent; others, like *lobber*, which was the slang term that the Indige used for the Lobstermen and ought to be fairly neutral in its value, was said with the sort of unadulterated venom that one would suppose was ordinarily reserved only for the worst *malakas*.

Only the strongest and most committed of miseries can withstand such a relentless onslaught of charity and hospitality, and Skinner found her resolve weakening. The hatred she felt towards the Emperor was forgotten quickly, of course; her anxiety about her future took longer, but it, too, began to evaporate after the fifth time that Pogo tried to tell his "Fat Trolljrman" jokes. Only an icy pain in her heart when she thought of Valentine remained. The thin layer of ichor beneath the silver plate on her eyes had dissolved her tears before they could reach her cheeks, but she'd shed them, nonetheless, and still sometimes felt more coming. It wasn't that she had *liked* Valentine, precisely. He had, in fact, been more than a little annoying. It was just that she missed him, as though she'd grown accustomed to his bumbling good nature. For all the petty inconveniences he'd caused (and Skinner couldn't help but feel guilty recalling them, knowing that he had lost his life seeking to provide her one great convenience) Valentine had been a good man, and the world always suffers when a good man dies.

Skinner coughed, and realized that she hadn't been listening to Pogo's joke.

"You see?" He was saying. "Because he wanted *grapes*. Haha!"

"Yes, it's very funny."

"I know," Pogo said. "I try and tell Jorgi" — this was the man that he'd stabbed in the leg two weeks ago — "This is a funny joke, I tell him. He doesn't listen, though. Stupid, huh!"

"Oh, Miss Skinner!" Karine's voice sprang up out of the forest of Indt. "Do you know this?" The indige girl passed her a wooden object, which Skinner ascertained to be some kind of stringed instrument; like a small guitar, but with a teardrop-shaped body. "I have seen you play something like it. Aga *bought* it —" she added, not disguising her contempt for Aga's poor financial decisions. " — but he doesn't know how to play it or even tune it."

Aga responded with an impassioned defense in Indt.

"Well, it's because you *are* an idiot, Aga. Miss Skinner, do you know anything about it?"

Skinner lightly touched the instrument, counted the frets, plucked at the strings. "Well, it's basically like my guitar, but with four strings, instead of six, and a little smaller. These three strings are tuned in fourths, this middle one is tuned to the third of the string below it." She plucked at the strings again, then fiddled with the tuning keys until they made a proper chord. "Not out of tune at all." She smiled slyly. "Good choice, Aga."

"Oh, please don't get him started, miss, or I'll never heard the end of it." The entire room—all twenty-two or so indige cousins held their breath expectantly. "Can...can you play it?"

"Karine, I can't. I don't even know..."

Pogo interrupted, saying something softly to Karine in their native language. Karine responded enthusiastically, then said to Skinner. "Please, miss? One song, just to show Aga how to do it, then he'll play it for the rest of the night."

Skinner grimaced at the thought of that, but relented. She hadn't had the chance to play for several days, and it wasn't all that dissimilar from the guitar. It was practically the same thing, really. "All right. I guess. Let's see. Something simple, obviously." She plucked aimlessly for a few seconds, then began to strum the chords for "By Sacred Text Redeemed"—an old rondel that had been one of her favorites. The instrument had a bright, jangling sound, that gave the song a sense of whimsy lacking in most interpretations.

After the first refrain, one of the men began humming a counterpoint in a low tenor. Another began tapping on the table. Two of the women joined in, taking turns switching between soprano and alto parts. They sang in Indt; the words flowed like water. The women invented melodic variations on the spot. More voices joined in, as the whole family took turns playing with the song. When there was a pause, Skinner grinned wildly, and began improvising her own tune, and a mad joy bubbled up inside her as she did, so that by the time the song ended she couldn't help but laugh out loud.

Skinner played again.

THIRTY-ONE

Fletcher had managed to preserve a fat cigar during the interminable voyage to the Dragon Isles, and he'd lit it up while they rowed ashore in the longboats. The cherry glowed red, almost unnoticed in the morning light, while the men passed it around and sucked on smoke. They were silent, grimly silent, unwilling to break the tension even for a laugh. Fletcher looked the worst—he was pale and twitched, and his eyes kept darting around, scouring the unforgiving landscape of the island of Karcaag, looking for Word only knew what.

Cook wasn't much better, though. He sat still, but sweated abominably; before the men had even clambered into the longboats, he was already soaked through with salt water. Even Sergeant Garret was dead silent, and the fact that the men were free from his constant haranguing was a small mercy.

Two thousand marines climbed onto the pristine white beaches. Rocky cliffs reared above them, a dusty trail switching back and forth across their faces. Atop the cliffs was the city of Kaarcag itself, walled, blocky, shrouded in mist and impenetrable. This was the home of one of the Dragon Princes, and whatever manner of creatures he shared his island with. It was surely not all reanimates, and yet Beckett found it hard to believe that there were men there, living, human men who would willingly submit themselves to being cattle for the Dragon Prince's thirst for blood.

The island was as dry as a desert. There was no life visible—no small scurrying rodents, no birds, hardly any plants except for the elephant roses, which looked like the dismembered feet of their namesakes. These had no blossoms or leaves, only thick gray stalks and roots that plunged directly into the rock. Far above, on the cliffline, some strange, twisted trees dotted the landscape.

The sun rose and beat heavily on the men as they disembarked. For two hundred years, the Sarkany Rend had plagued the empire, raiding Trowth's ships, campaigning against Trowth's ambitions, trying to seize territory claimed by the Empire. Only once, six months before, had Trowth ever delivered a resounding defeat to the Dragon Princes, chasing them from the nation's shores in a scheme engineered by Mr. Stitch himself — long mistrusted by the people of his country, Stitch had finally earned their acclaim by thrashing the armada of the same princes that many people believed he secretly served. After Abenhrad, there was no question whose side Stitch was on, and no question as to how much the Empire valued him.

Now, for the first time in history, Trowth controlled the Sanguine Straits. Though Stitch had cautioned against an expedition, Arcon III Vie-Gorgon vowed that he would strike at the very heart of the Dragon Isles. Such a feat was uniformly deemed impossible and, indeed, it proved to be so. Kaarcag was the northernmost of the Isles, practically an outpost, and the only piece within striking distance.

Beckett drew long on the cigar, felt the hot smoke lacerate his lungs. He could feel his heart jumping in his chest, and was unaccountably frightened that someone might notice his quickened pulse. He passed the cigar back to Fletcher and took his shift on the oars, as they beached the longboat. The men shipped their oars and leapt into the soft sand. They took twenty minutes to unload muskets, swords, cannons, and packs, and formed up at the foot of the hills. They had been told that the daylight hours were the best time to strike at the Dragon Princes, who must be asleep in their crypts when the sun rose. The island seemed deserted enough — there was widespread speculation, nervous chatter that flitted among the soldiers, that perhaps the main body of their forces was elsewhere. Perhaps the danger of the princes had been exaggerated through the years. Perhaps this wouldn't be so hard after all.

It was a lie, and they all knew it. You couldn't see the shores of Kaarcag, barren of life, of weapons, of fortification, and not know that Czarneck, the chimericist, was waiting for them.

They marched up the hill double-time, and when no defenders had appeared, the men grew confident. They told jokes. Beckett, to his dismay, was near the end of the line — what veterans called the column's ass. He could see a black river of marines on the march, eager to strike down Trowth's long-hated enemy.

"...I told him that's not my cutlery, son, that's my *knife*," Fletcher said, grinning, when the voices came. The men ahead surged back, and the drums beat an erratic time. "What? What is that?" Something was happening to the drummers up the line; some tried to keep tempo, others swung erratically about, trying to fight off...smoke? What looked like smoke, or some tiny foglets.

There was an ominous whistling then, and more men screamed. Dull thuds. And then bodies rose up from the dust.

Thousands of them, everywhere, clawing up from the ground, men with concave skulls (*Dummies*, Beckett had time to think, *they're called Dummies, men bred with holes in their brains*), bursting from the earth and setting about the marines with teeth and nail, some with guns that they fired aimless into the host, but their imprecision didn't matter, there were many, too many of them, ten thousand or more.

("What is that?" Fletcher asked again, before a bullet hit him in the side of the face. He stared blankly, still uncomprehending, as blood trickled from his nose.)

The tide turned and the men ran, Beckett trying to keep his feet in the vanished discipline and fleeing soldiers. They ran for the boats, as more dummies sprang up, sinking crooked yellow teeth into necks and arms.

(A dummy clutched at Beckett's arm, and he saw the thing's face, the livid purple dent about its left eye, the wall-eyed gaze, sweaty drooling thing, Beckett smashed at its face with the butt of its gun until it let go.)

More fog came then, green and swirling like a living thing. *It is a living thing*, Beckett realized this, too, as his mind had detached itself from the frenzied rush for the boats, commenting with distant curiosity. *Czarneck is the chimericist. Repurposing living things is his nature.* More teeth and hands clutched at him, while he tried to wrap his scarf around his mouth, to keep the gas out.

Cook stared at him, fallen to the ground. Beckett tugged at his arm. "On your feet," he shouted, voice muffled by his scarf, "come on, soldier, up!" The green fog crawled from Cook's nostrils, drawing blood out with it, suspending it in tiny drops in the air. More cannons sounded, and more detonations. The green fog rose in pillars, and reached out with crooked tendrils for tender lungs.

Blood landed on the soil, and the elephant roses bloomed in waves, slow explosions of tiny red flowers; the fat dry stumps sucking up the last of the living men. A carpet of red roses spread out from the trail, washed over the island's surface, followed the fleeing marines, as the dummies harassed them.

Beckett made it back to the boats, tried to drag Sergeant Garret back in with him. He held on to the Sergeant's arms, braced his body against the gunwhale, tried to pull him on board. Garret opened his mouth, but no sound came out, only a coughing sound (*Or is that the guns? Is he making any sound?*). Dark stains appeared beneath his nose, and at first Beckett thought it was blood, but it wasn't blood it was two thin, dark green vines that grew from inside his head and reached back up towards his face, sprouting thorns and scratching at his eyes. They wrapped around Beckett's arms, too, plunged their jagged thorns in and the pain was incomprehensible.

Beckett screamed but held on, held on as they crept up his forearms like fire and Garrett began thrashing madly, held on as the crept up past his elbows and he convulsed...tried to hold on but couldn't, he let Garrett go and the sergeant's weight wrenched the thorns free from Beckett's arms. Garrett fell back into the water, arms still reaching out, face still imploring for succor, vines and waves swallowing him up.

The sun beat down on them, all unmoved by the sight. As the longboat skimmed into the water, Beckett saw Kaarcag, once dead brown and gray, now red and beautiful with blood and roses in the morning light.

THIRTY-TWO

Back when there were still newspapers, agitators of various stripes and dispositions would often argue that one or more laws, or failures of law, or events or institutions or what have you were absolutely essential to the stability of the city. Essays on the subject—suggesting that a failure to support the new tariff legislation on linen would lead to the collapse of the Empire within the year, or that permitting the Working Woman to return to gainful employment would bring about the city's imminent doom, or that if the Public Theater's production of *The Country Midwife* were not cancelled at once then an entire generation of children would grow up to be moral degenerates—were actually quite common. In the cut-throat world of "printed materials sold on street corners," it was always the most alarmist demagogue who received the most attention, and therefore the highest sales. Consequently, Trowth's doom was predicted every three or four days, and so far these street-corner prognosticators had never quite seen their predictions born out.

Perhaps this is because no contributor to the broadsheet ecosphere had ever considered the fact that the Empire's integrity might rest on the back of one crusty old detective in the Coroners Division of the Royal Guard. Had broadsheets and streetcorner pamphlets still been legal, they would be filled with dire warnings about impending catastrophe, now that Elijah Beckett had disappeared. In truth, they'd probably be closer to the truth with these predictions than ever, as chaos swept rapidly through the city in the old detective's absence. Without Beckett's brutal, guiding will, the army that he'd assembled quickly dissolved into a mass of vigilantes. They attempted to continue with Beckett's raids, though guided now by fervor instead of intelligence. They raided docks and offices, started riots with gangs and stevedores.

Not a day went by without at least one bloody, vicious fight breaking out in the streets—some unacceptably close to New Bank or the Royal district. Of course, because there was no longer any news, no one had any idea where the fights were occurring, or when, or why. Numbers and violence were magnified by gossip, which served to be the only entertainment that anyone had left. It was fairly uncommon for people to leave their homes very often in the avalanche of rainfall that constituted late spring, but even these rare trips had been curtailed. People stayed in their homes, feeling besieged, making plans for escape or emigration, or otherwise simply hunkering down and crossing their fingers.

James Ennering, formerly communications officer for the 16th Quartermasters, formerly reconnaissance partner for Elijah Beckett, now found himself the *de facto* head of the remains of the Coroners. Most of the men and trolljrmen, and all but one of the therians, had abandoned the division after Beckett's disappearance. James and Gorud sat at what had been Beckett's desk in the old pressgang office. Thut Akh Dun, one of the three remaining trolljrmen, was helping them attend to the handful of arrest reports that were still coming in. It was humid in the office — spring was like that, as it seemed one could not go anywhere without tracking in a small river's worth of moisture — and James found it difficult to pay attention, perpetually distracted by the syncopated dripping of water from the eaves. Thun Akh Dun remained steadfast, though, in his determination to read every single report submitted by every single gendarmerie in Trowth.

With Becket gone, most of the gendarmes had stopped bothering to write reports at all; most of what came in now were notices from the more well-to-do districts, which had long been governed like police-states, anyway. Though even these notices were largely useless.

"Item: two men, miscreants. Arrested, administered corporal punishment, discharged," Thut Akh Dun said. "Item —"

"Wait. It doesn't say what they did? Their names?"

"No," Thut Akh Dun replied. "Item: one woman, prostitution. Arrested, incarcerated. Item: two women —"

The trolljrman was interrupted by a commotion at the door. James projected his hearing toward it immediately, rapping lightly across the intruders who were barging into the office. Knocker etiquette prohibited such a gross intrusion using the telerhythmia, but James Ennering was exhausted beyond measure, and no longer interested in knocker etiquette.

There were two men, large men with thick chests, dragging a third between them, a man to whom they shouted repeated unsavory epithets.

"Gorud..." James whispered. "Who are they?"

"One is Beckwith Harker, he was a gendarme captain. One is a man, I do not recognize him, but he wears gendarmerie apparel. The man they have prisoner is badly beaten, I do not know him. Ho, there!" Gorud raised his voice, using the remarkable capacity for mimicry in his species to do a serviceable evocation of Beckett's gravelly growl. "What do you think you're doing?"

The sound stopped the men in their tracks, but when they spoke, they spoke to James Ennering. "We picked this one up doing...uh. Loitering, I guess you'd call it."

"Loitering?" James asked.

"It is standing in a public place with an intent to commit mischief," Gorud provided helpfully.

"All right, Captain Harker," James said. "How did you know he intended...mischief? Thank you, Gorud."

"Uhm. Well, I mean look at him. Sorry, beg your pardon there. What I mean is, he looks pretty much like a miscreant. He was skulking, if you take my meaning, looked like he was up to something. Officer's discretion, anyway, sir."

"Fine," James shook his head. He couldn't afford compensation for the man if he'd been arrested wrongly, but at least he could speed up his release. "So, let's call him sufficiently punished, and now you can let him go."

"Beg your pardon, sir, but it's not the arrest that brings us here. It's what he confessed to."

"What he confessed to under duress, you mean? You're talking about the confession that you beat out of him?"

"Well, *sir*," Captain Harker said, not sounding particularly contrite. "Ordinarily I'd be in agreement with you about the unreliability of coerced confession. But this one might be worth listening to you. Here," Captain Harker seized the man by the hair and held his head up. "Tell him, then, what you told me."

The man coughed wetly; James couldn't see what he was coughing up, precisely, but he had his suspicions.

"I don't..." the man said, his voice thick. "I wasn't..."

"Tell him," Harker ordered.

"...I was supposed to. Scout. The palace. For routes in."

The office was at once dead silent.

"Why?" James asked quietly.

"I don't...know. For sure." The man coughed again. "A man hired me to do it."

"Tell him the rest," Harker spat. "Tell him your deadline."

The man swallowed heavily, hesitating, but knowing that he had little in the way of options. "He told me I had to be done. Before the first of summer."

The first. Shit, oh shit, James thought, a deadly anxiety churning in his stomach. The Emperor's Invocation. The only guaranteed, scheduled public appearance of the supreme head of the Empire. "Gorud. I need you to go and find Mr. Stitch. Now."

THIRTY-THREE

Beckett's lungs ached as he gulped in air, choking on the black brine of Cross the Water. He crashed in a bone-rattling heap on the fiery golden metal ground of the City of Brass, and somehow moved through it, melted brass towers swirling up around him, a cascade of color, accelerating rapidly as he fell, or rose, or moved, or else the world moved around him and he was the only place that was standing still. Eyes peered at him from crevices, but were gone in an instant. Black boneless fingers writhed and clutched at him, but had passed on before he could react. Long jaws and snaggle-teeth snapped in the dark. A circle of leprous green light lay beneath the City of Brass, and in an instant the towers were gone, high above him, shimmering clouds as he fell through clean, cold air to that glimmering green ground. Black stones gleamed under pervasive, sourceless light.

Beckett looked around him to see new towers made of black stone, windowless, crooked black fingers reaching up from the poisoned earth, clutching at the sky, stretching up and up. At the base of those towers moved things, incomprehensible things, things that were not so much shapeless as they partook of all shapes, all at once, agglomerations of limb and eye and mouth, utterly alien in construction. Beckett blinked, and in the fraction of a second that his eyes were closed, he saw long jaws again, and sharp teeth, he saw hands reaching out for him.

Blink. The basalt towers loomed again. Green lights like fireflies the size of fists floated in the dark, the eerie luminescence at the source of those mad figures, swirling around each other in an unfathomable dance.

Blink. Jaws and teeth, claws, closer, grabbing for him...

Blink. The towers were close now, close enough that he could reach out and touch them, touch the smooth stone foundations, the vast and seamless architecture. How could there be no seams? No individual stones? Were they carved from some single, vast source? A fallen meteor, the size of a city, etched over countless eons...

Blink. They had him, the hands took hold of him, sharp nails dug into his arms.

Blink. The city was all around him, dwarfing him to insignificance. The black forms of the City of Brass were here too, snuffling around in the dark, their boneless fingers, writhing like...*Leeches, their fingers are leeches*, Beckett thought, as behind them floated those incomprehensible forms with their green glowing, firefly-lights. *The Leech-fingered Men. Hobgoblins from children's stories, now I know I must be dreaming*, the men snuffled at the ground with faces that were just nests of hooked barbs, pulsing and quivering according to some invisible stimuli. The basalt towers shivered, and at once Beckett felt himself the object of their scrutiny, as though the featureless black surface housed innumerable imperceptible windows, through which glared millions of malevolent eyes. The leech-fingered men halted their aimless sniffing, and, as though they were all appendages guided by a single mind, turned their faces towards him. The firefly lights continued to bob in the dark, causing a strange and tangled mass of shadows.

Beckett tried to flee; he could not move so much as he could will the city to move around him. And yet all places appeared to be same place, all routes the same route. Black towers raced by, all leaning together above his head, reaching to some point in the infinite distance, and still he was surrounded by these buildings the height of mountains, by the swarms of leech-fingered men and their gnashing barbed faces.

Blink. The gnashing barbs were sharp teeth again, the green light turned black and cold...

Blink. Surrounded, he was surrounded by these things, as the green lights danced around him, inconsiderate of his presence, engaged in some inscrutable ritual, the invocation of some grand and alien intelligence. The leech-fingered men took hold of his arms, the slimy tendrils digging their sucking mouths into the skin, a thousand tiny pinpricks of pain, and he was sure that they would drain the life from him. They stretched him back, and he could see the tower tops above him, still endlessly reaching with geological slowness toward the shapes above...a circle like the moon, but fat and heavy in the sky and colored with swirls of blue and white.

Blink. Hands squeezing tight, tearing him apart, pulling, his heart felt like it was broken in half...

Blink. The lights floated above him, the shadowy mess of form that supported them writhed in silent confusion all around the edge of his vision, and though no limbs materialized from that sprawling chaos, still he felt something reach out to him, reach past the barrier of his skull and brain, place its toxic

193

fingers inside his mind, a greasy stream of substance that coiled up inside his head, piling upon itself, growing and throbbing in his ears and he screamed, *screamed* then...

...and saw gnashing teeth, each the size of his hand, black eyes and blue light casting the shadows of monstrous faces everywhere...

...felt brass inside his mind, cold metal gears that were stacked up and meshed together, turning and grinding his thoughts away, icy axles of metal thrust deep into his dreams, a machine built in his thoughts and it lurched to shuddering, limping life...

...and he was pulled from the icy water in an explosion of coughing and hacking, cold and pain falling on him like an landslide. His head throbbed like it was trapped in a vise, and there was a mortal agony screaming in his side. His hands and feet were completely numb, and his joints felt full of broken glass and shrapnel, shrieking with blinding pain whenever he tried to move. He lay on his back on a cold stone ledge, beside a river in a vast tunnel. A few fitful phlogiston lamps burned at regular intervals, providing a wash of eerie, flickering light around the people that surrounded him—men with long jaws and huge teeth, black eyes and grey pebbled skin.

Sharpsies, Beckett thought, barely able to form the word as he coughed up dirty river water and struggled mightily to get air into his lungs, *How can there still be sharpsies here?* He closed his eyes then, and it was dark. When he reopened them, he was somewhere else, next to a roaring red fire, stripped of his coat and jacket, listening to more sharpsies argue in their guttural, choking language. Beneath their arguments, faintly as though at some great distance, he thought he could hear gears whirling. One of the sharpsies turned its black eyes on Beckett; the old man tried to move, but found that his body had been weighted down with a hundred tons of lead. The sharpsie pressed a bowl to Beckett's lips, and he felt some hot liquid in his mouth. He tried to spit it back, but his body—desperately hungry and thirsty—betrayed him, swallowing the bitter broth down almost instantly. There was a faint, familiar aftertaste, the metallic tang of veneine...

He opened his eyes again, and the fire had burned down to warm coals, though the room was still stifling hot. *Where is this?* Beckett wondered, as he tried to move again, and still found his body impossibly heavy. Two sharpsies paced restlessly about the room with their springing strides and, briefly, Beckett thought he saw the hunched silhouette of a leech-fingered man. It was gone before he could work any saliva into his painfully dry mouth. He wanted to speak, to call out to his captors, but closed his eyes instead.

He awoke again, for a bare instant, just long enough to read his surroundings. Cold and dark, but aboveground now, it was night-time. Raining. More blue lamps, with no red fire to set off their eerie light. He was hunched painfully in a wooden wheelbarrow, his neck craned at an uncomfortable angle, his arm hanging over the side and quite devoid of circulation. A sharpsie in a long coat and a deep hood that was meant to obscure his enormous predator's teeth pushed the wheelbarrow, creaking along in the dark. The veneine kept him suspended, up and free from the cramped confines of his body. He was aware of the discomfort, of wanting to speak, of his nagging worry, but all of these things were true only at a distance. The only thing that was close to him now was a sudden nearness of the sound of turning gears, as though he were a few steps closer to the imaginary clock. He thought he should try to speak again, but the veneine sapped the urge, and he was content to float, as the light dimmed and he found himself in the dark, again.

"Beckett? Detective Beckett?"

There was a ringing in his ears, and his vision was blurred and muddled. Beckett cough and rasped. "What. What is...?"

"It is professor Helmetag, sir. Ernst."

Beckett bolted upright; his head spun and throbbed, but his vision cleared. He was laying on an operating table, in the warmly-lit corner of Wolfram Hall that had been staked about by professor Helmetag. The sound of spinning gears was gone, but still plucked at the corners of his awareness, now by virtue of its absence—a phantom of missing sound. The veneine high had faded, so now Beckett felt the traditional symptoms of a hangover: throbbing pain in his head, boiling nausea in his stomach, a disinterest in Ernst Helmetag's loud voice.

"Sharpsies," Beckett gasped. "Where...how did they...?"

Helmetag looked befuddled. "There are no sharpsies, here, no. There are no sharpsies in the city at all, I think."

"I saw...how did I get here?"

"You were crumpled up," Helmetag said. "On the doorstep. I thought you were a vagrant at first, I am sorry to say, and was going to report you to the gendarmerie. But I recognized...you have a, ah, a distinctive face..."

"What," Beckett said again. "What happened?"

"You were d—injured, badly. Nearly dead. I have certain...ah." Ernst scratched at his massive moustache. "Certain means. There was some vitality left in your cells that can be re-envigorated..."

Did I hallucinate the sharpsies? And the towers? Why would there be sharpsies in the city? "What do you mean, re-envigorated?"

"Envigorated, anyway. You must understand, it is a delicate thing, the line between the living and the dead, but you were certainly alive."

The old coroner put his face in his hands and sighed. *I would like for one year to go by*, he thought to himself, *without being nearly killed*. "It's fine. Thank. Thank you." His head hurt abominably. "I need...ah." He coughed phlegm from his throat. "Medicine. Veneine."

"Yes, that," Ernst nodded enthusiastically. "I hope you'll understand. You were in withdrawal, you see? This is a very stressful condition for the body, so it was necessary to administer...well, you understand, your veins, many of them were badly damaged, so I needed to take steps..."

Beckett looked up at him. "What steps?" Ernst said nothing. "What steps?" He looked down at his forearms. Affixed to the inside of his right arm, buried directly in the pale flesh and surrounded by livid blood vessels, was a round brass plug.

"It is sealed," Helmetag said quietly, "with ichor, much the way a knocker's eyeplate is. I have attached it directly to your radial artery." He fumbled in a pocket in his apron, and withdrew a few brass modules that looked like rifle shells. "Each one has a pre-measured amount of pharmacy—a combination of veneine, djang extract, and salt water. You plug it in, let me show you..." He set the shell again the plug in Beckett's arm and twisted it.

Beckett gasped as he felt a sting like a needle prick, and then a sensation of spreading cold that rapidly vanished. Immediately, his headache and nausea subsided, the metallic taste in the back of his mouth disappeared.

"You must be careful," Helmetag said. "These are smaller than what I think you must have been dosing yourself with. You *must not* increase the dosage, do you understand? Your body will acclimate, it will become very dangerous."

"How many do you have?" Beckett asked.

"You do understand, yes? You cannot let your craving for the drug determine how much you take..."

"How many?"

Ernst went to his desk and drew out a dark, walnut-colored box. "We use these for testing on animals. I can give you a hundred now, you cannot take more than five a day. You are still sick, yes? Your life is hanging on by a thread..."

If Ernst Helmetag had any further enjoinders to caution, Beckett was not inclined to listen to them. He took the box, gathered up his clothes, and set off into the cold rain. He did not notice the faint, distant sound of spinning gears had begun again.

Thirty-One

Have solved Chretien's problem with the eyes. The matter was trivial. Have simply built artificial eyes using lenses and a tympanum that is sensitive to light, attached to optical ganglions from a man picked from the gallows. Work on the thinking-engine continues.

--from the journal of Harcourt Wolfram, 1785

Skinner had, much to her surprise, fallen into a quite natural rhythm with the Akori—and, for their part, Karine's family were so burdened by numbers anyway that one more couldn't possible harm them. The men spent their days working or looking for work, and brought back what little money they earned. The women spent the days at home, attending to the responsibilities of the household, and kept the money close. With so many to provide for, it was necessary to see every penny spent to maximum effect.

Of course, Skinner brought a skill-set to this arrangement that was unlikely, to say the very least, and fairly impractical to be perfectly honest. It was a fairly unusual event that any member of Karine's extensive family required a secret passage found, a field agent communicated with, something listened to at an extreme distance, or a critically-acclaimed play written. Skinner was determined, however, not to become a useless appendage—and the Akori matriarchs were pleased with Skinner's efforts, even if she did not possess most of the skills necessary for governing a household.

It was decided on, eventually, that Skinner would be the one to take the daily trips to Market Street to purchase groceries. Her sense of smell and touch were expertly acute, making her ideally suited to sorting ripe fruits and vegetables from their counterparts that had been sitting for too long in the cart, and her bitter anger at the injustices of the world combined with a driving need to be useful for something made her a fearsome haggler. This was how she

197

found herself out and about in the city, two days before the Emperor's Invocation, squeezing *gogons*.

It was during this expedition that Skinner heard a familiar voice—a sweet voice, a voice that would have been irresistibly charming if that charm had not been calculated to within an inch of its life. A voice that oozed humor and wit in precisely optimal amounts. A voice, in other words, that could belong to no one other than Emilia Vie-Gorgon.

"Ah, Miss Skinner," she said. "What a pleasure it is to see you."

"Yes? I wish I could say the same." She chose one of the *gogons*—a particularly firm one, that did not seem to have any bad spots on its skin, and added it to what had become a considerable collection of the Indige vegetable.

"You are, no doubt surprised to find me here…"

"I should say that 'surprised' is actually a bit of an understatement," Skinner said. "I'm not sure I have the vocabulary to express quite how astonished I am to meet you here."

"…but I wonder if we could speak privately for a moment?"

Skinner took her burlap sack full of vegetables to the proprietor of the cart. "I don't think, Miss Vie-Gorgon, that that's very likely. In fact, I'm sure it's essentially preposterous. What could we possibly have to speak about? Two crowns," she said to the grocer, who was accustomed to a forceful parsimony from Skinner, and did not argue.

"I need your help with something."

This was so unexpected a turn of phrase that Skinner did not quite know how to respond. She considered simply walking away, considered screaming at Emilia Vie-Gorgon, considered throwing vegetables at her, but settled for a kind of spluttering disbelief, accompanied by a few choked-out words. "You…I…you what…?"

"Improbable as it may seem, I need help, and you're the only one capable of providing it. If we could adjourn somewhere more private, perhaps…"

"I don't think that I'm going to go anywhere with you, Emilia. And while I admit to being desperately curious as to what problem you could face that was so severe it would imbue you with the audacity to come to me asking for help, I find that I am equally moved to give your request the dispassionate rebuff it richly deserves. Good day." Skinner slung her bag over her shoulder and pushed into the crowd on Market Street, slashing viciously at feet and ankles with her cane in order to force a path.

She almost dropped her groceries when she heard Emilia's voice again, right beside her. The woman had a miraculous ability to move with a quietness that would put a cat, or a ghost, or the ghost of a cat, to shame.

"There is a substantial amount of money in it," Emilia began, but Skinner interrupted.

"If you think I've sunk so low that I'd prostitute myself for *you...*" She took a deep breath. "I do not need your money. And if I did need your money, I would starve before I took it."

"Oh, yes, I suspect you would," Emilia said. "But would you see someone else starve, to salve your pride? Your new friends have been very welcoming, haven't they?"

"What...how do you know...?"

"Just a peculiar coincidence, I'm sure," Emilia said, lightly. "Many of the Akori Indige work for my father, did you know? They've a long tradition of work as trainmen and engineers. Something about a resistance to the burns caused by free phlogiston. A lot of indige see employ on Vie-Gorgon trains."

"What are you saying, exactly?"

"Nothing. Why nothing at all! Except that it's fortunate that you've found so many friends who are lucky enough to find paying work in such bad times as we're now faced with." Emilia paused, becoming, yet again, a purely unreadable void. "And, perhaps, wouldn't you like to be able to give them a little more? Wouldn't it be worth it to you to contribute more to their livelihoods than doing their grocery shopping for them? I understand the Crabtree-Ennering-Vies have been building spacious new houses down by the waterfront—houses without leaks or mildew. Imagine if...well. Let me just say that I am willing to offer you let's say.." she lowered her voice. "A thousand crowns."

"A thousand...?"

"Up front. And another thousand afterwards."

Skinner hesitated, and hated herself for doing so, but...two thousand crowns... "What, precisely, would you expect me to do?"

"It's hardly anything at all, really. Just a bit of an errand that I'm afraid my schedule won't allow for. A cousin of mine is taking the train to Seagirt tomorrow, and, fool of a man that he is, he's forgotten one of his suitcases. All I would need is for you to take the suitcase to platform eight, and leave it there for him to collect."

"Aha. Really. And you're going to pay me two thousand crowns for this. For something that you already pay your porters and valets and such for. What's in the suitcase?"

"The contents are private, and the suitcase will be locked. I'd love to be able to tell you, of course, but the Vie-Gorgons in general, and my cousin in particular, greatly value their privacy."

Skinner wanted to be able to tell Emilia to carry her own suitcase around and, perhaps more importantly, where she could stuff her two thousand crowns. But the truth was that Skinner had already begun thinking of ways that she could spend it — of how far a sum like that would go in the hands of the Akori matriarchs. They could provide for their family for years on a sum half that large.

"Why do you need me for this?"

Emilia was dead silent again, the vacuum that she left behind filled immediately with the mélange of Market Street noise. "It seems that the Emperor has been growing increasingly…discomfited, these days. He's instituted a number of security precautions on rail travel. He's instructed the Coroners to search the baggage of any suspicious persons."

"I see. And you think that the Coroners are unlikely to consider me suspicious? And since whatever you've got in that little satchel is something you'd prefer the Emperor didn't see, you'd like me to carry it past the checkpoint for you."

"In a word: yes."

"In a word: no. I'm sorry Emilia…no, that's a lie. I'm actually pleased to tell you that I'm not interested in helping you, no matter how many crowns you dangle in front of me."

"I am sorry to hear that. Well, good day, Miss Skinner. And, do please offer my condolences to Pogo Akori."

"For what?"

"Ah, did I not mention that? Yes, I suppose I must have forgotten. I am such a flighty creature sometimes, you see? My father's been changing over to a new system of engineering on his major rail lines. I'm afraid a good portion of the Akori are going to be out of work by the end of the week."

"You…you would do that?"

"I? Miss Skinner, I don't have any power at all in this situation. You don't think I have my father's ear, do you? That I am directly involved in any of this?"

Skinner found her grip on her cane to be painfully tight, and her thumb hovering above the catch that would let her draw her slender sword from it. One quick slash and one quick thrust, and then the world would not have to suffer Emilia Vie-Gorgon. Emilia Vie-Gorgon and her poisonous treachery, her secretive ambitions, her callous, heartless manipulations…surely it would be worth it? Karine's family unemployed — a temporary hardship, at best. They'd find work again, wouldn't they? There was always work to be had for people willing to do it, and a few hungry nights were a small price to pay to put an end to Emilia Vie-Gorgon's diabolical machinery...

Wasn't it?

"I'll consider it," Skinner said, curtly, and took the narrow stairs down Baker's Close.

That evening, after a warm, spicy stew and a frankly astonishing amount of hot punch, while the Akori chatted about the day's events and told each other jokes, and demanded that Skinner play strings so they could sing along, a messenger arrived at the house in Bluewater.

He knocked crisply and briefly, but was gone by the time Karine had opened the door he was gone. "Miss Skinner," Karine called. "Someone left this for you." There was some muted, hasty discussion in Indt. "I don't know what it is. It looks like a suitcase? And a train ticket?"

THIRTY-TWO

Leaving the suitcase was, in terms of practice, a fairly painless process. The coroners on duty—James Ennering, Gorud, two trolljrmen and three humans that Skinner didn't know—offered her pleasant courtesies as she walked past the checkpoint unsearched. She handed in her ticket, went up to platform eight, set the suitcase down. Waited for a few moments, then left. All perfectly ordinary and simple activities that she had done many times before—speaking with people, carrying suitcases, offering tickets. Now, of course, these ordinary actions were wracked by paranoia; infusing every nerve-ending of her body with sheer terror and dousing her mind in quivering adrenaline, such that she was sure it must shine on her skin like a red beacon telling all passer-by that she was *involved* somehow, that she was guilty of clandestine activities, that she was *suspicious*. She found herself hoping, every time someone spoke to her, that they would notice her sweating, or her nervousness, and demand to search her bag. Every raised voice on the platform, every hurried footstep, became that of a dutiful coroner's, double-checking the last of the parcels, about to expose Skinner and her complicity with the Vie-Gorgons. It would be a relief if James had questioned her more thoroughly, and if he only had, she'd have been pleased to give up and put down the suitcase—which had now become an abominable, impossible weight in her hand—so that she could go to prison and finally ease her troubled conscience.

None of these things happened. It was strange to hear the grand concourse devoid of its usual murmuring ambience, but travel was light today, as many were dissuaded by the sudden appearance of the Coroners. Of course, because the papers had all been seized, and publishing had all been suspended, it was impossible for Skinner to know precisely why such draconian restrictions had been imposed. All she could do was listen to the echoes of her footsteps as she approached platform eight, and wish that she were more suspicious.

Skinner stood on the platform listening. A chilly wind had come in from the harbor. This was common for early summer; the oppressive, sweltering heat wouldn't come for a few more weeks. For now, though, if she hadn't been maddeningly preoccupied with her own troubles, she might have enjoyed that pleasant balance between the warm sunshine on her face and the brisk, salty wind.

It might have struck her as unusual that there was no one else on the platform. Nor, indeed, did there seem to be any trains running at all today. She could hear one, several lines away, moaning steam and creaking, but nothing else. No passengers chattered, no businessmen shuffled their feet. If Emilia Vie-Gorgon's cousin was waiting for his suitcase, he certainly didn't seem to be waiting nearby. Delicately, to avoid attracting the notice of any other knockers, she began to canvass the area with her clairaudience, in a slow, spiral pattern that gradually migrated away from her body.

Rats scuttled on the train tracks. Near the station's entrance, men muttered and made noise. That one train continued its symphony of weird train-noises. Nothing else. "Something's wrong," Skinner said aloud, startled by the volume of her own voice. She set the suitcase down and turned away; with great difficulty, she managed to keep an ear on the suitcase and track of where she was going.

"Everything all right, Miss Skinner?" James' voice. "Get your errand taken care of?"

"I...yes. What errand?"

James hesitated. "I thought...didn't Inspector Beckett send you out here? Or is it the kind of thing..." he dropped his voice to a whisper, "I understand if you can't talk about it."

"Beckett's here?"

"No, ma'am. He's on the train. With the Emperor."

The Emperor...? "James, what's going on?" The worry that had consumed her turned abruptly into a looming sense of catastrophe. Perversely, this seemed to actually calm her nerves; her body was less bothered by the threat of a real, imminent danger than it was by the illusory torments she'd composed for herself.

"You didn't know? I thought Beckett...there's been a plot against the emperor. We're moving him to the summer palace at Dunhill. You're not here for Mr. Beckett."

"I...am. Obviously. But Beckett doesn't tell me everything. Listen. There's a suitcase on platform eight, I need someone to go and get it. I have reason to believe it may be dangerous."

"Gorud," James said. The therian was on his way at once. "How do you know about this?"

"I've been moving in unusual circles, lately. I...would like to avoid running the risk of slander, but I think I may know who is involved in the plot against the Emperor."

"I...hold on." James extended his clairaudience out; Skinner felt the whisper of it as it brushed by her own sensorium. "It's Gorud. He says there's no suitcase."

"You need to get the Emperor off the train. Now."

"It's already left," James said, panic creeping into his voice. "And the clairaudient baffles are up. I can try and reach Beckett—he's in the last car."

"Well, do it, for fuck's sake," Skinner snapped at him. "We need to stop that train."

Thirty-Three

Beckett was huddled in the last seat of the last car of the emperor's train. The locomotive was a vast serpent of brass and steel and iron, belching black smoke and phlogiston fumes that smelled like blood and copper. It was decorated on the outside with the winged angels of the Hierologue; androgynous figures bearing swords and chains, blinded by the palm fronds wrapped around their eyes. Inside the train were exquisitely plush over-stuffed chairs, and a mural that extended through all eight cars, depicting the illustrious history of the Gorgon-Vies, all the way back to Demogorgon himself.

The train defied every law governing the sensible construction of a train—it was top-heavy, not at all streamlined, a machine designed for slow tours during which it could be *appreciated*. The Emperor's train was a train only technically; in reality, it was yet another monument to his power, and to the seemingly bottomless wealth he was permitted to devote to his comforts.

Beckett slumped in his chair, and rolled a brass veneine cartridge in his hand. He'd dosed himself only a half an hour ago, and could still feel the drug buzzing in his mind. It made him feel light, disconnected from his body. The only sensation that seemed to require immediate concern was the metallic bite at the back of his mouth, the part of him that craved more. It was early to inject another module into his system, if he wanted to keep to his five-a-day limit. Somehow, though, that idea didn't seem to be especially pressing at the moment. So what if he did take an extra one? Why should that really matter? He could take a sixth cartridge today, and start back again at five tomorrow. The damage to his system, between drugs and disease, was already immense—how could one more dose harm him?

The only thing that held him back was the sound of whirling gears he'd been hearing, lately. It was a troubling sound that seemed to grow closer according to how much veneine he was using. It was plainly a hallucination, Beckett didn't doubt that, but whenever he found his attention distracted by something, the sound caught at his ear as though it were real, making him start and look around suddenly, trying to locate its source. It was always the same sound, and it never quite went away—an endless, ubiquitous buzzing that gradually led him to the fanciful conclusion that he wasn't hallucinating it at all. He had sometimes begun to entertain the notion that the whirling gears really did underlay everything he saw. He imagined a vast network of gears beneath the streets, in the walls of the buildings, beneath peaked eaves and inside chimney-pots. He started to think of people or trolljrmen as kinds of automatons; skin on the outside, but inside filled with those same incessant mechanisms.

It was only in hours of weakness or extreme intoxication, of course, did Beckett give credence to these fantasies. He had spent a long time ignoring erroneous input that sometimes trickled into his senses, and so was generally unperturbed by the arrival of this new sound. Except that it occasionally grew unmanageably loud if he took too much veneine, making it difficult for him to hear what people were saying. This is why he hesitated, staring at the little brass module, and steadfastly ignoring the second and third-tier ministers with whom he was sharing the car.

Presently, he became aware of a faint tapping by his ear. It had the three long, two short cadence that knockers used for "attention," and the light hesitancy that Beckett had come to associate with James Ennering.

"Ennering," said Beckett, tucking the brass cartridge back into his pocket. "What is it?"

What followed was a nearly incomprehensible jumble of raps. Every knocker's sound was peculiar, and Beckett had just never been able to get the hang of James'—which taps were soft taps and which were strong taps, what empty air was hesitation and what was meant to indicate a purposeful space— and without being on the right track from the beginning, following a knocker's telerhythmia was heinously difficult.

"What...what? Stop. Just answer yes or no. There's a problem?" *Yes.* "Serious?" *Yes.* "At your end?" *No.* "On the train?" *Yes.* "Shit. Shit, shit. Do I need to stop the train and get the Emperor off?" *YES.* This was the most assertive Beckett had ever heard. "All right. Crap, hold on." At the front of the car was a small brass horn that, using a system of tympanums that Beckett had never fully understood, was able to communicate his voice from one end of the train to the other. He snapped to his feet and seized the horn at once, ministers eyeing him strangely. Beckett kept his voice low as he spoke—he didn't know the danger, precisely, and therefore didn't know who might be involved in it.

"Hello?" He said. "Hello, this is Beckett. There is an emergency..."

A burst of chattering feedback answered him, then resolved into a voice. "...hand off the button, if you want to listen. What is it?"

"This is Detective-Inspector Beckett. I have had word from my men that we are in imminent danger. You need to stop the train."

"What..." more feedback. "...danger?"

"I don't know what it is. I just need you to stop the train."

"...stop here."

"Yes, stop here," Beckett said, his voice rising. "Stop the fucking train."

"Soder Pass..." the voice came back. "...cking CAN'T stop..."

"Shit," Beckett said, inconsiderate as to whether he was speaking to the man at the other end of the horn or just to himself. If they were on the Soder Pass bridge, then the conductor was right—they couldn't stop, because there'd be nowhere for them to go. Just a train on a bridge, five hundred feet in the air over a rocky gorge. They wouldn't be safe until they reached the other side.

He drew his gun and, after a moment, fumbled the brass cartridge of veneine out of his pocket. He tugged his sleeve up to expose the plug on his arm—that strangely alien lump of brass affixed to his weathered skin. Beckett took a deep breath, then set the cartridge against it. Again, the sharp stabbing sensation, the spreading coolness that vanished almost at once. Beckett felt his head lighten and start to drift away, buoyed by the sound of gears and rushing water, and noticed with a vague indifference that this had been too much. He shook his head to clear it; his heart pounded in his ears and he smelt blood.

"Shit," Beckett said under his breath. He took hold of the grip of his revolver, squeezed it, made himself focus on the texture. He resisted the urge to close his eyes—he was leery of closing his eyes while on veneine, now—instead stared at the black, dull metal of the gun. "Shit, I don't have time for this," he said out loud, forcing his thoughts to dwell on the weight of the pistol, the straight lines of the barrel, the smooth grip in his palm. He tried to take a step and felt his legs wobble uncertainly, then gritted his teeth against the buzzing in his mind and threw open the door between the cars.

Outside the train cars was a small, iron-railed platform connected by chains and hitches to the platform of the next car. The space between the two was very small, but the drop between them, Beckett could see, was precipitous. The Emperor's train trundled slowly along Soder Pass—beneath the grate there were stiff iron rails and railroad ties—below that, only the lattice of girders that held the bridge up. There was nothing but those girders for a span of five hundred feet at least, as they crossed high above the otherwise-inaccessible Soder Gorge. Above, the blue vault of the sky, cleared of Trowth's persistent cover of pollution, stretched away to some infinite height, evoking that agoraphobia that lurked in the heart of all city dwellers.

The valley was dry and lifeless. Gray scree and stunted trees, barely visible at this height, crawled past below. Beckett noticed a sense of vertigo fluttering up from his stomach, but it contended with and lost to the veneine that had firm control of his mind. He crossed to the next car which, like the first, was stocked primarily with secondary ministers—third-cousins of prominent Family members, scrounging for whatever opportunity might present itself. The Emperor trailed men like this in his wake, like the detritus pulled after a ship. Beckett examined the pasty faces with their confounded and aghast expressions as he barged into their private coach. It was hard to imagine any of them masterminding a plan to assassinate the Emperor, Beckett considered, but easy to imagine any one of them getting involved. A new emperor meant new opportunities for advancement, and if there's one thing that third-tier Family members knew when they saw it, it was an opportunity for advancement.

Of course, I don't even know what I'm looking for. No one could have brought any guns onto the train. There were no oneiric munitions, no phlogiston munitions. *Tell me I'm not looking for a madman with a knife in his pocket.* There were a lot of pockets on that train to search. Beckett crossed ahead to the next car. *What am I even doing?* There was a full contingent of Lobstermen in the car before the Emperor's. The others—he saw as he moved through them—were filled with ministers, second ministers, sub-ministers, ministers-adjunct, secretaries to ministers-adjunct, and the assorted valets, servants, wives and mistresses that must necessarily accompany the members of a court. *I don't even know what I'm looking for,* Beckett thought to himself, as he threw about various vicious glares, in the hopes that someone with a guilty conscience, mistakenly believing that he'd been found out, would abruptly reveal himself.

He'd crossed all the cars but the last two—the one directly before him contained twelve Lobstermen, armed and armored, prepared for any eventuality, and so well-equipped to fend off assassins that they could hardly be helped and couldn't even be hindered by one old coroner with an out-dated Feathersmith revolver. Beyond that was the Emperor's personal coach, occupied by the William II Gorgon-Vie himself, a few trusted aids, and probably at least two mistresses. The Gorgon-Vies had fairly notorious sexual appetites, and an equally-notorious willingness to indulge them.

It was incomprehensible that the Lobstermen had been infiltrated—the Emperor's personal guard was composed of only the most fervently loyal soldiers, and only those who had already been serving for years. And it was equally incomprehensible that an assassin, intent on the Emperor's life, could get past one of them, much less a whole traincar full. This left two basic options: either someone in the emperor's personal retinue was an assassin, or else someone had planned this all out very poorly, and was stuck with a platoon of battle-hardened, blood-and-bone armored, invincible supermen between him and his target.

On the roof, maybe? Beckett wondered, as the train began to screech to a halt. *What...?* He flicked aside a curtain by the window and looked out—they were only halfway across the bridge. *Why are we stopping?* He snatched from the wall the brass horn that let him speak to conductor. "Why are we stopp—" Beckett began, but was interrupted by the tortured shriek of twisting metal. The train lurched—forward, then back, tossing the passengers helter-skelter. The floor buckled, knocking Beckett from his feet, as the front of the car actually raised into the air with the unimaginably loud, screaming, groaning sound of the train car being destroyed, a sound of unavoidable magnitude.

Like a wave, Beckett's car rose up and up, slowly coming to a stop and then pausing, for a bare instant, at the peak of its rise, to come crashing forward, hurling Beckett against the door which gave way beneath his weight. He fell out into the open light, and had to scramble to grab hold of the railing, gripping tight to keep from falling from the bridge. He watched his gun spiral away towards the stony valley bottom.

Ahead—below—the Lobstermen's car hung suspended, like a fly trapped in a spider web, in a vast, messy gnarl of... Beckett blinked, sure he was hallucinating again. Vines. They were thorny vines, crushing the car like an old tin cup, wrenching steel girders from the bridge, snapping about in the wind like slender whips. The car was fully twenty feet below, affixed to the shattered bridge by thick cords of vegetation. The platform Beckett was grappling with shifted suddenly, and he realized that the front end of his car was leaning perilously off the edge of the rails, dangling above the Soder Valley.

Fear still at bay from veneine intoxication—and, in a situation such as this, Beckett found himself hard-pressed to say whether fear or intoxication would be worse—the old coroner surveyed the scene. The Lobstermen's car had suffered the worst of the vines. Beckett could see men struggling, wrapped in thorny green, tiny red flowers blooming where the tendrils had found the gaps in their bone armor. The vines crushed bones and drove out breath and stabbed into veins like hypodermic needles. None of those men would survive; their lives were blooming red along the length of tangled vine.

Miraculously, the Emperor's car had managed to survive the...event. It was in place and firmly on the tracks, but caught by the vines and the weight of the Lobstermen's car. The forward engine shrieked and squealed and pumped blood-smelling phlogiston into the air, but the vines held fast. *What happened?* The vines...Beckett knew those vines from Kaarcag. They were a chimerstric weapon—a living entity transformed into a vehicle for destruction. The Sarkany Rend bred them, or grew them, or created them, somehow. *The Sarkany Rend...are they involved in this?* It was tempting to believe, but Beckett wasn't sure. With the explosion of heretical sciences in the last year, it seemed just as likely that some would-be assassin had gotten their hands on a chimerstry primer.

*I have to...have to do something...*his brain felt like it was mired in mud. He couldn't think straight, couldn't get his thoughts together. *What am I supposed to do?* The Emperor was alive, the plan had failed. *Unless...*

Beckett stared at the car with mounting horror. What if the plan had been to isolate the Emperor? The chimerstric weapon had been intended to neutralize the guard, while the assassin waited with the Emperor himself? Beckett tried to run down a list of the men and women that might be in the foremost car, while he scrabbled around, looking for a way to cross the gap. There was a girder, a few feet below him, that had been undamaged by the train's destruction. He tried to lower himself down a hanging railroad tie.

*Gradith Vie-Gorgon the Prime Minister. Minister of the Exchequer, something Rowan-Czarnecki. There's another Rowan-Czarnecki—under-minister of Health and Safety? The Emperor's personal physician. The two women...*Beckett had, in the past, insisted that all of the William II's mistresses be subject to background checks. The Emperor had conceded the need for it, and then promptly refused to ever supply the names of anyone he dallied with.

Beckett succeeded in easing himself out onto the girder—there was fully ten feet of length before he'd be able to reach a vertical handhold on the opposite side. The wind whipped at his coat. He was a very long way up, Beckett knew, and not a healthy man. Crawling across narrow metal girders, hundreds of feet below a stone valley floor was unlikely, to say the least. He had just taken it in his mind to turn back, perhaps find someone that could help him, maybe find someone who knew where there was a rope, when he saw tiny green tendrils wriggling from the steel by his hand. The tendrils flexed and grew, became thicker, blacker, began to extrude sharp thorns. They *reached* out for him, and he saw Sergeant Garret again, his face hacked together from whorls in the metal, vines climbing from his nose...

Beckett pushed off from the railroad tie and tried to run along the horizontal girder. He took one step, two—the vines were behind him now, crawling along after him, clutching—three steps—his balance was off, he could feel himself leaning to one side about to go over—four—the vines flexed again, tearing the girder from its place in the bridge, rocking it beneath his feet...

He fell forward, crashing chest-first into the vertical girder across from him, wrapping his arms around it like a drowning lover, his feet swinging in the open air as the rose-bedecked vines fell with his narrow bridge into the valley. Beckett stayed there for a moment, gasping with breath, squeezing the iron truss so tight that it would have been little surprise if he'd snapped a rib because of it.

Back across the now-impassable gap, a well-heeled man in a high-quality but disheveled suit leaned out of the car's rear door and shouted out. Beckett couldn't hear what the man said; blood was pounding so furiously in his ears, and this, combined with the illusory sound of machinery and the scraping, wrenching, shrieking sound that the malicious vines made as they continued to crush anything they lighted on, would make communication impossible.

"Get back!" Beckett screamed at him. "Get back! The vines live on blood! Get...get everyone to the end of the train, and get them off! Don't touch —"

A thin grin tendril whipped at the man's hand; he swore and snatched it away. An expression of horror occupied his face as he saw that the thin green vines with their bright red flowers were all around him, pulsing and writhing, and lashing out at him. He nodded to Beckett in curt acknowledgement of the warning, and then slipped back inside the car.

There was a groan of bending metal and then a series of high-pitched snaps as the vines that held the fallen car finally snapped. The coach swung, crashing into the supporting bridge; the entire structure shuddered, nearly shaking Beckett from his place, then it spiraled off into the gorge, cracking open and spilling forth its bloody, broken contents. It crashed like thunder when it hit, and the sound reverberated throughout the valley.

Almost at once, the engine and the Emperor's carriage began to sluggishly roll forward; the dead vines wrapped around their axels, deprived of sustenance, had begun to wither almost immediately, and were being shredded by the force of the train. Beckett spat, and began to climb up the iron rail.

It was not far, and there were evenly-spaced supporting rails at weird angles to the main one, and so should not have been too difficult. Nonetheless, Beckett could feel his shoulders burning, his hands cramping up, his legs turning to a weak jelly by the time he flopped up onto the railroad ties. The train car was still hindered by the vegetation, and only slowly picking up speed. The old coroner struggled to his feet, gasping at the sharp pains in his knees — pains that he had forgotten about almost entirely in the haze of his intoxication — and staggered towards the Emperor's coach.

He paused briefly to grab at a hefty stick of splintered wood — all that remained of a railroad tie that had been destroyed when the center of the bridge was lost. He jogged to keep up with the train, wincing at the persistent pain in his limbs, and trying to imagine the precise scenario that would need to exist inside the car in order for a foot-long splinter to be of much use. He did not succeed.

Lacking anything that resembled a strategy — and having been well-served by a lifetime of rash behavior — once Beckett had attained the platform on the rear of the coach, he just set his shoulder against the door and burst in. Perhaps he expected the element of surprise to give him some advantage that he lacked, or perhaps he considered it at least remotely plausible that William II's would-be assassin was standing directly behind the door. Of the many scenarios he considered — including an especially unlikely one that involved him knocking the assailant directly unconscious before he'd had time to harm anyone — none resembled the sight that lay before him.

The lush interior of the coach was in complete disarray. The heavy satin draperies, all in the deep purples and dark greens of the Gorgon-Vies and ordinarily hung about the windows to keep the car comfortably claustrophobic, were a shambles — torn from their rods and strewn about in mounds of lush fabric, along with paintings shaken loose from their moorings and shredded by their fall, chairs tumbled and broken, and a generous scattering of the razor-sharp remains of the Emperor's personal dry-bar. Glass crunched beneath Beckett's feet as he staggered into the room.

One body was spread out before him, dead. The man had been shot between the eyes, and the moist coil of his being was splattered liberally across the walls. A second man stood to the side; he was deathly pale, well-dressed and wide-eyed at the carnage, and a woman in a blue dress and an elaborate hairstyle had buried her face in his chest and was weeping quietly. The man Beckett recognized as the under-secretary to the Prime Minister; the woman he supposed was a concubine, but his eyes were drawn from them at once, to the center of the car.

The Emperor's coach, according to long tradition, was always divided into two sections — a kind of sitting room, where the Emperor might receive visitors and discuss matters of state, and beyond that a private room where, presumably, he indulged his insatiable sexual appetites in all manner of licentious and unspeakable ways. No one was ever permitted in the private room, and Beckett hoped that the man had had sense good enough to flee into it at the first sign of danger.

William II Gorgon-Vie was not in the car at all. Instead, at the door to his private chamber was another woman, buried beneath a small effusion of petticoats. Her head was turned at an impossible angle to her shoulders;

vertebrae pressed out against her skin, a grotesque jag of bone that made Beckett wince involuntarily. A look of choking horror was frozen on her face. *Dahran,* Beckett thought, absurdly. *That one's name was Dahran.*

Above the dead woman, looming in all its misshapen, patchwork monstrosity, reeking of ichor and enigma, was Mr. Stitch. It fixed Beckett with its brass, expressionless eyes, and said nothing.

What the hell do I do now? Beckett wondered. The sound of spinning gears in his mind had trebled and now threatened to overwhelm him. *Am I hearing...? Are those the gears in Stitch's head?* For a moment, Beckett was sure it was true — that the psychoactive venom in his veins had dissolved the boundary between his mind and the hulking reanimate, or that the invincible engine of Stitch's mechanical intellect had finally spilled over its borders and now had begun to leak into the minds of those around it. Self and object were undivided, now only decoration applied to the outermost edges of one incomprehensibly vast and turning mechanism, whose cogs and clockwork guided the destiny of all men.

"What happened?" Beckett choked, and the sensation vanished. He was Elijah Beckett again, wholly separate from that strange, unliving giant. He gripped his makeshift weapon tightly. "What happened here?"

"It was her," the pale man whispered. "She had a gun. Kept it hidden under her dress She ki...she shot Bertram. She wanted the Emperor..."

"You killed her?" Beckett said Mr. Stitch.

"She was waving the gun around like a madwoman," the man interjected. "We were all in danger. It was the only way. I swear...we're lucky to be alive."

"Where's the Emperor?"

Stitch spoke in its rasping, horrifically painful voice. "Safe." The reanimate took a deep breath, a sound like a crypt opening to the sky for the first time in centuries. "He. Is. Safe."

THIRTY-FOUR

Pogo ada Goan was ramo of the Clan Akori. This was a rank that put him somewhere below the headman — who actually still lived in Daeagea, the ancestral homeland of the indige — and, technically, slightly above the matriarchs of the Bluewater Household. This elevation in rank was a double-edged sword, of course; as a ramo, he was freed from the practical responsibilities of running the household, but, as a consequence, he was far less vital to that household's functioning than the matriarchs were. He filled a position among his fellow Bluewater Akori that was something of a cross between a priest and the captain of a ship. He communed with the ancestral spirits and the Genius of the Household, issued guidelines and directives to the matriarchs, but it was generally the mothers and aunts and sisters of the Bluewater Household that were responsible for the work, and received the accordingly high respect and adoration.

These days, Pogo knew, the ancestors had little to say. Since their demand that the indige migrate en masse from Trowth and return to Daeagea, they were silent almost to a one. This left Pogo with very little to do except engage, along with his brothers, nephews, and uncles, in honest labor. This was slightly embarrassing for a *ramo*, but Pogo had achieved a kind of bemused acceptance of it. Trowth was a mad place, and the needs imposed on his people there were mad ones; surely the Household's needs were greater than Pogo's sense of propriety?

He smoked a cigarette as he and his male family members sat strapped in the dark, hot, claustrophobic confines of the airship. This was an Akori clan ship, designed to resemble a gigantic *gava*-fish. Pale Trowthi claimed it smelled like rotten fish, due to the gasses that kept it aloft, but Pogo had never noticed such a thing. Besides that, these same Trowthi never complained about the smell of their chickens or the rotten green plants in their gutters, or when their

214

phlogiston soured and began to turn to vinegar, so undoubtedly their collective sense of smell was suspect.

The airship floated above the Soder Gorge at a leisurely pace, that represented the highest velocity to which it could reasonably attain. The pilot managed to maneuver the vehicle past the broken bridge, and a man from the coroners addressed the indige in less than perfect Indt.

"We am looking at men. To find. Finding. How is it..." the man said, then whispered something to the pilot, who muttered a response. "Identify. We am to identify men. Here." He gave a thick packet of papers to the man nearest him. "This list, to find the men. Yes? Question?" When no one responded, he returned to the cockpit.

The indige to whom the man had handed the papers immediately passed them to Pogo, who accepted leadership of the group as was his due. Leafing through the pages, he saw that they consisted of a list of Trowthi names and a number of fair sketches of people's faces.

"All right, cousins," Pogo sad aloud. "We are here to look for bodies. We are staying until we find everyone on the list, okay?" He tucked the papers into his belt, and prepared to rappel into the valley.

Pogo had grown up in Daeagea, among its mile-high stone towers and impossibly-tall trees. Heights never bothered him, and most of his people were similarly inconsiderate of the danger as they dangled on ropes far above the valley floor. A few who had been born after the Diaspora had never learned the exhilarating glory of the precipices of the homeland, and panicked a little at the descent. The other indige immediately mocked them and called them Trowers — city-boys, practically humans.

What did make Pogo nervous, he realized as he reached the bottom of the gorge, was the sense of the mountains looming up on either side of him. This was a sharper feeling than he suffered in the city; here, in Soder Gorge, there seemed to be nothing holding the gray granite sides of the chasm up. They could fall at any minute, burying all the Akori at the bottom of the pit, and then who would dig the bodies out? Not Trower men, who couldn't leave their city without mewling like infants at the great expanse of sky. No one would come for them, and the Akori men would all perish beneath the stone. Pogo smoked another cigarette, and nodded at this family that they should get to work.

Sorting through the wreckage of the fallen train car was hot, exhausting work, though at least the murderous thorny vines had died out. The indige were careful around them still, hacking the vines thoroughly before pulling them out of the car. It was unlikely that they could feed on indige blood, anyway — unlike the bright-mites that swarmed in the damp summer heat, which took sips from indige veins and then darted away, burning bright and phosphorescent blue.

Pogo's brothers dragged body after body before the ramo; the corpses smelled like salt and ocean water to indige noses, which made them fairly easy to find. And the maddening stench of ichor was unmistakable—how the Trower men could tolerate it was one more thing that Pogo would never understand. As the bodies were placed before him, Pogo checked their faces, if they were undamaged, or checked on his list of identifying marks if they were. He then spoke a short invocation to whomever might be the house guardian of these men. It was troubling to try to do this without knowing the spirit's name, but was better than letting them go into the next life with no chance at all for a family, even if heathen Trower men didn't know it. Perhaps they would prefer to be buried in a crypt somewhere, or set on fire; Pogo didn't know how the Trower men cared for their dead, but if he was to supervise, he would do his best to see them safely onwards.

By sunset, the indige were thoroughly exhausted, sweating silver bullets that hissed when they struck the hot rocks and smelled like vinegar. All of the names on Pogo's list were accounted for. He had insisted that the men keep looking for a while, just to satisfy his sense of completeness. He was about to call them in when a boy of sixteen ran up to him.

The boy had tattoos that indicated he was a Thoron from a Chapel Street Household: stylized seabirds and the double-eagle that the Trowthi-men used to mark their churches. He began speaking at once. "Ramo, ramo! I've found another—"

"Hap!" Pogo interrupted. He held up his hand.

The boy bowed his head, ashamed. "Forgiveness, ramo. I am Gad ada Sho, of Clan Thoron, Second Chapel Street Household, third son of Sorine Thoron, second cousin of Aran Akori. My father was Darag Thoron of…I do not know his household. He was born in the homeland, and died before I knew him."

"You are welcome, cousin. Many of our people have never known the households of Daeagea, there is no shame. What have you found?"

"Another body, sir. In a crevice in the rocks." He pointed to the south.

Pogo looked at his list, then thought fondly of the meal that would be waiting for him at home. *This man was not on the list, surely the Trowers don't care about him?* But then he thought of a nameless corpse, whose spirit was trapped in rotting flesh because no one had informed its ancestors of its death, and sighed. "Show me, boy."

Gad Thoron led Pogo close to the walls of the gorge, far from the shattered traincar, to a black crack in the rocks that was just taller than a man.

"What were you doing in here?" Pogo asked him.

"Ah," the boy said. "Forgiveness, ramo. It was hot, and I thought I would steal a few moments in the cool shade." He reached in to the dark, and heaved out a naked and badly-damaged body.

Pogo looked at this corpse. It was covered in black and purple contusions, and suffered from a kind of shapelessness indicating that many of its bones were broken. It was male, certainly, and very, very white. It had been a big man, with a barrel chest, thick legs, and broad shoulders. Its face was gone entirely, chewed off by animals, perhaps, no eyes or teeth apparent. There were livid red blotches on its skin where blood had pooled.

"How did he get in here?" Pogo wondered. "Could he have fallen from the train?"

"He must have been pushed in, ramo," said the boy. "He was far inside. There is blood still on the walls, you can smell the salt. It cannot have been long ago."

"Someone must have done it, and taken his clothes as well. Hup. Well. I will invoke his ancestors, then you can put him with the others."

"Yes, ramo," the boy said.

"Ancestors of what was once this man," Pogo said, not bothering to call out. If the Trower ancestors could not at least hear him this far away from their city, then they were likely to be thoroughly useless. "Sons of Gorgon and Demogorgon. Here is the soul of your child. I do not know if he was good or wicked, but if you have watched him, please reward or punish him accordingly. Set a place for him at your table, or, if he was wicked, find degrading work for him to perform among the many wicked and disloyal children that you likely already have."

Pogo nodded to the Thoron boy, who proceeded to drag the new corpse to the pile of corpses already recovered. Pogo decided that the day's labors were finished, and he called a halt. The men gathered downwind of the bodies, and passed around a jug of brandy and djang while they waited for the airship to return.

When it did float back into sight—looking at this distance for all the world like a great fish that, unaware of the divide between ocean and sky, had simply swum up towards the clouds—the coroner on board refused to come down. He called down to Pogo to ask if he was sure of the identification—forgetting that he'd actually assigned this task to Pogo's cousin, or else not being able to effectively distinguish between indige. The ramo couldn't hold this against him; without thorough description, Pogo had a hard time telling Trower men apart.

"We've found them all, yes," Pogo called up.

"Good. Burn it then."

"What?" Burn the list? Or burn the bodies?

The coroner waved at the pile of bodies. "They dead. Burn. Phlogiston."

Pogo shrugged; he and his family covered the many corpses with sticky blue phlogiston, and set it alight.

Thirty-Five

"Okay, hold this. Hold it tight, okay?" Skinner said. "What are you going to do with it?"

"Mummy," Jaine Akori said. She was six, and clever, but much more proficient at Indt than she was at Trowthi. "Aikiat da aga da'an?"

"Mummy what?" Skinner asked, holding Jaine's hand closed around the stack of hundred-crown notes. She had decided to keep only two hundred from her first payment from Emilia Vie-Gorgon. She suspected that, now that the assassination attempt had failed, and now that Skinner could identify Emilia as being involved, the second payment would not be forthcoming.

"Bring to mummy," Jaine said. "Jana agad. Osheed?"

"Osheed is right, honey," Skinner replied. Eight hundred crowns would take the Akori a long way, and two hundred might be enough to give Skinner a head start, at least. She had no illusions about what would happen now. "And what do you tell mummy?"

Jaine obediently recited the message Skinner had given her. "Thank. You. Very. Much. From. Miss. Skinner."

"And if she asks where I went?"

"You had to go. To be safe. You can't come back."

"And?"

"Uhmmm. Don't follow!"

"Good girl." Skinner patted her on the head. "You wait here for mummy to get home, okay?"

"Okay! Where are you going?"

Skinner shrugged. "I don't know. But even if I did know, I don't think it would be a good idea to tell you." The girl said nothing. "Though I guess I could probably tell *you*, and it wouldn't matter that much. Never mind. Wait here for mummy, okay? And make sure you give her the money. Okay?"

"Gan. Okay!"

Skinner left the house in Bluewater for the last time. It was, as to be expected in Trowth during the summer, raining. Not the razor-sharp jags of calcium that would rattle on the roofs in late summer, fortunately, but a steady, warm rain that, if not for the stifling humidity, would have been quite pleasant. Rain clattered on slate roofs and cobblestones and had soaked her through to her socks in a few moments.

The truth was that Skinner didn't know, at all, where she would go. She didn't have any friends left in the city and now the trains were all closed down, so she couldn't even go back to her family if she wanted to. As a woman alone, she couldn't rent lodgings except in the most dismal and dangerous of locales, and she wasn't sure how to find those anyway. But she absolutely could not stay with the Akori.

It's not that she doubted that Emilia Vie-Gorgon could get to her without any collateral damage. Killing an emperor was one thing; killing an unemployed knocker living in a ghetto with a family of immigrants was something altogether different. It's just that Skinner wasn't fully certain that Emilia would *bother* not causing collateral damage. After all, wouldn't a bomb serve to disguise who the target was? Anonymous bombs obscured even their own intentions. Was it to kill a person? To cripple the gendarmerie? To strike out against the Empire, or against the indige?

The very thought made Skinner wonder just how much Emilia had been involved in the other attacks. It was hard to say, because what little Skinner knew of it had only come from the broadsheets — and one could fully rely on the papers to exaggerate outrageously whatever scant details they managed to get a hold of — but the thought had accompanied a mounting terror. If Emilia was involved, the extremity of her willingness to do harm was staggering. Commissioning a scandalous play was almost absurdly childish compared to what the Vie-Gorgon girl was capable of.

And Skinner knew that Emilia was involved in the assassination attempt. There was no way that she would permit Skinner to live.

Skinner let her telerhythmia rattle along the walls as she found her way towards the heart of Trowth. She knew that people often confused the sound of telerhythmia with the sound of a heavy rain, but no knocker had difficulty sorting them out. The telerhythmia was clearly sharper and crisper, the echoes jumped out at the ear and snagged attention in a way raindrops didn't. She made her way through mostly deserted streets, guided by her preternatural senses, until she came to the cramped doorway that led to Backstairs Street.

Backstairs might have actually been a street at one point, a short connecting alley between a courtyard and Watchmaker's Close perhaps, but once Irwin Arkady had catastrophically changed the topography of Trowth, someone had had the bright idea to build a staircase here. What Backstairs had been called before it was a stairway was a piece of information lost to the abysms of history and apathy. Skinner paused at the top of the stair, stretched her clairaudience down its length. She heard nothing but the labored breathing of a far-off transient and the omnipresent drip of water and leaking pipes.

The Arcadium wasn't the best choice, it was just her only choice. The summer meant she had little chance of freezing to death, and the sheltered tunnels would provide some protection from the worst precipitation that Trowth had to offer. All she had to worry about was catching scrave from a plague rat. Or being attacked by a vampiric foglet. Or being stabbed by a beggar. Or, obviously, being found and murdered by Emilia Vie-Gorgon's assassins.

But at least she wouldn't be rained on.

As she stood at the top of Backstairs Street and prepared to embark on her new life as a vagrant, she checked again for the footsteps that had been following her for the last half-mile. Footsteps, much like telerhythmia, jump out to a knocker's ear; they were a sound that floated right to the surface of the world's sea of noise. It was a mistake to try and take a knocker by surprise if you were just going to follow them. Two sets of steps, evenly-spaced. Heavy, purposeful. Booted feet, men's feet, walking steadily towards her. Skinner reached out with her clairaudience to ascertain what she could about the men. One ground his teeth. One was smoking. Based on a man's gait and how high above the ground his breathing was, Skinner could estimate his height. Based on the volume of his footsteps, she could guess at his weight. These men were both much bigger than she.

"There," one said, softly, not realizing how absurd it was to whisper while Skinner was listening for him. "There she is."

At least, Skinner told herself, *it's not a bomb.* She fled into the Arcadium.

Pogo Akori eventually established the story of Skinner's absence, at no small difficulty, from his sister Trine. Trine, of course, wanted to go after the Trower-woman right away. She called him a heartless monster when he said no, said his soul had turned to black filth like the soul of a Trower, that his grandfather would be ashamed of him, and offered many other colorful and cruel insults. Pogo remained philosophical on the subject. Was the Trower woman in danger? Perhaps. But it was her danger, and she would know best how to solve it. If they pursued her into the night, they would likely do more harm than good. And, after all that, Skinner had been trying not just to preserve herself, but to preserve the Akori, as well. If they followed her and were harmed, would this not make her sacrifice meaningless?

"We will do what we can when we can," Pogo insisted, "But we will not follow her, because she *asked us not to*." And that was that.

When a tall, rangy Trower man in a deftly-tailored but somewhat rumpled suit arrived at the Akori household later that day, Pogo was true to his word. While his family glared at the stranger, Pogo insisted in broken Trowthi that no, only indige lived here. No one named Elizabeth Skinner. No Trower women at all. The man believed him, or seemed to, and his face took on a disappointed air as a consequence. He offered his apologies and left them with a pamphlet that he had drawn from a pocket inside his coat.

Pogo Akori, in order to improve his command of the Trowthi language, spent a great deal of time reading, and this practice had given him a keen hunger for words—a hunger that had only sharpened since the day that the Emperor had shut down all of the presses. Maybe the stranger was a murderer, but Pogo had sent him on his way with no clues as to Skinner's whereabouts; he considered his obligation discharged, and so there was no point in not enjoying the chance to read.

He settled into his chair while the children shrieked and the matriarchs gossiped as they cooked, and began to leaf through the pamphlet the man had left. Pogo saw, with some surprise, that it was the script for a play.

It was called *Theocles*.

Thirty-Six

The engine is complete. The body that Chretien has built is serviceable, at least. We have envigorated the entity earlier this evening. I can hear a faint buzzing from the engine, which I have installed in its skull. The eyes, of course, are without expression.

And yet, I feel certain that the creature is looking at me.

--from the journal of Harcourt Wolfram, 1785

Beckett stalked along the streets of Trowth through the steady summer rain. Dark crevices looked back at him from beside the street, beneath which lurked the Arcadium and, he knew now, any number of attendant dangers. There were eyes, he was sure, in those dark corners, there were men waiting for him with purple dents in their foreheads, ready to scream their fervent fealty to the Dragon Princes. Crooked streets and crooked buildings loomed over his head, sometimes bedecked with the flowers and birds of the Crabtree-Daior household architecture, sometimes they were squat and square like the Gorgon-Vies', but the most disconcerting of all were the long narrow arches and peaked roofs that belonged to the Vie-Gorgons. As Beckett walked deeper and deeper into the city, those sharp black gaps looked more and more like teeth or talons, at rest right now, but humming with a need to reach out and commit murder, as though the city were a great beast only resting lightly on its haunches to lure other, less wary cities to their destruction.

It was too hot for his coat and Beckett had left it at home, wearing his pistol openly on his belt. He had kept the scarf wrapped around his cadaverous mouth and nose, but his empty eye socket still glared with blind menace at anyone that saw his face. He mindlessly fumbled with the empty brass cartridges in his pocket. Among them was a new cartridge, one he'd had specially made by the scientists at the Croft.

"You've been using too much of the veneine," Helmetag had told him. "We don't know...you understand, we don't know how it reacts to what else is in your system? This is dangerous." But he handed the cartridge over, anyway.

Beckett couldn't recall quite how many doses of veneine he'd had today, and he had some vague notion that he should wait until some of the drug cleared out before he tried the new pharmacy. *Not yet*, he thought, *not yet*. There was an anxiety that had been gnawing at him, displaced by the constant rumbling of those damnable gears, and he was on his way to meet his source.

The death of Dahran the concubine wasn't an end, he knew that much. She'd been hired, driven by whatever noble purpose or base greed at her core, it was too late to find out now. Someone had planned the attempt and Beckett was determined to find him. The Emperor, convinced now of his safety, had rescheduled his Invocation, and would be delivering it from the palace, as planned. Beckett had less than a day to forestall another assassination attempt. It was troublesome, trying to put pieces together like this, while his head spun and whirled. The ground pitched like the floor of a ship and while Beckett knew that *something* was wrong, he couldn't gather his thoughts enough to guess as to what it might be. He now did the only thing he could think of; desperately ready to try anything, he now went back to where he imagined this had all began. Just a little more information and he'd be ready.

He clutched tight to this one thought, and it buoyed him through the messy swamp of confusion that mired his mind. *There will be answers here*, he thought as the city around him blurred and stretched. *I will find the answer here*, he insisted, as the sky fell away above him, torn away from the earth by the fall of steady rain and left to float loose and slippery high above the world. *Answers*. Deformed faces looked out at him, strange animals nuzzled garbage in the gutters.

Beckett paused at the intersection of Cartwright and Galley Hill, confused. The buildings were suddenly alien to him, not the grey stone of Trowth at all but the red-brown bricks of Kaarcag—shook loose from his past by the veneine that buzzed in him—dotted with tiny windows that hid inhabitants whose nature and needs could only be guessed at. The coughing, choking sound of guns in the distance made him reach for his pistol; as he turned, he saw black basalt towers, tall and potent with nameless peril. Gears thundered and the towers stretched higher, hoisted by some invisible machine.

We never came to Kaarcag, Beckett thought to himself as he drew his gun, *We never made it up the hill*. "I've never been here!" He shouted aloud. Gears spun, and at the same time the city was silent as the dead of night. The ground thrummed beneath him.

"What is that?" Fletcher asked at Beckett's side. He turned to see the young man staring blankly, as blood poured from his mouth.

Something scurried among the narrow alleys. The silhouette of a man resolved at a bend in the road and Beckett knew without looking that he would have that hideous red-purple crease in his forehead, that place where mind and will had been removed by the Dragon Princes. "Don't come any closer!" Beckett fired a shot off; it ricocheted with a white spark from the wall near the man's head. "Stop!"

More shuffling footsteps echoed from the walls behind him and now something new accompanied them—a kind of wet sucking sound, like a handful of slimy worms writhing against each other. More dummies appeared, brainless automatons, shambling from the dark corners of the world, and on top of the roofs misshapen shadows with hands like nests of leeches watched and reached out.

Above, the constant cover of clouds and pollution had vanished, revealing a fat green moon that hung in the sky like a rotten cancer, surrounded by wicked pinpricks of white stars. Beckett fired his gun again and shoved past the dummies, as the gears in his head built to a crescendo, drowning out the sound of his own feet slapping on the cobblestones and yet not at all drowning out the sound of the footsteps that pursued him, pursued him as he ran through the streets of Kaarcag. Grim windows watched and thorny green vines roiled at his feet, lashing out at him, sharp barbs hungry for blood.

Beckett found stairs—he didn't know, couldn't remember if there had been stairs at all in Kaarcag, only the trail that wound up towards the fortress-city. The red-brown stone was everywhere, stone colored by rust and blood, a city made of death and entropy, lit by the gangrenous moon. He slipped and fell, knew that he'd banged his arthritic right knee badly, but found himself so far detached from his body that he could not even feel the pain from it. He skidded down slick rust-colored stones and landed on his back with the wind knocked from him.

He tried to move as a figure appeared before him, but found himself paralyzed. The figure was tall, inhumanly tall and thin. It wore chainmail and black robes and the peaked helmet of the old Saaghyari. Its face was a skull, empty of flesh except for a few withered scraps, dark pits where there should have been eyes, and teeth that belonged to an animal—long and sharp and gleaming white in the dark. It carried a sword in skeletal hands, a sword that it raised above its head.

"Czarneck," Beckett whispered.

The Dragon Prince dissolved into smoke, taking the strange scene with it. Kaarcag was vanished, and in its place was dim, smoky, dirty Trowth. Soberly-dressed men and women stood on the sidewalks, watching Beckett as he gasped for breath and rolled to his feet. No one raised an alarm; passers-by darted sidelong glances at the fallen man, then coughed and discretely turned away. Beckett just glared at them, holstered his gun and looked up.

Vie Abbey stood before him at the top of its hill, just as the wave of rocky architecture that was the city of Trowth began to peter out. From this distance and in the dark, it looked for all the world like a bundle of black knives, thrusting impotently into the entrenchant air. While Beckett still stumbled through the murk of his own imagination, Vie Abbey remained his one constant certainty. He staggered up the hill towards it, sure the he heard that ticking clockwork echoing in the seams where the Arcadium became the Abbey's labyrinthine undercroft. He shoved the grammateurs aside as he entered, demanding to be let in to the repository of heretical texts. He waved his bronze coroner's badge and, when that failed to produce the desired effect, waved his revolver instead. No longer interested in their permission, he pressed on, deep into the belly of the stone beast, kicking doors open when they barred his way, forcing the terrified priests to unlock them if the doors proved too sturdy. He clipped one man behind his ear with the butt of his pistol, but in the moment that he did it, he could not remember why.

The world felt like it was slipping away, shivering on its axis, only a moment from dissolving into water and revealing some occult, terrible but truer world beneath, a septic sewer of viscous real upon which foul, miserable Trowth was a fractionally-thin skein, like an oil slick. What monstrosity lurks beneath us, that our world is but a shadow of its wickedness? Beckett ignored the grammateurs as they demanded that he swear the oath of secrecy, tuned out their shrieks as he seized the log book. The pages were practically decaying in his hands. He saw Valentine's name at the top and for a moment saw Valentine himself, standing opposite the book, looking at him with imploring eyes.

Imploring what, though? Vengeance? Justice? Compassion? What does a ghost want from the living world at all? The page was yellow and brittle, and Beckett understood why Valentine had never turned it. Perhaps it was the understanding that the ghost sought, for now he was gone, replaced by a bishop in splendid robes, painfully officious and furious at Beckett's intrusion and violation of protocol. He screamed and roared, and probably threatened to excommunicate the coroner. He called for the guards, who did back away when Beckett threw his badge at them. He grabbed at the coroner's arm, but thought better of it almost at once. Beckett ignored him, and turned the page.

The name he saw, the last name signed before Valentine's own, nearly stopped the old coroner's heart. The world shattered and vanished, time became a twisted knot. Beckett's life disappeared and he wondered then if he had known anything at all, or if he had always been groping blindly in the dark.

That name.

Beckett fumbled the new cartridge from his pocket, a small glass capsule, filled with a glimmering green fluid. Etherized flux. The reagent of the daemonomaniacs. He pressed it to the socket in his arm, and felt the sparking pain of heresy in his veins.

Chris Braak

THIRTY-SEVEN

Egg and his partner, (who was called Six-Fingered Will, despite having the ordinary, requisite allotment of ten digits), were not supposed to actually have to kill the woman. Their principal, who always contacted them anonymously, had assured the two thugs that they were a contingency plan, set in place only in the unlikely event that Elizabeth Skinner seemed like she was going to abandon the house in Bluewater. Whatever plan was in place, it was supposed to occur with a minimum amount of participation from Egg and Will, the go-to strongmen for the Dockside Boys.

Plans change, however, and Egg at least was phlegmatic about unexpected events. He considered himself a kind of philosopher among hooligans, adapting to a new scenario with intellectual aplomb, ready for whatever the world might throw his way. He didn't expect the universe to change on his behalf, is how he thought of it, and that made it easier for him to deal with the problems that necessarily beset him and his fellows.

Six-Fingered Will was noticeably *less* phlegmatic. He complained bitterly when Egg insisted that Skinner was leaving the Bluewater House for good. He offered that they should give up following her, and just report back that they'd lost her. He asserted that he didn't like the rain, and it was surely no good for his health to be wandering around in a warm summer shower. Six-Fingered Will was not the man with whom Egg would have preferred to do this job, but he adapted.

They pursued the knocker to the entrance of Backstairs Street, and watched her cock her head to one side, like a cat.

"There," said Will. "There she is."

The woman at once disappeared into the dark down the stairs.

"Do you think she heard us?" Will asked.

Egg shrugged.

"Do we really have to kill her? She's as good as dead down there, anyway. Blind girl down in the Arcade. I heard there's sharpsies there."

Egg shrugged again. He was growing less and less tolerant of Will's complaints. "We'll do it. Come on, it won't take long. Hurry, before we lose her."

The two men jogged towards the doorway and down the stairs. They followed the sound of her footsteps — after a moment of consideration and heated argument about precisely which direction said footsteps were coming from — down one dark, covered alley, and through a curved connecting tunnel, past a bronze statue that vaguely resembled either a man on horseback, or possibly three women dancing.

"Is she heading towards the river?" Will asked, and Egg shushed him. The soft susurrus of the Lesser Stark, one of the many small tributaries of the greater Stark, could be heard below the roads that had been built above it. Egg listened closely for the telltale sound of echoing footsteps, trying to sort them out from the random, quiet cacophony that was the sound of city life. He heard, some distance away, a sharp, precise rapping sound.

"That way," Egg muttered, taking them deeper into the Arcadium. He had her now, he was sure. The sound of her shoes, the rustling of her skirts, the tapping of that weird clicking noise the knockers made. He could even see her shadow flickering in the messy whorl of blue light from the phlogiston lamps. Egg slipped his hand inside his coat and took a hold of his knife.

It wasn't that he *liked* killing people, women especially. It's that it was good money, and from an early age, Egg had realized he was good at not feeling bad about things. And since a man has to earn a living, he needs to take advantage of the assets he has available.

"Here, what's this?" Will said, as the two men rounded the corner. Will knelt down and drew a skirt out from a puddle of petticoats. "She's walking around in her bloomers?"

Egg's eyes narrowed and he looked around. They were in a fairly large Close, with side-streets leading off in four more directions. Two of them were pitch dark, their lanterns burned out or broken by vandals.

"She's left her shoes, too," Will snickered. "Maybe this won't be such a bad time after all."

"Shut up," Egg snapped. A wave of knocking swept through the close, echoing off the walls, compounding on itself until it began to sound like thunder. Will swung around wildly, imagining that the source was nearby. Egg, by coincidence, looked up at the hanging lamp that cast blue light into the Close. Its metal frame was rattling alarmingly fast; the key that controlled the phlogiston flow was shaking in its socket as the knocking grew louder — and then, abruptly, the key fell out.

Phlogiston poured into the lamp, ignited by the filament, and exploded in a burst of blinding, blue-white light. When their vision cleared, the two men found the close almost impenetrably dark. The knocking continued, softer now, and proceeded down the alley directly ahead of them.

"Shit," Will muttered. "Did she do that? I didn't know they could do that."

"Shut up and follow—wait..." There was a second clicking now, from the other alley. It didn't sound quite the same...was it an echo? "Wait. We'll split up. I'll go down this one, you take that one. She can't be far, not if she's running without shoes on. She'll cut her feet on something soon enough, and we can just follow the blood, then."

"Yeah," Will said. "All right." He muttered something under his breath and took a few steps into the dark, making him practically invisible to Egg.

Egg set his hand along one of the stone walls and slowly made his way down the alley. He could see, at some remove, another lantern, its light a faint pinprick in the dark. A trick of the shadow and the distance made it seem to throb. "All right, miss. We know you know about us. Come along then. We don't want to do nothing to you, you know? We're just sent to talk. You're going to hurt yourself, stumbling around in the dark like this." Inwardly, he thought, *Shit.* He knew they'd catch her eventually—she'd stumble into a dead-end, or something. But the Arcadium was huge, and it could easily take all night.

"Ow, fuck!" Will's voice echoed off the walls.

"What? What is it?" Egg shouted.

Will growled wordlessly, then responded. "She's. Ow, she fucking *stabbed* me. She has a knife or something. She's here."

"You have her?" Egg turned around and ran back towards the entrance to the alley, heedless of the pitch darkness.

"No, *idiot.* Fuck. Fucking—if I had her, wouldn't I say I had her? She's *near* here—"

"What—" Egg began, when his ankles struck something hard. He tumbled forward, knife skittering from his hand, cracking his elbows against the stone. He slid a few paces, not quite fast enough to crack his head open on the wall opposite. "Shit! What was..." Footsteps. Bare feet slapped on the stone, just for an instant, back the way he'd come. They were obscured almost at once by another wave of sourceless knocking. "Bitch. Crafty little bitch. Will, are you all right?"

"Yeah." Will's voice was close enough to startle Egg. He squinted, and could just make out the other man's shape in the dark. "She got me good, though, right in the arm. She's got a knife — "

"Never mind," Egg got to his feet. "Never mind that, we know where she is. Just follow me, all right?"

"Right," Will put his hand on Egg's shoulder as they started down the alley again.

"Here, now," Egg called out. "That was clever. That was very clever. You could have hurt someone pretty bad with a trick like that. We aren't mad though, are we, Will?"

"No, we aren't mad," said Will. "Just come on out and we can talk about how mad we aren't. No troub — "

Egg felt Will's hand disappear from his shoulder. "Will?"

"Hrrkggk," Will said, and the sound of a body collapsing onto cobblestones was unmistakable.

"Will, shit," Egg knelt down and groped for the body of his partner. He felt the man who was now very still, and very limp. "Now you've done it," Egg said. "Now — agh!" White-hot pain lanced through his shoulder as something sharp broke his skin, and something horribly foreign entered into his body. "Fuck!" He screamed and twisted, taking the blade with him, slapping at it with his free hand.

It was definitely a sword, a slender sword jammed nearly to its hilt in the muscle underneath his armpit. He swung his good arm out and, by what could have only been blind luck, struck human flesh. "Got you!" He shouted grabbing the thrashing body and finally getting a hold of a wrist. It was the woman, he was sure of it. "Got you, you fucking cunt bitch. I'm going to break your god-damn — " sharp pain in his cheek; Egg let go instinctively and clapped his hand to his face. He tasted blood, trickling into his mouth. "Fuck, did you just fucking *bite* me?"

Another wave of knocking echoes obscured the sound of her movements. Egg, blinded by rage now as well as darkness, stumbled to his feet and took off down the alley, where he imagined his quarry must have fled. He ignored the pain in his face, ignored even the distractingly-uncanny sense of the sword embedded under his arm. His calm unflappability gone, Egg barreled into the dark, towards that blue light, surrounded by the haze of knocking.

Egg skidded to a halt beneath the blue phlogiston lantern, which illuminated only a frustratingly small circle in the otherwise pitch black Arcadium. "Where the shit are you?" He shouted.

"Here, idiot," a woman's voice called from some distance way. He could just distinguish her silhouette. "Are you coming, then? Or did you prefer to stay here and bleed?"

The wounded man roared again and charged towards her like an angry bull, his imagination momentarily flush with images of the tortures that he'd inflict on the stupid, skinny little knocker when he got his hands on her. He was so angry, in fact, that he did not notice that the shape he was charging towards, which did indeed seem to be resolving into the shape of a woman, didn't seem to be moving in the face of his advance. He also didn't notice that she seemed to be illuminated not by phlogiston at all, but by the vague, watery yellow light from a full moon half-eclipsed by clouds.

He didn't notice any of those things; all he noticed was that the woman was nearly in reach, and that his desire to crush her neck with her bare hands was irresistibly strong. Consequently, he was surprised when, at the very last moment, she spun away from him, and he staggered out into the moonlight. He slipped and nearly fell, caught himself at the last second with a hand on the stone wall.

Egg looked out to see that he was standing on a ledge, ten feet above the Stark, which roiled cold and swift beneath him. *She was leading us back to the river*, he thought, just as a heavy weight crashed into his back. He lost his balance and fell, face-first, towards the dark water. *Bitch*, he thought again, as the cold water hit him and the current dragged him along to knock him senseless among the rocks.

Elizabeth Skinner stepped back away from the ledge. She was sorry about losing her sword, but there was little for it now, she knew, as she made her way back to retrieve her shoes.

Thirty-Eight

If the sun was up, Beckett didn't know it. His eyes suffered a new time and a new universe; even the blind eye could see in this weird new world, that shimmered beneath a light that seemed to come from somewhere in the depths of his own skull. Past and present had come together in a still picture that showed all moments as one moment. The flow of time had collapsed like a bridge above a river, leaving only a jumble of steel and concrete, sinking into the depths without order or context. Gone was the menace of the desiccated Dragon Princes and in its place a strange pastiche of memory and conjecture. Kaarcag towered to his left, the red brick fortress-city atop a mountain that grew above Trowth and reached out towards the moon and the black shapes that crawled across its surface. The royal palace roiled to the right, a bubbling congeries of towers and arches and buttresses. Beckett seemed to see not just the palace itself, but the palace as it was when it was first built, and simultaneously every version and variation that had existed since then. They displaced each other, fought for prominence in his eyes, and all the while beneath the palace rumbled the Clock, the grand ticking Clock, the inexorable grinding spinning whirling Clock that governed all of Trowth with its immutable predictability.

Beckett found that he could look back down the Royal Mile and see his childhood there, spread out in crystal-clear relief. His father dying, eyes red and nose bleeding because of the blood fever. His mother wept, her loss eternal. His first day of work in the factory where he breathed in the aerosol fluxion that had poisoned him. The day he first joined the Royal Marines.

The slaughter that was the Kaarcag Expedition crawled up the imaginary hill that led to that stone city. Muzzle flashes were frozen spots of bright white light; clouds of smoke rose from the men's guns who, trapped in the amber of Beckett's memory, had no hope of eluding the brain-dead dummies that fell upon them. Beckett's ship floated on the mirror stillness of the bay, where

Sergeant Garrett was endlessly torn apart from the inside by those chimerstric vines.

The vines crawled from the water and up to the elevated train tracks, where Beckett could see the shattered coach from the royal train, could see himself paused in the middle of his desperate lunge across the broken tracks above the Soder Pass. Beckett saw himself stabbed above the Stark, saw himself falling into the icy river, saw himself pulled from it by strange figures. He saw Anonymous John and his sickening blank visage everywhere; above the river, on the bay, at the factories. He saw him peering out of windows and looking down from ledges, saw him lurking in back alleys and beneath the streets. Anonymous John moved, but was only the faceless tool of another guiding hand.

The gendarmerie exploded, a flower of shimmering silvery light, like the northern aurora, a pulse of pure unearthly dream emanating from a muddy, filthy stone cocoon. The daemonomaniac, horribly contorted in the basement of the Raithower House, which was somehow still whole but turned in such a way that both inside and outside were visible at once, and also *not* whole, but burning blue and red, a fountain of fire frozen in winter. In the city center a column of white light struck out against the sky, the explosion of the *Excelsior*, a shockwave of irreality preceded from it, turning lungs to glass and causing strange sculptures of still ashes. It was echoed in the distant mountains by light and avalanche, the launch of its twin the *Montgomery*. Men in boiled-leather breastplates fought with snaggletooth sharpsies, held aloft above Vlytze Plaza by time out of joint; some leaping, some thrown from their feet by the detonation of the translation engine. And always, that same hand was visible.

The road he walked looped back around itself, took him in circles around the city, or else it took him through his life which circled around itself, manipulated and transformed by that merciless hand. How much of his life was managed in this way? How much of the life of the city was under this invisible sway? How much of the Empire?

Where the sun rose in the east was an empty square, awash in the sunlight of the First of Summer, devoid of the Emperor and the crowds who would hear his invocation. Above it, or behind it, or before it was that same square, packed with men to hear the Emperor ban the printing presses and cripple the flow of information that was the lifeblood of the city. Only there still was information, pamphlets and documents and quartos everywhere, they fluttered in the sky like snowflakes or flocks of birds, cartwheeling above Beckett's head, suspended before his eyes. They were papers about heresies, about chimerstry and daemonomania and oneiristry. They were seditious pamphlets about the Emperor's tyranny and how loyal citizens must raise their hands against him. One was a play about a man who thought he was only doing good but who had himself become a tyrant and a monster, and who was still guided by that omnipotent omnipresent hand.

At the end of the road the two grand statues of Gorgon and Demogorgon stood, old and new images superimposed atop one another — now they were worn beyond recognition, now rendered in exquisite detail, two vast figures decked in armor but they were not men at all, not indige or sharpsie, but something else, something strange, something incomprehensibly alien. They were gone, empty space where statues once stood, and they returned, all points along the timeline existing at once.

Some small part of Beckett's mind was lucid somehow, despite the shock and the staggering amount of drugs he had imbibed. It was sure that he had gone quite permanently mad, that the rest of his mind was damaged beyond repair and would never be quite the same again. And it wondered how even the least among the daemonomaniacs could withstand even the barest touch of the infinite mind of the Daemon, the omniscient but unthinking mind that knew every speck of dust, every atomie of the universe. Sublimation into the aethyr would be a mercy.

Gorgon and Demogorgon stepped aside as Beckett approached, or else the road widened as he came near the palace and forced them apart, or else they had never truly been there in the first place. Beckett walked or stumbled, he could not say which — perhaps he floated, buoyed along by the strangeness that burned in his veins — through the main square which now was crowded with open faces that looked upon him with concern. Was it now? He was not sure but supposed it must have been. Hundreds of faces looked at him, and scattered among them were those hideously flesh-colored spots of blankness that were Anonymous John.

Beckett ignored them and no man made a move to stop him. He wondered at this only briefly, until the lucid flash in the back of his mind pointed out that he still carried his gun in one hand, and had somehow regain his coroner's shield, which he now waved about. Men fell away like water before the prow of a ship and Beckett wandered as in a dream up the stairs and into the galleries that surrounded the square. These were meant for diplomats and advisors, ministers and members of parliament, the wealthy scions of Esteemed Families, but no one tried to eject him from these honored rooms. He ignored the moustached men in their clean suits, cavorting with their wives and mistresses. Ignored the Crabtree-Daiors and the Rowan-Czarneckis and the Wyndam-Crabtrees, the Daior-Vies and the Ennering-Vies and the Rowan-Vies. Sadness may have touched his face as he passed by the Vie-Gorgons, a sympathy for their mutual loss; even through his delirium, Beckett felt the bitter sting in his heart still when he thought of Valentine, saw Raithower House a frozen eruption in the midst of the city, but the old man was consumed now.

Consumed with the desire to see the source of that strange hand, consumed by the need to follow the sound of turning gears, the gears of the great royal Clock that thundered beneath him, the gears that turned in the heads of men and women, the gears that grew louder and faster and more frenetic, more dangerously swift, the deadly high-pitched whine of a machine on the brink of self-destruction. Beckett staggered, bereft of any more personal will, carried instead by the aggregate power of his visions, into a private gallery with no chairs, only a low table on which sat singed folders filled with clippings from the broadsheets. A gallery that looked out upon the podium where the Emperor, against all tradition, would offer his Invocation three days after the first day of summer. A gallery where Beckett found the mind made of turning gears that was behind it all, behind every movement of the cities innumerable tiny cogs.

The source of the horrors he had seen, men murdered, destroyed by heresy and science, all designed and directed by a cold, dead hand. The monster that had seized the Empire by the throat. The thing that owned the name, the last name signed in the Black Library's book.

Mr. Stitch.

Thirty-Nine

Some five hundred years before the present day, during the first Gorgon-Vie dynasty, Owen II Gorgon-Vie officially broke from the Goetic Church at Canth, and established himself as the First Voice of the Church Royal. This new church was identical to the old church in virtually all respects, save two fairly significant ones: the first was that Owen II had the final say on all matters of theological discussion within the Trowth Empire; the second was that the many tithes that had previously been sent to the Holy Convocus of Canth would now be sent directly to the royal treasury. It was a very controversial arrangement, and the only person that could be said to be thoroughly pleased with the situation was Owen II himself, who was now both temporal and spiritual Emperor, and required to answer to no higher authority but the divine Word itself.

This arrangement was scandalous, outrageous, and completely unacceptable to the many Esteemed Families, yet, peculiarly, none of them saw fit to change the policy when their own scions had control of the Imperial Throne. So, the Emperor's position as head of both church and state persisted well into the present day, where it formed the basis of the Coroners' authority to pursue and execute heretics — ever since that venerable branch of the royal guard was established by Adelwulf Vie-Gorgon and Mr. Stitch a hundred years prior.

The Emperor had very few specific duties in his position as de facto Convocus, leaving most questions of grammar and the Word to the Subvocum of Vie Abbey. He did, however, appear once every year on the first of summer (or later, in the case of repeated assassination attempts — a situation that occurred, perhaps, more often than might be thought healthy), to deliver the Invocation to the people of Trowth.

By tradition, any free citizen was permitted to attend the Invocation, and hear the Emperor bless the city and the Empire, calling for the favor of Divine Providence on himself and therefore, by extension, his people. Though some emperors were more public figures than others, all emperors must, at some time, present themselves for the Invocation.

Even William II Gorgon-Vie, outrageous tyrant that he was, did not dare risk Divine Disharmony by banning the public from this most sacred of events. He permitted the citizenry—men and women dressed in their finest clothes (some clothes, obviously, were finer than others), indige and trolljrmen, even a scattering of therians filled the square, blessed themselves, looked up to the balcony from which the emperor would appear. As was custom, even the beggars were permitted inside the palace walls for this, which was how a sickly old man, dressed in rags and with a matted, disgusting beard—a man who smelled very much like he'd spent time rolling in an open sewer—was permitted into the crowd that gathered before the Emperor.

William II Gorgon-Vie's one break from tradition was a concession to security—twenty-five Lobstermen, on guard, encircling the square and looking down on it from the galleys above. They each carried a long-pin rifle, and eyed the crowd with ichor-envigorated eyes, fully prepared to gun down anyone that behaved suspiciously. It was generally felt, among the Emperor's advisors, that this concession should be sufficient.

Elijah Beckett, Detective-Inspector of the Royal Coroners, was having trouble understanding very much of anything that was happening anymore. He heard gears, spinning so fast that he was sure they must soon fly apart. And he saw Mr. Stitch, the grotesque, undead giant, standing as devoid of expression as a statue. But he somehow saw Mr. Stitch outside of time now—Mr. Stitch at once here, the architect of the murder and mayhem that had dogged the city for a year, and Mr. Stitch in the past. The Mr. Stitch that had founded the Coroners, the one that had engineered the Dragon Isles expedition, why? At this weird remove, divorced from his own present senses, the long arc of Stitch's planning became, if not obvious, more clear.

If a man needs an army to fight heresy, he starts by finding men who have been hurt by it. And if he cannot find men who have been hurt by heretic science, he makes them. A simple solution, almost elegant, if morally repugnant. A kind of point A to point C solution only possible by a mind essentially unencumbered with pity or concern.

Many things still didn't quite make sense, and Beckett wasn't sure if they ever would, wasn't sure if the plan he was looking at was simply too big, too long, too intricate to reveal itself to him. Why? Why all of this? He realized a moment later that he'd asked it aloud.

Stitch turned to him, dead muscles creaking, brass eyes fixed. "I must. Defend. The Empire."

"From what?" Beckett held up his gun. "From *what*? You did this! You were the one...the one spreading heresy. The one that told Anonymous John where to get the oneiric weapons, the one that...you're defending Trowth from yourself?"

"No." Stitch replied, simply. The anguish that sounded in his throat seemed more of an affectation, a byproduct of his dead lungs, than moved by real human concern. "There is. Something. Worse." The hulking reanimate gestured out at the assembled throng, distant voices like the waves of the ocean, all unaware of the sinister mind that looked on them. "They must. Be. Ruled."

Beckett staggered back against the wall and sank down to the floor; his strength ebbing from his body. He wanted to spit his denial in Stitch's teeth but he was afraid that maybe it was true. He remembered Anonymous John, telling him about the Clock that secretly governed the soul of Trowth. He thought about the byzantine bickering, the intricate waste of confusion and bureaucracy that mired him down. About the Emperor, who for all the honor of his office was little more than a clown in fancy dress, preoccupied with his mistresses, squeezing every cent, every iota of goodwill, every dram of happiness from the city. He had become a tyrant; a man that confused the expression of his power with his own ego.

The Feathersmith pistol in Beckett's hands was ice cold. He wondered if he were really feeling it at all, because the pain of that cold stabbed right through the numb tips of his fingers. He imagined that the gun was not cold at all, but that it had become cold to his mind, which insisted on its coldness no matter how he held it. He wondered if...the men he'd hurt...all this time, and it was never for the city, for the Empire, only some microscopic part of Stitch's catastrophic plan. He saw the girl, Agnes Cooper, saying her prayers and weeping because of the harm her mind had suffered. Alan Charterhouse, banished from his own home because of Beckett's swerving devotion to his duty. Dozens of heretic scientists gunned down, and for what?

All this misery, for nothing. Lives lost and wasted, it was all obscene. It was too much, Beckett knew. Every second the fades ate away at him from the outside, and every second the drugs burned him up from the inside, a black acid on his soul. And now this.

"What about me?" He whispered staring at the barrel of his gun.

"You," said Mr. Stitch. "Are. No longer. Necessary."

Something lurched in him, and he saw himself at a distance, saw himself taking other paths into the gallery, taking a wrong turn here, hesitating a fraction of a second there. He saw himself on the gallery across the way, overlooking the gathered crowd. He saw the Emperor beginning his Invocation, saw a filthy beggar drawing his guns, saw the Lobstermen gunning him down before he had a chance to fire.

Beckett's mind was trying to flee, into the past, into the future, into alternate possibilities; anything to escape this one inevitable moment. But there was nowhere else. Beckett wanted to weep, but he knew he didn't have that in him anymore. He cocked his gun instead.

The filthy beggar man stood alone in a small circle in the square. The pressure of the crowd was not quite sufficient to overcome the olfactory counter-pressure of his stench, and this gave him some elbow room. He grinned green scraver-teeth and gabbled in what could only have been the incomprehensible gibberish of the mad or senile. He ignored the finer-dressed men and women who, through some peculiar effect of the dynamics of crowds, managed to gradually shift as far from him as possible, creating a spectrum or stratification of the people gathered for the Invocation.

The Emperor appeared on the balcony, dressed in a black suit, resplendent with medals commemorating wars he'd never fought in and honors he was only vaguely aware of. He wore his thick, black-tinted glasses, which was somewhat gauche, but hardly without precedent. He seemed to have paradoxically gained weight since his harrowing experience on the train, and seemed a little sallow, but besides that, hardly the worse for wear. He raised his arms, somewhat stiffly, and called out to the gathered mass.

"Hail, men of Trowth! We stand in harmony with the Word!"

As the speech began, the filthy man reached beneath his ragged costume and began to draw two beautiful, silver-plated revolvers. The Lobstermen saw him at once, but in the precise moment before they fired, *another* gunshot rang out from a gallery above the square.

The Lobstermen all turned to face it, moved to protect the Emperor, to engage the assailant, confusion setting in as they drew a bead on their new target, only to hear more gunshots, dozens of strange echoes. A man in ragged shirt-tails, with a morbid visage, a face so ravaged by disease that it looked like a skull—a man with a black iron revolver firing wildly into the crowd. He appeared in a half a dozen places simultaneously, unrestricted by the laws of physics.

The Royal Guard fired back instantly, as they attempted to ascertain the nature of this new threat. Their bullets struck the strange phantoms, which dissolved into jagged, fractured lines of causality.

And in this moment of distraction the beggar aimed his revolvers and fired both of them, round after round into William II Gorgon-Vie's chest.

Gunshots rippled across the square, the grim-visaged man appeared and disappeared, each causal doppelganger finally being borne down beneath the Lobstermen's gunfire.

The man who smelled like sewage was tackled hard by the men around him. He was beaten soundly, but not killed. They held him tight, instead, intending that he should be taken into custody.

After some moments of pandemonium, during which the milling crowd turned to near-deadly panic in its attempt to escape the confines of the square, the gunfire ceased. The strange man's spectres had all disappeared, the mad beggar was restrained, the Lobstermen cautiously ceased their fusillade. The crowd had almost completely evacuated the Royal Square.

When the Lobstermen attained the balcony where the first shot had been fired, they found Elijah Beckett comatose and half dead, and Mr. Stitch. The huge reanimate had been shot in the head five times. The miracle difference engine that was its conscious mind was now a fine scattered sand of impossibly tiny gears. Its body stood, still vital and held in place by the heretical chemistry that had created it. Its brass eyes betrayed no evidence of the changed condition.

The men held the Emperor's real assassin to the ground and discovered that his beard was false, and had only been glued on. The looked up towards the Emperor who, despite having eight holes in his chest, was still standing. He cocked his head to the right, again and again. Opened his mouth to speak the same words over and over:

"We stand in harmony with. We stand in harmony with. We stand in harmony with."

From the bullet wounds in his chest, black ichor bled in thick, gummy rivulets down his suit.

Forty

It was some days after the incident before Skinner was finally able to meet the Emperor's would-be assassin. He was being held under arrest at a temporary facility in New Bank, a townhouse owned by the Vie-Gorgon family. Skinner was admitted, dirty, disheveled, and haggard as she was—having been wearing the same clothes since her untimely departure from the Akori household—with a minimal amount of fuss. Someone had indicated to the men on duty that she might be expected. She strode in, her telerhythmia furiously rapping on every available surface. It ruffled papers into the air, nudged chairs out of position, and swung a portrait of Farrier Vie-Gorgon so forcefully on its nail that the painting fell from the wall and crashed to the floor with a resounding *thunk.*

"You," Skinner said, as she entered.

"Hello!" The man replied.

Skinner walked up to him and slapped him across the face. When he did not immediately respond, she began hitting him in the chest and stomach. She caught him a good blow to the solar plexus, and he doubled over and began coughing. "You asshole. You irresponsible miserable stupid *asshole.*"

"Here, I thought—"

She punched him, hard, right in the face. Not quite hard enough to smash his nose completely, but enough to draw blood, and enough to knock him back into the small sofa in which he had been lounging. "You've been missing for months. For fucking *months,* I thought you were *dead,* you fucking bastard!"

"Yes, but—"

"For months, you let everyone think that you're dead, and then what? What's the first thing that you decide to do? How do you announce your presence to the rest of us peons? Is it with a letter? A note? No! You try and kill the bastard *Emperor.*" Her fury spent, Skinner sat down with a huff in the chair opposite. "You are lucky I lost my sword, Valentine, or I would stab you in your neck."

"I think you broke my nose," Valentine said. She couldn't see that his face was still yellowed with old bruises from the beating he'd already taken during his apprehension.

"Good." Skinner crossed her arms and effected a scowl; the silver plate across her eyes spoiled the effect somewhat, as it tended to cause all of her expressions to blend into "serious but enigmatic." After a moment, she asked, "How did you know, by the way? That he was a reanimate?"

"Look...I'm sorry about all of that." Valentine leaned back against the couch and held his nose. "I'm sorry I didn't tell you, but my plan was kind of dangerous, you know? I didn't want you to be implicated, because I didn't think that both of us should go to jail, and then I couldn't *find* you...ow, Skinner, my nose really hurts."

"*Good*," Skinner asserted. "What plan?"

"Yes," rasped a new voice from the door way. "What plan?"

Elijah Beckett looked somewhat the worse for wear. He was wearing his gray suit, as usual, but had put on his heavy gray overcoat to stave off a chill. His hair was thin, and his good eye had a pronounced dark circle beneath it. The skin that was left visible was paper-thin and pale, before it dissolved almost entirely into vivid gore. The whole right side of his face had been consumed by the fades, down nearly into the bones, exposing spongy red marrow in his cheeks and jaw. His speech was slurred faintly; his lips seemed to have trouble forming words. "What plan?" He asked again.

"Beckett..." Valentine whispered, his voice tinged with awe. He managed to collect himself. "It was nothing to do with...with the thing. That I did. It was for Skinner, I was trying to do her a favor —"

"Then how did you know about the Emperor?"

"I..." Valentine paused. He wiped the blood from his nose, sat up straight in the chair. "I just. I knew."

Skinner wondered about that. About Valentine, watching his family's business seized, his mother and father and brothers and sisters driven into exile. Had he worried about her, too? Stuck without a job, without prospects, shoved aside despite all her hard work by an ungrateful emperor? Had he seen what William II had made of Trowth? Had Valentine known at all?

"You knew," Beckett repeated. He sounded as though he had barely any strength left at all. "You knew. Because you went back to the abbey, and looked in the book. You saw Stitch's name, you saw that he'd been to the Black Library.

Realized he must have been responsible for the heretical pamphlets we'd found. Put it all together. Somehow."

"Somehow," said Valentine, after a long, pregnant moment. "Yeah."

"So, your plan didn't really have anything to do with the Emperor?" Skinner asked. "What were you doing?"

"It didn't at first," Valentine replied, his voice unaccountably cold. It warmed as he spoke, though, almost to the point that he sounded like the old familiar Valentine. "At first I was just doing Skinner a favor, like I said. It was dangerous, but I just realized, I knew where we kept some of the old presses. There were a couple in an old printer's shop in the Arcadium that no one had used for a few years. So, I thought, 'Well, Skinner just needs money from her play, right? And nothing's more popular to read than something you're not supposed to.' So...I...well, I printed up a bunch of copies of *Theocles* and started selling them."

"You sold my play?"

"Well, eventually I started paying people to sell it. You...ah, you made a lot of money, Skinner. Anyway, the Committee on Moral Responsibility was getting dangerously close, so I had to clear out. It was then...that was when I got the idea about the log book. I'd been kind of preoccupied, you know?"

"Good enough for me." The old man slumped in a chair. "You'll be cleared today. You'd have been out yesterday, really, except that there's been some...ah...administrative confusion."

"Because of the new Emperor?" Skinner asked. Emilio Vie-Gorgon, Valentine's cousin and Emilia's brother, would certainly be crowned. Eventually. Some question remained as to what precise timeline that auspicious event would proceed along.

"No," Beckett replied. "All of the ministries of Trowth function fairly well, emperor or no. They run on a kind of inertia. Most of the trouble comes when he tries to interfere. No, the problem is with Stitch gone, no one's sure who to deliver the reports to. The Ennering kid can't read them, and I don't want them."

"What...what was really going on here, Beckett?" Valentine asked.

"I don't know for sure. But. I think that Stitch has been...'sword and fuck, I think it's been responsible for everything. The pamphlets, definitely. The attacks...the attack on the Emperor. It replaced him with a reanimate. It's been trying to get control of the Empire for two hundred years, at least. "

"I think," Skinner added, "that Emilia was involved, as well. I'm sure that Stitch intended for me to right this play — though, frankly, whether Stitch was using Emilia, or she was using Stitch, I don't know."

With a groan and a crackle of his joints, Beckett managed to hoist himself back out of his chair. He stood and hesitated for a moment. "I don't...I don't know what to do anymore. They want me to retire."

Skinner was on her feet immediately. She took a step towards him, ready to...she didn't know what. Talk him out of it? Elijah Beckett was the bedrock of the Coroners, was in some way the foundation of her *understanding* of the coroners — what it meant to put duty above all things.

And yet, for Word's sake, he was *old*. He'd been giving of himself, sacrificing life and comfort and basic human contact in the name of the Empire since before Skinner was born. If there was any man in the world who deserved a rest, surely it was him.

Instead of saying anything, she threw her arms around the old man and hugged him tightly, resting her face on his shoulder. After a moment, Valentine stood and joined them, hugging the two of them equally tightly.

It was perhaps past all reasonable supposition to imagine that, after this small display of human affection, Beckett himself might actually raise his arms — such as he could raise them, given the circumstances — and return the embrace. Certainly, any man or woman observing the scene who had even a passing familiarity with Beckett and his life would be forgiven for believing that no such thing was possible.

The natural world, however, is full of surprises.

Some time passed before Skinner finally spoke. "So. Now what do we do?"

"My nose is still bleeding," offered Valentine. "I think I should probably take care of that."

"Yes," Skinner allowed. After a moment, she asked, "Valentine. Just...just how much money did I make?"

EPILOGUE

Emilio Vie-Gorgon became Emperor Emilio VI Vie-Gorgon at the end of that year, without raising any particular commotion. The throne of the Trowth Empire had, by long tradition, generally been passed back and forth between the Gorgon-Vies and the Vie-Gorgons whenever one or the other suffered from an insufficiency of heirs, and parliament's approval had been long accepted as something of a rubber stamp. Emperors, it was understood, behaved according to the nature of their office, rather than the nature of their families, and so aside from certain pointed changes in civic architecture, one emperor could be relied on to be as good as the next.

During his coronation, Emilio treated his subjects to a speech that was so widely-praised afterwards as to have fallen almost immediately into the collective of quotations that mediocre men used to bolster their positions in tavern arguments.

Said the Emperor: "The days of dread and sorrow are now behind us. With bold hearts and omnipotent industry, Trowth shall stand astride the world, shall cross the oceans, shall rule a kingdom upon which the sun shall never set. Let no man say it cannot nor it should not be, for we say that it must be. If there is any passion that will deter us, it is fear. Fear of the magnificent destiny that awaits the great people of this rugged isle, this seat of power, this glorious empire."

Neither at the time, nor ever after, did more than three people in the world realize that this speech drew quite liberally on an early, unperformed draft of *Theocles*.

Following his coronation, the Emperor first immediately dismissed the Committee on Moral Responsibility. He secondly reinstituted the Estimation of the Comstock Vie-Gorgons, returned their property to them, and permitted them to reopen their printing houses, after making it quite clear that the press was only free so long as it served the pleasure of His Majesty. He thirdly declared that it pleased His Majesty to remove certain pieces of literature from the Black List, among them the aforementioned *Theocles*.

Finally, Emperor Emilio VI Vie-Gorgon, by imperial decree, lifted the ban on the employment of women by industry in Trowth. He did not go so far as to grant the suffrage that was still in high demand among fairer sex, but it was widely accepted that this was a positive first step. And among those in the know, who suspected that Emilia Vie-Gorgon might have an unusual amount of influence over her sibling, it was considered an extremely optimistic sign.

During the following Armistice, Valentine Vie-Gorgon married Elizabeth Skinner. While it was a great disappointment for Valentine's mother, father, brothers, sister, aunts, uncles, and cousins to see the youngest scion of the Comstock Vie-Gorgons marry so far below his station, it certainly came as no surprise. Indeed, upon great reflection, they allowed that marrying a lovely, intelligent, and professional woman was probably the most sensible thing Valentine had ever done. Elizabeth Skinner Vie-Gorgon was welcomed into the family, and if she was welcomed with some certain caution, rather than the customary joviality bespoke by such an arrangement, she was welcomed nonetheless.

Elijah Beckett, after many persuasions both tender and severe, surrendered finally to his retirement, and adjourned to the small village of Kyloe on Stark, and there kept to a small but well-appointed manner house subsidized by monies from Comstock Street. Finally relieved of the tedious weight of his lifelong burden, he listened to his old-fashioned music, snapped irritably at the young indige woman who had been employed to look after him, complained about the moral decay of the Empire and the strange fashions and disrespectful behaviors of the young people of the village, and otherwise engaged in all manner of similar pursuits peculiar to retired old men.

This state continued for some time until, during the deep and dreamy sleep brought on by the veneine, Elijah Beckett very quietly, very peacefully, very painlessly, slipped off his ravaged mortal flesh, and died.